THE CRIMES OF
CHARLOTTE BRONTË

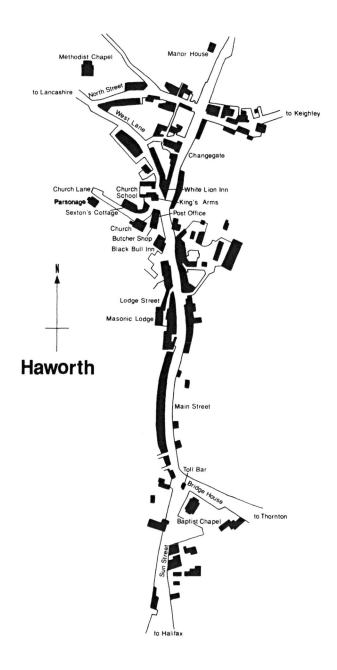

Methodist Chapel

Manor House

to Lancashire

North Street

West Lane

to Keighley

Changegate

Church Lane

Church School

White Lion Inn

Parsonage

King's Arms

Sexton's Cottage

Post Office

Church

Butcher Shop

Black Bull Inn

N

Lodge Street

Masonic Lodge

Haworth

Main Street

Toll Bar

Bridge House

to Thornton

Baptist Chapel

Sun Street

to Halifax

THE CRIMES OF
CHARLOTTE BRONTË

The secret history of the mysterious events at Haworth

James Tully

Robinson
LONDON

*Para mi querida J . . . – whom
I met when she was but seventeen
and have loved deeply for some
fifty years*

Robinson Publishing Ltd
7 Kensington Church Court
London W8 4SP

First published in the UK by Robinson Publishing Ltd 1999

This paperback edition 1999

Copyright © James Tully 1999

The moral right of the author has been asserted

A copy of the British Library Cataloguing in Publication data
is available from the British Library

ISBN 1-84119-131-0

Printed and bound in the EC

10 9 8 7 6 5 4 3

Introduction

My name is Charles Coutts, and I am a partner in the firm of solicitors Coutts, Heppelthwaite and Larkin, which was established in 1788 by my great-great-great-great-grandfather, Henry Coutts.

Henry began his practice from one room which he rented in a large four-storied building in Keighley, Yorkshire. He prospered, and, over the centuries, more and more rooms were acquired until, in 1926, my grandfather bought the freehold of the entire property. Then, three years ago, we received an offer for it which we could not refuse.

Some developers were willing to pay a considerable sum in order that they might demolish the building and then use the entire, very large, site for the construction of a shopping mall. Actually we were, in effect, made two offers. We could either have the total amount in cash, or have our pick, at a favourable price, of a spacious suite of offices in a new block which was nearing completion, and receive the balance.

I discussed the matter with the other partners at some length, and in the end we realized that we should be foolish not to jump at the proposal. Our premises needed a lot spending on them, and they were already costing the earth to heat and maintain. It was a heaven-sent opportunity to cut our losses and move, and that was just what we did – after opting for the 'part-exchange' deal.

As we had anticipated, the changeover was a major upheaval. To move one's home is bad enough, but to clear such a large building of all the junk which had accumulated in over two centuries was a nightmare. It had been decided that it would be best if we dealt with the removal floor by floor, and transferred to our new offices gradually. We began, therefore, with the two large attics.

Many years had slipped away since I was last up there – as a small boy during the Second World War – and, remembering what it was like then, it was with some trepidation that I ascended the rickety stairs to make an inspection.

What I beheld, when I finally managed to force open the first door, confirmed my memories – and my worst fears. The rooms were packed from floorboards to rafters. It seemed that my forebears had been unable to throw away anything whatsoever, and it was going to be a task of gargantuan proportions to sort through what was there.

I undertook the supervision of the work myself, mainly because I did not wish anything of value to be discarded, but also because I was interested in my ancestry and the history of the firm. In other words, as I overheard one of my partners say, I was 'both acquisitive and inquisitive'!

It was a slow business but, with the help of four stalwart workmen, I was able to make steady and rewarding progress. A couple of containers of rubbish went off to the tip, but there were many other items, some genuine antiques, which we sold at prices which astounded us.

There was, however, one piece of furniture which I earmarked for myself. It was a handsome George IV bureau/bookcase, which I thought would stand nicely in my study. I gave it a rough wipe with a rag, made sure that it was free from woodworm, and then had it taken to my home where it was stored, temporarily, in the garage.

What with the move, and other matters, it was some weeks before I was able to get round to a closer inspection. Eventually, however, a weekend arrived when I had the time to give it a good cleaning in order to see whether any restoration would be necessary.

I lowered the flap which formed the writing-top, and then removed all the drawers before starting work. It appeared to be in good condition, and I was feeling quite pleased with myself as I beavered away with cloth and polish. Then, suddenly, as I was rubbing the side of the large central section, there was a loud 'click' and, to my utter amazement, the bottom of the section swung up.

2

What was revealed was one of those secret compartments so beloved by nineteenth-century craftsmen. The base of the middle section was false, and obviously I had touched something which released what was, in fact, a carefully hinged lid to the hiding-place below.

Among other bits and pieces, it contained various documents which, I was to discover, had been placed there by my great-great-grandfather who died, suddenly and quite unexpectedly, in 1878. All had been of a highly confidential nature at the time, but most were now no longer so and need not concern us here. However, the contents of a brown paper parcel have intrigued me ever since I read them, and have given me many a sleepless night.

The parcel measured some twelve inches by ten, and was about three inches thick. It was sealed with red wax, imprinted upon which was the name of our firm, and tied neatly with white tape, the knot of which was also sealed and bore the signet of my ancestor James Coutts. On the front of the parcel, in his magnificent copperplate handwriting, were the words: 'Statement sworn to by Miss Martha Brown of Bell Cottage, Stubbing Lane, Haworth, on January 8th, 1878. Not to be opened until after her death, and that of Arthur Bell Nicholls, Esquire, of Hill House, Banagher, King's County, Ireland.'

It was the stuff of which murder mysteries are made and, never having seen similar phraseology before in my professional career, my curiosity knew no bounds. I was filled with anticipation as – oh, so carefully – I slit open the parcel and examined the contents.

They consisted of a pile of rather tattered old school exercise books, one of which, I found later, had been used as something of a diary by Anne Brontë.

At the end of the final paragraph, on the last page of the books, there was a deposition that what had been written in the books was true. That was followed by a form of wording which authorized James Coutts or his successors to use the information contained in the books in any way they saw fit, but only after the deaths of the signatory and Mr Nicholls. Below that, and witnessed by James Coutts and one of his clerks, was the

3

signature 'Martha Brown', written in a good hand for one who, I was to discover, had been a mere servant woman.

I had to read the books several times before I had a proper appreciation of the enormities which they detailed. Apparently Martha Brown had been a servant in the employ of the legendary Brontë family of Haworth – which is some five miles from Keighley as the crow flies. Among other things, she claimed that most of the Brontë family had been murdered, and that she was privy to one of the killings. What she alleged she had witnessed made startling reading, especially as part of it was self-incriminatory, but, if it was all true, I understood why she had seen fit to have her testimony signed and sealed.

Was it true, though? Or *could* it be true? Although their former home was so close to mine, I must confess that I knew very little about the Brontës. I had once accompanied my wife, under sufferance, to Haworth and the Parsonage – but had thought the best part of the trip was our visit to the Black Bull afterwards! From holidays in Cornwall, I also knew the house in Penzance in which Mrs Brontë had lived until she married. That, however, was the sum total of my knowledge of the family. As for the literary works of the three daughters, I had heard of *Jane Eyre* and *Wuthering Heights* but had never read them.

What Martha Brown deposed was to alter all that. Clearly I needed to check on all the available evidence. I wanted to know why she had chosen James Coutts' firm, and whether what she had told him was in keeping with the known facts about the Brontës.

The answer to my first query was easily discovered. I found that our firm had acted for the Haworth Church Trustees on many occasions, a fact of which Martha might have been aware both from working at the Parsonage and being the daughter of the sexton at Haworth. It was logical, therefore, that she should have come to us, and the senior partner would have been the only person to whom she would have imparted such extraordinary information.

As for my other question, I began on the premise that James Coutts must have thought that there was at least *some* truth in

4

what she had confided. Otherwise, from what I had read of him, he would probably have sent her packing with a stern warning ringing in her ears. I then embarked upon what was to become a lengthy process of research, but it did not take all that long to come to the conclusion that there was something seriously amiss with the generally accepted legend of the Brontë family.

It all seemed far too good to be true. Three almost saint-like sisters – Charlotte, Emily and Anne – live with their stern, but equally saint-like, father in a grim parsonage in a wild part of England. After very little formal schooling, and not until they are all far into their twenties, each writes – in the very same year – a romantic novel which sells well. Within ten years they are all dead, but they live on in their books – which continue to sell well nearly 150 years after the last sister's death.

Interwoven with their lives is a young and handsome curate who arrives, very coincidentally, at the start of the year in which the novels are written. He eventually marries the eldest sister who dies, tragically, whilst carrying their first child. Husband, heartbroken at the loss of his one true love, vows that he will care for her aged father for the rest of his life. This he does, for six long years, until the venerable, white-haired patriarch finally departs to meet his Maker.

The sad and lonely widower then rides off into the sunset to try to find some meaning in Life. Curtain down; not a dry eye in the house.

Of course, being Victorian, the story has to paint a moral, and this is provided appropriately by the sisters' brother, Branwell Brontë. He is intelligent, artistically gifted, and shows great promise. However, he falls in with bad companions and is easily led into a life of debauchery. Inevitably he comes to a sad, but only to be expected, end through his addiction to drink, drugs and gambling. Let that be a lesson to us all, and an encouragement to sign the Pledge before it is too late!

I fear that, according to Martha Brown, the reality was very different. The Brontës were *all* fallible, and subject to short-comings as are we all.

Having checked her story, and what Anne Brontë had

5

written, against the known facts, I was in a dilemma. I had been able to discover nothing which contradicted what she had to say. Initially I had made my enquiries merely to satisfy my own curiosity; but now that I had done so, and become convinced of the veracity of the documents, what should my next step be?

Probably the easiest thing would have been to have destroyed the books, or at least kept the whole matter to myself. Nobody would have been any the wiser, and the 'authorized version' of the Brontë legend would have continued to be accepted. On balance, however, and only after a great deal of thought, I decided that the statement and the 'diary' were historical documents which should be made public.

Here, then, is what Martha recounted all those years ago. As it incorporates all the facts that Anne recorded, I have seen no reason to quote verbatim from *her* book. I have other plans for that highly valuable document.

In order to make Martha's deposition understandable, and to provide readers with background and other information, I have replaced the more obscure of the old Yorkshire dialect words, inserted some punctuation and added, at the end of each chapter, comments on the results of my research – to distinguish them from Martha's text the reader will find my initials [*CC*] at the start of each of these sections. The Biblical quotations at the start of each chapter are my idea, and were introduced in order to break up Martha's continuous narrative and because they seemed appropriate. Essentially, however, the tale belongs to her.

I am very conscious of the possibility that the publication of this account may cause offence in some quarters. That, I am sure, was not Martha's intention, and it is certainly not mine. I shall therefore be sorry if such proves to be the case. It is merely that, as her statement fits all the known facts, I feel I have an obligation, especially to the Brontës, to let it be known.

So come along with Martha and me, step by step, and see what you think. If, as I did sometimes, you find anything which is difficult to accept, compare it with the popular version and then with the facts and see which you consider the more reasonable.

Obviously each reader will come to her or his own conclusion, and there will probably be many who, initially, will doubt Martha's tale – as indeed I did. However, after asking myself what she had to gain by inventing such a story, I approached it with an open mind and all I ask is that you do the same.

If, in the end, she has achieved nothing more than to cause you to doubt the traditional Brontë story I am sure that Martha Brown's spirit, and those of the Brontës too come to that, will rest more easily.

Chapter One

'Lo, mine eye hath seen all this, mine ear hath heard and understood it.'

Job 13:1

My name is Martha Brown, and for over 20 years I was servant to the Brontë family at Haworth Parsonage. During my time there I witnessed and overheard many things that have stayed unknown to the world outside, and I was told of other matters by my Father and the Reverend Arthur Bell Nicholls, who was Mr Brontë's curate for about 16 years. Even so, there were happenings that were not fully clear to me at the time, but so much has come out since the Brontës died that I can now see the whole picture.

For a long while now what I know has been a burden to me and, as I have not been too well of late, I now feel that it is high time that I set my mind at rest. I shall ask that what I write is not read until after my death, and even then it should not be made public if Mr Arthur Bell Nicholls, now of Hill House, Banagher, King's County, Ireland is still alive. Although he has much to answer for, he has never rendered me any harm and I do not wish any ill to befall him through me.

What I have to say begins in 1840, when I was only just over 12 years of age. My Father, John Brown, was a stone mason in Haworth. He was also the Sexton of the Church there and Master of the Freemason Lodge. We lived in a cottage called 'Sexton House' in The Ginnel – near the Church and right next door to the National School, where I also went to Sunday School. Father used a barn across The Ginnel from the Parsonage for his work.

I was very happy with my Mother and Father and sisters until shortly after my 12th birthday, when Father told me that

8

as I was the oldest I would have to earn my keep. He said he had had a word with Mr Brontë and I was to work at the Parsonage and live there. Life was never the same for me after that.

There were many tales about the Parsonage, and I was very ill at ease on the morning that I had to start my job, so Father took me by the hand and we walked there together, carrying the bits and pieces that I was taking with me.

First of all we met the Parson, Mr Brontë, and his dead wife's sister, Miss Branwell, who had come up from Cornwall to look after the family when Mrs Brontë died nearly 20 years before the time that I am talking about. Mr Brontë was only 63 then, with Miss Branwell being but a few years older, but they both seemed *very* old to me, and I was a little afraid of them. Mr Brontë spoke to me kindly enough though, as did Miss Branwell after him and Father had left the room. She showed me the kitchen and the other rooms downstairs, and then took me to meet Mrs Tabitha Aykroyd.

In truth, Miss Aykroyd – as we called her – knew *me* very well, as I did her. She was a village widow-woman who was nigh on 70 then, and who had worked at the Parsonage for 15 years. The Brontë children looked upon her as an aunt, and called her 'Tabby', but talk in the village had it that, at one time, she had had a very different friendship with Mr Brontë. Now, though, the years were catching up with her, and also she had had a fall and broken her leg which was not mending as it should, so Father and Mr Brontë had agreed that I should be taken on to help out.

The work at the Parsonage was hard, and the house dreary and damp with no curtains at the windows because Mr Brontë was afraid of a fire. I had to get up very early, and I slaved for many hours, doing all manner of rough jobs, some of which I *hated*, from scrubbing the flags with sandstone, which often left my hands bleeding, to making ready the vegetables, and all for only 2/3d a week which I had to give to Mother with naught for myself but what she chose to give me from time to time. As I got older I was to be relieved of many of the worst jobs by younger girls, and I would be allowed to work upstairs,

9

becoming something of a maid to the sisters. However, I did not know that then and I was very unhappy.

Night after night I was kept working to all hours. I would trail upstairs so tired out, and many a time in tears. I had to share a bedroom with Miss Aykroyd, and that had not bothered me when first I was told about it for I was used to sharing with my sisters in our crowded house. When it came to it though, I did not like it one jot. Miss Aykroyd snored a great deal, and often moaned, I suppose from the pain in her leg. But it was not only that – she got up two or three times in the night to pass water and made such a noise that some nights I had barely any sleep and would start work tired out already.

At the start it seemed that I could do nothing right, and I was always being scolded. Miss Aykroyd was crochety and had little patience, but she was old and I was able to get away with some things with her. No, it was Miss Charlotte who was the bane of my life. She was always snooping around the house and poking her nose into things that were not rightfully her business, and she took to ordering me about and watching to see that I did not get a moment's rest. I also heard her complaining to Miss Branwell about me, and I began to wonder why she was so down on me, but it was not until I said about it to Father that I understood. He told me to take no notice, and said that she was probably trying to get back at him through me as she blamed him a lot for Master Branwell's drinking. Father and Master Branwell both loved to drink at the Black Bull, and were also members of the Freemason Lodge of the Three Graces.

It was all right for Father to say take no notice; he did not have to put up with her. As fast as I finished one job I was given another, and if anything went wrong, such as me breaking something, you could be sure that she would be on the spot. Then she would give me a good scolding, no matter who else was there, and say that the cost would be taken out of my wages. I would feel myself becoming redder and redder, and would have a job holding back the tears. Many was the time when I swore to myself that I would get my own back on her one day.

It was Miss Emily who, without the others knowing, usually came to my aid with a kind word, a hug, and little treats, and

10

she saw to it that nothing ever was taken from my wages. She was the only person who took the trouble to explain to me how jobs should be done properly, and to give me a kind word when I did well. Happily for me, it was her who was in the kitchen for most of the time, as she loved cooking and doing jobs around the house, whereas the others seemed to think such things beneath them. As time went on I grew to love her dearly.

Little by little I became more able, and I also became very good at hiding my true feelings from Miss Charlotte. It was all 'Yes, Miss' and 'No, Miss' with a smile on my face – even though I usually put my tongue out, or worse, to her back – and gradually she came to think that that was the real me, and stopped tormenting me so much.

The years passed, and I grew stronger, but even so it was still hard work, and many were the times when I told Father that I wanted to leave the Parsonage to do something else, and be more amongst girls of my own age. I had my mind fixed on going into one of the mills, where most of the girls I knew were working, but Father would have none of it. I know now that he was right, and that the hours there were even longer and the work far harder than I suffered at the Parsonage, but at least I would have had a few laughs instead of the grimness that was my lot in that dreary house.

As time went by, though, things became a little easier and in the end I was as taken for granted and unnoticed as a piece of their old furniture. Rarely did anyone tell me off, and I was allowed to be privy to a lot that was hidden from other folk. I have kept most of what I learned to myself for all this time, but now it is only right and proper that folk should know what really happened over the years in that awful place.

I suppose it was during the year of 1845, when I was 17, that things began to go wrong for the family, although it was hard to see it at the time.

The first thing that happened was that a new curate came to help Mr Brontë out. He was the Reverend Arthur Bell Nicholls, and when he arrived there was quite a stir of interest both in the Parsonage and the village. I knew more about him than most though, for Mr Brontë had arranged with Father that

11

he should lodge in our house – as though it was not full enough already – but I was still surprised when I saw him.

Mr Nicholls – for even after all we have been through together I seldom think of him as anything else – was a handsome man. Then he was 27, about Miss Emily's age and some 2 years younger than Miss Charlotte. He was well-built, with a full beard. Like Mr Brontë, he had been brought up in Ireland, but he spoke in a lovely soft voice that was quite unlike the harsh Irish accent of Mr Brontë and his daughters.

I got to know him quite well early on, what with him living with my family and being in and out of the Parsonage all the time. He was very agreeable and, when he wished, he could be quite the charmer, but there were other sides to his nature.

Very often he would seem quite down, and Mother told me that then he would go off for long walks on the moors from which he would come back more cheerful. There was no doubt in my mind, nor indeed in the whole village, that he had an eye for the ladies, and it seemed to give him great pleasure to make himself agreeable to even the oldest and most cross-grained of the women in the parish – though I had a good idea of his true thoughts.

I knew that he was lonely, because at the Parsonage he was treated much as I had been when I first went there. He told Father that Mr Brontë and Miss Charlotte rarely spoke to him, and that only Miss Emily had shown him any kindness and gone out of her way to make him feel at home. There were no young men of his class in the village, and though Father had tried to befriend him at the outset they did not get on very well. Father loved his drink, and he was often at the King's Arms or the Black Bull, but Mr Nicholls was not interested in mixing with the villagers socially, especially in a tavern, and I always noticed his face set when the Freemasons were mentioned.

Mind you, Father would not have been so well-inclined towards him then had he known of some of the things that Mr Nicholls got up to with me from time to time when nobody was about.

It started with him putting his arm around my shoulders in a

12

fatherly fashion, and sometimes he would pat my bottom in jest. Then he took to creeping up behind me when I was busy and tickling me in the ribs. I am very ticklish, and used to wriggle and try to stem my laughter, and then, somehow, his hands would be on my breasts giving them a gentle squeeze. I was quite taken aback when first it happened, but put it down to being by chance. When it happened quite often though, I knew it was not. Still, I never made anything of it – indeed I rather liked it and, although it would have been very immodest of me to have let him know that, he must have sensed how I felt.

One day he tickled me when I was on my hands and knees scrubbing, and somehow we finished up on the floor together with him on top of me. I could feel the hardness of him, and feelings that I had never had before swept over me. To this day I do not know what would have happened next if we had not heard Miss Charlotte clip-clopping across the flags. Mr Nicholls leaped to his feet and was out of the door in a flash, whilst I quickly put my dress to rights and took to scrubbing as if possessed.

All along, though, I knew that to him it was but a bit of play with a servant girl, especially as I had noticed that he had been trying very hard to get into Miss Charlotte's good books right from the very start. He would take any chance to talk to her, putting on all his charm as he did so. I just could not understand this, because even her best friends – such as she had – would not have called her anything like pretty, or even handsome. In truth, to me she looked very much like an old pug-dog that Father once had. That being so, you would have thought that she would have been more welcoming of his attentions, but she was not and sometimes she was really quite rude to him. Not only that – I heard her pass nasty remarks about him to Miss Emily, and I know from seeing some of her unfinished letters to her friends that she was quite down on him to them as well.

It seemed to me that the only man she had any time for then was one that she used to write to in Belgium.

*

13

[*66*] Here, I think, we should pause for a closer look at Charlotte who, to my mind, is the key figure in the Brontë puzzle.

I have explained how, when I started upon the research for this book, I knew practically nothing about the Brontë family, and had read none of the sisters' works. Therefore I had no preconceived ideas but, as I became more and more involved with my research, I was able to put some flesh on the bare bones of my knowledge.

Most of the recognized information about the Brontës comes from Charlotte. Her letters – and those from her friends – form the basis of most research, together with the first biography of her, written by another famous novelist, Mrs Gaskell.

Mrs Gaskell presents a sometimes inaccurate, almost always biased, and frequently over-sentimental picture of her subject. The letters, however, are invaluable because they tell us about Charlotte's true character. Fortunately, when they wrote them she and her friends had no way of foreseeing that successive generations would read them, and be able to compare them, one with another, thus allowing them to place what they wrote in context.

Let us make a start with her appearance.

Most people who know anything about Charlotte prefer to think of her as she was presented in the portrait by George Richmond. That, however, is a very flattering likeness, to say the least. It should be borne in mind that Richmond would have wanted to please the successful authoress, who was by then in a position to recommend him to the rich and famous. For something nearer the truth we should listen to those who knew her well, her two lifelong friends, Ellen Nussey and Mary Taylor.

Talking about Charlotte at the age of fifteen, Mary Taylor said: 'She was very ugly.' Ellen Nussey said: 'Certainly she was at this time anything but *pretty*.' Her 'screwed up' hair revealed 'features that were all the plainer from her exceeding thinness and want of complexion'. She looked 'dried in'.

Even Mrs Gaskell was not flattering. Listen to her description of Charlotte, when she first met her in 1850: 'She is (as she calls

14

herself) *undeveloped*; thin and more than half a head shorter than I, soft brown hair, not so dark as mine; eyes (very good and expressive, looking straight and open at you) of the same colour, a reddish face; large mouth and many teeth gone; altogether *plain*; the forehead square, broad and *rather* overhanging.'

In the same year, G.H. Lewes, a well-known writer of the day, described her as 'a little, plain, provincial, sickly-looking old maid'. She was only thirty-four!

Let me not be misunderstood. Nobody can be held responsible for what Nature bestows upon them, only for what they do with, or to, it. It was not Charlotte's fault that she was short, thin and plain; all I am trying to do is peel away some of the layers of myth which have been built up around her.

Now that we know how she looked, let us examine her character.

Basically she was a domineering and ambitious child who became a domineering and ambitious woman. I attribute that to the fact that she had a poverty-stricken upbringing in a bare and poorly furnished parsonage which left her with mental scars from which she never recovered.

She was the plain daughter of an eccentric – to put it mildly – Irish parson, who herself spoke with an Irish brogue. Very early in her life she developed an inferiority complex which never left her. She went to Roe Head School where most of the other girls were from better-off families. They were better dressed than she, had better homes, more influential parents and more money. The only ways in which she could offset her feelings of shame and inferiority were to tell herself that she was intellectually superior to them, and to attempt to dominate them and become the centre of attention.

As she grew older she became determined to acquire money. In that she was encouraged by her father, who also thought that life owed him more than he had achieved. For a woman in those days, the usual way to a comfortable life was by making a 'good' marriage, and upon that Mr Brontë pinned his hopes for his daughters. In reality, however, there was little hope of his dreams coming to fruition – the sisters being who they were and living where they did. The only young men whom they were

15

likely to meet, and who were remotely acceptable socially, were curates, and Mr Brontë wanted something better.

Charlotte also wanted something better but, as Martha observed, 'the only man she had any time for then was one she used to write to in Belgium'. This was M. Constantin Héger, at whose school in Brussels both Charlotte and Emily had been teachers in 1842 and 1843. Charlotte was passionately in love with him.

M. Héger was only seven years older than Charlotte. Already embarked upon his second marriage, he was sexually experienced and had awakened in Charlotte that latent sensuality which, once aroused, was to increase until it tended to dominate her whole being. Martha realized what had happened only too well, even though Charlotte always concealed her passions beneath a demure, and apparently rather prudish, facade.

Although, of course, we can never be absolutely certain how far that affaire finally went, all the indications are that Charlotte and M. Héger eventually became lovers in every sense of the word.

One of those signs is contained in a letter which Charlotte wrote to Emily on 2 September 1843. She told of how she had gone into the Catholic cathedral in Brussels and asked if she might make confession. At first the priest refused, because she was a Protestant, 'but I was determined to confess'. He finally agreed that she could do so, but only in the hope that it would be a first step 'towards returning to the true church. I actually did confess – a real confession.'

Now what on earth could have affected Charlotte so much that she just *had* to confess to a Roman Catholic priest? Her father would have been furious to think that a daughter of his had done such a thing. I submit that the reason was that she was so weighed down with guilt about her adultery with M. Héger that she was desperate to unburden herself.

Charlotte promised the priest 'faithfully' that she would go to his house every morning, in order that he might do his best to convert her to Roman Catholicism but, of course, she did nothing of the sort. She could not risk having M. Héger identified as her lover.

Unfortunately for Charlotte, Madame Héger eventually became suspicious, and Charlotte had no alternative but to leave the Pensionnat.

Charlotte came back to England early in January 1844. In July 1844, she wrote to M. Héger complaining about his 'long silence', but his failure to write can hardly be wondered at. Clearly he had been 'warned off' by his wife in no uncertain terms, and had finally come to his senses once the physical temptations offered by his tiny admirer had been removed.

Charlotte ended her letter: 'Once more good-bye, Monsieur; it hurts to say good-bye even in a letter. Oh, it is certain that I shall see you again one day – it must be so . . .'

When October arrived she wrote again, asking if he had received her two previous letters, but there was no reply.

The year 1845 dawned and, still having heard nothing, in January Charlotte once again put pen to paper. 'Day and night I find neither rest nor peace. If I sleep I am disturbed by tormenting dreams in which I see you . . .' She asked him to be frank with her, to tell her if he no longer had any interest in her and had forgotten her, and went on to tell him of 'the torments which I have suffered for eight months'.

It was passionate stuff indeed, and by then M. Héger must have been praying that Charlotte would stop writing altogether. In an attempt to lessen his problems, he proposed that she should send any future letters to the academy, the Royal Athénée, where he was Professor of Literature, but that did not suit Charlotte at all. Whether she had hoped to profit from any dissent which her letters were causing between husband and wife, or whether she simply felt humiliated by the suggestion, we can but conjecture. However, she had finally got the message and, to M. Héger's undoubted relief, she never wrote again. Some idea of what he thought of her, in the latter days at least, may be gained from the fact that he used her letters for laundry and shopping lists.

Chapter Two

'What is this that thou hast done?'
Genesis 3:13

M r Nicholls came to the Parsonage in May of 1845, and Miss Anne came home the next month. I hardly knew her because all the time I had been at the Parsonage she had been working as a governess for a family at Thorp Green Hall in Little Ouseburn, not too far from York, and I had seen her only when she came home for a few short visits. She was a quiet little woman, and something of a mixture of Miss Charlotte and Miss Emily. Miss Aykroyd told me that she had been in love with a curate before Mr Nicholls – a Mr Weightman. I had not known him as well as I knew Mr Nicholls, but he had been a handsome man and I know we were all upset when he died for he was only 26. Miss Anne would have been 23 then, and I well remember how sad she was when she came back for his funeral. After that it was said that she took no further interest in men.

All in all, that must have been quite a bad time for her because her aunt, Miss Branwell, died but a few weeks after Mr Weightman and so she was soon back at the Church where he was buried for the funeral of the woman who had really been mother to her. Oddly enough, though, her death hardly bothered *me* at all because we never really had much to do with each other, although she was good enough to me in her way and never put on me as Miss Charlotte did.

On the other hand, Miss Anne was always very kind to me. She never went out of her way to speak to me, but when our paths crossed I always felt as if I was talking to someone more of my own age and ways, and I was never as uneasy as I was with Miss Charlotte. Even so, she was nearly always sad and serious, and there were certain things that not even Miss Aykroyd would mention in her company.

One of them was why she had left the family at Thorp Green Hall after being with them for 5 years. There was such a mystery about it that we were all agog to know what was behind it, but the family never talked about it in front of the servants, and there was many a time when, quite out of keeping, they would stop talking if one of us came within earshot. It was only when Master Branwell came home without warning in July that a little of what had passed began to leak out.

Seemingly he had been working for the same family as Miss Anne – Robinson their name was – for just over 2 years, as tutor to the young son there. From what Father said – and Master Branwell told him nearly everything – he had been doing very well there, and so it came as a bit of a shock to find out that he had been told to leave.

He told Father that it was because Mr Robinson had found out that he was carrying on with Mrs Robinson, but Father took that with a pinch of salt for he knew Master Branwell's nature and said to us that he had never even been *seen* with a woman other than his sisters.

I never did know how Father found out the truth. He had Freemason friends all over, and so it may have come from one of them but, on the other hand, Master Branwell often told him secrets when they were drinking together. All I *do* know is that I heard Father telling Mother that Master Branwell had been sacked because of something to do with the Robinson boy, and that Miss Anne had resigned from her job because of what had been going on.

Certainly Miss Anne was quieter than ever once her brother was back, and Miss Charlotte would have nothing to do with him at all, even though it was said that she had always been closer to him than the others when they were children. Only Miss Emily seemed to have any time for him, and it was her who cared for him when his health failed after he came home. She told me that he was quite ill, and I know from what I overheard that he went night after night without any sleep at all, which I can now understand if he was worried about the truth of why he had lost his job coming out.

Mr Brontë was more than bothered about him, and one night

he sent me with a message to Father to come to the Parsonage. To this day I do not know of all that passed between them, but the upshot was that Father was asked to go with Master Branwell on a holiday in the hope that a change of air and everything else would help him to get better.

I was there when Father told Mother what was to take place. She sniffed, and then said sharply that that was like asking a fox to look after a lamb but, at the end of July as I recall it, off they went to Liverpool and North Wales. To tell the truth, Master Branwell *did* seem a little better when they came back, but any good that the time away may have done was soon lost because I know from Father and what I saw that he straightaway took to drinking even more, and that he was dosing himself with laudanum.

Even so, I noticed that when he was forced to be sober because of lack of money he was scribbling away in some old exercise books from the Sunday School. It was in no sense a surprise to me therefore when Miss Emily told me that he had had some poems printed in the *Halifax Guardian*, especially after I had seen her rewriting what he had set down so that folk could read it. Then – in September I think it was – he told Father that he had finished the first part of a three-parts book but, shortly after, he said that he had given up the idea.

Instead he went on in his same old ways for nearly a year. He was very often so drunk that he did not know what he was doing, and acted so silly, but at the end of May, 1846, things took a strong turn for the worse.

Mr Robinson died on the 26th and a few days later his widow sent her coachman to Haworth with a message for Master Branwell. He was not at the Parsonage at the time and so the coachman was directed to the Black Bull as being the most likely place to find him. Sure enough, there he was, and several villagers witnessed what happened next.

From all accounts, the envelope was handed to Master Branwell who opened it and read the letter inside. Then he seemed to have a seizure and became almost as a person possessed, rolling on the floor and making terrible noises. Father was called from his yard, but it was ages before he could calm Master Branwell and try to find out what was up with him.

Master Branwell would not let Father see the letter, but he told him that it said that Mrs Robinson would get nothing from what her husband had left if she had anything more to do with him. The story was that Mr Robinson had added that wording to his Will and so Mrs Robinson had told Master Branwell that she would never see him again. Weeping, Master Branwell raged to Father that Mr Robinson's Trustees hated him, and that one had said that if he ever saw Master Branwell he would shoot him.

It was not until many years later, when Mr Nicholls told me the full story, that I found out that there never was any such wording in Mr Robinson's Will, and that Master Branwell had made up the tale to hide what the letter *really* said.

Seemingly, and in spite of the story that Master Branwell put about, he had been sacked for misbehaving with young Edmund Robinson and matters came to a head following the time when the Robinsons went on holiday leaving Master Branwell in charge of the lad.

The boy must have said something when he finally joined his parents at Scarborough, or else it must have been evident that something was amiss, because a doctor was called in and he questioned Edmund closely. Then, on that very day, Mr Robinson wrote the letter ending his job to Master Branwell, who was given no chance to speak up for himself nor sought one.

It would seem that the sacking and the fear of what had *really* happened becoming known came as a terrible shock to Master Branwell. He dreaded his family and friends learning the truth, and that is why he made up the tale about Mrs Robinson. The whole business sent him to pieces completely, and he sank into a long bout of drunkenness during which he told the truth to Father.

I never learned *all* the ins and outs of it, but I know that Master Branwell was very down at the time, and he told Father that he felt a total failure. He had no money; his family and most of his friends would have nothing to do with him; he was

21

not able to find any work and his state of mind did not permit him to carry on with his writings. It seemed to him that he had nothing to lose and so he wrote to the Robinsons saying that he would make the whole scandal common knowledge were he not paid to keep silent.

I cannot imagine what Mr Robinson must have thought when he first read that letter, but after thinking about it he must have been fearful of everyone knowing what had happened. As Mr Nicholls pointed out to me many years later, even if young Edmund had been an innocent victim in whatever took place there would have been a blight on his future, but had he been a *willing* partner . . . well it was all too awful to think about.

Be that as it may, the upshot was that from then on, and with only one short break, I know now that Master Branwell got regular payments of 20 pounds from the Robinsons' doctor, Dr Crosby, for the rest of his life.

The short break in the payments came after Mr Robinson's death, when his widow had to explain them to the Trustees of his Will. According to Master Branwell, they were powerful people who surrounded Mrs Robinson and hated him like Hell, and it seems that they were filled with horror when they found out the facts. Mrs Robinson was told that Master Branwell's bluff should be called, and that the payments would cease forthwith, and he was told of that in the letter delivered by the coachman.

Once I knew all that, I could understand why Master Branwell had gone into such a fit in the Black Bull, and I saw that it was a tantrum made up of anger and hopelessness – anger because of the actual message, and hopelessness because he was always being beset by folk that he owed money to and he had great need of that from Dr Crosby.

For days he just laid on his bed, and I was not allowed into the room to clean or tidy it. He never went out and, on the rare times when he came down for something to eat, he just bolted his food and left. It was evident to us all that he was thinking about something important but, of course, we did not know what it was.

22

After a time, and with money that he got from his father and friends, and from somewhere else that I shall write about later, he began to go out again. His manner was not the same though and he seemed Hell-bent on making away with himself. Father said that he was drinking more, and I began to find no end of laudanum bottles under his bed. As for his bedding, it was an absolute disgrace, and after Miss Aykroyd complained it was Miss Emily who took over the washing of his linen and the making of the bed.

Things went from bad to worse, and at the end of 1846 there was a shameful day when the Sheriff's Officer called at the Parsonage and told Master Branwell, within the hearing of us all, that he must either pay his debts or go to prison.

Then, almost overnight, he was more cheerful and his usual self. At the time none of us could understand what had wrought the change, but Father and his other friends knew and, in the end, I also learned what had happened.

It would seem that his very bad need for money finally decided Master Branwell to start his blackmail again. He went to see Dr Crosby and said that if the payments were *not* restarted the whole terrible story about him and Edmund would come out. Dr Crosby then met the Trustees, and made them see that Master Branwell meant what he had said. He was backed up by Mrs Robinson who, by then, was thinking not only of her son but that her chances of getting wed again would be harmed if the scandal came out.

In the end the Trustees were made to see that they would have to agree to Master Branwell's demands and, in June, 1846, he had a very careful letter from Dr Crosby saying that the payments would be restarted.

I always felt very sorry for Master Branwell. He painted some lovely pictures, and I used to love hearing him play the organ in the Church. Not only that, but folk said that his poems were every bit as good as his sisters'. He was always a gentleman towards me, and at times he could be very funny – sometimes having us all in fits in the kitchen. Father said that nobody could tell a tale like him, and folk always sought him out, especially in the Black Bull and other public houses. Had he

23

been reared in a normal family, and with a mother's love, it is likely that he would now have more fame and respect than his sisters.

Be that as it may, in writing so much about Master Branwell I have gone ahead of myself and now I should really go back to 1845, when all the family was at home for the first time in years.

[*66*] So there the Brontës were, in this year of 1845, all at home again and all, in their own eyes at least, failures. None of them had any idea what to do next, and certainly the village in which they lived was hardly likely to present any inviting opportunities.

In the nineteenth century, Haworth was a particularly squalid and disease-ridden place, which drew attention even in an era when unsanitary conditions were regarded as normal. It was a remote place, and life was hard.

The Parsonage was a rectangular stone house which stood at the top of the long, and steeply ascending, cobbled main street. It faced east, and was exposed to the gales which often pounded that part of the country. The front door was opposite the western door of the church, which was about a hundred yards away. On three sides of the house was the overcrowded graveyard, which must have presented an awesome spectacle to the children when they were young.

Behind the Parsonage, the windswept moors sloped upwards to the horizon. They were attractive during the summer, but in the winter they presented a particularly bleak appearance.

The interior of the house was equally cold and dreary, even in good weather. It was stone-paved, damp, with few floor coverings. There was no indoor sanitation, and the only drinking water came from a polluted well.

At that time there were only four proper rooms on each floor. On the ground floor, to the left of the front door, was the sitting room behind which was a storeroom. To the right was Mr Brontë's study, with the kitchen at the rear.

Upstairs there were four bedrooms, and a small box room which was above the downstairs passage. That tiny room,

24

which measured only 9 feet by 7½, had originally been designated as the children's 'study' – a rather grandiose title for such a cheerless little den which had no fireplace and faced east, overlooking the graveyard. It was now Emily's bedroom, in which she had to make do on a camp bed.

There was little comfort, and no privacy. That had not mattered overmuch when they were young, but must have been irksome in that year of 1845 during which Charlotte was twenty-nine, Emily twenty-seven, Anne twenty-five and Branwell twenty-eight. Their father was sixty-eight, and nearly blind. Branwell was drinking to excess, taking drugs and gambling.

There is strong evidence to suggest that Branwell behaved improperly towards, or with, the thirteen-year-old Edmund Robinson. That tends to be supported by Anne who wrote: 'During my stay I have had some very unpleasant and undreamt of experiences of human nature.' An affaire between a man and a woman, even an adulterous one, was hardly in the category of 'undreamt of experiences' nor, one would think, would it have been considered, as she also put it, 'bad beyond expression'. It is virtually certain that the main reason for Anne's resignation was her knowledge of Branwell's misconduct with young Edmund.

It is significant that Charlotte was totally unforgiving.

For most of his life Branwell had been closer to Charlotte than to his other sisters, and she had thought highly of him. In the years immediately prior to 1845, however, she had become more and more disenchanted with her brother, and the Thorp Green Hall business was the final straw. After that she did not speak to him for weeks on end, and then only if there was no way of avoiding it. That hurt him bitterly, especially as he probably knew or guessed what she was writing about him to Ellen Nussey.

On 31 July 1845, for instance, she told her friend: 'I found Branwell ill: he is so very often owing to his own fault.' On 18 August: 'My hopes are low indeed about Branwell – I sometimes fear he will never be fit for much – his bad habits seem more deeply rooted than I thought . . .' On 4 November: 'I wish

25

I could say one word to you in his favour, but I cannot, therefore I will hold my tongue.'

Charlotte had absolutely no time for him, and did not, at that time, care who knew it. There was no question of loyalty to her brother, nor of keeping his problems within the family. That must have had an adverse effect on how people treated him, but in the event it was a self-defeating exercise, because the more he was shunned and denied employment the more he drank.

It was only after his death that Charlotte came to realize that he might not have continued his life of dissipation had she not been so harsh with him, and if she and her sisters had taken him into their confidence more fully. She was to feel guilty about her treatment of him for the rest of her life.

Charlotte herself was doing virtually nothing in 1845. She was still distraught at being parted from M. Héger. Her long-suppressed sexual passions had been aroused in Brussels, and she could not come to terms with her celibacy. She did not like Haworth, or the local people, and felt that her world had now come to an end. Day after day she hoped desperately to receive a letter from her former lover, but she suffered constant disappointment.

I suspect that she also felt rather lonely, and somewhat estranged from the rest of the family. Earlier in their lives the four children had tended to separate into two couples, Charlotte and Branwell, and Emily and Anne. Now, however, she was disenchanted with her brother and, following Anne's return, her sisters had taken up where they left off. Charlotte was therefore a rather solitary being in her own home, and was becoming increasingly anxious to do something with her life.

For her part, and quite to the contrary, Emily was more than contented with her lot. Being at home, and near to her beloved moors, was all that she really asked from life, but, between her domestic chores, she was now writing poetry as well as revising and sorting some of her previous works. How she felt as a woman we can but guess. Generally she is regarded as having been more domesticated than her sisters, and there had never been even a hint of a romance. Branwell was the only man whom she had known really well, and he was not a very good example of the species. She knew that her sisters had fallen in love, and she must have experienced sexual stirrings herself. Her poetry from this period reveals a sublimated passionate nature, and is quite different from her earlier love poems. However, any yearnings which she may have felt were concealed from the world by a no-nonsense facade.

As for Anne, she had qualities which were seldom revealed – especially at home. In 1845, after returning from Thorp Green Hall, she was merely living her life quietly, but she was a keen observer of people and events. I have often wondered what went on in that quiet little mind. She must certainly have regretted leaving some of the advantages of working for the Robinsons because, although the Parsonage was home, it must have seemed very drab and squalid after five years in a mansion.

One can but imagine what the atmosphere in the house was like at that time. What a mixture of emotions, mostly repressed, in which fact and fantasy merged and four breasts held secret, and sometimes passionate, longings for they really knew not what.

Chapter Three

'I will write upon him my new name.'
Revelation 3:12

Looking back over all those years it seems to me now that, her concern for Master Branwell apart, Miss Emily was the only one in the Parsonage who was happy in 1845. For strange to say, although she was contented and placid by nature, that Summer she was in love for the very first time. Even stranger to tell, she had fallen in love with Mr Nicholls, and she believed that her love was returned. I had noticed that she never made any remark when Miss Charlotte was going on about Mr Nicholls, but I did not find that at all out of place for that was her way. Later, though, I began to think that there might be another reason for her silence because word was getting about that she had been seen on the moors in company with her father's curate.

As soon as I heard that I began to keep my eyes open for signs of anything passing between them, and I found that there was indeed something in the gossip. I would see Mr Nicholls start off up to the moors from our house and then, a little later, Miss Emily would leave the Parsonage. They never took the same paths, nor did they ever come back together, but, even without taking any mind of what else some of the villagers said they had seen, I had but to look at Miss Emily's face when she came back to know that there was something in what was being said.

The talk got to such a pitch that Father took me to one side and asked me what I knew. Well, that made me very ill at ease for I thought much of Miss Emily and did not wish to say anything that might harm her, but also I did not wish to lie to Father. I felt myself going redder and redder as I dithered about what to say and in the end he let me be, but I knew that I had given him an answer by my manner.

Soon, however, Summer was drawing to a close, and everyone began to dread the prospect of another bleak Winter at Haworth – but no one more than me.

In later years, Miss Charlotte was to say that it was at some time during that Autumn that she 'accidentally' came across Miss Emily's poems. It made me smile when I heard that for I know for certain that she never came across *anything* by chance. She was always snooping about, and many are the times that I have seen her going through her brother's and sisters' things when she thought nobody was about.

After she had found the poems, Miss Charlotte had the idea of bringing out a book with some of each of the sisters' poems in it. That livened things up for a while, and kept Miss Charlotte off my back, but, sadly, she did not ask Master Branwell to take part. I think it was sad because such an interest at that time might have been the making of him.

Anyway, the book was put together, but letter after letter came saying that no one was interested in it, and so I heard Miss Charlotte coaxing her sisters into paying to have it published. She got her way in the end, but not very easily for none of them had much money and I heard 2 or 3 tiffs about it. As it happened it proved to be money ill-spent, and there were more cross words when only 2 of the books were sold. They had enjoyed doing it, though, and I know that Miss Emily in particular had gained pleasure from the making of it, but for a reason very different from those of her sisters.

I have had friends who fancied themselves in love, and it seemed to me that all they wanted to do was talk about whoever had taken their fancy, even if they were only simple village lads we had all known for all our lives, and taking no heed when it was evident that they were boring everyone else beyond belief. Poor Miss Emily was not able to talk about Mr Nicholls though. Although she must have longed to tell someone, even her sisters, of the feelings that were so new to her, her normal quiet nature would not have allowed of it and, in any case, I know now that Mr Nicholls had made her see that their love should be kept secret. What with that and her fears about what would happen if what was going on came to light – especially from Mr Brontë – she had not felt able even to speak her lover's name. That all changed, though, when the book of poems gave her a perfect excuse.

It came about in this wise, and I can vouch for every word, for I was there at the time.

The three sisters were in the sitting room one evening when I went in to lay the table and make up the fire. I heard Miss Charlotte going on about how it was not fair that men writers seemed to get their books published more easily than women did, and she said that *they* might have more of a chance with *their* book if they were to let it be thought that they were brothers and not sisters. I think that at first she was speaking only in jest, but Miss Anne took it in serious fashion and asked why they should not think of something of the sort. Miss Emily thought that a good idea, but said that if they took on different names they should at least keep their true initials – and the others agreed.

It was evident that the surname would have to begin with a 'B', but whilst her sisters puzzled over which one to choose Miss Emily had no such problem. She saw her chance and snatched at it by suggesting the middle name of the man most on her mind, Arthur Bell Nicholls.

For a little while there was total silence from the others; in fact it was so quiet that I put down the coal-scuttle and turned around, thinking that I had been making too much noise and they were all looking at me. At that moment, though, Miss Charlotte and Miss Anne both burst out laughing. Miss Emily went red, but soon saw that they were not laughing at her, but were just amused at the idea. They told her that it was a very good choice, and it was agreed.

Then came the question of which Christian names they could use that would *sound* as if they were men's, but without of necessity being so. Again they all thought, but once more it was Miss Emily who came up with the answer. She said that if they were going to use Mr Nicholls' middle name, why not use the letters of all of his names and see what they could think of? She was not certain that it could be done, but the others thought that it was another amusing notion and they decided to try it.

Of course, it was Miss Charlotte who, as usual, decided to go first, and she wrote all the letters of Mr Nicholls' names on a piece of paper and studied it:

ARTHUR BELL NICHOLLS.

It was at that moment that I just had to speak out. In the usual way of things I always laid the table before making up the fire and tidying the hearth, but as they were using the table I had seen to the fire first. Now, having washed my hands in the kitchen, I came back to find that I was late in setting the table and would be even later in popping home for a minute the way Miss Charlotte was taking her time about things. I just could not waste my off-time standing about whilst she thought, so I nerved myself and then, in a whisper, I asked Miss Emily if they were going to be much longer.

Well, a whisper it may have been, but I should have known that Miss Charlotte missed nothing. She gave Miss Emily no chance to answer me but, with her face set, just snapped at me that I should hold my tongue and wait.

In my usual way, I went red, but this time it was out of great anger at their selfishness and at having been spoken to like a piece of dirt and put in my place. Still, I could do naught about it, so I just flounced away and sat myself down on a little chair in the corner.

It seemed to me that Miss Charlotte then seemed bent upon making me wait even longer than would otherwise have been the case. She looked at the piece of paper for an age, and then broke off from her thinking to ask if she might use the same letter more times than it came up in the names. For my part I could have told her what she could do with them all, and it would not have been very ladylike, but instead I was made to sit mute whilst her sisters told her that she could, and then to watch, in temper, as she went back to her thinking.

There was a long, long silence and, if the truth be told, I was at the stage of walking out of the Parsonage there and then never to return — in spite of what Father might have to say — when, at last, my tormentor, as I often thought of her, said in a

31

loud voice that she had chosen 'CURRER'. Her sisters asked her where she had got that from, and I must say that *I* wanted to know as well and so I pricked up my ears to hear her remind Miss Emily that it had been the surname of one of the founders of the first school they had gone to. She then turned to Miss Anne and told her that it was her turn – which did not seem to please Miss Emily who was, after all, the next in age – and said that, if possible she should use only those letters that were left after what *she* had taken out.

Miss Anne took Miss Charlotte's piece of paper and, on a piece of her own, she wrote the letters that were left:

ATHBLLNIHOLLS

She gazed at them as if transfixed.

It was fortunate for me that she took nowhere near as long as Miss Charlotte had done, and she very soon gave *her* name as 'ACTON'.

From what they all said then, and from what I have learned since, that was the name of a lady poet of the time, and so they all thought it was a very good choice for a book of poems. The only trouble was that it could be used only if the 'C' that Miss Charlotte had taken could be used again, but nobody spoke against that, especially as Miss Charlotte had already done the same with an 'R', so 'ACTON' it was.

Then it was Miss Emily's turn and, in spite of the time ticking away, I could hardly wait to hear what she would choose. Mind you, there was not much left to go on, and I remember thinking at the time that Miss Charlotte probably told Miss Anne to go before Miss Emily so as to make the last turn harder. What was left was:

HBLLIHLLS

Miss Emily copied those letters down very carefully, but seemed to be thinking all the time she was writing, and indeed she must have been because, in barely any time at all, she said that she had chosen 'ELLIS'. The name seemed to please her very much, and I was dying to know why, but I did not get the chance to find out that night for, all of a sudden, time seemed to be important to Miss Charlotte and she said briskly that they should not dally any longer but should get ready for the meal. It was probably spite on my part, out of the mood I was in, but it seemed to me that she was not very pleased that Miss Emily had managed a name so quickly.

The next day I bided my time until she was doing some ironing and then asked Miss Emily who 'ELLIS' was. At first she seemed a little taken aback that I knew anything about it, but then she remembered that I had been there and seemed pleased that I wanted to know. She said that she very much admired a Sarah Ellis, who was not only a writer and a poet but had also started a school for young ladies called Rawdon House. 'We'll have to see about getting *you* in there one day, Martha,' she joked, and then, smiling away to herself, she put away her ironing and left for the moors – and Mr Nicholls.

I should say that on the evening when the names were chosen what the sisters were on about was of little interest to me. I listened carefully enough, for I had naught else to do, but all I could really think about was that I was going to miss my break at home through being so late.

When they at last left the room I gave a long sigh of relief and had the table set quicker than ever before. They had left behind them the scraps of paper that they had worked out the names on and, rather than take them and lay them somewhere, I just poked them into my apron pocket for the time being so that I could get on the faster. It was only when I got home that I found them still there, and so I put them to one side meaning to take them back, but I forgot to pick them up again. Nobody ever asked after them, and somehow they finally found themselves into one of my old exercise books.

It was not until years later that I found them again, and they sit before me now as I write, silent witnesses to the tale I have just told and bringing back so clearly all the memories of that night and the temper I was in. Over the years I have heard many accounts about how the names were chosen – some of them very silly indeed – but I am now the only one who knows the truth of the matter, and that is why I have taken the bother to tell the full story.

Seeing the interest that there is in the family these days, Mr Nicholls has told me that probably I could sell these little pieces of paper for a lot of money. Perhaps I shall, for I am forced to live very carefully, but, for the moment at least, looking at them brings back such memories of the sisters and my own early days at the Parsonage that I cannot think of letting them go.

That year of 1845 meant so much to the family and me that I like to have some little mementoes of those times about me, especially as they serve to remind me of the other happenings that I had better get on and tell about.

[*66*] Every aspect of his new position and surroundings must have come as something of a cultural upheaval to Nicholls. This was his first curacy and, with little idea of what to expect, he seems to have been quite shocked at the cheerlessness of the Parsonage, his lodgings, and Haworth village. (Knowing what the Parsonage was like, I think it is safe to assume that Brown's house was even more undesirable: at least the outside privy at the former was a double-seater!)

Nicholls was a bright young man, only recently come from undergraduate life, and the civilization and delights of Dublin. There is no evidence that he had any sense of vocation, and it seems likely that, as with so many before and since, he entered the Church only because it presented the prospect of a secure and undemanding life. Now he was not at all happy with his surroundings, especially as the lack of professional people meant that he was without any congenial male company.

It was therefore almost inevitable that he should have been drawn to the opposite sex for solace and companionship and, as it would have been unthinkable for him to have been associated with any of the village girls, that he should have turned his attention to the Brontë sisters.

His first approaches were to Charlotte, and rumours about the couple were still going the rounds over a year later. Indeed,

34

in 1846, Ellen Nussey actually asked Charlotte if it was true that she was engaged to Nicholls.

Charlotte's reply was scathing: 'A cold far-away sort of civility are the only terms on which I have ever been with Mr Nicholls.' In that same letter, and still referring to curates, she stated that: 'They regard me as an old maid, and I regard them, *one and all*, as highly uninteresting, narrow and unattractive specimens of the coarser sex.' The redolence of sour grapes is unmistakable, and perhaps smacks a little of the lady protesting too much.

She may very well have thought little of Nicholls a year before, but then she was still hoping against hope that something would come of her relationship with M. Héger. By 1846, however, the case was altered. She had been forced to the realization that there was no future for her with her erstwhile lover, and would have welcomed any overtures from her father's assistant. The trouble was that, by then, she was too late – he had turned his attentions elsewhere.

Maybe Nicholls first made a set at Charlotte because he detected her sensuality, and he may also have heard whispers about M. Héger. However, he does not appear to have been very distraught at being rebuffed, perhaps because Charlotte was not exactly a personable woman.

Instead – Martha tells us – he sought consolation with Emily, who was the only other daughter at home at that time. She was his age and, being the sort of woman that she was, she had been kinder to him than Charlotte from the outset.

There can be no doubt but that Emily was the most attractive of the three sisters. In later years, former servants at the Parsonage would declare that she was the prettiest of the children, with beautiful eyes and sensuous lips. She was also the tallest, and had 'a lithesome graceful figure'. Nevertheless she was a very reserved young lady.

It has been suggested by more than one writer that she had lesbian tendencies. I cannot subscribe to that view. All the signs are that she was a passionate woman, but that her shyness with strangers was so pronounced that any male overtures had been doomed from the start. That had not prevented her from keeping a watching brief over her sisters' affaires however – which was a habit that had earned her the nickname of 'The Major' from Anne's admirer, Mr Weightman.

It is probable that the unfortunate attachments of her sisters had increased her natural reserve towards men but, in addition, her father was always very sarcastic about would-be suitors and Emily would have wished to avoid being the butt of such comments. Instead, she had sublimated her natural instincts with her poetry, but Nature has a way of triumphing when the conditions are right and this, with Emily feeling very much the Cinderella of the family, was just such a time.

While Charlotte was mooning over M. Héger, and cudgelling her brains for schemes to make money, it was Emily who, as usual, was overseeing the running of the house. She must have been very lonely, especially when Anne was still away, but that was nothing new because, generally speaking, she had been a very private and rather introverted person for the whole of her adult life. Now her main relaxation was to walk over the moors, and it does not take a great effort to imagine her solitary figure wandering across that vast expanse of wild countryside.

Then Nicholls arrived, and one lonely spirit recognised another.

At first Emily felt little but pity for him, and sympathized with his situation, but he constantly sought her out and soon his gentle words began to have their effect. Dormant yearnings were awakened and, despite herself, she began to respond in ways that she would not have thought possible. Came the day when she, the most matter-of-fact and down-to-earth of the Brontë sisters, realized that she was deeply in love.

One has only to read the diary note, written on her twenty-seventh birthday, to feel her general pleasure with life: '. . . merely desiring that everybody could be as comfortable as myself as undesponding.' To those not knowing of her secret love, her happiness and optimism seem remarkable in view of her apparent situation, and that of her family.

I have written 'secret' love, because secret it had to be. As well as keeping it from her father, Emily did not wish her sisters to know what she was up to either, especially the domineering

Charlotte. She could not have borne her, of all people, to be privy to the secret. From past experience, she knew that Charlotte would immediately start offering advice, and would probably use the opportunity to go on, even more, about M. Héger. Then there was the fact that her sisters would have derived great amusement from knowing that 'The Major', of all people, was in love, and that would have been unacceptable to such a proud woman.

Nicholls also had good reason for requiring the matter to be kept quiet. Whatever he felt for Emily at that time – and Martha believed that he was genuinely fond of her – he had no intention of tying himself to such a girl, and such a family.

So they met, as they thought, in secret and, whilst sometimes it was possible to steal a few moments of privacy in the Parsonage, it was usually upon the moors that they came together because of their mutual love of walking over that majestic landscape. On occasion, the villagers remarked that Emily appeared 'transfigured' when returning from her absences there. She had loved those open spaces all her life, but now they held an additional delight.

Of course it was too much to hope that their meetings would pass unnoticed. There were always villagers about on the moors, but the inquisitive eyes of one seventeen-year-old girl saw more than most.

Martha was equally shrewd in her observation of Charlotte's devious discovery of Emily's poems. Charlotte was not averse to being 'economical with the truth'. In her 'Biographical Notice of Ellis and Acton Bell', which appears at the front of the 1850 edition of *Wuthering Heights* and *Agnes Grey*, she wrote: 'One day, in the autumn of 1845, I accidentally lighted on a MS. volume of verses in my sister Emily's handwriting . . .' Now that has to be a blatant lie. Emily poured out her soul in her poetry, and that introverted young woman would never, ever, have left such works lying about for anyone to read, especially inquisitive Charlotte.

There can be no doubt whatsoever that she would have put her poems away in her desk as usual. Charlotte had been consumed with curiosity to know what she was writing, but was forced to bide her time in order to find out. Then, when her sister had gone for one of her long walks, her patience was rewarded. We gain some idea of the time which she needed to pry into everything when we learn that there were about forty poems to read!

I find it very telling that Charlotte did not put out her tale about 'accidentally' lighting on the poems until Emily was long dead.

Chapter Four

'Oh that my words were now written! Oh that they were printed in a book!'

Job 19:23

As I have said already, Master Branwell was in a poor state on his return to the Parsonage, but he took to writing in his sober moments because, as he said to Father, he knew he had to do *something*. He had no job, and little chance of getting one, and money was very short.

He also told Father that, whilst with the Robinsons, he had learned from some of his writer friends that writing a 'novel' – whatever *that* might be – was a way of making money and so, in his spare time, he had made a start on one. It had been put aside of late, but now he had taken it up again.

Taken it up he may have done, but it was only for short spells because for most of his time he was in no fit state to do anything worthwhile. In his drunken mind, though, he had finished his book already and was well on the way to becoming a rich and famous writer, and I myself heard him rambling on in that vein.

Of course, with her ears and eyes *everywhere*, it was not long before Miss Charlotte heard of what he was going around saying, and Mr Nicholls told me in later years that, not knowing the full truth of what her brother was going on about, she was tormented by the thought that there might be something in it. She and her sisters were writing nothing, and the book of poems was still being sent back by publishers, and just the thought that what I have heard her call her 'disgusting brother' might outshine them all gave her sleepless nights.

Of course, I knew little of that at the time, and therefore I thought it just one of Miss Charlotte's many ideas for making money – which usually came to naught – when I heard her ask

39

her sisters whether or not they thought that they might write their own books. I only realized how much it meant to her when I saw her face set when she heard their answers. Miss Anne told her that she had already been writing whilst with the Robinsons, and had, in fact, almost finished a tale. Then, as if not to be outdone, Miss Emily chimed in to say that she already had an idea for a book.

Miss Charlotte went pale and then very red, and called them 'a pair of slyboots'. She had clearly been very taken aback. She had thought that she was coming up with a new idea only to find that her younger sisters were well ahead of her. I learnt later that the discovery did nothing to endear them to her; it simply added to her feelings that they were in league against her. She wondered why they had said nothing before she raised the matter, and felt that they might all leave her behind in the race for fame and fortune. Now she felt that she just had to carry on with her plan that they should each write a book, if only to keep an eye on what the others were up to.

Thus it was that, around November, 1845, they all set to writing in earnest.

That was easy for Miss Anne, who was already well on with her book, and soon it became less difficult for Miss Charlotte. I had seen some of the little books which the sisters had written as children with Master Branwell, long before I went to work at the Parsonage, so all of them knew something of the proper way of writing.

The only one of the sisters who seemed to have real trouble was Miss Emily. To my mind, she had not even thought about writing a book, let alone have an idea for one, when Miss Charlotte first came up with the idea, but said that she had simply to tease her sister. Either that, or her idea for a book just had not been good enough. Be that as it may, there were several times, when we were alone together, that she told me that her mind was a total blank, and that she had no idea of what to write about.

Then, all of a sudden, she was off and there seemed to be no stopping her, with her scribbling away faster, and for much longer, than her sisters. I have even seen her taking her papers with her when she went off up to the moors. I could not imagine that she was doing much writing up there, especially with Mr Nicholls about, and I put it down to the fact that, after the business with the poems, she did not want Miss Charlotte 'accidentally' discovering what she had written. Mr Nicholls has told me that I am right about that, but also that he would look at what she had written and make some changes.

After her death, there were tales that Miss Emily had not written the book herself, and at those times I scoffed at such ideas and said that the people were liars – for I could vouch for having seen her writing it. Now, though, I am not so sure, because Mr Nicholls told me that it was Master Branwell's idea in the first place, and so many others have come forward with what seem to be true accounts that the book was, in part at least, Master Branwell's.

In recent years Mr Nicholls has also felt able to confide in me about the worries that Master Branwell began to cause him and Miss Emily at that time.

The first was when he told her that he knew about her meetings with Mr Nicholls. She could not think of how he had found out, but perhaps it was because everybody had become so used to treating Master Branwell as if he were not there – much as they tended to do with me at times – that she and Mr Nicholls had not taken care when he was about. Some folk make the mistake of thinking that those in their cups do not notice what is going on around them, but it has always seemed to me that a part of their mind keeps going as normal. Many were the times, when I was a young girl, that I passed remarks – sometimes about him – when my Father had had a drop too much and I thought that he would not notice, but was taken to task by him the next day.

Be that as it may, however Master Branwell knew, knew he did, although at that time there was little enough *to* know, but even so Miss Emily did not want anything of her friendship with Mr Nicholls to be bandied about. There can be no doubt but that she was already in love with him, but what passed between them then was very mild and she had in no way made her true feelings known to Mr Nicholls. I suppose that with the

41

way she had been brought up, her natural closeness and her lack of dealings with men, things could not have been otherwise. Certainly she needed a great deal of wooing and, from what I knew of her and from what Mr Nicholls has told me, at the start she would have been put off by anything but the most gentle and innocent of lovemaking.

By then it was 1847, and life at the Parsonage was going on in much the same old way except that Master Branwell's state was getting worse. I could see that he was lonely, and Father said that, at long last, he was having to face the fact that he would never amount to much. Seemingly he was full of self-pity, saying that he thought himself ill-suited for drudgery and blaming that on the fact that he had been too much petted through life. Their mutual friend, Mr Leyland, told Father that Master Branwell had written to him saying that he was an utter wreck and, being without hope, was in mental agony.

Certainly his drinking was even more of a disgrace and the talk of the village, and I knew for a fact that he was taking far more laudanum than ever because I saw the bottles. Miss Anne seemed to look upon him with horror, and I heard Miss Charlotte call him 'a shameful burden', which I did not think was a proper thing to have done when servants were in earshot.

Then, in May I think it was, Master Branwell became much quieter, but when I remarked about that at home Father said it was not to be wondered at because he had got to the end of a large sum of money which he had got in the Spring, and had therefore to restrict himself to some degree. However, that state of affairs was too good to last because, as Miss Charlotte said, he just had to have his drink and drugs, and seemed willing to do anything to get them.

I knew from gossip in the village at that time that he was going to almost anyone trying to borrow money, but folk had had enough of him and he had no luck. I suppose that is why he decided to make demands of Mr Nicholls.

Before that he had often had small sums from Mr Nicholls, who has told me that, although he had little enough money for himself, he had not minded parting with the odd coin or two to keep him quiet and get rid of him. Now, though, he was not asking but demanding, and those demands came more often and for much larger sums than Mr Nicholls could provide. Then when Mr Nicholls refused him altogether, his desperate state drove him to start to make nasty threats to Mr Nicholls about his friendship with Miss Emily. He told him that he would tell his father they were meeting on the moors if Mr Nicholls did not pay him.

Well, as Mr Nicholls has said to me, what choice did he have? He knew that Mr Brontë would probably have a seizure if he found out that one of his daughters was walking out, or worse, with his assistant. Mr Brontë wanted his daughters to marry money, and he would not have allowed any of them to wed an assistant with hardly a penny to bless himself with. Mr Nicholls knew that he would have been dismissed, and that, coupled with unclear tales of misbehaviour with a Minister's daughter, would have made certain that he did not get another job in the Church.

He knew also that it was important to keep Master Branwell quiet about what he and Miss Emily now thought of as 'her' book. They both had the constant worry that Master Branwell would decide to take back what he had written and make it public – leaving her with nothing. So Mr Nicholls paid up, not knowing that in doing so he had taken the first step on a path that would lead to misery and death.

[*CC*] As far as Emily was concerned, I can quite believe that she found it difficult to begin her novel. She was not as worldly as her sisters, and was unaware of many of the frailties of human nature. All she knew was that she was possessed by inexpressible yearnings from which she was constantly tempted to seek relief. She wanted so much to keep up with her sisters, and therefore did not relish the prospect of having to confess to Charlotte that she had never had an idea for a novel, and most certainly was not writing one. From what Martha hints at, and others have actually stated publicly, it seems apparent that finally, in utter desperation, and because the emotions expressed were so akin to her own, she resorted to plagiarism.

It is well known that Emily wrote fair copies of his writings

43

for Branwell when they were younger, and Martha has told us that the practice continued into their adult lives. Perhaps her help was even more essential then, because heavy drinking, and the subsequent bouts of *delirium tremens* from which he suffered, were hardly conducive to good handwriting. Thus Emily had come to know upon what Branwell was working when he gave her the completed part of his novel for tidying up.

That is not to say, however, that she did not already have a good idea of the subject matter. Branwell, unlike Emily, was never one to keep anything to himself and had bragged about his writing to his sisters and others, albeit only in the vaguest of terms. To whom, though, had he spoken in more detail, in search of approval and praise? Certainly not Charlotte; he had been wounded deeply by the way in which she had treated him since the Robinson business, and it was obvious that she was avoiding his company.

Anne, also, had made her opinion of him quite clear. She had been horrified by what had happened at Thorp Green Hall, by what he had become, and by what he was doing to the family. It was also because of him that she had been obliged to leave a post which she enjoyed and return to cheerless Haworth.

No, it was to Emily, always his friend, that he looked for approbation. Apart from anything else, he had spent more time alone with her in recent years, and there was a great deal of rapport between them. The worst that Emily is known ever to have said about her brother was that he was 'a hopeless being', and I think that even that was merely a passing comment. I also consider that, unlike his other sisters, she was inclined to believe his tale about an affaire with Mrs Robinson. Anne may have told her the truth, but that would not have been something which Emily would wish to believe. She had a great deal of pity for Branwell, and would have sympathized with what she thought to be his plight because of what was happening between her and Mr Nicholls.

Nevertheless, her predicament compelled her to desperate measures. Having seen Branwell's incomplete manuscript, she realized the potential of the story, which was set in a location very dear to her heart. I do not think that she would have set out to steal it, but she found herself in a dilemma, and the finishing of a novel which might otherwise have gone uncompleted seemed an ideal solution.

She sought Nicholls' advice and he encouraged her: he realized the financial potential of a successful novel. So she took the incomplete story and finished it with the active advice, collaboration and corrections of Nicholls, from whom I do not think even Charlotte and Anne were averse to seeking help. Branwell was consulted from time to time, but only to placate him, because he was under the impression that Emily was merely writing his thoughts whereas, in essence, she took the idea from him and then wrote most of the book which she later entitled *Wuthering Heights*.

I fear that some readers may regard all of this with a degree of scepticism. If, however, they examine the evidence objectively, and disregard the myths which tend to surround the Brontës, they will find corroboration of what Martha asserted.

In 1845, Branwell had some poems published in the *Halifax Guardian* and started on a three-volume novel. In September of that year, he told his friend J.B. Leyland that he had finished the first volume, but at the end of the following month he informed another crony, Grundy, that he had abandoned the project, and those apparently conflicting statements have led to some confusion. Fifty-eight pages of a novel entitled *And the Weary are at Rest* were discovered after his death but, as there *were* only fifty-eight pages, they cannot comprise the finished volume of which he told Leyland. It is, therefore, logical to suppose that they made up the *un*finished work which he mentioned to Grundy. That, however, prompts the question of what happened to the completed volume – but more of that in a moment.

Much later, in 1867, William Dearden claimed that in 1848 he, J.B. Leyland and Branwell each agreed to write something which would be read aloud in the Cross Roads Inn, which was situated between Haworth and Keighley. They met on the appointed night, but Branwell had to apologize, saying that, by mistake, he had brought the opening chapter of a novel he was writing instead of the special piece which he had composed.

According to Dearden, Branwell then proceeded to read out the first chapter of *Wuthering Heights*!

That is not all. In his book *Pictures of the Past*, Grundy wrote: '. . . Brontë declared to me, and what his sister said bore out the assertion, that he wrote a great portion of *Wuthering Heights* himself. Indeed it is impossible for me to read that story without meeting with many passages which I feel certain *must* have come from his pen. The weird fancies of diseased genius with which he used to entertain me in our long talks at Luddenden Foot reappear in the pages of the novel, and I am inclined to believe that the very plot was his invention rather than his sister's.'

I find it more than frustrating that Grundy did not *name* the sister who confirmed Branwell's claim, but all the signs point to it having been Emily.

There is more. Edward Sloane, of Halifax, told William Dearden that Branwell had read to him, portion by portion, the novel as it was produced, at the time, insomuch that he no sooner began the perusal of *Wuthering Heights*, when published, than he was able to anticipate the characters and incidents to be disclosed.

Staunch supporters of Emily have poured scorn upon all those statements, especially as they were not made until all the Brontës were dead, but they are not being objective. They will listen to nothing which tends to detract from the popular Brontë image. However, an impartial observer will ask why all those men should have lied. They had absolutely nothing to gain by so doing, and their statements were not only made independently but were separated by an interval of twelve years. Actually, the mere fact that they *did* wait until the family was dead tends to strengthen my belief in their veracity. We should ask what the results would have been had they spoken out whilst the sisters were living. Their assertions would have served merely to fuel the arguments about the authorship of the sisters' novels which raged when they were first published, and that would have caused distress to the family, and to Emily in particular. The men would not have wished that to happen, especially in view of Emily's many kindnesses to their friend Branwell.

Is there not, also, the ring of truth in what they said? One can well imagine poor befuddled Branwell producing in 1848 something which he had written three or four years earlier and declaring that it was the first chapter of what he was *then* engaged upon. Sloane's statement, that Branwell read the story to him chapter by chapter, as it was written, lends credence to my belief that Emily consulted him whilst she was writing. Were that the case, he would have known how she was progressing, and it would not have been difficult for him to smuggle chapters out of the Parsonage as they were completed.

In addition to all that, there is very convincing literary evidence which indicates that Branwell was involved in the writing of the book.

I have been struck very forcibly – and much as Grundy was with his friend's *spoken* words – by similarities of phraseology between certain passages in the novel and some in letters written by Branwell.

There is also the mute testimony of the book itself. The first three chapters are related by the character Lockwood and tell of his personal experiences, but then there is an awkward change of literary style. One is introduced to Nellie Dean, Lockwood's housekeeper, and the rest of the story is *her* tale to Lockwood – who then recounts it to the reader. I can think of no more likely reason for the change than that a female writer took up where a male left off.

Most writers about the Brontës will *hint* at the possibility of Branwell's having had a hand in *Wuthering Heights*, but none, as far as I am aware, have stated categorically that they themselves believe in his involvement. Well Martha did, and so do I. I think that he had roughed out the novel, had actually written the first three chapters, and had then abandoned it. I further believe that it was finished by Emily with some help from Branwell, but far more from her lover, the Rev. Arthur Bell Nicholls.

I find it most significant that the original manuscript of *Wuthering Heights* has never been traced. It is common knowledge that Charlotte destroyed some of Emily's manuscripts after her death. Why, however – if in fact she did – should she

47

have done away with that particular one? The book had been published, so there was nothing, on the face of it, which should have been withheld from the public. One explanation could be that, if Emily had retained Branwell's originals, Charlotte did not want it to be seen in whose handwriting the first three chapters were. An alternative, or additional, reason may have been that Nicholls' notes and suggestions were written in the margins.

Who knows, the manuscript may very well turn up one day. Stranger things have happened. If Charlotte simply concealed it, instead of destroying it along with the others, it could very well have fallen into other hands when the Parsonage was vacated after Mr Brontë died. Perhaps, at this very moment, and just as with Martha Brown's statement, it is lying in some dusty Yorkshire attic unknown for what it is.

There are conflicting statements and opinions about whether or not Branwell knew of his sisters' writings, and of their eventual publication. Charlotte said that he did not, but I feel that that was not so – and that she had a very good motive for lying. Had people known that he suspected what they were all doing, but had been excluded, some blame for his misconduct might have been apportioned to the sisters, and to Charlotte in particular – and that would not have done at all.

Commonsense tells us that Branwell could not *not* have known of their writings. There they were, in that small house, all scribbling away night after night; even in his worst moments he was not as obtuse as that. Also, apart from any discussions which he may have had with Emily, we know that he advised Charlotte on the everyday practicalities of dealing with publishers.

Emily was the only one who stood by him. That was due partly to her natural compassion, but mainly because she felt badly about appropriating his story. It was always she who tried to conceal his worst excesses from their father, and on occasion she had been known to run to the Black Bull and tap on the window to warn him when the old man was on the warpath. At other times she carried him upstairs when he was drunk. Then there was the notable time when he was discovered unconscious on his blazing bed, which he had accidentally set afire whilst under the influence. It was Emily, alone, who got him out and extinguished the flames.

In actuality, though, it is probably true to say that nobody at the Parsonage *really* had much time for him, literally or metaphorically; he just drifted along in his solitary world. Emily would probably have responded to his questions about what had become 'our' book by consulting him on certain aspects of it, but only to keep him quiet and compliant. She had no wish to upset him for not only did he know that 'her' book was basically his but, as Martha tells us, he was privy to her other secret which she considered far more important.

Chapter Five

'There is death in the pot.'
2 Kings 4:40

There was great excitement at the Parsonage at the end of that year of 1847.

Miss Charlotte's book, called *Jane Eyre*, was printed in October and, by what she went about saying, it went well straightaway. Then, 2 months later, Miss Emily's book, *Wuthering Heights*, and Miss Anne's, *Agnes Gray*, came out bound together in one volume. I heard Miss Charlotte say, with great pleasure in her voice, that the other 2 books were not going as well as hers, but Miss Emily told me that they were selling nonetheless, and that was the main thing.

The whole business was marred, though, because some folk said that all 3 tales had been penned by the same person, and Mr Nicholls has told me that that was probably because *he* had had a hand in all of them and it showed.

Apart from being cross about what was being said, Miss Charlotte was cock-a-hoop at having her story in print. Straightaway she wrote to some well-known writers telling them about her book, and when she gave me the letters to take to the post she went to great pains to tell me how important the people were. I cannot remember all the names, but Thackeray and Lewes have stuck in my mind. She then began another book, which I now know was called *Shirley*.

On the other hand, Miss Anne, as usual, said very little about *her* book, but stuck grimly to writing another that I had seen her busy on for some months. I had not dared to ask Miss Charlotte what *her* new book was about, but I felt able to do so with Miss Anne. She did not answer me directly, and now I know why. It was called *The Tenant of Wildfell Hall*, and it

50

would seem that she got her ideas for it from Master Branwell's conduct.

As for Miss Emily, well, her manner was very odd once the early excitement was over, and I was at a loss to understand it. It was evident that she had been contented enough to send her book to be looked at by the publisher, and I remember her saying that she was going to write to him about a second book that she had in mind. Then, though, shortly after *Wuthering Heights* was printed, she withdrew into herself completely and nobody, not even me, could get a word out of her. That both puzzled and bothered me greatly, for I thought I had become something of a favourite with her, and it seemed to worry Miss Charlotte as well because she remarked upon it several times. The trouble was that neither of us knew what Miss Emily did, and only later did we find out that the fact of the matter was that she felt very guilty about Master Branwell.

She had watched him sinking deeper and deeper into misery because he felt such a failure, and because he was lonely and his family wanted naught to do with him. Yet there *she* was, now a known writer because of a book which was, at the very least, founded upon a story that was his.

As I know from having seen some of her earlier poems, Miss Emily had always had great pity for outcasts, so I know full well how much stronger must her feelings have been for her own brother – with all his faults. It is true that she was kinder to him than were his other sisters, but now she knew that that had not been enough. She had not realized what awful feelings she would have of letting him down once the book was published, and now she wished with all her heart that she had had nothing to do with it.

Her deep feeling of guilt was not made less when Master Branwell learned that his sisters' works had been printed. He had always thought of *Wuthering Heights* as being his path to money and respect, and had never dreamed that not only would it be stolen from him, but that his part in it would not be told. It all hurt him very much, and Miss Emily told Mr Nicholls, who later told me, that Master Branwell spoke to her about it, but only gently and seemed more sad than angry that she, of all

51

people, could have done that to him. What he did not know, and Miss Emily could not tell him, was that she would have been very happy to have told everyone of his part in it – in fact she had wanted very much to do so – but Mr Nicholls would not have it, and by that time she could gainsay him nothing.

Mr Nicholls has told me that he had a slight hope that some of the cash from the book might come his way, but he knew full well that if Master Branwell's name had been put to it in any way he would never cease demanding a share of the money. So, very much against her nature, Miss Emily gained a pledge of secrecy from him by way of half-promises and a few shillings from Mr Nicholls.

Of course, it did not work, and Miss Emily, with all that she knew of her brother, should not have expected that it would. Everything was well whilst Master Branwell was sober, but when he was not – which was most of the time – he could not help dropping a word or two to his friends about his part in the book.

It did not take Miss Emily very long to realize that the promise of secrecy that he had made to her was almost as worthless as all his other promises, because he really was in a bad way for most of the time. He had fits of the drunken shakes in the Talbot and the Old Cock taverns in Halifax, and went weeks without proper sleep or food. Then he became even more desperate for money when Mr Nicholson, the landlord of the Old Cock, told him that he would have him arrested for debt, and Mrs Sugden at the Talbot began to complain about the great amount that he owed to her.

Father seemed very put out by Master Branwell's troubles at that time, but I never knew the full story until Mr Nicholls told me. All I knew then was that I had overheard Father saying that Master Branwell was telling all his friends that he felt wretched and weak, and was nearly worn out.

I got some idea of what this meant when Master Branwell gave me a note one day and begged me to take it posthaste and secretly to my Father. It was only a folded piece of paper, and I never could stop myself from sticking my nose into where it should not be, and so I read it as I made my way to Father's barn. The writing was very bad, and there were many blots of ink. At this distance of time I can no longer recall all the words, but what *does* stick in my mind is that he asked Father to get him 'Fivepenceworth of Gin', and promised to pay him back out of a shilling which Mr Brontë was due to give him on the morrow.

Father was pleased to see me, but his manner changed when he read the note, and he pursed his lips in the way he had when he was cross. I knew that he was far too busy to be bothered in such a fashion because he was not even going home for his midday meal. Instead, he contented himself with taking bread and some cheese or meat with him when he went off in the morning. Sometimes my Mother or one of my sisters carried some hot broth down to him at noon, but usually he made do for the whole day with what he had.

Anyway, knowing me better than I knew myself, he looked at me straight and asked whether I had read the note and, as I could hardly ever lie to Father, I told him I had. He nodded, and then, pledging me to silence, he placed a sixpenny piece in my hand and told me to go to the back door of the house part of the Black Bull and get the Gin, saying that it was for him.

I scurried off and did as I was bid, and then took the Gin to Master Branwell, who was shaking so much he was like to have dropped it, but was very thankful for it.

I have gone on at some length about this because the happenings of that day are so printed on my mind for 2 reasons in particular.

The first is that, whilst I had kept the bottle hidden, and had managed to get it up to Master Branwell without being seen, I was stopped by Miss Charlotte when I came back down the stairs. She gave me a right telling off, saying that she had been looking for me for nigh on a half-hour, and asked where I had been and what I had been doing upstairs at that time of day.

I was so taken aback by the way she spoke to me that all I could do was stutter that I had been on an errand for Master Branwell, and I was thankful that she did not ask what the errand was. Instead, she gave me another good scolding and told me that going errands for Master Branwell was not one of my duties, and that if he asked me to do anything else for him I should seek leave from her or one of her sisters first. Of course, I bit my tongue whilst she was ranting on, but my mind was going pell-mell. I thought how ugly she looked, with her little red face all twisted up, and how much I disliked her voice. Above all, I hated even more the airs and graces which she had always taken upon herself. In that very instance, I wondered who she thought she was. She and her sisters did not pay my wages, yet I was expected to seek leave of them before I did anything for their poor brother, who was only a year younger than her and older than the other two.

It was then that my real hatred of her was born, and I vowed to myself that one day I would get my own back.

My other memory is about the penny change that I had after getting the Gin. The next time I saw Father he asked me if all had gone well with the Gin, and then for the penny. I told him of what had befallen me with Miss Charlotte – which did not please him one whit – but try as I would I could not remember what I had done with the penny, and I could not find it. I looked everywhere, but it never did come to light and I do not know to this day whether or not Father believed that I really had lost it and not spent it, although I have always hoped that he did. On my next pay-day, I offered him a penny out of the little that by then I was allowed to keep, but he would not take it.

As it happened, Master Branwell never did ask me to run any more errands, which was probably just as well for I had made up my mind that if he did I would, and to the Devil with Miss Do-As-I-Say. In fact, he hardly seemed to speak to anyone in the Parsonage, but just got worse. One day I peeped at a half-finished letter which Miss Charlotte was writing to her friend Miss Nussey. She had written that Master Branwell was 'the same in conduct as ever; his constitution seems shattered', and that just about summed it up. All he seemed to do was drink whatever came to hand, and Father told Mother that he placed no limit upon who he would try to beg money from – but usually without much luck.

In the end, although he had gone farther and farther afield for his drinking, he could get no credit at public houses, and

Father said that even his best friends tended to avoid him when he was at his worst. I heard him ranting to Miss Emily that their father now gave him hardly anything, but I did not know how hard pressed he had become until much later, when Mr Nicholls trusted me fully and felt able to tell me most things.

It would seem that he just did not know which way to turn for a penny, because even the money that he was expecting from Dr Crosby was already promised to Mrs Sugden and Mr Nicholson. It must have seemed to him that his only hope lay in Mr Nicholls, for it was to him that he turned, but in a manner that was far more ugly than before.

Had he but known it – or perhaps he did – he could hardly have chosen a better time to up his demands, for by then Miss Emily and Mr Nicholls had become lovers in the fullest way.

Looking back, I see now how different Miss Emily became at about that time, and it is apparent to me that her first going with a man had been a wonderful happening for her, and one that changed her life. Mr Nicholls has told me that there was nothing she would not do for him after that first time together, and he took great advantage of that. Yet again he forbade her to mention their relationship to anyone, especially her sisters, and that would seem to have been another reason for her strange silence that folk noticed. She did not even go to London with her sisters when, in the Summer of 1848, they went to see Miss Charlotte's publisher. I had often wondered why she did not go, for *I* would have leaped at the chance, but Mr Nicholls has told me that he was against it because he thought that a constant watch should be kept upon Master Branwell.

Knowing much more now of Mr Nicholls' true nature, I am able to see how trapped and angry he must have felt after Master Branwell had been to see him with his threats, and he has told me that he was not only angry with Master Branwell but with himself for being so foolish as to let matters come to such a pass.

According to him, his dalliance with Miss Emily had gone much further than he had really wanted it to, and things had been made much more difficult by the writing of *Wuthering Heights*, although Master Branwell's silence about that did not seem as important as it had. Mr Nicholls has confessed to me that he still held out a slight hope that some of the money from the book might, somehow, find its way into his pocket, and so he wished to keep Miss Emily happy and untroubled but, that apart, he had not cared overmuch if Master Branwell blabbed about his hand in it. However, it was a much different kettle of fish when it came to the threat of telling Mr Brontë, and all and sundry, of what was going on between him and Miss Emily.

He was not sure just how much Master Branwell knew. If, somehow, he knew everything, that could lead to ruin, and so he had to be kept quiet at all cost, but how? Mr Nicholls was already feeling the pinch, especially after paying the previous sums to Master Branwell out of a wage of less than £100 a year, and there was just no chance of him being able to afford more. In any case, Mr Nicholls knew enough of the world to be sure that rarely are blackmailers satisfied, and therefore he could see that Master Branwell's demands would go on for as long as he drew breath.

Mr Nicholls became very sad when he told me of these things. He said that he had never really wanted anything more than a quiet, comfortable life, but then it seemed to him that Fate was bent upon taking away from him even the little that he had. When he had tried to explain to Master Branwell that he just did not have the cash his words had fallen upon deaf ears, and it had seemed that what he called 'the nasty little sot' was about to ruin his good name, his job and his future.

He said that he told Miss Emily how he felt, and found her almost as desperate as he was. She managed to scrape a little more money together to keep her brother quiet for a while, but by then she too had come to see that he would never be satisfied, and she was worried to death about how it would all end. That, of course, was something that was in Mr Nicholls' mind all the time, but he was angry that Miss Emily should be so burdened because he thought a lot of her.

They lived in daily fear that, although it was to his gain to say naught, Master Branwell would nevertheless tell all when he was drunk, and the constant worry began to tell on Mr Nicholls. He said that he was not able to put his mind to his duties, and he wandered around like a man in a daze. Indeed I know that to be true, for I well remember Father asking me if I knew what was amiss with him. Of course, I did not know then, though I sensed that it was something to do with Miss Emily. In fact, I did not know until so many years later that none of it seemed to matter, but here is what Mr Nicholls told me.

He said that for two years he had watched Master Branwell going downhill, in the hope that he would die an early death. That would have been to everybody's gain, and was much to be wished for. However, he had not obliged, and by the time that I am writing of Mr Nicholls could see no end to the troubles that he caused him and Miss Emily. He worried over the matter for weeks, but the only answer that kept coming to him was that Master Branwell should die, and quickly. That, he said, was when he was finally driven to see that the tight spot he was in could be righted only by stern action, and that he should take matters into his own hands. It was evident to all that Master Branwell was drinking himself into an early grave – he would just hurry things along a little.

Mr Nicholls told me that he was surprised that he suffered no doubts or misgivings once he had decided to murder his tormentor. His Faith had never been strong but, in any case, with Master Branwell seemingly bent upon destroying himself, it seemed that what he had in mind was really a kind of mercy. Anyway, he felt he *deserved* to die.

Mr Nicholls had disliked Master Branwell on sight for what he was although, oddly enough, he had been somewhat jealous of his popularity and some of his ways when in company. However, the dislike had deepened gradually as he came to realize that Master Branwell and his friends were laughing at him behind his back, and I can vouch for that because many was the time when Father mimicked him and made us all laugh,

Then Mr Nicholls learned a great deal of what had really happened at Thorp Green Hall, and that sickened him. Dislike had become hatred as Master Branwell's goings-on became worse, and the blackmail started, until the time came when Mr Nicholls loathed the sight, smell and sound of him. Master Branwell had come to stand for everything that Mr Nicholls hated and despised – but above all he feared him for the harm he could do.

I once asked Mr Nicholls why he had thought it necessary to kill him, thus putting his own life and soul in peril, when, as we all knew, Master Branwell was slowly killing himself. He looked at me a little sadly, and then said something like: 'But that was the whole point, Martha my dear, he was doing it *slowly*. Left to his own devices, he might have gone on for years, and that was something that I could not bear to think about.' Of course he was right, and I felt a little foolish for asking.

Having decided what he was going to do, Mr Nicholls wasted no time in putting his plan into action. On Friday, 22nd September, 1848, Master Branwell was out and about in the village, and very much his usual self. The next day, though, he was forced to take to his bed – which, in itself, was not unusual for him – but by Sunday morning he was dead!

As Mr Nicholls had supposed, nobody was surprised by his sudden passing, and the village doctor, Dr Wheelhouse, signed the death certificate without a second thought, although Father, who knew about such matters, was of a mind that a postmortem examination should have taken place.

Master Branwell was buried in his father's Church. I was not allowed to go to the funeral, but Father did and he said that it was very moving, and that there were a fair few folk there. What surprised many though was that, of his three sisters, only Miss Emily went. Miss Charlotte said that she was ill, and Miss Anne made the excuse that she had to stay home to look after her.

I did not hear any of that until after the funeral, and so I wondered why they were not there instead of sitting at home whispering together. I saw no signs of Miss Charlotte being ill, and certainly she never took to her bed. Even if she had, there were enough of us in the Parsonage to have seen to her wants for the short time the service took without Miss Anne staying away as well.

I thought it all very sad.

*

58

[*GG*] Writer after writer states that Branwell died from tuberculosis – more commonly known as 'consumption' at that time. That, however, just is not true, and is yet another example of how the accepted Brontë legend feeds upon itself. I have a copy of Branwell's death certificate before me as I write, and it gives 'Chronic Bronchitis, Marasmus' as the causes of death.

Now I must confess that, although I am an amateur criminologist, the medical condition of 'Marasmus' was not one with which I was familiar. It necessitated reference to a reputable medical dictionary. The definition given therein was 'A progressive wasting, *when there is no ascertainable cause*'. (My italics.) It was not until much later that a pathologist friend of mine told me that 'Marasmus' is one of those high-sounding terms employed by doctors when they really have no idea of from what a person has died!

That same friend and I have given a great deal of thought to what substance Nicholls may have used if, in fact, Branwell Brontë *was* poisoned.

Obviously, the first one at which we looked was laudanum, otherwise known as tincture of opium, because it is well documented that Branwell was addicted to it, and addicts can, within moderation, drink it like wine – the only effect being one of stimulation. In those days it was said to be a preventive against consumption, and it was also used widely as a sedative, even for babies.

For Arthur Nicholls, the advantages of administering an overdose of laudanum would have been that it was widely available, cheap, easily administered and left no odour on the breath. Also laudanum has other important properties. A lethal dose does not cause death until seven to eighteen hours after being taken, and the effects may be postponed for several hours more if it is taken with alcohol.

How very easy it would have been. Branwell would drink anything alcoholic, especially if it was free, and so all that Nicholls would have had to do was wait until he was approached for more money and then offer his victim, say, a few brandies which were laced liberally with the drug. Branwell would have been appreciative of the drink, and Nicholls would have had ample time to be elsewhere when death occurred.

Could he have used arsenic? Again, it is a possibility. It would have fitted the bill almost as well as laudanum, and better in some respects, but we shall discuss poisons later, and in more depth.

I consider it of great importance that I have been unable to discover any mention of Branwell being ill just before his death, except that he had a cough. Indeed, on 9 October 1848, Charlotte wrote to Ellen Nussey saying that *'neither the doctor or Branwell himself thought him to be so close to death'*. (My italics.) Yet, even so, the good doctor did not see fit to arrange an autopsy. He merely fudged the death certificate, and Arthur Nicholls and the Brontë family breathed a collective sigh of relief – albeit for different reasons.

Following her brother's death, Charlotte was instantly, and very conveniently, stricken with 'bilious fever', and was therefore, she said, too ill to attend Branwell's funeral.

As Martha has told us, Anne did not go either. Such behaviour was only what one would have expected in the light of their opinions of their brother, and despite some of the hypocritical terms in which Charlotte wrote about him after his death. Compare her letter to Ellen, of 4 November 1845: 'I wish I could say one word to you in his favour . . .' with that to W.S. Williams, of 6 October 1848: 'When I looked on the noble face and forehead of my dead brother . . .' and one sees vintage Charlotte.

However, many were genuinely grieved by his death. Emily wrote a moving poem about him which she called 'The Wanderer from the Fold', and in later years his friends were at pains to correct the erroneous portrait which had been painted of him by Mrs Gaskell. Leyland and George Searle Phillips testified to his lively conversation, his wit, his poetry, and his thoughtful discourse. Phillips also contradicted Mrs Gaskell point blank: 'But, even when pretty deep in his cups, he had not the slightest appearance of the sot Mrs Gaskell says he was.' It was a description which she probably obtained from Nicholls.

I think we should allow another friend to have the final word on Branwell, for I feel it to be the truest. Grundy wrote that Branwell 'was no domestic demon; he was just a man moving in a mist who lost his way.'

Chapter Six

'My punishment is greater than I can bear.'
Genesis 4:13

M iss Emily, then, was the only sister who went to Master Branwell's funeral. Being the woman she was, she would have done so anyway, but I know now that by then her feelings were so mixed up that she could never have stayed away.

She already felt guilty about stealing his idea for her book, but now she was burdened by something far more terrible, for she had found out that her lover had murdered her brother. (How I know of this, I shall tell later.)

Mr Nicholls has since told me that it was not his intent that she should know anything about what he had in mind, for he knew that nobody could be trusted with that kind of secret. He had therefore gone about his plan with care and very quietly.

After much thought, he had decided that the only way to kill Master Branwell was by means of poison, but knowing that to buy it in Haworth was out of the question he went to Halifax to do so, and did it under another name and dressed as quietly as possible. In order to account for his absence, he had given it out that he was going to visit his friend, Mr Grant, who was the curate in the next parish, but he was undone by one of those strange chances that no one can foresee.

It so happened that Master Branwell was drinking in Halifax that day and he, of all people, saw Mr Nicholls coming out of the apothecary. He was forced to return to the Parsonage sooner than he had reckoned, because he had run out of cash and credit, but even so he was well drunk and had to be helped upstairs by Miss Emily. She asked him where he had been to get in such a state, and he told her Halifax – but then went on to say, with a laugh, that he had seen her sweetheart coming from the apothecary's shop there, and that he was not wearing his normal clergyman's garb.

Of course, Miss Emily did not believe him, thinking that what he had said was just part of his drunken ramblings, but a little doubt must have stayed in her mind because I remember that much later she asked me if I had seen Mr Nicholls about on the day before and how he was dressed. I had not, because I would have been busy about the Parsonage, but I thought that her questions were so strange that, in a roundabout way, I quizzed Mother that evening and she told me that he had gone out in clothes that we had all seen hanging in his wardrobe, but had seen him wear but a few times before.

I told that to Miss Emily, but she did not seem very interested and said that her questions to me had been only in passing. However, I know now that she had been both puzzled and worried. Her first thought had been that Mr Nicholls was ailing and, not wishing to worry her, had gone to an apothecary outside the village for some medicine. It would seem that she did not mention the matter to him straightaway. She merely asked him how he had got on with Mr Grant, and he told her that he had spent a pleasant day with him. He said nothing more, but his answer, and the manner of it, lulled any worries which she had.

It would seem, therefore, that it was only when Master Branwell died so quickly and unexpectedly, and within but a few days of Mr Nicholls' day out, that her mind went to another possibility and she began to think with dread of what he might have done. It was a notion that so took hold of her mind that she was not able to rest until she had found the truth, and it was then that, I realize now, I was once again caught up in the matter – albeit without knowing.

On the evening of the day of Master Branwell's death, Miss Emily took me to one side as I was washing the dishes. She was far from her usual self, and spoke in such a low voice that I wondered what was amiss, but she simply took an envelope from her pocket and said that she had an urgent message from her father for Mr Nicholls, and would I run home and hand it to him without delay.

I was somewhat puzzled by that, because I had carried messages from Mr Brontë to Mr Nicholls several times before, and to Father, but he had always handed them to me himself. Also, the name of the person that the letter was to had always been written on the envelope whereas there was no name on this one, and indeed it did not look or feel like one of Mr Brontë's which were bigger and stiffer. Still it was none of my business, and I remember thinking that Mr Brontë may have been so upset by his son's death that he had had Miss Emily write his message for him.

I hurried down the lane to our house, went to Mr Nicholls' room and handed the letter to him. He did not open the envelope in front of me, but within minutes I heard the back door close and he went out. I thought that he was going to the Parsonage to see Mr Brontë, but then, as I was taking the chance of a quick word with Mother in the kitchen, I saw him making his way to the moors and it came to me that he was off to meet Miss Emily.

Of course, I have been able to put these happenings together in proper fashion only since I learned the full truth, but even then I thought it all rather odd.

I know now that it was at that meeting that Miss Emily taxed Mr Nicholls about her fears that he had murdered her brother. He has told me that what she said shook him to his core, but that he was able to manage a laugh and tell her not to be so silly. It was only when she told him that he had been seen leaving the apothecary's at Halifax – without saying who had seen him – that he was forced, little by little, into telling the truth. Only later did she tell him that it was Master Branwell himself who had pointed the finger at him.

Mr Nicholls has told me that, at first, he had wanted to lie and say that he had been to the apothecary for some sort of potion for himself, and he thinks that he might have got away with that. However, he was thrown into such a state of mind by her unexpected questions that all he could think of at the time was that if she went to the authorities with her fears he would soon be identified by the man who had served him. Then, if Master Branwell's body was dug up and the same

64

poison found as he had bought, he would be sure to be hanged.

Only after he had told her all did he realize that he had been in no danger, because then it was evident that Miss Emily's passion for him would not have allowed her to betray him. He was quite right in thinking that for I now know that Miss Emily told Miss Anne as much, and that she, poor woman, was being torn asunder by her feelings, and that she would never be able to live at ease with the fact that the man she loved had killed her brother.

People have always said that Miss Emily caught a chill at Master Branwell's funeral, but I do not recall any such thing. All I know is that she became very, very quiet after it and only pecked at her food, like an ailing sparrow. They also say that she never left the Parsonage again until her own death some 3 months later, but that also is wrong, as anyone who knew Miss Emily well will tell you.

As I remember it, she did have a bit of a cough, but nothing that troubled her overmuch, and I know for sure that she carried on meeting Mr Nicholls for at least a month after Master Branwell died because he has told me so and he has no reason to lie at this distance of time. He said that she seemed to need to talk to him because she was finding it very hard to live with what she knew, especially as she was not sleeping well because of her cough, and her darkest thoughts came in the small hours.

For his part, though, Mr Nicholls has never shown any sense of regret to me. He says that, as far as he was concerned, what was done was done. Nothing could have brought Master Branwell back, and it was good riddance to bad rubbish. He found it impossible to understand how Miss Emily was feeling, and often he had little patience with her.

When he was like that, it dismayed Miss Emily beyond belief. It was a side of him that she had not seen before, and it was then that she came to believe that he was tiring of her and was carrying on with her just to keep her quiet. If that was so, it is little wonder, I feel, that she drew more and more into herself. Not only that, but she began to act so oddly that Miss

Charlotte became concerned about her, even taking the trouble to remark upon it to me – of all people. I think that, knowing that Miss Emily often talked to me, she was hoping that I knew something, but even if I had I would not have told *her*.

As it happens, I now know that Miss Emily *had* felt the need to tell someone of what ailed her. That someone was Miss Anne, who wrote down everything, which, as I shall explain, I have read myself.

I do not think that Miss Anne would have been as shocked by what she learned as most folk would imagine. In fact, I doubt very much whether she would have been shocked at all. She, more than anybody, knew what Master Branwell had been up to at the Robinsons, and that is almost certainly why she felt she had to leave her post there with so little warning. His conduct had dismayed and horrified her, and she felt no pity for him whatsoever. Since then she had been sickened by the way he was going on, so why then should she have been put out when she discovered that someone had helped him to the early death that he was heading for anyway? I think that her main feeling was more likely to have been one of amazement – amazement that it was Mr Nicholls who had done the deed, and amazement that her quiet sister was carrying on with him.

As for Miss Emily herself, Miss Anne tells us that she seemed to feel better after their first talk, but then she became far worse for, as well as her old worries, she was then bothered because she had told all to Miss Anne, and time after time she begged her to say naught to anyone.

There is a saying that it never rains but that it pours, and often I have thought that Miss Emily must have had that feeling if what Miss Anne wrote next is true.

As I have said, by then Miss Emily and Mr Nicholls had been lovers in the fullest manner for the best part of a 12-month, and so it was almost certain that, sooner or later, the time would come when she would have reason to think that she might be with child. That time came now, and it drove Miss Emily to the point of madness.

She seems to have kept her fears to herself for as long as possible, but the time came when she just had to tell Mr

Nicholls, and he was shocked to the core. He has made it clear to me that by that time he was already tired of Miss Emily and her worries, and he had never had any notion of being tied to her. Now he felt that she was a threat to him and his future, and although he had some choices none of them was very pleasing to him.

He could, of course, have accepted things and wed her, but that prospect filled him with horror because, tired of her as he already was, he could not face the notion of being married to her – and with a child to boot. Even putting his feelings to one side, his pay was quite small in his eyes, and he knew of others who were finding it hard beyond belief to support a wife and family on such a pittance.

According to Miss Anne, Miss Emily was very much cast down by the short shrift that he gave her. It seems that there was no tenderness or thought for her, and certainly no sympathy for the plight that she found herself in. In fact he seems to have blamed her alone for their problem. He steadfastly refused to marry her, and even went as far as to say that she should go and see one of the women who were known to do away with unwanted babies.

That seems to have shocked Miss Emily more than anything else, and I can quite see why that should have been. She loved all living creatures, and her whole upbringing and nature would never have allowed her to take part in what to her mind would have been murder and what was, in any event, an unlawful act. She refused, and begged Mr Nicholls to change his mind, but he would not be moved. It was only then, so she told Miss Anne, that she came to the full knowledge of how little she now meant to him, if indeed he had *ever* felt anything for her, but her plight was desperate and she could not afford to take 'No' for an answer.

She told Miss Anne that it was only after days of pleading had proved in vain that she was driven to take a leaf out of Master Branwell's book, and she told Mr Nicholls that she would tell of his hand in her brother's death if he did not make an honest woman of her.

It is not so long since that I asked Mr Nicholls how he felt

67

when she told him that, and, apart from his words, I could tell from how he spoke that even after all this time he still feels how shaken he was. As he said, he felt that he was going back to the blackmailing nightmare from which only Master Branwell's death had set him free – and worse. Suddenly he felt totally lost and with no way to turn.

He tried his hardest to reason with her, and I have little doubt that he used all his old charm – which I know more than a little about – but it was no good. In her way, when her mind was firmly made up about something, Miss Emily stood her ground with a steady will, and he was able to do nothing against it although it filled him with rage. Seeing that he was doing no good, he decided to change his manner. He made a show of weakening, and begged for time to think, and that seemed to soften her towards him, for she agreed.

It was not time to think that he wanted though, it was time to plan, because, in his heart, he already knew what he had to do. Just as Master Branwell's death had ended one vexation, so Miss Emily's would rid him of the danger that *she* now posed.

In his own words, that he spoke to me in quite a hard voice, he knew that she would have to go.

[*CC*] At first sight, I thought that Martha's suggestion that Emily was pregnant, or thought that she might be, was almost beyond belief, but as I conducted my research certain facts emerged which gave credence to it. Therefore, although I appreciate fully how preposterous the whole idea will appear to Emily's fans, all I can ask is that, like me, they keep an open mind.

As we shall see, Emily refused steadfastly to be examined by a doctor, or even to try a prescription sent by one, until the day she died. Nobody, however, not even her sisters, has ever given a reason for such an apparent aversion to the medical profession.

Charlotte was in frequent correspondence with Mr W.S. Williams, who was a reader for her publishers, and in a letter dated 22 November 1848 she commented upon Emily's attitude: '. . . my sister would not see the most skilful physician in

68

England if he were brought to her just now, nor would she follow his prescription.'

On the following day she continued in the same vein to Ellen Nussey: '. . . she declares "no poisoning doctor shall come near her." '

I find it hard to understand why Emily should have felt as she did. I can find no mention of her ever having been ill, during her adult life, until then, and so she could have had no adverse personal experience likely to have set her against doctors. What, then, could have been the reason for her behaviour?

One explanation may be that she had lost whatever faith she had in Dr Wheelhouse and his colleagues after she witnessed his inaccurate diagnosis of the cause of Branwell's death. Were that the case, then the phrase 'poisoning doctor' may well have been the result of a subconscious connection between whatever killed her brother and the doctor who failed to detect it.

In the normal course of events, I would have expected Emily to have scoffed at the idea of a doctor when she was in the early stages of whatever ailed her. It would have been very much in character for her to have scorned the idea of 'a cold and a cough' meriting any consideration. However, there is no obvious reason why she should have refused even 'the most skilful physician in England' when she began to feel *really* ill, unless she was, indeed, pregnant – or even supposed that she was. In either of those events there would have been a very good, and apparent, motive.

Older readers will remember – and it is not *that* long ago – when to become an unmarried mother was one of the quickest ways of becoming ostracized and reviled. Being the daughter of a clergyman, Emily would probably have suffered more than most, and then there would have been the child to consider. The present trendy term 'love-child' had not been invented then, and any issue would have carried the stigma of 'bastard' and been denied some entitlements in law.

Certainly this would account for Charlotte's curiosity about the change in Emily's manner. In a letter dated 29 October 1848, she told Ellen Nussey that her sister's 'reserved nature

69

occasions me great uneasiness of mind. It is useless to question her, you get no answers.' Unfortunately, she does not say what form her questions took, and we do not know, therefore, whether they were just general enquiries about what was the matter with her, or something more specific.

Of course, whatever the reason for her questions, she should have known that she was the last person in whom Emily was likely to confide. However, Emily obviously needed to unburden herself to *somebody* and it comes as no surprise to learn that that person was Anne.

We have seen how close Emily and Anne had been for all of their lives, sharing pleasures and troubles alike. It was therefore perfectly natural for Emily to turn to Anne when she was more distressed than she had ever been, and, as we shall see, Martha had good evidence that, having sworn her to secrecy, Emily poured out her soul.

Chapter Seven

'We have made a covenant with death, and with hell
are we at agreement.'

Isaiah 28:15

M r Nicholls has told me, and I believe him, that he did not come lightly to his decision to murder Miss Emily. He was not really an evil man. He was simply a weak, idle and vain person who felt driven to do the things which he did by anything which seemed to be a threat to him and his quiet way of life.

He began to give Miss Emily small doses of poison whenever that was possible, whilst all the time carrying on as lovingly as he had at the start of their friendship. As Miss Emily told Miss Anne, that made her hope against hope that she was mistaken in thinking that Mr Nicholls no longer loved her, and slowly part of her really came to believe that he would marry her after all – she just prayed that he would not leave it too late. She felt that she had to see him every day, and I can vouch for the fact that to do that she never once took to her bed during the whole of her illness.

Each day she arose at 7, and stayed up until 10 in the evening although, as she became weaker, she was not able to keep on with her walks on the moors. Therefore it was arranged that, as an excuse for their regular meetings, Mr Nicholls would call at the Parsonage every day to collect the dogs for exercise.

As he says, that suited him very well as the agreement not only did away with the long, and sometimes tearful, talks that Miss Emily always wanted to have, but also gave him more chances for giving her the poison.

He has told me that he called at the Parsonage only at times when there was little chance of anyone being in the kitchen. Then it was an easy matter to dose whatever Miss Emily was going to drink or eat. There was little danger of anybody else being affected because, as everyone knew, Miss Emily planned her own meals and they were almost always different from what the rest of us ate.

As for Mr Nicholls sneaking into the kitchen, as soon as he told me that I recalled one or two times when I had come upon him without warning in the quiet of the afternoon, and he had seemed somewhat startled and had had to make excuses for being there. I smiled to myself as I remembered that and he, sensing what was in my mind, smiled back.

Of course, I knew naught of any of that at the time. All I knew was that Miss Emily seemed unwell, but I thought that there could not be much up with her because there was no talk of doctors, and she went about her business in the house much the same as usual at the start. Little did I realize how much worse she was becoming, but Miss Anne did, and she also knew why Miss Emily dared not permit a doctor to be called in, even had she been so minded. Nevertheless, she writes that she was very much of the opinion that all would be well if only Mr Nicholls could be urged, or forced, to marry Miss Emily and thus give her the will to live.

Miss Anne did not think, from what Miss Emily had told her, that Mr Nicholls could be coaxed, and she admits that she knew that she was not the one to talk to him to try to force his hand. Seemingly she had tried to steel herself to speak to him, but it did not work. That does not surprise me at all, because we all knew that she was not very good at that kind of thing.

It would seem that she worried over the business for weeks, and all the time Miss Emily was becoming weaker before her eyes. In the end she could bear it no longer and made up her mind that there was nothing else for it but to tell Miss Charlotte. She did not want to do so, and she knew that it was the very last thing that Miss Emily would have wished, but she could think of nothing else. There would have been no holding her father had she gone to him and told him that Miss Emily was with child by Mr Nicholls, and so it was to her elder sister that she went and told the whole of what Miss Emily had told her.

To my mind, in the normal way of things Miss Charlotte would have been the best person to deal with the matter. The trouble was that very little was normal in that family, but nevertheless out it all poured.

Miss Anne told of how Mr Nicholls had done away with Master Branwell, and that Miss Emily knew of it, and of how Mr Nicholls and Miss Emily had become lovers, and now she fancied that she was expecting but Mr Nicholls would not marry her.

I can just see Miss Charlotte's face as she listened, almost without believing, to what Miss Anne had to say. Quiet, shy Miss Emily carrying on with their father's assistant, and under her very nose at that! So *that* was who she had been seen with up on the moors, and then it would have come to her why Mr Nicholls had never made any more advances to *her*. He himself told me, much, much later, that, years on, Miss Charlotte had admitted to him that after she had got over the man in Belgium she would have been very pleased to have had an approach from him. Indeed, as he had noticed, she had made her feelings clear, albeit in a careful way, but he had made no move because by then his eyes were firmly on Miss Emily.

Time and time again I have wondered whether Miss Emily really *was* with child, or whether it was simply that what had ailed her at first had upset her monthly showing – as has sometimes happened with me. We shall never know now but, as Miss Anne wrote, Miss Charlotte did not care either way. The mere notion that her sister thought that she *might* be was enough to show her how far things had gone between them, and she was *so* angry with them both. Knowing that Master Branwell had been done to death seems not to have bothered her at all – indeed she burst out to Miss Anne that she was *glad* he was dead. All that seemed to have been on her mind was what in the world could be done about the present mess.

Miss Anne tells us that she was quite taken aback to see that Miss Charlotte, who was usually so level-headed at such times, seemed to find it hard to think straight. I can but hazard a guess about how she felt, but knowing her as well as I came to, I feel sure that her main feeling was one of jealousy.

As far as I know, she had had nothing to do with a man in that way ever since she came back from Belgium. I recall Miss Emily telling me that she often heard Miss Charlotte tossing and turning in her bed, and now I can understand why. Mr Nicholls is a man who attracts the attentions of women, and her thoughts of him, so near yet seemingly not noticing her, must have cost her many a sleepless night, and now she knew that, all that time, her sister had been enjoying the love that *she* needed so badly. Now Miss Anne was expecting her to help bring about their marriage – she would have seen them both dead first!

No, Miss Charlotte would have had none of that, but the thought of what had been going on must have made her very angry because Miss Anne says that she stormed off straight-away to have it out with Mr Nicholls.

Now it so happened that he had been closeted with Mr Brontë in his room that morning, but he was just leaving as Miss Charlotte came down the stairs. From the kitchen, I saw her take his arm and half pull him along to the sitting room, but then the door slammed and although I could hear her voice I could not make out the words.

Mr Nicholls has told me that he can now recall that meeting with some good humour, but that he was fully taken aback at the time to find out that Miss Emily had let the cats out of the bag, and that both her sisters knew everything. However, Miss Charlotte gave him no time to think, as she lashed into him with great fury, no doubt thinking of herself very much as a woman scorned.

Right from the outset she took no care to keep her voice down, and so I can recount at first hand a lot of what was said, because, by that time, I, inquisitive as ever, was at the door trying very hard to hear what was going on, whilst all the time taking care not to be caught.

It was quite a long meeting, and I could not be at the door for the whole of the time because other folk were about, but I heard enough to understand something of what was going on, and Mr Nicholls has since filled in the gaps for me.

As I have said, at first he was totally taken aback, and was so afeared that he was not able to think properly as her words poured out. Slowly, though, as she ranted on, he came to see that there was more to her anger than what she was going on about. He could not believe it: 'the spiteful little woman', as he called her, was *really* jealous!

At the outset he had tried to hush her, because there were at least 4 other people in the Parsonage at the time, but to no avail, and he had been forced to let her carry on. However, there finally came a moment when she seemed to run out of breath and to be a little calmer, and then he was able to make himself heard.

I know only too well how good with words Mr Nicholls has always been, but then he must have been at his very best. Although I could hear him talking in his lovely Irish voice, he was speaking too softly for me to catch the words – and I very nearly pushed the door open as I was leaning against it straining to hear. He has told me what he said though, and it went something like this. Seemingly, he explained that he had never felt anything for Miss Emily, and that was why he would not marry her. He had been lonely, and it was only because Miss Charlotte had rebuffed him that he had sought friendship elsewhere – it was not something that he had *wanted* to do.

Mr Nicholls smiled a little as he remembered how his words had calmed Miss Charlotte, almost as if they were magic to her ears, and she had been forced to admit that she *had* spurned him. From that moment on, he said, she acted almost as if *she* was the one at fault, and the time came when she even seemed to believe that it was Miss Emily who had made the running in their friendship.

Knowing Miss Charlotte as I did, I cannot but think that usually she would have taken a lot of what he said with a pinch of salt, but it is evident that she heard the words that she wanted to hear, and they were enough to make her heedless of any doubts that she may have had. It must have been then that she began to see that she, plain as she was, could make that handsome man hers if she thought and acted with care.

The talking went on for quite a while longer, but Mr Nicholls says that he had sensed something of what was going on in her mind, and he thought that a turning point had been reached, but it was only when he placed his hand gently upon hers and she did not withdraw that he knew that an unspoken agreement had been reached.

The problem of what to do about Miss Emily was still there though, and about Miss Anne as well, come to that, but by then he was ready with his answers. I can well imagine how he put on his best soothing voice as he pointed out that Miss Emily might not be with child at all, and that if she was not something else must be ailing her that seemed to be getting worse. Miss Charlotte was not so sure though. What *she* wanted to know was what Mr Nicholls had in mind to do if she *was* expecting, or if she recovered from whatever else might be wrong with her.

They were questions that needed direct answers, and Mr Nicholls has confessed to me that for a moment he was not sure what to say. Then, feeling a sureness that had been coming back to him the longer they talked, he decided to take a chance. Gently, very gently, he put it to her that one answer could be that he should help Miss Emily along just as he had helped Master Branwell. Of course, he did not tell her that he was already doing so – he was just sounding her out – and he said that he held his breath as he awaited her reply.

When it came, however, he was not really surprised. It was very much as he thought it would be, although she put on a good show of being shocked, and told Mr Nicholls that he should put any such notion right out of his mind. They should wait a while and see what happened. Mr Nicholls has told me that it was very much the answer that he himself would have given in her place because it allowed her to play for time and safety. Should Miss Emily die of a natural cause that would be all well and good. However, she must have known that, if that looked unlikely, Mr Nicholls would take up his poisoning ways again, but if he did and she had not been part of it she would never know for sure that he had, and could always tell herself that her sister had died naturally.

As I have said, Mr Nicholls was not deceived because it was the sort of answer that he had expected from careful, sly Miss

Charlotte. He simply pretended to agree with her, safe in his knowledge that Miss Emily would not be a problem for much longer, and that he might expect no bother from Miss Charlotte when she died.

From what he says, there was a little kiss on the cheek when they parted, each knowing what was on the other's mind, but I knew nothing of that because at that moment I had had to creep quietly back to the kitchen.

I heard Mr Nicholls leave though, and a few minutes after that Miss Anne was closeted with Miss Charlotte in the same room, and with the door once again closed tight. However, I was busy getting the vegetables ready with Miss Aykroyd; so any hopes of getting back to listen were dashed, and it was not until some months later that I learned what had passed between the sisters.

According to what Miss Anne wrote, Miss Charlotte told her that she had spoken to Mr Nicholls and had told him, very firmly, that she would make his misdeeds known unless he married Miss Emily. That, she said, had quite taken him aback and he had said that he would marry her just as soon as she was well again. Miss Anne took that as the truth for, after all, she had no reason to doubt her sister, and her mind was set at rest. Not only had she been able to share the secrets that had burdened her so much, but now there was to be a happy outcome.

Of course, Miss Emily knew naught of any of this, and certainly she did not know how angry Mr Nicholls was with her for blabbing to Miss Anne in spite of her promise to him to keep everything secret. On the outside, though, he kept up his show of loving care, and Miss Emily became quite sure that he would marry her as soon as she was well enough.

That Winter of 1848 was a very cold one, and in December it was bitter. I would dress as warmly as I could, and sometimes I even wore my mittens, but it did no good and the Parsonage was always so cold once you were away from the stove or a fire. I was plagued with chilblains, and everything froze up. On several mornings I had to let the bucket drop quite heavily into the well to break the ice. The dark days dragged by, and with each one Miss Emily got worse until she looked nothing more than skin and bone.

Miss Charlotte put on a show of concern about her, and she told folk that she had sent away for something for her sister to take, but it was all an act. One day I asked Miss Emily if the medicine was doing her any good, but she looked at me askance and asked what I was talking about. I felt myself going red, for it was evident to me that she knew naught of any medicine and that I had opened my mouth too widely, and stammered that I must have been mistaken for I thought she was taking something.

As Christmas neared we were all kept very busy getting things ready for the Feast, both at the Parsonage and at home. It was always a happy time for me, and I was quite caught up in the general excitement. I was 20 by then and, in particular, I was looking forward to having some time off so that I could get to the 2 dances that were to be held in the village.

It makes me sad to think of it now, but in all the hustle and bustle most of us tended to forget about poor Miss Emily, and many a time since I have wondered how she must have felt seeing everyone elso so happy. Mind you, she was never one to complain, and so it was simple for us not to notice how very much worse she must have felt, poor woman. Taken up with myself, I now recall prattling on about my own concerns, and telling her about one certain lad that I was hoping to see a lot more of. Once she smiled and said I was a comely lass, and that she had little doubt that I would soon be leaving them to get wed. I always feel a strong sense of guilt when I recall that talk because it was on the very next day – the 19th – that, to my great surprise, I was told by Miss Charlotte that I was to hurry for Dr Wheelhouse and ask him to come at once.

As I say, the errand came very much as a surprise to me for, many times, the latest being when I had asked her about the medicine, Miss Emily had told me that she had no time for doctors and so I knew that something had to be very much amiss for her to have changed her mind.

I ran as hard as I could, holding my skirts up out of the mud as I went which made a lot of folk turn and look at me, especially some lads, but I did not care. Miss Emily had always been very kind to me and it was the least I could do.

It was quite a way, and I was puffing, and quite hot for a change, when I got to the doctor's house, and I had to catch my breath before giving the message to the housekeeper who answered the door. I waited in the hall for what seemed an age before he came out, but he was soon ready, with his coat and hat on, and his little carriage had been brought round so we were quickly back at the Parsonage.

Somehow I knew as we hurried up the path that something was very much amiss. The front door stood wide open, and everything was so very quiet. As we got inside I could see Miss Anne at the end of the hall, near the bottom of the stairs, and she seemed to be weeping. At that moment, though, Miss Charlotte came out of the sitting room and said quietly, 'I'm sorry, Doctor, but you are too late.' She told me to go into the kitchen, and then led the doctor into the room where, with the door being ajar, I could see Miss Emily lying on the sofa, with Mr Brontë sitting in a chair pulled close to it.

I walked across the hall to the kitchen and by then Miss Anne was in a corner and I could see quite clearly that she was indeed weeping, but I said naught. In the kitchen, Miss Aykroyd sat at the table, also weeping, and with her head in her hands, whilst a young girl – whose name I now forget, but who had worked with us for a short time – stood as if not knowing what to do with herself.

Of course, I knew by then that Miss Emily had passed on, but I asked the girl when she had died, and she told me that it must have happened almost as soon as I had left, because she heard Mr Brontë calling for Miss Charlotte whilst I was running down the path.

It was a terrible day, and then, what with the funeral and all, Christmas was a very sad time. I still went to my dances, but my heart was not really in anything and I must have been a disappointment to the lad I had my eye on because he seemed to want naught to do with me after that.

That, though, was the least of my worries because, even though I knew very little then, I felt that something very bad was going on, and I wondered what the New Year would bring for us all.

[*GG*] As usual, most of what we know about Emily's symptoms comes from Charlotte. She stated that Mr Williams had recommended two fashionable London doctors whom Emily might consult, and that when Emily had rejected their services he had suggested that she might turn to homeopathy for relief. He advised that Dr Epps be consulted, and therefore, in her reply of 9 December 1848, Charlotte sent a description of what she said were her sister's symptoms in the hope that Dr Epps would prescribe by mail.

Now the symptoms which she listed coincided neatly with those of consumption, many of which she would have remembered, as both her elder sisters had died of consumption when she was a child – but there was one important, and interesting, omission.

On the very next day after replying to Mr Williams, Charlotte wrote to Ellen Nussey and told her about her letter of the day before. She stated that she had written to 'an eminent physician in London', and had given him 'as minute a statement of her case and symptoms as I could draw up'. Note that word 'minute'. Earlier in her letter to her friend, Charlotte told her: 'Diarrhoea commenced nearly a fortnight ago, and continues still. Of course it greatly weakens her, but she thinks herself it tends to good.'

So there we have two sentences devoted to diarrhoea in the same letter to a friend but, amazingly, there was not a single mention of it in the 'minute' statement sent to a doctor on the previous day! Is that not strange?

One could understand the omission had it been the other way round and she had mentioned it to the doctor and not to the friend. I do not suppose that diarrhoea would really have been considered a proper subject of correspondence between two genteel Victorian ladies, and therefore it would not have been surprising had Charlotte not mentioned it to her friend. On the other hand, it would not only have been acceptable but very

80

relevant to have included the symptom in a letter to a medical man. It was a most peculiar omission but, as we shall see, there was a very good reason why it was not included.

I think that we may safely assume that Emily did not suffer from diarrhoea during the early stages of her 'illness' because, in that same letter to Dr Epps, Charlotte told him that her sister had occasionally taken 'a mild aperient'. Now one does not take a laxative if suffering from diarrhoea, and so we know that only one of the two statements is true. Either Charlotte was lying about the aperient, and Emily was subject to diarrhoea throughout the whole of her illness, or she was telling the truth. If she was *not* lying, then her sister must have been slightly constipated during the first two months of her incapacitation, but was affected by constant diarrhoea from the end of November.

There are two important reasons why I have gone into this matter at some length, distasteful though it may be. The first is that, if Charlotte was *not* lying about the aperient, the onset of Emily's diarrhoea coincided with the beginning of the poisoning. Then, secondly, comes the question of why Charlotte concealed her sister's distressing symptom from Dr Epps because – let there be no mistake about it – conceal it she did. Now why should she have done that? The answer, to my mind, is simple. It is because diarrhoea is a very common and well-known symptom of irritant poisoning, and Charlotte did not wish to alert Dr Epps to the possibility that all was not as it should have been.

Actually, she need not have worried herself. Diarrhoea often occurs during the later stages of tuberculosis, but it would seem that she did not know that.

All this, of course, goes a very long way in confirming what Nicholls told Martha, namely that Charlotte had every reason to suppose that Nicholls might be poisoning Emily, but that she did nothing about it.

It was two days after her momentous meeting with Nicholls that Charlotte sent the list of symptoms to Dr Epps, yet for nearly three weeks Mr Williams had been anxiously advising action on Emily's illness, and suggesting that she be introduced

81

to homeopathy. In her letters of 22 November and 7 December, Charlotte had told him that she had discussed his suggestion with Emily, but that it had been rejected. Personally, I doubt whether the subject was ever mentioned between the sisters.

Only after the meeting with Nicholls did Charlotte's self-defence mechanism click into action, and she decided to continue the correspondence and send the list. Beyond all reasonable doubt, her reasoning must have been that should Nicholls, in fact, poison Emily to death and then, somehow, be discovered in his crime, she would be able to show that, despite anything he might say, *she* knew nothing of what he had done but, on the contrary, had tried to help her sister. Therefore, I submit, it was for that reason, and that reason alone, that the list was sent but, because she did not wish to queer Nicholls' pitch, she omitted any mention of diarrhoea.

Chapter Eight

'Their feet run to evil, and they make haste to shed innocent blood.'

Isaiah 59:7

T he year 1849 arrived, but the New Year did not seem to make much difference to anyone. There was never any especial regard paid to a New Year during my time at the Parsonage, and in any case the weather carried on as cold as ever, with folk seeming to have little on their minds but keeping warm.

For my part, I must say that I was more taken up with my own matters than perhaps I should have been. I realize now that I was being selfish and unfair but, because of Miss Emily's death and all, Mr Brontë had not given us our usual Christmas gifts and it did not look as if we were going to get them. It was Mr Brontë's custom to hand each of us an envelope with some money in, which I knew that Miss Emily used to get ready for him, and I had been counting on it for a linsey-woolsey skirt that had taken my fancy. I had given Mr Whitehead a few pence deposit on it just before Christmas, and had promised him that I would pay the rest and collect it by New Year. Now I could not, and I did not know what to do.

So things at the Parsonage went on much the same as ever, but I must say that it was strange to start a New Year with two of the family gone. Mind you, there seemed to be less work, although Miss Charlotte did her best to keep us slaving away at this and that. She did not seem to miss Miss Emily though, and hardly ever mentioned her unless someone from outside the family was about, and then I wondered how she could make up such tales about how sad she was. I thought it odd at the time, though, that she seemed to take to me more. Now I began to get smiles, and indeed she was altogether less dour than usual. She also took to talking to me, and sometimes she would quiz me about the lads in the village I had walked out with from time to time, and quite often I found that I was becoming a little red at some of the things she asked me. Of course, I know now why that was: she thought she had Mr Nicholls where she wanted him and was allowing him hardly any peace.

He has told me that he tried to put on as good an act as possible of returning the advances that she made whenever she could do so safely, but that he never felt anything for her at all. Any interest that he may have had was only of the body, and there was very little of that, with him doing only what he felt was expected of him. All the time, though, he wondered what she had in mind for the future, and dreaded it lest she was set on marriage.

That is not to say that he was not fairly content with his lot. As he has often told me, with Miss Emily's death he felt that he was no longer under threat, and he could put up with her sister's attentions, although sometimes they were a bit too much. He knew that as long as he did not upset her she was now no danger to him, and he began to sense – much to his relief, he said – that she did not have wedlock in mind. Of course, it was always possible that something might happen to change her mind about that, and he knew that then he would be unable to refuse her, but he began to think that even that might not be too bad. He knew that she had quite a lot of money by then, and there was another book on the way. Not only that, when the old man – as Mr Nicholls always called Mr Brontë to me – died, and that surely could not be too far off, he would expect to step into his shoes. As he said to me with quite a laugh, money and his own parish and a quiet life was not at all a bad prospect should the worst have happened, and even Miss Charlotte would have had to keep her mouth shut then.

Both of them were therefore quite at ease with their under-standing and, indeed, their lives in general, but then, as is so often the way, something came along to put an end to their contentment.

This time, seemingly, it was Miss Anne who was the prob-lem. I know for a fact that she was nearly out of her mind with grief when Miss Emily died, and I can well understand that because she had not only lost her sister but her lifelong best friend as well. I do not suppose that the fact that she was not feeling well herself helped either. She had been saying just before Miss Emily died that she had pains in her side, and then she had a very bad cold and fever. Dr Wheelhouse came to see her, but he seemed to me to be as doddery as ever. He said that she should be blistered, but Miss Emily told me that, if anything, that had made her sister feel worse.

Over and above everything else though, I sensed that something was bothering her, and in the light of what happened later I now have a good idea of what it was. She seems to have stayed longer in her jobs than her sisters did, and I suppose that that had given her a better insight into how folk behaved behind their own closed doors, and she had probably seen a great deal more of the wickedness of the world than they had. That, I feel, was why she began to think how well it must have suited Mr Nicholls to have Miss Emily die and, knowing that he had poisoned Master Branwell, she kept wondering if he had done the same to her sister.

Later, Miss Charlotte told Mr Nicholls that Miss Anne had said to her that she tried to put such thoughts from her, but they kept coming back, and the time came when she felt that she just had to do something about them.

She went to Miss Charlotte with her fears but she, of course, pooh-poohed them, but underneath she became very alarmed when Miss Anne said that she was thinking of telling their father everything now that Miss Emily was dead and could no longer be hurt by what she had to say.

Mr Nicholls has told me that Miss Charlotte hardly knew what to say to her sister, and she ran straight to him to see what he thought. They had a long talk, and then she went back to Miss Anne. She pointed out to her that if she *did* go to their father, and he reported Mr Nicholls, Miss Emily's memory would suffer when the story got out. Not only that, the whole sorry tale would be bound to leave a stain on the name of Brontë, and the whole family, but especially their father, would suffer.

It seems that Miss Anne was affected by what Miss Charlotte said, but it was evident that she was not happy with matters and Mr Nicholls has confessed to me that he became very disturbed. His words to me were: 'I wondered if the whole nightmare would never end.' Miss Charlotte was making constant demands upon him, and he was then having to make calls to the Parsonage almost every night, which is something I can vouch for because I saw him when he called and all of the family at home had seen him going to the Parsonage, and one night he was so late in coming back that Father, just in from the Black Bull, asked him whether something was amiss with Mr Brontë. What we did not know at the time, though, was that that was just about when Mr Nicholls had decided that he could put up with Miss Charlotte, but was worried to death about what he was going to do about her sister and her worries.

Miss Charlotte seems to have done her best to console him, and told him that she did not want him to worry. She said that she would see to it that Miss Anne kept quiet and that, in any case, the way things were going it did not seem that she was long for this world anyway. It took some time to calm him, but in the end it was agreed that Miss Charlotte would keep a close watch on Miss Anne, and would tell him if anything arose that he should know about.

According to Mr Nicholls, he and Miss Charlotte became a little easier in their minds as the weeks wore on, because it did indeed seem as if Miss Anne was following in Miss Emily's footsteps to the grave. Even so, they felt the need to stay watchful, because there always seemed to be something which looked as if it would cause bother – and it was not long in coming!

When Miss Emily was ill, I heard Miss Charlotte say several times that the weather at Haworth was 'unfavourable for invalids'. Well Miss Anne must have remembered that because soon, and quite without warning, she said that she thought that a visit to somewhere warmer might be better for *her* health. I remember thinking that a move to somewhere warmer would be better for *all* of us, and when she started to go on about visiting her relations in mild Penzance, in Cornwall, I was very envious, although the thought of journeying so far – Father said it was well over 300 miles – was not to my liking.

I heard Miss Anne talking about going to Cornwall, and I could not, for the life of me, understand why Miss Charlotte was struck so pale. Now, of course, I know that she and Mr Nicholls did not want Miss Anne out of their sight *at all* lest she told someone of what she knew, and that danger would have been even greater were she with kindly relations and all that far away. Mr Nicholls has told me that the notion really bothered them – but then they were given a helping hand.

If my memory serves me right, Mr Brontë was 71 then, and very, very odd at times. Still he was no fool, and like all of us he knew that Dr Wheelhouse was not a very good doctor. One day I was working in the hall and I heard him talking to Miss Charlotte about Miss Anne. He said that he was not satisfied with what Dr Wheelhouse was doing, and that he thought that half the time he did not know what he was talking about. After much thought he had decided to bring in another doctor, and so he was writing to a Dr Teale who, it seems, was the surgeon to Leeds General Infirmary, to ask him to come and see her. Miss Charlotte wondered what that would cost, but Mr Brontë said that his mind was made up and the letter would go that day.

We had to get the Parsonage really spick and span for when the great doctor came, and then, when he did, Miss Charlotte told all of us to keep out of sight and be as quiet as possible. Afterwards she gave it out that the doctor had said that Miss Anne was suffering from consumption, but that it had not gone too far and could be stopped. She said also that he had forbidden 'the excitement of travelling'.

By the end of March Miss Anne did not seem much altered – in fact, if anything, to my mind she was a little better – and one day she told me she was very happy because Miss Charlotte's friend, Miss Nussey, had asked her to go and stay with her for a while. I do not think Miss Charlotte was very pleased about it though, because when I said to her that it might do Miss Anne good she just grunted and said it was far too soon for her to think of such gadding about. I could not understand that, nor why Miss Charlotte was always telling folk that Miss Anne was worse than seemed to be the case. Sometimes she made out that her sister was almost bedridden, and I know that Miss Anne was none too pleased about it when she found out.

Then there was the time when Miss Anne found out that Miss Charlotte had been reading her letters when she was out of the room, and had said that she would answer them for her if Miss Anne wished. I was cleaning the stairs, and they did not know I was there, and I heard Miss Anne tell Miss Charlotte, very sharp like, that she was quite able to take care of her own affairs and that she wished that Miss Charlotte would stop poking her nose into them. Miss Charlotte made no reply that I heard, but the next moment she just bustled out of the bedroom. She brushed past me without a word, and I could see that her face was even redder than usual, and her lips were pursed shut very tight.

I think that Miss Anne must have felt well in herself because she was always saying to me that she felt like going off to Scarborough after Easter, when it was a little warmer, and once I heard her say the same thing to Miss Charlotte and ask if she would go with her when the time came. All that Miss Charlotte had to say was: 'We'll see,' and I could tell how that damped Miss Anne's spirits. Next thing I heard was when, a week or two later, Miss Anne told me that she was thinking of asking Miss Nussey to go with her instead.

She must have done so, because one day I went in to make the bed and Miss Anne was sitting on it, and it was clear to me that she had been shedding a tear or two. I thought that she must be feeling unwell. I asked her if I could bring her anything, but she said that it was all right, it was just that she had had some disappointing news, and it was then that I noticed that she had a letter beside her on the bed. A moment later she said that Miss Nussey had written to say that she could not go away with her before June and so, as she had set her heart upon going before that, she did not know what to do. I nearly said that if she wanted someone with her she could take me! I had never been more than 15 miles from Haworth in my life, and had certainly never seen the sea.

The next thing I knew was that Miss Charlotte had said that

88

she would go with her after all, but the weeks went by and it did not happen.

In the meantime Miss Anne gradually grew worse, and I think that the disappointment and being made to stay in Haworth had a lot to do with it. She was very down all the time, and I watched her grow thinner and thinner almost by the minute, but still she managed to keep going and she went out every day.

Mr Nicholls has told me that he and Miss Charlotte were very concerned about her at that time. They knew she was in an odd state of mind, and they had become more and more worried as to how much longer she could be expected to hold her tongue, but things seemed to come to a head when she told Miss Charlotte that for some weeks she had believed herself to be near death, and that the awful things that she knew had become a burden that she could no longer bear. She felt a great need to confess to someone before it was too late, but she was unsure of what to do. She did not know whether to tell their father everything, or whether it would relieve her state of mind if she made her confession to a clergyman outside the parish.

It seems that that made Miss Charlotte run straight to Mr Nicholls. She told him that she did not think that Miss Anne could be kept silent for much longer.

As for Mr Nicholls, he made no secret to me that that was the moment when he began to think that Miss Anne also would need to be helped to an early death. He told me that with quite a sigh, and it was apparent that it was not a thought that he had enjoyed. Nevertheless the notion that she might let everything out at any moment was never far from his mind, and the more he thought about killing her the more he came to see that her death might not be a bad thing for him in other ways.

At first he felt that the best thing would be not to tell Miss Charlotte what he was set upon doing. He pointed out to me that with Miss Anne out of the way Miss Charlotte's hold over him would be very much less, as Miss Anne would not be there to back her up, and she might therefore stop him from going on with his plan. However, he soon came to see that she would have to be told, for the simple reason that he would need her help.

You see, his trouble was that, unlike with Master Branwell and Miss Emily, he had no way to put anything into Miss Anne's food – but Miss Charlotte could, and it would be very easy for her, but would she do it?

Mr Nicholls closed his eyes when he came to that part, and it was clear to me that he was reliving his state of mind at that time. When he spoke again he said that he had not known how to bring up the matter with Miss Charlotte, although he *did* know that he would need to lead up to it very gently indeed.

He never went into the whys and wherefores of how he got round to coming out with it, but he said that when he finally got to the point Miss Charlotte did not seem all that taken aback. That seems to have surprised him, but it did not me. I see now, from the complete change in her general manner then, that she must have been besotted with him, whereas I know that Miss Anne had been vexing her with her illness, her worries and some of the things that she had said. I well remember that, only a few weeks before, Miss Charlotte had come into the kitchen and slammed down a plate and cup, so hard as if to break them, saying that Miss Anne gave herself the airs of a saint. Miss Aykroyd was most displeased, not only by what she had said but also, I think, because she had said it in front of me. She scolded Miss Charlotte for saying such things about her sister, and then sent me off for some wood. That was only an excuse to get me out of the way though, for when I listened at the door I heard her carrying on to Miss Charlotte as nobody else would have dared to do.

Then there was the fact that, as we all knew, Miss Charlotte had been looking forward to leaving Miss Anne at home to care for their father whilst she journeyed around and met important people, but now that her sister had become something of an invalid she found herself tied to the Parsonage and what she would sometimes call 'awful Haworth'.

Above all, and knowing Miss Charlotte as well as I did, I would think that she had never forgotten how Miss Emily and Miss Anne had kept her out of their lives whenever possible. From time to time she had made catty remarks to Miss Anne about that in my hearing. All in all, then, I feel that her thoughts would have been that she owed Miss Anne naught, but I doubt very much if she would have wanted to become mixed up in murder. Against that, though, she would not have wanted to take the chance of losing Mr Nicholls.

Mr Nicholls has told me that she did not give him an answer straightaway, and he took that as a good sign. He thinks that she held back because she thought that if she took a direct part in Miss Anne's death she would place herself in his power, but it was evident to him that she wanted to help him because of the threat that Miss Anne was to him, and she thought that something should be done. However, she drew back at murder, and took her usual way out when she had something of moment to decide – she tried to slow matters down whilst she thought.

That time, though, she was not able to, because Mr Nicholls pressed her for an answer and, in the end, she was forced to say that she would help, but Mr Nicholls told me that, even whilst she was saying so, he knew that she was hoping to get out of it. It was evident to him that she would put it off for as long as she could because she said that, to her mind, it would not be long before Miss Anne died a natural death anyway – and that would have let her out of it.

One thing was sure though, either way she would die.

[*CC*] For Nicholls and Charlotte it was certainly a fortunate coincidence that Anne was apparently forbidden to leave Haworth just at the very time when that possibility was what they feared most. On a balance of probabilities, however, it would seem that Charlotte misused Dr Teale's words. As the illness had not reached an advanced stage, then surely it is common-sense to suppose that a move to somewhere warmer, and where the air was purer, would have been of benefit. I find it very contradictory that, on 30 January, she should suggest, in a letter to Ellen Nussey, that during the *following* year 'an early removal to a warmer locality for the winter might be beneficial' to her sister. If that statement is pursued to a logical conclusion it is clearly nonsensical. Were Anne's health still to be a cause for concern a year later, it follows that her condition would be no better, and probably worse. Yet there was Charlotte implying that 'the excitement of travelling' would then be of no consequence, which prompts the question of why, in that case, it should have been considered deleterious a year before.

In the event, the ploy succeeded. Anne stayed put, and that was that problem solved.

Unfortunately, however, Charlotte's relief was short-lived because the well-meaning Mr Williams intervened again. It will be recalled that it was he who had recommended that 'two fashionable London doctors', who were Drs Elliotson and Forbes, should see Emily, and that, when Charlotte told him that her sister had rejected that idea, he had suggested Dr Epps and homeopathy. Well now he recommended that Dr Forbes, who was physician to the Queen's household, be consulted on Anne's behalf.

Significantly, Charlotte did not reply to him. Instead, on 22 January 1849, she wrote to his employer, George Smith, but once again rejected Mr Williams' advice. This time it was on the grounds that Mr Brontë had declared his 'perfect confidence' in Dr Teale but, in point of fact, it is very doubtful whether Charlotte ever mentioned the matter to her father, any more than she had in Emily's case. What happened was that, with a singular lack of originality, she imitated the Dr Epps episode.

It is a little difficult to follow, but this is what she did. She asked George Smith if *he* would tell Dr Forbes of Dr Teale's diagnosis, and then ask the former for his opinion on what the latter had said.

George Smith would not have been pleased to have been burdened with such a chore. He had a publishing business to run, and that gave him quite enough to do without having such tasks imposed upon him. Also he must have thought, as I do, that Charlotte's request was rather a tortuous way of going about things, and have wondered why on earth she was involving *him*. Either she shared her father's faith in Dr Teale or she did not. If she did, then why was she bothering to have another physician consulted? If she did not, then she had two obvious options open to her. *She* could have done what she was asking

George Smith to do, or she could have asked Dr Forbes to visit the Parsonage in person and examine her sister himself. Of course, had she adopted the latter alternative, and had she been telling the truth when she said that Mr Brontë was satisfied with Dr Teale, she would have needed to be prepared to face her father's wrath. Surely, though, that would have been a small price to pay were she genuinely concerned about Anne.

There is, therefore, no logical reason why she should have involved an outsider. Instead we are presented with yet another example of Charlotte's self-defence mechanism. Were her sister to die, she wanted no criticism levelled at *her* which might then have led to closer examinations of other sensitive matters. *She* wanted to be seen to have done *her* duty, and that would have been achieved had she been able to give the impression that she had made an approach to Dr Forbes. Only two people other than her would have known that the consultation had been through a third party, and had involved such an unnecessary but, importantly, time-consuming procedure.

We see something of what I am getting at in her letter to Ellen Nussey, of 30 January 1849, in which she wrote: 'A few days ago I wrote to have Dr Forbes' opinion,' thus deliberately giving the impression that she had consulted him herself. She went on to say that he disapproved of any change of residence for the present, so that now, according to her – and her alone – there were *two* doctors of the opinion that Anne should not leave the Parsonage. It was all very convenient, much *too* convenient some may think, and we shall never know the truth of it. Nevertheless, it was the result which counted, and the result was that Anne stayed put.

February came, and Charlotte wrote to Ellen to thank her for a respirator which she had bought for Anne. In that letter she expressed the curious hope that 'the respirator will be useful to Anne in case she should ever be well enough to go out again'. One can but be driven to wonder at her motive for expressing such a hope, because it is almost as if she was preparing Ellen for Anne's early demise. Only a fortnight before she had told Mr Williams how much better Anne was, and on 2 March she wrote: 'My sister still continues better; she has less languor and weakness; her spirits are improved.' One tale for him, to put off any further mention of doctors, and another for her friend.

We now know that, in confirmation of what Martha said Anne told her, that Ellen Nussey did indeed invite Anne to come and stay with her, and there is also some confirmation of Martha's account of the row between Anne and Charlotte about the latter interfering with the former's correspondence.

From what is now in the public domain, we know that Anne was quite capable of writing her own letters – indeed she wrote to Ellen only a week after the letter which I am about to discuss – but it had been Charlotte who thanked Ellen for the respirator, and it was Charlotte who now replied to Ellen's invitation. She began with an ambiguous phrase: 'I read your kind note to Anne . . .' Now what, precisely, was *that* supposed to convey? It could be construed as meaning simply that Anne had read the note and then passed it to Charlotte. Alternatively, and more probably, it could have been worded in that way in order to give the impression that Anne was too ill to read anything for herself and that Charlotte had therefore read the note to her. Charlotte was usually very precise with her words, and we should therefore look askance at such loose phraseology.

The letter to Ellen continued: 'Papa says her state is most precarious,' although whether he made any such remark must be in doubt because, as we have seen, it suited Charlotte's purposes very well to exaggerate her sister's condition. She then went on to the main purpose of her letter, which was to say that, in a month or two, and were she well enough, Anne wished to 'go either to the seaside or to some inland watering place'. In that event, Charlotte would be unable to accompany her, as she would be needed at home to look after father, so would Ellen take her place?

That part of the letter is surprising and, to a large extent, contradictory. Surprising because we know that Nicholls and Charlotte wanted Anne where they could see her, and contradictory because it made a nonsense of the impression about Anne's 'most precarious' state which Charlotte had been so anxious to convey.

94

Certainly she and Nicholls would not have wished to have Anne go off with Ellen, or anyone else come to that; so why did Charlotte write such a letter? Well, the reason is really quite simple: it is just that she did not want *Anne* to answer Ellen's invitation. One can imagine the conversation which took place when it arrived, and Anne's expression of her wishes.

Charlotte: 'What a good idea. I shall be writing to Ellen tonight; I'll ask her if she'll go with you, shall I? I'm sure she'll agree.' It would have seemed so natural, and Anne would have been saved the bother of replying. So Charlotte *did* write, and she *did* put Anne's proposal to Ellen. She had no alternative, because Anne would have expected a reply, but there was method in her apparent foolishness, and in the solving of this problem we see Charlotte at her most devious.

Having told Ellen of Anne's wishes, she went on, in the same letter, to raise what she described as 'serious objections' against Ellen falling in with them. She wrote that it would be too terrible were her sister to be taken ill far from home and alone with Ellen. 'The idea of it distresses me inexpressibly, and I tremble whenever she alludes to the project of a journey.' (Well that part, at least, was true!) 'If a journey *must* be made then June would be a safer month – if we could reach June . . .' Charlotte asked Ellen if she would: 'Write such an answer to this note as I can show Anne.' Then came the devious part. She also asked Ellen if she would, at the same time, write another, private, letter to her, Charlotte, 'on a separate piece of paper'. Oh what a tangled web we weave . . . !

Ellen did as she had been requested. She wrote to Anne and said that *she* would go, but her 'friends' had advised her against doing so, and May was a trying month, and she was expecting visitors before the end of May anyway – every excuse under the sun. Charlotte must have been well pleased with the results of her machinations, but her pleasure soon turned to dismay when Anne, to her credit, would have none of it. She wrote to Ellen herself, and told her that if *she* could not accompany her she hoped Charlotte would. In doing that she no doubt hoped to force Ellen's hand, but she did not – much to Charlotte's satisfaction. However, Charlotte was well aware of how deter-

95

mined Anne was to get away and so she appeared to bow to the inevitable and stated that she *would* go with Anne, even if that meant that their father would have to fend for himself. That was because, as we know now, Charlotte had come to the conclusion that, if Anne was really set upon going, *she* was the one who would have to accompany her to ensure her silence.

Even so, Charlotte still played for time. In a letter to Ellen, she said that she *would* go with Anne, but only were she of the same mind in a month or six weeks. She suggested that Ellen might join them.

At first it puzzled me as to why Charlotte would have wanted a third party present should she be the one who had to kill her sister. However, it was not long before I saw why. Obviously she had come to the conclusion that, were it absolutely necessary, she would be willing to carry out the deed, but she was worried lest anything should go awry at Scarborough which would place her under suspicion. Even if everything should go according to plan, she felt that a few malicious tongues would be bound to wag. What would be needed, she thought, was an independent witness to events who would be able to testify on her behalf should that become necessary.

On 16 April, Charlotte also wrote to Mr Williams. Her main reason for doing so was because he had, once again, recommended homeopathy, but this time the idea was rejected outright. However, she also told him about the proposed trip, and said that she felt torn between the two duties of either going with her sister or staying with her father, but that it was 'Papa's wish' that she should accompany Anne.

One cannot help but wonder how true that was because it is clear, from numerous examples, that if Charlotte wanted something badly enough she got it – with or without her father's consent. She never had any compunction about going off and leaving the old man – even when he was older and frailer – and had raised the question of his welfare only as an excuse to try to keep Anne at home.

So Charlotte agreed to go, but still she played for time because, secretly, she hoped that all talk of journeys was academic, and that her sister would be dead by then.

Chapter Nine

'Set thine house in order: for thou shalt die, and not live.'
Isaiah 38:1

T he days passed, and Miss Anne's health did not seem to get any worse but I noticed that she was becoming quieter and quieter, and she seemed very sad. I would try to cheer her up with funny tales about village folk who she knew, and sometimes she would give a little smile. It was evident, though, that something was troubling her mind, and one day she told me that she had a feeling that something bad was going to happen. I asked her what she meant, but she said that she did not know, she just felt very ill at ease.

What I did not know until Mr Nicholls told me was that him and Miss Charlotte felt then that she was becoming more and more of a threat to them, and that even Miss Charlotte had had to agree with him that the sooner she was out of the way the better.

The trouble for them, though, was how her death could be brought about in a short time without causing folk to talk. Everybody had taken it for granted that Master Branwell would finally drink himself to the grave; and Miss Emily's death had passed with no one saying anything; but were a third member of the family to die in the Parsonage in under 8 months it would be bound to cause a stir. Even Dr Wheelhouse might have been forced to take notice.

Mr Nicholls has told me that they talked about the matter a lot, but it was him who found the answer in the end. He told Miss Charlotte that if she could keep her sister quiet for a while, in the hope that she would soon die a natural death, then all well and good. They would give her a little longer, but if not she would have to go and they would have to take their chances.

Seemingly, Miss Charlotte told him that she thought she could do that, but only for a short time, and she agreed that if Miss Anne did not then seem to be sinking fast Mr Nicholls' plan would have to be the answer. That meant that Miss Charlotte would have to go to Scarborough with Miss Anne – for that was where she was now set upon going – and it would be up to her to give Miss Anne the fatal dose of poison there.

When May came Miss Anne seemed much better though, and I was so pleased for her. At the time, and not knowing what I know now, I thought that Miss Charlotte was pleased as well because she told some of us that she and Miss Nussey had made plans to take Miss Anne away to Scarborough and that, nearer the time, she would tell us what she wanted us to do in looking after the house and Mr Brontë whilst they were away.

That made me even happier, because the Parsonage was always a very different place when Miss Charlotte was away. We were all more cheerful then, without her nosing about and finding fault and giving us more work. It was odd, though, because we all seemed to work much harder when she was away, and certainly we got far more done and more quickly. Also we were able to sort out our hours to suit ourselves, and that meant that we could have time off if there was something special that we wanted to do.

I think it must have been on May 23rd that they left, because I know it was on a Wednesday about that time of the month. There was great excitement at getting their boxes ready, and even Miss Charlotte seemed in high spirits and was talking to everybody for a change. I asked her how far it was to Scarborough and she said it was about 100 miles, but that they were going on a train and that Miss Nussey would join them at Leeds. We were all allowed to wave them off, and then we helped Mr Brontë back to the house and went about our work with very light hearts.

A week passed, and a lovely week it was. Everyone in the Parsonage was in good spirits, and it was so warm and sunny. I remember that I even went for a long walk on the moors one night with a lad from Stanbury who I had been seeing, on and off, for a time.

It was a week to the day after they had left that we were all called together by Mr Nicholls. Such a thing had never happened before and we had a feeling that something must be badly amiss, and wondered why Mr Brontë was not talking to us himself. It so happened that I was the last to get into the sitting room, and I thought that Mr Nicholls was looking black at me because of that, but I soon came to see that he had on what I always called his put-on face that he usually kept for sermons.

He spoke very slowly I recall, in his lovely deep Irish voice, and began by saying that Mr Brontë had that morning had some very bad news which had so upset him that he had asked Mr Nicholls to impart it to us. Then he told us what it was, and we could not believe what we were hearing. He said that Miss Anne had died at Scarborough 2 days before, and went on to say that it was felt that it would cause Mr Brontë even more hurt if her body was brought back to Haworth, and so Miss Charlotte would see to it that she was buried at Scarborough straightaway.

As I have said, we found it all very hard to believe, especially as Miss Anne had looked so much better when they set off, and we were all in tears. Miss Anne had been such a quiet, gentle soul, and now not only was she dead, but she was to be buried miles away amongst strangers. Somehow it did not seem right.

Mr Nicholls made no mention of how Miss Charlotte was feeling. All he said about her was that it was her who had written with the bad news, and that her and Miss Nussey were seeing to the funeral and she would be home later. In the meantime we were all to carry on with our work as usual, except that he wanted us to pay special heed of Mr Brontë.

So it was yet another sad time at the Parsonage, with folk coming and going all the while to see Mr Brontë. That meant extra work for us, but none of us cared because we were all so sorry for the poor old man. Of course, at the backs of our minds, was the thought that we would soon have Miss Charlotte back. Apart from Miss Aykroyd, I do not think that any of the others knew that there was little love lost between her and Miss Anne, and so they all expected that she would be back in tears as soon as possible to comfort her father.

To their surprise, though, but not to mine, that did not happen. Another week passed without sight or sound of her, and it was only when my Father asked Mr Brontë about her that we found out that her and Miss Nussey were going to have a long holiday together. That caused quite a lot of talk in the village. Miss Charlotte was not generally liked there, and folk felt that she should have come back to her father instead of gadding about in foreign parts.

When all came to all, it was going on 4 weeks after Miss Anne had died before she came back, and although she tried to put on an act for others it was evident to us in the Parsonage that her and Miss Nussey had had a very good time at different places on the coast, and that she was not at all sad at the loss of her sister.

Later, I learned from Mr Nicholls that she told him that she had dallied because she dreaded having to come back to the Parsonage and 'awful Haworth'. The only things that had brought her back, she said, was knowing that he was waiting for her and that she now had no brothers or sisters to spoil her life.

In point of fact, she could hardly have done anything else but come back, but in the light of what was to happen later she would have done better to have stayed away.

[*CC*] It would appear that Nicholls never told Martha what, exactly, took place at Scarborough. Certainly she gives no details, and therefore it is necessary for me to fill this gap from the information which I have unearthed.

On 16 May, Charlotte sent Ellen the time of the train to Leeds that she and Anne would be catching, and warned her that she would be shocked at Anne's condition. It does not appear that Anne appreciated just how quickly she was declining, and Charlotte did not want Ellen to make any remarks which would bring the truth home to her. The last thing that Charlotte needed at that stage of the plan was for Anne to panic and start thinking yet again about unburdening her guilty conscience.

100

Ellen was told that Charlotte was making no special arrangements for anybody to look after papa – which was a far cry from when she had been unable to go away with Anne because she had to stay at home to care for him! Apparently 'Mr Nicholls' had offered his services, but papa would not hear of it. That would have surprised nobody as, according to Martha, it was common knowledge that Mr Brontë had very little time for his assistant.

The day for their journey duly arrived, and the three women travelled first to York and thence to Scarborough, where they arrived on 25 May. Anne could not have felt ill on the following day because she drove a donkey cart on the sands for an hour, and she was obviously quite well on Sunday 27 May also. She walked to church in the morning – and quite a walk it was – strolled on the beach in the afternoon and, as Ellen was to tell Mrs Gaskell, the night was passed 'without any apparent accession of illness'.

Anne arose at seven o'clock on the Monday and performed most of her toilet herself, 'by her expressed wish'. After that, as Ellen would say later, nothing untoward happened until about eleven that morning when, all of a sudden, Anne spoke of feeling a change. 'She believed she had not long to live. Could she reach home alive, if we prepared immediately for departure?'

It was all very abrupt, and totally unexpected. One moment Anne was, apparently, quite well, the next she felt so ill that she believed herself to be at death's door. Surely, then, it was between seven and eleven o'clock that morning when Charlotte administered the fatal dose. I have wondered often whether Anne suspected what her sister had done to her, and whether that was why she wanted to get home if at all possible. She may have felt that she would be safer in the Parsonage.

A doctor was summoned, and there can be little doubt but that he was primed by Charlotte before he saw the patient. One can almost hear her: 'It's my sister, doctor. She has had tuberculosis for months. I'm very worried about her because there's a history of the disease in our family – in fact my three other sisters died of it.' What doctor would have suspected anything sinister, especially when the words came from an apparently prim and respectable little spinster? It would have sounded so innocent, and the doctor would have examined Anne with the probability of consumption planted firmly in his mind. Any signs of vomiting or purging could then have been mistaken for the symptoms of tuberculosis in a late stage.

We do not know how thoroughly he examined her but, almost immediately, he told Anne that she was dying. He called back two or three times, but there was little he could do to save his patient and she died at about two o'clock in the afternoon.

It is worth noting that, apparently, very few people at the guesthouse thought Anne to be particularly ill; 'Dinner' was actually announced through the half-open door to her room just as she died!

Her death certificate states that she died of 'Consumption. 6 months. Not certified.' Now that information could have come only from Charlotte. No doctor's name appears on the 'certificate', obviously because he was not prepared to certify the cause of death, but, yet again, no postmortem examination was held.

Anne's death was actually registered two days after the event, and by Ellen Nussey.

Charlotte must have been both relieved and quite pleased with herself. Her sister had been disposed of neatly, with nobody suspicious; she had an independent witness to the death; and she had even arranged matters so that Ellen's name, and not hers, appeared on the death certificate. Arthur *would* be pleased. Now all that was needed was to tidy up the loose ends.

Nicholls and Charlotte had made their plans carefully. They were determined that there was not going to be another Brontë funeral at Haworth, with all the accompanying publicity. Were too many people to get to know of Anne's death too soon somebody might start putting two and two together, and the dangers of exhumation were very real. They had, therefore, decided that Anne would be buried at Scarborough, quietly and as quickly as possible – and that was what happened.

Anne died on 28 May 1849. Charlotte wrote to their father on

102

the following day, told him the sad news, and *informed* him that his daughter was to be buried so soon that he would hardly be able to arrive in time for the funeral. She did not *consult* him, he was *told*. Now I find that peculiar, by any yardstick. Had everything been above board, what was the rush? There was ample time to consult her father, and to ascertain his wishes, because the mail then was far quicker than it is today. By what right did she take it upon herself to have her sister's remains interred so far from home? The excuse given at the time was that it was felt that it would upset the old man too much to have yet another family funeral at Haworth. That is rubbish. Mr Brontë was a hard old nut and, if Charlotte is to be believed, he had been prepared for Anne's death for some time. Why, it was only two months earlier that he had been quoted as saying that he considered his daughter's situation 'most precarious'. No, it just will not wash. Anne was buried at Scarborough because that was part of Nicholls' plan, and for no other reason.

The doctor who attended Anne offered to go to the funeral, but Charlotte was not having *that* and his offer was declined, politely but firmly. In the event, the only people present at the church were Charlotte, Ellen, their old headmistress, Miss Margaret Wooler, who lived in Scarborough, and one of Ellen's female neighbours who just happened to be visiting the town and would not be put off.

Charlotte then went through the motions of ordering a headstone for her sister's grave, but she wasted little time on the matter. The inscription reads: 'Here lie the remains of Anne Brontë, daughter of the Revd. P. Brontë, Incumbent of Haworth Yorkshire. She died, Aged 28, May 28th 1849.' It will be noted that there is not one word of sentiment. Charlotte was quite content to use up four words to inform the world of what her father did for a living, but there is no commendation to the Lord, no 'beloved daughter', not even a 'Rest in Peace'. So much for Charlotte's oft-expressed protestations of her affection for her sister.

Charlotte stayed in Scarborough for twelve days after Anne's death. However, she did not bother to ensure that her instructions about her sister's headstone were carried out. Instead, she and Ellen made their way down the East Coast. It was to be three years before she returned to Scarborough, and even then it was only because she happened to be in Filey, and was able to pop over on a day trip. At that time she told Ellen that she wanted to see that the headstone was all right, saying that the matter had long 'lain heavy on my mind' – so heavy, in fact, that it took three years for her to get round to doing anything about it!

In the event, she discovered that there were no less than five errors in the lettering, and therefore 'gave the necessary directions'. She never visited her sister's grave again and, to this day, the stone still gives Anne's age at the time of her death as twenty-eight, whereas she was actually twenty-nine. What more can one say?

Chapter Ten

'Let him kiss me with the kisses of his mouth.'
The Song of Solomon 1:2

Now I must set down some happenings which are not to my credit, and I would like to leave them out, but they form such a part of what was to come that I cannot do so.

We all noticed the change in Mr Nicholls once Miss Charlotte and Miss Anne had left. He was much more like he had been when he first arrived – light-hearted and full of cheer, and talking to us all when he made his daily visit to the Parsonage to see how Mr Brontë was. Oddly enough, as I thought at that time, he seemed in even higher spirits after the news of Miss Anne's death came, although he put on a different face when he was out.

Of course, he had many chances of speaking to me and knew a lot about me because he was living at our house. Sometimes he would start talking to me about almost anything, and would really get me laughing with his tales of when he was a lad in Ireland. At times he would place his arm around me, seemingly without thinking, and once he even tickled me as he had done in his early days.

I suppose he was about 31 then, and I was 10 years younger. He had always attracted me greatly, and he seemed to have been somewhat drawn to me as well, but I was just a servant and he had given his serious attentions to Miss Emily and Miss Charlotte. However, with Miss Charlotte away, and looking to be so for quite a while, he seemed to take more notice of me and I was quite pleased and flattered.

On my side at least, it was all very innocent, but then came the day, whilst Miss Charlotte was still away, when, for I think the first time ever, we found ourselves completely alone in our house.

It had been a warm and sunny day, and that evening I had some time off from the Parsonage. Father had a Lodge meeting and Mother had told me that her and my sisters would be walking over to my Aunt's cottage for what sounded to me as if it would be a pleasant time. I had said that I would join them if I could. Miss Aykroyd had agreed that I could have some time off and so, as soon as I had finished work I hurried home as quickly as I could, and just as I was.

I had had a busy day, what with all the sympathetic callers about Miss Anne, and I was hot and sweaty and I could barely wait to get home to get washed and changed into some of my best clothes. It was usual for me to wash from the ewer and basin in my sisters' bedroom whenever I was home but, knowing all my family to be out, and Mr Nicholls with Mr Brontë at the Parsonage, I decided to do so in the kitchen rather than have to go through all the bother of emptying the basin and refilling the ewer again afterwards.

As it happened, there was already a bowl of clean water in the sink and so I took off my dress, slipped my shift to the waist, and then bent over and put my hands in the water and splashed my face. It was bliss, but then, in an instance, I was almost turned to stone because I felt two hands cupping my breasts and a body was pressing hard against me from behind. Half-blinded by the water, I swung around in a panic, my hands lashing out, but then I felt my wrists grabbed tightly and heard Mr Nicholls saying softly that it was only him, and that everything was all right.

My senses were still all at odds though, and I pulled and pushed trying to get away, whilst all the time he was holding me tighter and forcing me hard against the sink. Then I felt him pressing a cloth to my face and I thought he was trying to smother me until I found that he was now holding me with but one hand and was trying to dry my face and hair with the other, whilst all the time kissing the back of my neck. I found myself becoming calmer, but I could feel his hardness and then, without a thought on my part, I turned and was returning his kisses with a feeling as wild as his.

As I write this now, I feel all the madness of those moments coming back to me, and my face is becoming warm even at this space of time. I do not wish to set down in full all that happened next – let it be enough to say that we ended up on the stones of the kitchen floor and when, but a few moments later it seemed, we got to our feet again we both knew that things would never be the same between us after that.

I remember that my body seemed to be burning all over, inside and out, and, grabbing up my clothes, I fled up to the bedroom and lay on the bed with so many thoughts rushing through my mind. I must be honest, I was not a virgin at the time for I had let myself go with two lads in the past. Never, though, had I known such fever as at this time and, in between hoping that I would not find myself with child, my mind was awhirl wondering what the future would hold.

All the time I was lying there I was wondering if Mr Nicholls would come upstairs, but he did not. I heard the splashing of water from the kitchen, and then the back door went and, creeping to the window, I saw him striding up to the moor as if he had not a care in the world.

When I had collected myself, I went down to the kitchen and, after emptying and refilling the bowl, I washed myself all over – but this time with the doors bolted and the curtains drawn, and all the time with my ears cocked for the smallest sound. Then I dressed and did my hair, and walked across the village to my Aunt's cottage, feeling all the while that folk had but to look at me to tell what I had been up to.

I do not know how I got through that evening, and Mother must have had her thoughts because she said I was flushed and asked if I had a fever. Ever since, I have wondered whether she sensed what I had been about, and whether she ever spoke of it to Father.

The next time I saw Mr Nicholls I felt my face burning like fire, but he made no mention of what had passed between us. Only later in the day, as he came out of Mr Brontë's room, did he take me to one side and ask me if I was all right, and we arranged to meet that very night.

After work that night I went home, washed and did my hair most carefully, with one of my best ribbons holding it back. I

107

even dabbed on a little perfumed water that one of my sisters had given me for my birthday. I looked at myself in the little glass and, though I say it myself, and even though my face was so flushed that it seemed as if I had painted it, I thought I had never looked prettier. Of course, one of my sisters had been watching through the door and, having seen what I was about, she wasted no time in running down to Mother and telling her that I was off to meet a lad. Thank goodness Father was out when I came down, because he would have wanted to know more, but all Mother said was to enjoy myself but be careful – and I knew what she meant.

Just as he and Miss Emily had done, Mr Nicholls and me made our own ways up to the moor and there, by a little waterfall, he took me in his arms very gently and said all the things that I had been hoping he would say. It ended with us making love again.

We had several more meetings like that before Miss Charlotte came back – and then they stopped. This saddened me, but it did not surprise me, as he had warned me that they would have to. When I pressed him to say why, he said there was a lot he could not tell me, but that I should trust him and all would be well.

I had to be content with that, but I was very puzzled, until something happened that explained a lot of things, and later led me to think of what might be the truth of the matter.

It all began like this. Me and Mr Nicholls had been trying to make the most of it before Miss Charlotte came back, and 2 nights before she was due we went to the moors a bit earlier. Little did I know, though, that that evening would stay in my mind for ever, because we were to make love in a way such as I have never known.

At first Mr Nicholls was so gentle, for we were both sad that our times together were to end. Slowly, though, our other feelings got the better of us and we ended up with not a stitch on and touching and kissing each other all over until I was beside myself with wanting him. Afterwards we lay together quite out of breath, and with me feeling all drained, but I had never been so at ease.

That night I slept more sweetly than for a long while, and

was up even earlier than was my custom, and started work feeling very different from how I normally did. I was content with the world, and so full of good spirits that I took it upon myself to undertake a chore that I had been dreading ever since I got over the news of Miss Anne's death. I went to her room, stripped off all the bedding – even though I had put clean on when she left – and took it downstairs for washing. Then I went back and set about tidying up and putting her things in some semblance of order. Everything was higgledy-piggledy after all the excitement of her getting off for her holiday, and I did not really know where to start, but start I did and, being inquisitive, I quite enjoyed rootling around amongst her things.

I looked at some of her old writings, and then poked around in the chest where I knew she had some keepsakes and other things dear to her heart. On top were some things of only passing interest to me but, just underneath them, I found her writing-desk. I got it out carefully, because it was a lovely box, and then set about having a closer look. I had never been able to do so before because Miss Anne always locked it and put it away carefully when she was not using it, and so I knew little about it and I was filled with curiosity.

To my great surprise, I saw that its tiny key was still in the lock. Now that was indeed unusual because, as I have said, Miss Anne was always so careful about locking it, especially of late, that I had often wondered what was inside to be guarded so well. All that I could think of was that she had hidden it away in a hurry in the last-minute rush to be off, and had quite forgotten to take the key.

The desk was locked, and so I turned the key but still it would not open, and it was only by jiggling it around that I found that it seemed to open in the opposite way from what I thought it would. I unfolded the desk, but there was nothing that caught my eye on top, nor in the secret little drawers underneath and between the inkpots. Then I lifted the flap, below which I had often seen Miss Anne slip things, and found several papers, all about things private to her, and a small bundle of letters tied up in ribbon. I read one, and found that it was a love letter from Mr Weightman, who had been the curate

109

when I first started work at the Parsonage, but who had died young only 2 years after. Everybody had always known that Miss Anne thought a lot of him, and she was never really the same after he died. All the letters were from him, but I read only the one and tied them back up again.

Then, underneath everything else, I found one of the thicker exercise books that used to be given out to the older children at the Sunday School. I hardly expected it to hold anything worth reading, but I opened it and found that page after page was covered in Miss Anne's neat handwriting, but writ so small that I had to squint my eyes to read it.

I read but two pages, but that was enough to tell me that it seemed to be something of a diary of happenings that made my heart beat so fast it was like to burst. There was no time to read it all and so I placed it under my skirt and then went and hid it with my things in my bedroom.

It took days for me to read it all, for I could do so only when nobody was about. Once Miss Aykroyd asked me what I was doing and I had to tell her that I was going through some of *my* old exercise books as I was thinking of throwing them out. What I read, though, would not have been found in any of *them*. It was far worse than some of the magazines about murders that Father sometimes left lying about the house.

I found out that Mr Nicholls had poisoned Master Branwell, and that Miss Emily had thought that she was with child by him when she died, and that Miss Anne had told Miss Charlotte everything, but she had done nothing except swear Miss Anne to secrecy. Then came pages of her wonderings about whether Mr Nicholls had poisoned Miss Emily as well and whether, in spite of her promise to Miss Charlotte, she should tell someone else, lest something happen to her.

It seemed to me, though, that she might have been content with doing nothing more had she gained a measure of relief from writing everything down but evidently she did not. Her later words were about not being able to understand why Miss Charlotte kept putting off the holiday with her and why, at the last, *both* her and Miss Nussey were going with her when Miss Nussey had, at the start, made it quite clear that it was not

110

possible for her to go. The writings ended with her hopes that Scarborough would do her good – little did she know, poor girl.

One thing above all stood out in my mind when I had finished reading; I could not, for the life of me, understand why Miss Charlotte had done nothing when Miss Anne went to her, but had made her pledge herself to keep quiet. Surely, I thought, Miss Charlotte would have wanted to have Mr Nicholls brought to book. It nagged away at my mind, and then suddenly it came to me that she was holding it over him, and all became clear to me, though it was to be years before I learned the full story from Mr Nicholls' own lips.

I sat there, the book in my lap, not knowing what to think or do. My first thought was to show it to Father and let him decide, but then it came to me that he did not like Mr Nicholls one jot, and that it was like to happen that he would have him sent to the gallows. I could not bear to think of such a possibility in the light of what was happening between us, and so I resolved to do naught. I was always taught 'Least said, soonest mended', and that seemed to be the right thing then. Next day I put the book back where I had found it, and tried to put what it held from my mind for the time being, although it was clear to me that what I now knew might one day stand me in good stead.

I never said a word about it to anyone then, but what I had learned was to change the whole way in which I regarded Mr Nicholls and Miss Charlotte. With Mr Nicholls I no longer found myself in awe of him, and I went into our lovemaking far more sure of myself and of him. As for Miss Charlotte, no longer did I put myself out to please her, nor did I suffer her scoldings as before – even though they were far fewer than they had been when I was younger. Instead, I began to stand up to her when I knew I was in the right and, to my surprise, she showed me more regard for it and talked to me more than she had ever done.

However, I must not get ahead of myself, because I have not yet told of what went on when Miss Charlotte finally came home.

Much later, Mr Nicholls told me that it was clear to him that Miss Charlotte had found it a long time to be away from him, and she was even more pressing with him than before. Of course, I knew naught of that at the time, but he had warned me that we could not meet when she was around.

He also told me that Mr Brontë wanted his company more and more, and that he found it harder to get away. Looking back, I just cannot understand how foolish and besotted I must have been to believe him. It was evident to most folk that Mr Brontë had little time for him, and that for two pins he would be rid of him except that he needed his help. But believe him I did.

It was also much later that he told me of the tale that Miss Charlotte had spun him when she came back. He said that he had looked at her askance when she said that Miss Anne had died of a natural cause, and had felt confirmed in what he was thinking when, having asked for the poison back, she told him that she had thrown it over the cliff at Scarborough. Nevertheless he could not be sure if she had used the poison; so he made out that he believed her, and put on a show of looking pleased that all had gone so smoothly. For her part, it seems that she had been most worried about how the news of Miss Anne's death had been taken in Haworth and thereabouts, but he was able to calm her fears and tell her that there had been no talk that he knew of, and that her father had accepted everything – but little did either of them know what was said in the village behind their backs!

Miss Charlotte put on a good act to all and sundry about being so sad at Miss Anne's death, and how much she missed her, and so on and so on, but she did not pull the wool over *my* eyes. On top of what I had always thought and known about her, I now saw her quite clearly for the nasty little woman she was. Miss Anne's book had shown me that she knew what had happened to Master Branwell and Miss Emily and, to tell the truth – and I am not being wise after the happening – I had already begun to have secret thoughts about Miss Anne's death.

Knowing her as I did, I did not think it at all odd that one of the first things that Miss Charlotte set about was to go through

112

Miss Anne's things. I had often seen her poking around her sisters' private belongings when they were alive, if she thought that no one was about, and so it did not surprise me when she spent hours sorting through Miss Anne's clothes and other bits and pieces. Nor was I mazed when one day I crept in whilst she was out and found that Miss Anne's book was gone. All I thought was: 'Well if she didn't know it all before, she now knows what *I* know.'

After that I thought and thought about it all, because the only person in danger from Miss Anne's book was Mr Nicholls, and we all knew how very cold Miss Charlotte had always been to him. When I first read Miss Anne's book I had wondered why she had not told on him, but now that it had disappeared, and again nothing had happened, the reason suddenly became clear to me: Miss Charlotte was in love with Mr Nicholls. I knew for certain that she would use the book to bind Mr Nicholls to her even more closely and for as long as she wanted. Now, more than ever, I saw why he was not meeting me so often, and I understood his late nights at the Parsonage and so many other things.

From time to time I had seen them standing close together and deep in talk in different places downstairs in the Parsonage. On the times that they had noticed me, which they did not every time, they had stepped apart and said something loudly for my ears and then gone their ways. When they did not see me they kept talking for ages. I had thought that they were worried about Miss Anne or Mr Brontë, or some such thing.

Then, shortly after she got back, there was the time when she was going on about something or other and she said 'Arthur' instead of 'Mr Nicholls'. It was the very first time I had ever heard her call him that, and she knew what she had done as soon as the word was out of her mouth. She went redder than I had ever seen her go, even in temper, and said, very quickly: 'Oh, I mean Mr Nicholls of course.' I had wondered about that at the time, but now, as I have said, I suddenly understood a lot of things and I did not like what I knew. I had thought that Mr Nicholls really felt something for me, in spite of the differences in our stations, and I had begun to have secret dreams. Now, though, I felt that I had just been silly, and that he had simply been dallying with me because, whatever his true feelings for me, he had to dance to her tune. Far too late, I wished that I had kept Miss Anne's book instead of putting it back.

I tried to get Mr Nicholls alone to see what was what, but there always seemed to be someone about and we could contrive but a few words at a time. All he said was that he would see me as soon as he could. I knew that would not be likely to happen as long as she was there, and no one knew how long that would be for because, although she kept on about how she was going to travel later in the year, just as soon as she had finished the new book that she was writing, we did not know how long that would take her.

July came and I resolved that I would wait no longer. I had not seen Mr Nicholls alone for more than 2 minutes at a time since *she* came back after Miss Anne's death, and it just was not good enough. I wanted to know *from him* where I stood. I thought about the matter for a long time and then I wrote a note and placed it in his hand one day as we passed in the hallway in the Parsonage. In it I said that I wanted him to meet me, without fail, in the Church that evening. I chose the Church because I thought that nobody else would be there, and even if they were they would think naught of Mr Nicholls and me being there at the same time, me being the Sexton's daughter and all.

I wondered whether he would heed my note and so it was with heart beating that I hurried along the lane, past our house, after I had finished work. I took the long way round the back of the Church to the little side door, because I did not want to be seen going in the front. As quietly as I could, I opened the door, went inside and looked around me. Nobody was there, and my spirits sank, and then I saw Mr Nicholls by the Vestry door waving to me.

He looked very worried, and the first thing he did was to ask me if I was all right. Since then he has told me that all day he had been in fear that I was with child – so I can understand now why he seemed so afeared. I told him that I was quite all right, except that he seemed to have no time for me of late and I

114

wanted to know why. At that, he locked the door and took me to the long seat that ran along the wall.

Speaking very softly, and looking into my eyes all the while with such a tender concern, he pledged me to secrecy and then said that Miss Charlotte had a hold over him. He could not tell me what it was, and he hoped to break it soon, but in the meantime he dared not see me whilst she was about lest it got back to her. Of course, I did not let on that I knew what her hold was, I just listened to him talking so gently in that lovely smooth voice. He told me that he really cared for me, and were I patient for a couple of months it seemed that we would then have plenty of time together because she would be away a lot then.

There was nothing I could do but agree to bide my time. I could gainsay him nothing, and when he drew me down we made love in such a way that I felt sure that his feelings for me were all that he said they were.

As it happened, Miss Charlotte finished her book in the August, but she did not go on her travels until the October. After that she was away, on and off, for several weeks and Mr Nicholls was as good as his word. We managed quite a few meetings, in the Church and the School and on the moor – although it was a bit cold up there. Twice we even made love in the Parsonage – the first time on the night of the very day when she first went away – but I was always ill at ease doing it there, although somehow it used to excite me more than anything else.

Then Christmas came and she was back, and Miss Nussey came and stayed well into the New Year. There was no chance at all of our long meetings, and in any case he did not seem in a very good humour although I did not know why.

It was a long miserable time after Christmas. The weather was bad, and it was very dark and cold morning and night, and I longed for Spring to come because Miss Charlotte was dropping little hints that she would go away again then. In the meantime my days seemed endless, and I seemed to have little wish to do aught. Father became quite concerned about me, but I told him I was all right, it was just that Winter was getting me down and I longed for warm days and light nights.

115

In March 1850, she did indeed go off again, somewhat earlier than I had thought she would, and she was away for several times after that. I do not know what she got up to on her travels, but she was always going on about the men she had met and stayed with, and hardly ever made mention of women. Once, though, when I was alone with her in the sitting room, and she was going on as usual about all the important men she had met, she gave little hints that she thought that one or two were would-be suitors. She looked at me as if waiting for me to say something, but I said naught. I was thinking that she must be mad to think that, but it was evident that she did.

I do not know who else she dropped like remarks to, but once, when she was away, I was making up his fire for Mr Brontë and he asked me outright if I had heard talk of his daughter getting wed, or if she had said anything to me. It was not unusual for him to talk to me – in fact he seemed to have quite taken to me as the years went by, especially with two of his daughters dead and him being left so much alone and all – but never before had he spoken to me of family matters and at first I did not know how to answer him.

For a start, I wondered whether *I* had said anything in passing to make him wonder about her, but I did not think I had. Then it came to me that he could have got it from Miss Aykroyd, or indeed anyone else in the village if she had been going around dropping hints or making little slips with them, as she did with me about 'Arthur'. One of her troubles was that she was such a chatterer, when she was trying to seem important to folk, that she never knew when to stop.

At first, whilst I was thinking what to say, I made out that the rattle of the coal from the scuttle had stopped me from hearing all that he had said; so when he asked me again I was ready to say straight out that I had heard nothing of the kind. Even so he looked at me in that quizzing way of his and I do not think that he believed me. From then on he seemed to go into himself and did not seem at all well, and we were all most concerned about him.

When she finally came back, in the July I think it was, she asked me how things had been whilst she had been away which,

116

by then, had become the usual thing because, little by little, I had come to be the one who was really in charge of the household, what with Miss Aykroyd being so old and the others younger than me. I told her that all had been well, except that her father had been ailing of late. She wanted to know what the matter was, and by then I was so sure of myself that I told her what I thought it might be. Only a few months before I would have said that I did not know, but now I came straight out with it and she did not like that one whit.

Had she known what was going on between her 'Arthur' and me I supposed she would have liked that even less, but perhaps it was just as well that she did not for, one way and another, she had enough trouble in store.

[*CC*] Here we have reached a period of Charlotte's life of which Martha knew only the Haworth part, and in order to appreciate her tale fully it is essential to be aware of what Charlotte was doing elsewhere.

In 1849 she completed her second novel, *Shirley*, which opens with a cruel satire upon three curates, whose characters were, allegedly, drawn from life. Later, however, a fourth curate, the Irish Mr Macarthey, is introduced, and the original of that character was Nicholls. *He* is 'decent, decorous and conscientious'. Unlike the others, he labours 'faithfully in the parish; the schools, both Sunday and day-schools, flourish under him. He has his faults; what many would call virtues.' In addition, he is 'sane and rational, diligent and charitable'.

There is absolutely no reason for 'Mr Macarthey' to be in the book at all, and when one remembers Charlotte's views on curates generally, and the period during which this part of the book was written, who can, in all conscience, doubt what was going on between her and Nicholls?

Shirley was well received, and gave Charlotte the financial independence for which she had always striven. Now, therefore, she resolved to travel, in order to meet famous people and ingratiate herself with them. She felt that she had outgrown Haworth and, as we have seen, she had realized that there was

117

nothing to keep her at the Parsonage if she did not wish to be there. Nicholls was not going anywhere, and she no longer made any pretence of anxiety about entrusting the welfare of her father to servants.

Charlotte began her travels modestly. In November 1849, just after *Shirley* was published, she journeyed to London where, for a fortnight, she was a guest at the home of the mother of George Smith, her young and good-looking publisher, and met Thackeray and Harriet Martineau, the authoress.

The circumstances of the visit to the Smiths provide yet another example of her flawed character. During her time at the Pensionnat Héger, she had been treated most considerately by a Dr Wheelwright and his wife and family. The Wheelwrights had settled in Brussels with their five daughters, all of whom attended the Héger establishment, and they had often asked Charlotte and Emily to tea.

In 1843, the Wheelwrights moved to London, but contact was maintained and then, in 1849, they invited Charlotte to stay with them on her next visit to the capital. That she had fully intended to do because, no matter how much money she acquired, Charlotte was nothing if not 'careful', and hotels could be expensive!

Then, however, she received the invitation from George Smith, who was obviously of far more use to her, both in publishing her works and in introducing her to those whom she wished to meet. Also she found his offer flattering, and therefore it was accepted with alacrity. No one can blame her for that, but the way in which she referred to the Wheelwrights in her letter of acceptance is unforgivable. On 19 November, she wrote to George Smith thanking him for his invitation, which she was pleased to accept. That was all that was required, and had Charlotte confined herself to those few words no criticism would be possible – but she did not. She could not bear to lose an opportunity of implying how wonderful she was; nor could she resist trying to identify with the class of person she was addressing, if she considered them in any way superior to herself.

After her words of acceptance, she went on to say that, at

first, she had thought that she would have to decline, 'having received a prior invitation some months ago from a family lately come to reside in London, whose acquaintance I formed in Brussels. But these friends only know me as Miss Brontë, and they are of the class, perfectly worthy but in no way remarkable, to whom I should feel it quite superfluous to introduce Currer Bell; I know they would not understand the author.'

Oh, the condescension!

I cannot help but wonder what the Wheelwrights thought of that letter, when Charlotte's correspondence was published after her death.

Next March she was off again. She went to stay with Sir James and Lady Kaye-Shuttleworth, at their home at Gawthorpe Hall, near Burnley in Lancashire. Sir James tended to regard her as his protegée, and had called upon her at Haworth earlier in the year. Charlotte loved her association with what she regarded as the aristocracy and, even more, she loved crowing about it, despite the reservations which she professed. For months, she went on and on, to all and sundry, about her connection with the Kaye-Shuttleworths, and about her visit.

On 16 March 1850, she wrote to Mr Williams that she did not 'regret' having made the visit. Then she just had to gild the lily. 'The worst part of it is that there is now some menace hanging over my head of an invitation to go to them in London during the season.' My word, we *had* come up in the world! 'Some menace' indeed. She would have been over the moon at the possibility, and one wonders just how much angling she had had to do to secure the invitation. However, and yet again, it gratified her to demonstrate to the lower classes just how sought after she was, and how terms like 'the season' now sprang so readily to her lips. As she was to write later to George Smith, 'Aristocratic notice is what I especially crave, cultivate and cling to.'

Her travels continued. Charlotte was having a marvellous time. In April she paid another visit to Ellen. Then, in June, she was in London again. First, she stayed with the Smiths, and then with Dr Wheelwright and his daughter, Laetitia. Obviously the Wheelwrights had their uses after all. She dined with Thackeray, and sat for the portrait being painted by George Richmond.

From London she went, directly, to stay with Ellen again. She did not wish to go home because the Parsonage was being re-roofed; too bad about 'dear papa'!

After that visit, she once again avoided Haworth and went to Edinburgh, to spend two days with George Smith and his sister. That must have pleased her greatly, because I really think that by then Charlotte had convinced herself that she was quite desirable.

What though, I wonder, were Smith's thoughts about Charlotte? He was almost eight years younger, good-looking and comfortably off. Living, as he did, in London, he could have had his pick of many of the eligible young women there – and probably did. It is ludicrous, therefore, to suppose that he felt physically attracted to Charlotte, and the only logical conclusion at which one can arrive about his attentions to her is that his interest was solely professional. He was making money out of her, and there was the strong probability of more – not only from any future works of her own, but also from those of her dead sisters. That being so, he would not have wished to upset her, but probably regarded her importunings with some amusement.

Charlotte should have been worldly enough to know that, but all the indications are that eventually she deluded herself into thinking that he loved her for herself.

When she finally arrived back at Haworth, she was told by Martha that her father's 'recent discomposure' had been caused, in part, by 'the vague fear of my being somehow about to be married to somebody'. Now Mr Brontë may have been many things, but a fool he was not. If he thought that his daughter had received 'some overture' then he would have had good reason for such a supposition. In the event, Charlotte 'distinctly cleared away' his fears, but how had he come by them in the first place?

Later in the year, in September 1850, Ellen told Charlotte that she too had heard rumours that the latter was to marry and,

120

although Charlotte scoffed at the gossips, I suspect that what Ellen had written was a little too near the mark for comfort. Probably conjecturing that her friend had done her own share of gossiping, Charlotte did not answer that letter and Ellen was forced to write again, later in the month, asking what was wrong and why she had received no reply.

One is driven to wonder how the rumours had started. It may well be that they had been caused by Charlotte's sojourn with the Smiths, and her visit to Edinburgh – but few people knew of those. A stronger possibility is that they had originated in suspicions which the villagers may have had about the relationship between Charlotte and Nicholls, and which had spread farther than Haworth. As we know from Martha, it would have been very difficult to keep anything completely secret from the servants in the Parsonage – and servants talked.

Another likelihood must not, however, be overlooked. It would not have been beyond Nicholls to have whispered a few ideas in her father's ear whilst Charlotte was gadding about, because Nicholls had no intention of seeing her marry, as then there would always be the possibility that she would tell her husband what she knew.

Nicholls realized that her father did not wish Charlotte to marry *anybody* really, and therefore he may have invented rumours to tell the old man, or have fanned the flames of anger when he heard tales elsewhere. Were that indeed the case, he could have had no idea of how such a policy was to backfire on him.

However, what occupied Charlotte most in the final quarter of the year was one of her favourite occupations – the acquisition of money. Her publisher had suggested that he produce a reprint of *Wuthering Heights* and *Agnes Grey*. She was asked to edit *Wuthering Heights*, and how she enjoyed that opportunity to get back at Emily. Her treatment of her sister's book shows her at her most spiteful. She savaged it, altering many scenes and modifying the dialect, and her revenge for imagined slights would have been especially sweet if Nicholls was present while she performed her treachery. Poor Emily must have turned in her grave.

Chapter Eleven

'Though he slay me, yet will I trust in him: but I will maintain my own ways before him.'

Job 13:15

It did not seem to bother Madam – for that was how, by then, I had come to think of her, but not in a nice way – that her father was out of sorts. She had used to make such a song and dance that he could not be left alone, but now she did not seem to care, and no sooner was she back than she was off again. Of course, *I* did not mind one jot as that left me in peace at work, and it also meant that Mr Nicholls and me had more chances to meet, and that was about all I lived for during that lovely summer of 1850.

He was always so light of heart when she was away, and I just wished that we could go out together openly and just be happy, but he said that that could not be, and I understood what he meant. Instead, we had to meet in out-of-the-way places, or where we had good reason to be at the same time if we were seen. Sometimes we took little chances, but it really was not worth it because we were both uneasy all the while and our time together was spoiled. Not that *I* cared overmuch about being seen, for I would much rather have had things out in the open, but, as I have said, I knew that that would not do for his sake. Even so, that did not stop me from wishing, and I longed for the day when things would be different.

Then *she* came back, bringing Autumn with her, and the terrible thought that Winter was almost on our doorstep. Our meetings became fewer, and I was back in the everyday rut of work at the Parsonage and village life in Haworth. I think that what got me down most was the unfairness of it all. Whenever she came back she not only took my man away from me – for that was how I saw it – but I had to put up with having her

122

about all the time telling me what to do. She tried to do so in a nicer way than she had when I was younger, but even so I was at her beck and call and I hated it.

Soon it was November, and cold and dark, and I seem to recall an East wind bitter enough to cut you in half. I always hated the Winter, but that one sticks in my mind because Madam told me she would be away for a week or two over Christmas – never mind how her father was – and so I would be in charge of the Parsonage as far as anything that mattered went, and I was of a mind to make the most of it. It would be nice to be rid of her – especially as she had been in a black mood for weeks – but that apart I meant to see more of Mr Nicholls, and I really looked forward to that, and cheering him up, as he had begun to look so down.

As it turned out, all my hopes came true and Christmas 1850 was one of the nicest that I ever had. With Madam away, and only Mr Brontë and Miss Aykroyd to look after, there was nowhere near as much work to do and so I had more time to make everything ready, myself included.

One thing in particular that pleased me was that we had our Christmas gifts from Mr Brontë just as before, but with about twice as much in them as we had expected.

It came about like this. As Christmas was nearing I had said in passing to Mr Nicholls that I hoped we would get our money that year. He had asked me what I meant, and I had told him how we had got nothing for the last 2 years. He was very concerned, and said I should leave it up to him. Then, without saying what he was going to do, he went to see Mr Brontë. Without mention of my name, he told him he had learned that the staff had had nothing the year before and were wondering if they were going to get anything that year.

Seemingly Mr Brontë was most put out, and said that the deaths of Miss Emily and Miss Anne must have put the matter out of his mind. Mr Nicholls told me that the mention of the deaths seemed to affect the old man greatly, and he was pleased to take up Mr Nicholls' offer to make up the envelopes, as I had told him had been Miss Emily's custom. Mr Nicholls then got enough money from Mr Brontë to make sure that we all got about twice as much as usual, but he saw to it that *I* had even more! He pledged me to secrecy about that though, because he did not want it getting back to the others, but said that I *should* have more than them anyway because now I was really in charge of everything.

The extra money was a boon. I was able to buy some things I had wanted for a long while, and I was able to make it up to my family for having had naught the years before. On top of all else though – and what pleased me more than I can say – I was able to buy a present for Mr Nicholls. It was a pocket-book, and it cost a lot, but he still uses it to this very day. He said that I should not have bothered, but it was evident that he was very touched when I gave it to him, although he was very put out that he had bought naught for me. That did not bother me – my present was in seeing him so pleased – however, within the week, he gave me a little brooch of Forget-Me-Nots and I was so happy that I could not stop crying. It made me very sad though that I could not wear it, for everyone would have wanted to know where it came from. I had to hide it away carefully for many years, but now I am rarely seen without it.

Then, after Christmas, *she* came home and a long miserable time began.

I had hoped that she would come back from Miss Nussey's in better spirits than when she went, but she did not. Indeed she was very down, and snapped at everyone including, as he told me, Mr Nicholls. He said that he had told her off about it, and that she had said she was sorry, but she felt so tired after all the work she had done before December.

Anyway, what with her being as she was, and me having but rare meetings with Mr Nicholls, and the nasty weather, I was glad when the Spring of 1851 came with the promise of warm and light days ahead.

I recall that it was about that time that *her* spirits lifted as well. That came about after a young man who was something to do with her books came to see her. When he had gone she was cock-a-hoop and hardly seemed able to wait to tell folk that he had proposed marriage to her. *I* thought she was making it up, but Mr Nicholls did not and I could not understand why it seemed to upset him so much. When I said that to him I was taken aback at how he snapped at me and said I did not know the half of it. It was so unlike him to speak to me in such a manner that I must confess that I snapped back. I told him that I was not going to be spoken to like that, and that perhaps he should tell me what I did not know, but he would not and I did not like that.

Later I tried to cheer him up by telling him that she was making plans to go away again in the May, but that seemed to displease him even more and I wished I had kept my mouth shut. Seemingly she had not told him, but she had to put me on notice because she said that she would be gone for some weeks and there was a lot to be thought about. Even so, I could not understand why he should be so cross-grained, because *I* thought it such good news. With her away, and the better weather coming, he and I would be able to spend far more time together and I was really looking forward to it. However, he would not come out of his gloom, and that upset me because I did not know what was going on and I felt I should.

When she *did* go I hoped he would change, but he did not and I became very out of patience with him, so much so that I picked up with Tom Oliver, a lad from Oxenhope.

His father was the carter, and sometimes Tom used to do some of the deliveries himself. Although he was a bit younger than me, whenever he came to the Parsonage on his own he used to make a point of staying longer than it took and talking to me. Sometimes, when nobody was about, I would ask him into the kitchen and give him a drink because it was nice to have someone different to talk to and he made me laugh with his tales. He was a good-looking lad, and very quick, and we so took to each other that he started to ask me to go out with him. Well, I had always said 'No', although he would have had the use of his father's cart, because the only one in my mind up till then had been Mr Nicholls. But when he got to being so cross I made up my mind to teach him a lesson, and the next time I was asked out I went.

Tom called for me at our house one evening, and I was ready for him. I had taken a lot of care with my person and I knew that I was looking at my best, and that showed in his eyes when he helped me up next to him. What *really* pleased me though was that he had brought me a little posy tied with ribbon, and I could not but help giving him a peck on the cheek for it. That made him red, but we both laughed and it was then that I noticed Mr Nicholls glowering at me.

Mother and one of my sisters had come to the front door to see me off, and he must have wondered what all the hulla-baloo was about because he had come down and was standing behind them. They could not see his face, but I could and it was as black as our grate. That pleased me even more than the posy, and I thought 'Serves you right' as we set off in high spirits with me waving all the while until we had rounded the corner.

We did not go far that night, either in miles or in other ways, but as time went by we went to places that I had never seen, and sometimes we would stop at inns where I would wait outside whilst he brought the drinks. I began to allow him to become more and more familiar with me but, mind you, I never allowed him the liberties that I allowed Mr Nicholls, although the little that I did allow seemed to please the lad quite enough.

Of course, in a place like Haworth, it was but a matter of time before *she* got to hear that I was 'walking out' as she put it, and for some reason it seemed to please her greatly. She always wanted to know where I had been or where I was going, and she took to lending me little things of hers or her sisters to wear. Then when Miss Nussey came to stay at the Parsonage in the Summer she must have told her because she would sometimes pull my leg about my beau.

All in all, that was not a good time for poor Mr Nicholls. I was not seeing him, and Miss Nussey – who for some reason he seemed to dislike very much – was there. It did not surprise me at all, therefore, that later he went off to Ireland for a while, but it mazed Madam.

He had not told her, or me come to that, that he had arranged the holiday with Mr Brontë a couple of months before – about the time I had started seeing Tom Oliver – and I did not find that out until later. He had said naught to anyone in Haworth,

126

and so we all felt at that time that he was going because he was out of sorts with us all.

Long after, he told me that the main reason why he went off was to give Miss Charlotte a taste of her own medicine. If she thought it was right and proper that she could just clear off at a moment's notice whenever she thought fit, leaving him to watch out for her father, he thought he would let her see if she liked it when the shoe was on the other foot. To use his own words, as far as I can recall them, 'She thought she had me fast, and I wanted to show her that she had not.' He did say, though, that if *I* had not been so flighty at the time he would probably have stayed and taken it out on her in other ways – because he had ill afforded the cost of the journey – but I told him that that was his own fault. In the light of other things, though, I think that the real truth of the matter was that he needed a little quiet to think in because, although I did not know it at the time, his way of life was not to his taste but he did not know how to change it.

He was away for 6 whole weeks, and *she* was out of sorts with everybody for most of that time. She kept making nasty remarks about him, and I wondered what had gone amiss between them. Once, in quite an innocent fashion, I asked her when he was coming back and she snapped at me that she did not know and hoped he never would, but that it was none of my business anyway.

From time to time, however, she seemed more at ease, and she went back to offering to lend me little things to wear when I was going out. Somehow, though, I was able to put her off without her taking offence. I had long since made up my mind that I would take nothing more from that little Madam, what with her blowing hot and cold to me in accord with her moods. Also I had not liked her telling Miss Nussey my business, and I had the feeling that they were laughing at me behind my back.

Then Mr Nicholls came back, and it was as if a great load had been lifted from her mind. He, though, seemed as displeased as he had been when he left and hardly spoke two words to me in the first few days he was home. That made me think that he was still out with me about the lad, although when I had the chance

127

to ask him what was wrong he said that it was naught to do with me. Even so, I thought that I had taught him lesson enough and I made up my mind to finish with Tom Oliver.

I did not like doing it to him as we had had some good times, but I felt it just had to be – Mr Nicholls apart. Tom had been becoming very earnest, and had begun to talk of us being wed some time. That was not to my liking at all though. I had no wish to end up as a carter's wife stuck in a place like Oxenhope – or even Haworth, come to that – my mind was set upon better things.

Tom did not take it very well at all – in point of fact he turned quite nasty once he found that he could not get me to change my mind. He said that I had taken him for a fool, and that I would make him a laughing-stock with his family and mates. Seemingly he had been putting it about that we were going to wed, and now he felt that I had let him down. When I told him that I had never thought of such a thing he became very angry and said that I had just led him on for his money.

That did it. We were not far from our house so I was off the cart and in the door in a trice. I suppose that it was true that I had used him simply to get back at Mr Nicholls, but I had never wanted him to spend the money on me that he had always been bent on doing – in any case, he had had good value for it.

Later I found out that he had told some of his mates what we used to get up to from time to time, and had made up even more, and I was more angry than I have ever been in my life. The next time he came to the Parsonage on business I smacked his face hard, and did not care who saw me. I have not spoken to him again to this day. In time he married a lass from Thornton, and then took over from his father when he died. As I understand it, they have had 6 children out of which 4 died, and his poor wife now looks old before her time, and is living the kind of life that I had been in dread of – so I have never cried over *that* spilled milk!

Of course, it soon got round our gossipy village that Tom and me were not going out together any more, but even so I made a point of telling Mr Nicholls myself. He put on a show of not being bothered either way, but I could tell that really he was pleased and it was not long before we were contriving the odd meeting, but not as often as I wanted.

Autumn went, and yet again there was the prospect of a long, cold, dark Winter. I *hated* the very thought of it, and was really down. I should have counted my blessings though, because in October and November everyone in the Parsonage and our house was taken with illness. If it was not one thing it was another, and as fast as I got over something I fell for something else, and it seemed that we were all taking it in turn to be bedridden.

In between my spells of being laid up I had, of course, to work, and it was more miserable than ever. The Parsonage was ice cold, and there was more work, what with people being in bed and all the fetching and carrying for them. I felt very weak and down, and could manage hardly a civil word to anyone. Then, of all things, I did not have my monthly showing and I was worried and felt worse than ever.

The only thing that went any way to giving me some cheer was that *she* was taken worse than any of us. Of course, she had a doctor in to see her – the rest of us just had to get on with it – but he did not really seem to know what was up with her. Her being laid up really seemed to cheer Mr Nicholls though. He was having a rough time like the rest of us – with a terrible cold and cough in particular – but he never took to his bed, and he was not out of sorts in his mind with it as we all were, and he went out of his' way to try to cheer me.

It was only very much later that I came to think that, somehow, he may have had something to do with *her* illness, which was quite unlike anything else that was going around – especially as she was very ill again after Christmas when most folk were better again.

Christmas had been a very quiet time, with most folk content just to be indoors with no work, either in bed in the warm or huddled around the fire. Of course, *I* had to work, but not for as long as on other days, and I did manage to meet Mr Nicholls once after Evensong.

Thankfully, *all* my troubles had cleared up and so I was feeling much better and looking quite my old self. Certainly Mr

Nicholls seemed to think so, for he was very ardent and made me feel quite wanted.

So the New Year of 1852 came, but one person who was not pleased to see it was *her* for, as I have said, she was laid *very* low again. I did not suspect then what was up with her, and the doctor did not seem to know any more than me. Apart from all else, her mouth was in a state such as I have never seen before or since, and it made me feel quite off just to look at it. She could eat nothing at all, and broth and suchlike had to be taken from a feeding cup. We had to do *everything* for her, and her bed-clothes sometimes had to be changed twice in one day. I *hated* it; what with her mouth, and the smell and the washing I felt sick at times and like to faint.

In the end, thank goodness, she came to something of her usual self – at the end of January, I think it was – and then, to our great joy, she managed to get over to Miss Nussey's for a couple of weeks. She was quite recovered when she came back, and very much her old self, and that made me think even more about what might be happening to her in the Parsonage. Straightaway she went back to her writing – and to Mr Nicholls – and that did not please me, but I just had to put up with it and try to make the best of things.

Slowly, very slowly it seemed that year, Spring was at last upon us, and after such an awful Winter I could at last begin to think about warm days and sunshine – and evenings with Mr Nicholls. Well the warm days and sunshine came, but I saw Mr Nicholls only on and off, and then it was but for very short times. You may imagine then how cheered I was when, in May, she told me that she would shortly be going to the seaside. Once again I wished that *I* was going, but still it was good news because she would be away and Mr Nicholls and me would be free of her for a while. I could not wait for her to be off.

It was a blissful time for me whilst she was away. There was little work at the Parsonage, weather that I loved, and no *her*. Mind you, I was quite put out, and just could not understand it, when Mr Nicholls suddenly went away for a few days during that time. He warned Mother that he was going, but he did not tell me and when I asked him where he was off to all he would

130

say was that he was going to see a friend of his who was also in the Church. Knowing him as well as I did by then, I thought I sensed something in his manner that told me that he was hiding something – but that may just have been imagining on my part.

Anyway he was only gone for 3 days and then, a week or so later, *she* came back and settled down to her writing again. She seemed very happy, and was very talkative with me, but it was not long before her mood changed.

For a start, Mr Brontë was taken with some kind of fit that left him with one arm very bad, and hanging by his side, and he could talk only out of the side of his mouth. He could not eat properly for a while either, and we had to make beef tea for him in a feeding cup until he got back to a little of his old self. *She* had to do all the feeding, with a tiny spoon, and she would get very cross about the time it took when she thought she ought to have been writing. Once she asked me to do it, but I did not feel it was my place to do something like that and said so. She was not very pleased, but she had, perforce, to take what I said – that I was there only to see to the housework, and was not a nurse.

Then there was some kind of row between her and Miss Nussey. I never got right to the bottom of it; all I know is that Mr Nicholls has told me that she was spreading tales about *her* and him, and so he took steps to put an end to their friendship.

I think, though, that the main thing was that Miss Charlotte was very down about how she was placed with her life. After all, and never mind about all that she had had to say about the men who wanted to wed her, nobody had and she was fast becoming an old maid, and I do not think that the prospect was very pleasing to her. Mr Nicholls has told me that she acted very odd to him at the time. One minute she was all around him, but the next he could scarce get a word out of her.

All I knew at the time though was that something was amiss between them, and that Miss Nussey seemed out of favour. None of that touched me though. I was out and about as much as possible that Summer, and Mr Nicholls was always all right with *me* – although some times more than others. We did not

131

meet *that* often, but when we did it pleased me greatly, especially when he told me of things that were going on in the Parsonage that I should not otherwise have known of.

I never knew what Father or Mother knew or suspected at that time, or indeed later, but I well remember Father saying that I seemed very well informed about certain matters, and he asked me how I knew one particular thing. I cannot recall what it was, but I know I felt myself going red, and wondered whether I had been prattling overmuch. I told him that Miss Charlotte and Mr Brontë talked to me at times, but I do not think that he was deceived because, with a queer little smile, he asked me: 'And does Mr Nicholls talk to you as well?' In spite of myself, I felt my whole face and neck come afire – which was always my giveaway – but all I answered was 'Sometimes', and the matter passed off.

Then, yet again, the Summer was gone, and the leaves were blowing every whichway. There was the smell of Winter in the air, and soon we would be busy making plans for Christmas. There was never any reckoning Miss Charlotte though with the way she was, and so I should not have been so surprised when she said that she was off to Miss Nussey's for a week – but I was. It was not that I minded – very much the other way – it was just that it came so sudden.

So off she went, and then Mr Brontë gave me word that she was going on to somewhere else from Miss Nussey's and would not be back for at least another week. That left me in charge for longer than I had expected, and I made the most of it in more ways than one. What I could not understand, though, was why Mr Nicholls was in such a bad mood again, and there was no talking to him when he was like that.

I tried to get round him on the very few times we were alone, but his mind seemed elsewhere and he would have none of it and I really did not know what to think, or what he was talking about when once he snapped that he was not putting up with it any longer. I thought he was getting at me in some way, and I recall the tears filling up in my eyes, but he said that it was *her* that he was on about. He would say no more, but somehow I knew that there was going to be trouble before Christmas.

132

What I never dreamed of, though, was how bad it would be, nor how much *I* would be affected.

[*GG*] The 'young man' who, Martha tells us, proposed to Charlotte was James Taylor, one of George Smith's employees.

Charlotte had met Taylor first when he called at the Parsonage to collect the manuscript of *Shirley*, back in 1849. She did not trust the post, she said, and had asked if it could be collected. Perhaps she had the notion that George Smith would come in person, but it was obviously a prospect which did not appeal to him. All other considerations apart, a journey from London to the West Riding of Yorkshire was not something to be undertaken lightly. Taylor, therefore, was nominated for the chore, which was to be carried out on his way back to London from holiday.

He could not have been too enamoured with the idea either, and the thought of changing trains, and then having to hire some form of transport for the last four miles to Haworth, must have cast something of a cloud over his vacation. It would have been some consolation, I suppose, had he been able to look forward to a break at Haworth before resuming his journey, but Charlotte made it quite clear that that was out of the question. In her letter to Mr Williams dated 24 August, she told him that she 'would with pleasure offer him [Taylor] the homely hospitalities of the Parsonage for a few days' – and then went on to make every excuse under the sun for why that would not be possible. So poor Taylor arrived at the house, was given not only the manuscript but a great pile of books to add to his luggage, and was then bundled back on his tracks. It would no doubt have been an entirely different story had it been George Smith, but Charlotte was not having an employee stay at the Parsonage!

In the light of subsequent events, it is apparent that Taylor, an ambitious young man, very quickly summed up what he thought to be the situation. He saw a frustrated female, living in a frightful place miles from anywhere, and lacking congenial male company. Charlotte was Smith's most successful female

133

novelist, unattached, with more money than he was ever likely to make, and the potential for making more. In addition, he was very well aware that she was thirty-three years of age and, if the medical history of the family was anything to go by, unlikely to make old bones. All in all, he decided that she would be a good catch, and he entered into correspondence with her upon his return to London.

I find it rather amusing to note that one of the excuses which Charlotte made for not replying to his letter sooner was that she had 'been kept more than usually engaged by the presence of a clergyman in the house.' What *had* Arthur been up to?

Now, some two-and-a-half years later, a situation had arisen which caused James Taylor to act. Messrs Smith, Elder and Company had decided to send him to India for five years and apparently he asked Charlotte to marry and accompany him but, as Martha says, she declined. She evidently still had her matrimonial sights set on his employer, and her immediate sexual demands were satisfied by an apparently subservient Nicholls.

In view of this, she was clearly shaken when Nicholls went off to Ireland, because she actually mentioned him in a letter to Ellen, stating that he had asked himself to tea on the eve of his departure! In the normal course of events, one would never have expected her to waste time in writing about a mere curate – we have seen what she thought of the breed. Is it also not a little surprising that her father's assistant could feel so sure of a welcome that he had no misgivings about inviting *himself*? Had there not been something between him and Charlotte he would have received very short shrift from her for his temerity. I find this little slip of hers quite revealing. Normally she kept Nicholls out of her correspondence completely, and misled everyone with her flirtations with Smith and Taylor. Now, however, the thought of Arthur leaving was so traumatic that she allowed the veil to slip a little. She had detected that all was not well with him, and wondered what he had in mind.

Nicholls left Haworth during the last week in July, and spent almost six weeks away. Charlotte continued to be affected by his absence, so much so that she could not prevent herself from telling Ellen when he was due back. It was a lip-gnawing time for her, because she could not be sure about what he was doing in Ireland, nor indeed whether he intended to return. If he did not, she had no idea what she would do, because without him she faced a very bleak future. In her heart of hearts, she feared that George Smith would never marry her – especially as his mother did not think very highly of her – and Taylor was in India for five years. No, without Nicholls all she would have to look forward to was a dreary existence at the Parsonage, enlivened only by holidays and the occasional visitor.

However, and to her great relief, Nicholls did come back, and things continued as before, although if he was discontented when he left he was positively querulous about returning to the old routine. Ireland had made him more unsettled than ever.

During October and November 1851, and just as Martha recorded, the entire household was affected by illness and Charlotte was tied to the Parsonage. She began to write her novel *Villette*, but became quite ill with what the doctor was said to have diagnosed, mysteriously, as a 'highly sensitive and irritable condition of the liver'. There is good reason to suppose that Nicholls may have been to blame for that – maybe even trying out a poison that he had obtained in Ireland, and was new to him. There are many accounts of habitual poisoners employing this practice in order to discover the effects of different doses of fresh substances.

In the New Year of 1852 she was *very* ill, and told Ellen that she had been 'brought to a sad state'. She blamed her indisposition on the pills prescribed by the doctor which, she said, contained mercury. Be that as it may, her mouth and tongue were ulcerated. The doctor, a Dr Ruddock, stated that 'he never in his whole practice knew the same effect produced by the same dose on man – woman or child . . .' – but then he had never had a patient who was receiving additional 'treatment' from Nicholls!

Charlotte *must* have had her suspicions of Nicholls, as she knew that if he disposed of her he would be a free man, but apart from being very careful about what she ate or drank, what could she do? Eventually, and very wisely, she decided to get

135

away from him and the Parsonage. At the end of January she went to stay with Ellen Nussey for a fortnight and, probably as she had anticipated, made a complete – and somewhat miraculous – recovery. Then it was back to Haworth and *Villette* for four months. She could be very single-minded when money was in prospect!

At the end of May she had another break, and crept off quietly and apparently alone to Filey for a whole month. That has often made me wonder whether she *was* there – well for the *whole* period anyway, in view of Martha's statement that Nicholls disappeared mysteriously for three days during that time. It would have been an ideal opportunity for her and Nicholls to have spent some time together away from prying eyes, and would explain why she went without telling Ellen. Certainly it was unusual for Charlotte to be staying away completely on her own and, equally certainly, Nicholls was very much in her thoughts during that first week.

In a letter to her father, and in the full knowledge of how much he disliked his assistant, she mentioned Nicholls no less than three times! That, I consider, is a clear indication of how full of him her mind was. She went on and on about him, telling Mr Brontë how she would like Mr Nicholls to see a church which she had visited – and that Mr Nicholls would have 'laughed out' at the behaviour of the singers and the congregation – and ended by asking him to give Mr Nicholls her 'kind regards'.

One can but imagine the unholy thoughts which Mr Brontë may have had about that request, but surely it must have occurred to him that his daughter seemed rather obsessed with his assistant?

We shall never know whether the pair of them did, in fact, meet at Filey, but it would have been a good opportunity for them to sort out their differences, because there can be no doubt but that their relationship was at a crucial stage. As Martha has told us, Nicholls did not seem at all contented with his lot. He was idle, and not at all ambitious, and in normal circumstances he would have jogged along, from curacy to curacy, until he acquired his own living and a suitable wife.

136

However, things had not been normal for him since he had set foot in Haworth: he had murdered two people, but had gained nothing – not even peace of mind. The years were slipping away, and he was trapped in a miserable place, at the beck and call of an unattractive little woman – and unable to pursue any other. He would not be able to take up any better post that might become available, and was therefore condemned to a life of near penury. On the other hand, however, Charlotte had a great deal of money. She was able to gad about at will, whilst he was left as nursemaid to her father, in addition to carrying out many of the parochial duties for which the old man, not he, was paid.

Nicholls could see no way out except one, but he did not really want another death on his conscience if it could be avoided.

For her part, Charlotte wanted little more than for the situation to continue unchanged, but she realized that something was amiss with her lover and was probably rather fearful of him, especially if she suspected that he had poisoned her. She still had lingering hopes of marrying 'well', but until that time Nicholls was convenient. One thing had surprised her though; she had discovered that she was just a little jealous when he disappeared to Ireland, and now, despite the hold which she had over him, she felt a pressing need to discover what was wrong and how he could be placated.

Another major source of contention was her friendship with Ellen Nussey. I have no doubt that Ellen had long suspected what was going on between Charlotte and Nicholls. She had visited the Parsonage on many occasions, and it would have been impossible for her not to have noticed the little signs which betrayed their intimacy.

She had already begun to hint at the possibility that someone other than Charlotte – and she could only have been making a veiled reference to Nicholls – was reading the letters which she sent to the Parsonage, and immediately a nerve was touched. Charlotte was *most* indignant. On 25 August, she wrote to Ellen and assured her that 'there is certainly no one in this house or elsewhere to whom I should show your notes.' She went on to

137

say that if she appeared to write with restraint it was because she had nothing to say. Ellen would not have been deceived by that, however. She knew that Charlotte *always* had something to ramble on about.

On 5 October, Charlotte wrote to Ellen refusing yet another invitation to stay with her, and expressing the vague hope that when they met next it would be at Haworth. Then, and within only four days, there was an incredible volte-face and Charlotte was literally begging her friend to come.

We can but speculate upon what brought about that abrupt change of mind. Charlotte was a very determined lady who rarely changed her mind about anything. I have the feeling that the whole business is symptomatic of the emotional volcano which was concealed from the world by the seemingly placid facade of Parsonage life.

Chapter Twelve

'I have chosen thee in the furnace of affliction.'
Isaiah 48:10

M r Nicholls seemed to get worse the longer Madam was away and so, for the first time ever, I was almost pleased when she came back. Oddly enough, though, they seemed to want nothing to do with each other, and I was driven to wonder what was going on.

I knew that Mr Nicholls was not happy about her keeping on going away, leaving him to, as he put it, 'wet nurse' her father, but I just could not fathom what else was wrong between them.

Since Miss Anne's death he had become quite a regular visitor to the Parsonage, especially when *she* was away – which came to be more and more often. At those times it had become his custom to spend an hour with the old man each evening just before Mr Brontë went to bed, and slowly it became his habit even when she was at home. The only difference then was that he sometimes joined her once her father was tucked up and out of the way – but I did not know that for certain until much later.

Neither did I know then what I am able to set down now – all this came to light only when Mr Nicholls felt sure of me, and told me no end of things.

It seems that he had been very unhappy with his life for a long time, but could do nothing to change things because of the hold that Madam had over him. When she was away he was spending night after night without sleep for worrying what she was up to. He was not at all sure that she would not let something out to somebody, if only by chance, and seemingly he was always fearful that her money might gain her a husband, and the money would then go to him, whereas Mr Nicholls

139

would have had naught but her silence – if that – in spite of all he had gone through to please her.

In the end it came to him that he should wed her himself. He told me that when the notion first came to his mind he almost laughed out loud at it, but then, as he thought about it, he saw that he had much to gain and little to lose if he did so. Not only would he have her silence for as long as she lived, but all her money would become his. Also he would no longer have to put up with hole-and-corner meetings, and he would be the one in charge which would leave him nicely placed to take over the parish when old Mr Brontë popped his clogs.

The more he thought on it the more he liked the idea. Although it would not be as he had hoped his life would turn out, nor would she be the bride he had pictured for himself, nevertheless beggars could not be choosers. All in all, he made up his mind that he would do it.

When he told me what his thoughts had been all those years before, I asked him if he had ever had a mind to the chance that she would turn him down. He said that he had given much thought to that as well, and had then made up his mind that if she did – and just wanted things to stay as they were – he would have none of it and she would have had to have done her worst.

Seemingly his reasoning went something like this – if she *did* make up her mind to tell on him it would be only her word against his, and he would have to take his chance. If things looked black for him he would go to Australia – which was something he had often considered anyway, and long before his troubles came upon him – or go back to Ireland and take ship from there to America.

Anyway, he made up his mind to have it out with her when she came back – but then he could not get to speak to her when she did. He told me that all he could think was that she must have known he was angry with her when she went away, and then when she decided to stay longer she must have had it in her mind that that would make him worse. Whatever the reason, when she came back she had tried to keep out of his way and that *had* displeased him. He tried to speak to her to arrange a

140

meeting, but she always said that they would do that later – and then there was always an excuse.

In the end, after 3 days of being put off in such a manner, he made up his mind that he *would* see her, by her leave or no, and so he invited himself when he knew that she would be at tea and on her own.

After he told me that, I cast my mind back and then I knew why she had been so put out at that time. I recalled him coming to the Parsonage and asking me if she was having her tea. When I said that she was he did not say another word, but almost pushed past me and went in and slammed the door. I heard her say something out loud, and then she came out so quickly that I had not had time to get back to the kitchen. Without so much as a 'Please' or 'Thank you', she just snapped at me that Mr Nicholls would be joining her, and that I should bring extra things for him, and then she was back in the room and the door slammed again.

When I had made up a little tray for him I tapped on the door and went in. They were both sitting with faces set and saying not a word, and I got no reply when I said something or other, and not even a 'Thank you', so I just went out again – giving the door a little slam of my own.

On purpose, I made a loud noise on the flagstones as I went back to the kitchen – but I did not go all the way. Instead I took off my clogs, crept back and put my ear close up to the door. It was all in vain though because I could not make out the words.

Mr Nicholls has told me that he tried to tell her that he wanted a quiet word on a certain subject. However, she made a pretence of not knowing what he meant, and kept prattling on about one thing and another whilst giving him his tea, and put him off until the time when she knew he had a meeting with her father and would have to go.

I heard a chair scrape and so I rushed around the corner out of the way. Then the door was opened and Mr Nicholls came out and bang went the poor door again. He did not look my way, but I could see that his face was angry as he went across the passage to Mr Brontë's room.

After a while, I went in to see if I could clear away and, for something to say, I asked her if the tea had been all right – but she just snapped 'Yes', and so I was none the wiser as to what was going on.

Mr Nicholls was still with Mr Brontë after I had washed up and put the things away, and then I was so busy with this and that that I did not notice how the time was passing.

As far as I can gather, what happened that day was that when Mr Nicholls went in to see Mr Brontë he fretted and fumed until he could get away from the old man, and he was almost beside himself with anger when he did and was able to go in search of Madam.

He could not find her and so – and I remember this *very* well – he came to me in the kitchen and I told him that I had heard her go upstairs. I thought that would be the end of it, but I was wrong. Without another word, he stormed off and, to my great surprise, he almost ran up to her bedroom and, before the door was closed, I could hear him nearly shouting at her. I had never heard of such a thing. Of course, I wasted no time in hurrying up there myself, but I dared not go too close to the door; so I hid just round the corner and tried to hear what was going on.

As it happened, I could hear very little, but he has since told me that he let loose with all that had been on his mind – some of it for years. Much to his surprise, though, she just sat there and said naught for quite a long time. When she did finally open her mouth she spoke quietly and steadily, but what she had to say was very much to the point. He has told me that she shocked him to his marrow by telling him of Miss Anne's book, and that she had it hidden away for use against him if need be.

He said he was so taken aback that for a few moments he could think of nothing to say, but then he recovered himself and recalled his plan. Without any more ado, he told her that if *that* was how she felt, he would be out of the country as soon as he could, and she would then be free to do her worst.

That, as he tells it, stopped her in her tracks, much as she had done to him. They just sat there looking at each other, because they knew that neither had the edge on the other, and each wanted to hear what the other had to say.

For my part, I just heard it all go quiet, and wondered what they were about – and in her bedroom and all – and I must say that what I pictured made me so angry that I could have spit. Slowly, and as quietly as I could, I inched along to the door with my heart beating 13 to the dozen lest I stepped on a creaking board. I pressed my ear close up to the door, and I could hear them speaking very quietly, and that made me feel even worse as I could not hear what they were saying and all manner of thoughts came to me in the darkness there.

They went on and on, and in the end I just had to go because there were so many things still waiting to be done downstairs. Only years later – as I keep saying – when Mr Nicholls told me the full story did I learn that once they had cooled down they had a long sensible talk. Each of them was as honest as they could afford to be, and in the end Mr Nicholls came out with his proposal of marriage. She did not answer him straightaway though, and it was only when Mr Nicholls began to get cross that she said 'Yes'.

They must have been up there for quite a while because I did not see Mr Nicholls any more that night. I took Mr Brontë and Miss Aykroyd their suppers, made up the fires, and then tiptoed up and tapped on her door to say that her supper was ready. She did not come to the door, but just told me to leave it on a saucepan, and so I said 'Goodnight', had my own supper and went to bed wondering what they were up to and not very happy at all.

When Madam appeared next morning I eyed her all the time. She looked very tired, and I could see that she was very ill at ease, and that made me wonder all the more what, if anything, was afoot. I did not see Mr Nicholls all day, and that made me cross because I wanted so badly to know what was going on but I felt he was keeping out of my way.

I do not know how I got through that day, waiting for something to happen, but nothing took place until after supper, when Mr Brontë was still alone in his room waiting, as I thought, for Mr Nicholls to turn up. To my surprise and disappointment, though, Mr Nicholls did not come for his usual time with him. Instead I saw *her* go into his room, and I noticed that she shut the door behind her, which was not usual

143

unless folk wanted to talk about something very private. I was dying to know what she had to say to him that was so secret, but I could get nowhere near the door because Miss Aykroyd and the young girl we had taken on were about, and so I had to wait on.

In fact, though, it was a good job that I did not have my ear pressed against it because she had not been in there for many minutes before the door was flung open and she was out again. I was just coming along the passage as she flounced out, and I could see that there were tears in her eyes and her face was all red and set. She made as if to go up the stairs, but when she saw me she stopped stunt and went into the sitting room.

The next time I saw her was when, the following morning, I saw her making her way to the Church, and I felt that she was almost surely going to see Mr Nicholls. She was gone a long time, and I did not see her come back, but she came into the kitchen to see how dinner was getting on and I knew that something was very wrong because she looked much the same as she had done on the night before. She said very little to me though, and I had only short sightings of her for the rest of the day.

I lingered about that evening, making up jobs, until well past Mr Nicholls' time to come and see Mr Brontë, but he did not come and so, as I did whenever I could, I popped home for a minute or two.

When I got to our house Mother put her finger to her lips and shut the kitchen door fast. I wondered what on earth could be wrong, but she told me that Mr Nicholls had come back from the Church at dinner time in a black fury and had gone straight to his room and was there still. He had eaten naught, and had not opened his door when Mother tapped at it to see if he was all right. All he had said, very shortly, was that he *was* – Mother said he did not sound it – but would require no food that day.

He must have heard my voice as we moved along to the living room, because only a short time after I had got there he came down and gave me an envelope and asked me if I would take it to Mr Brontë. I wanted to ask him why he was not going to see him at the Parsonage that night, but he looked so pale and drawn that I could not. My heart quite went out to him, but with my family there I could say naught of what I felt.

I took the letter back with me and gave it to Mr Brontë, and later on Madam went and spoke with him again. She did not seem very happy when she came out and was in such a bad temper for the rest of the night that I was glad to get to bed out of it all.

The next night I popped home again and Mother told me that although he had taken some food at dinner time he had not been out of the house all day. She said that she did not think he was sick, but he looked very wan and seemed most troubled about something.

I took off my coat and began giving Mother a hand in the kitchen, and then I was more than pleased when she asked me to tap on Mr Nicholls' door to see if he wanted any supper, as I was dying to speak to him.

For a moment or so after I knocked there was no sound, so I knocked again and called his name and then the door was opened straightaway and there he stood. Though Mother had warned me, I was quite taken aback by how ill he looked, and I must have shown my feelings because he gave a sad little smile and said he did not feel as bad as he looked. I asked him about supper, and he said he would have some, and then he asked how long I would be there as he would like me to take another letter to Mr Brontë.

I could not help myself, I just *had* to know what was going on, so I came straight out with it and asked him. In a whisper, he told me that him and Mr Brontë had had a good row and that, in a temper, he had given in his notice. Now, though, he was writing to take his notice back.

That pleased me greatly, because the heart had gone right out of me for a moment at the thought of him going, but then I took the bull by the horns and asked what the row was about. He did not answer me directly, but just said it was over a trifle and that I should not worry about it. He did ask me, though, to say naught to anybody about what he had told me.

I stood there for a few minutes whilst he finished his letter and then took it back downstairs with me. Mother wanted to know what had taken me so long, but I just said that Mr Nicholls had asked me to wait whilst he finished a letter to Mr Brontë and so that passed off.

When I got back to the Parsonage I took the letter in and gave it to Mr Brontë, and next morning he handed me one from him to Mr Nicholls. He asked me if I would take it home there and then, rather than wait until evening, and so I hurried down the lane with it just as I was.

Mother told me that Mr Nicholls was out the back and so I went out of the kitchen door and found him just standing there looking at naught so far as I could see. I handed him the letter, and although I knew I should not have done so with Mother about I stood by him as he read it. Then, in a low voice, he told me that all was well, but to my mind he did not look it. His teeth were pressed so hard together that his face looked to be set in stone, and I knew that whatever the row had really been about we had not heard the end of it.

Christmas was nearly upon us though; so I put all that to one side. That time of year was always a happy one for me, and I had had some pleasurable ones at the Parsonage, but somehow I was looking forward to this one more than usual. However, there was to be no happiness in my life that year because, on the very next evening after I had taken Mr Brontë's letter to Mr Nicholls, Father came in and, looking more directly at me than any of the others, asked us if anyone had heard anything about 'our lodger' and Miss Charlotte. We all looked at him with blank faces, but my mind was already running ahead of itself as I wondered if what I knew about them had somehow got out. What I was thinking was cut short though because Father, with his words tumbling on the heels of those that had gone before, gave us the news that broke my heart and my dreams in an instant.

He said that he had called in to see Mr Brontë on Church business and the old man had been so out of sorts that he was very concerned and had asked if something was amiss. Mr Brontë had looked at him for quite a time and had then said that Father might as well know that Mr Nicholls had proposed marriage to his daughter!

146

Father said that he could not help himself and had said that he hoped Mr Brontë was not going to agree to such a thing. On the instant, Mr Brontë had started half out of his chair, and his face had gone so red that Father thought his head looked fit to burst. Then the old man did something that nobody had ever known him to do before, he *swore* and half shouted that he would *never* permit such a thing, and that he had told 'that b—— Nicholls so'.

It was so unlike Mr Brontë that Father had spent the next half-hour soothing him before he felt able to leave.

I hardly heard those last words though because I was in such a daze, and everything seemed very distant for a moment, with the room going round me. Then the tears had come to my eyes, and I flung out of the room before I made a fool of myself.

Later on I found out that that had served to make Father and Mother more sure that something or other had been going on between me and Mr Nicholls, as they had thought for some time, but nobody said anything that night.

I spent the next little while in the bedroom trying to put my feelings in order before going back down. Then I splashed my face and went downstairs and put my coat and bonnet back on. I put my head round the door quickly to say that I was going back to the Parsonage to see if Mr Brontë was all right, and then I was out of the house and down the lane, sobbing fit to burst.

I did not go back to the Parsonage. I went up to the moor, and wandered there in the cold and damp whilst I tried to sort out my feelings. Try as I would, though, I could think of naught save how Mr Nicholls had let me down, and I could not believe that he had been so two-faced. He had told me that she had some kind of hold over him, and I had had a good notion of what it was after reading Miss Anne's book, but still I could not see how he had come to even think of *wedding* her.

Within a day or two the news was all over the village because, seemingly, Mr Brontë had told every person he had spoken to. I do not know if Madam knew then of how the word had spread, but somebody – Miss Aykroyd I think – must have told her at some time as when we were alone in the kitchen she said to me that no doubt I had heard tell of what folk were saying. I looked

147

at her straight and said that I had, but that I did not believe it. That did not please her a whit, and she said nothing more, though I could see that she wanted to.

As for Mr Nicholls, I had seen him in our house but there had been no chance to talk to him properly there, and he stopped going to the Parsonage altogether. I was firm in my intent to see him though, and so I did what I had done before. The next time I went home I put a note under his door saying that I just *had* to speak to him, and that I would be in what we called our own place on the moor at a certain time a little later that night.

When I got there I saw that he was there first, and he came walking towards me as I drew near. He went to take me in his arms, but I would have none of it and started in straightaway to tell him what I thought of him. The words just poured out, and the tears as well, until at last I just dropped down on a rock – talked out and snivelling.

He sat down beside me and put his arm and part of his cloak around me, and then he began to talk in the way that I had never been able to withstand. Kissing me gently on the cheek from time to time, he swore to me that he had been forced into his action by things that were outside his ordering and that I could not begin to understand, and that he could not tell me of. Softly he begged me to believe that he had had no choice for what he had done, and said that I should trust him whatever else might come to pass. All I wanted to know though was how all that had happened had left *us*.

Thinking back, it is evident that he had given our meeting a lot of thought beforehand because, without any waiting, he had the right words ready. He told me that *nothing* would come between us, even though things might not be easy for us for a while. I did not really know whether to believe him but, like many a silly woman before and since, I was hearing the words I wanted to hear and I felt so drawn to him that we ended up making love up there, in the mist and the cold and the wet.

As was only to have been expected, that Christmas was not a good one for Mr Nicholls. It had soon got around that Mr Brontë had put his foot down and there was to be no wedding, and everyone seemed to know that Mr Nicholls had put in his notice and then taken it back as well. All the village seemed to be laughing at him behind his back, and Father went around calling him and making things worse, and so, even though it was usually a happy time for me, not even Mr Brontë's Christmas money really cheered me up because I did not like to see Mr Nicholls a laughing-stock. Only after the holiday did I feel any better, and that was when Madam told me that she was going to London.

As far as I can recall, she went away in the first week of that New Year of 1853, and she did not come back for about a month. I used that time to think about Mr Nicholls and me, and to try to be at peace with things, but also we were able to be together and that helped to calm me down and make ready for whatever was to come.

One thing I could not put out of my mind, though, was the chance that, somehow or other, Mr Nicholls and her *might* wed after all. It was a notion that I could not bear, and I did not know how I would ever stand the thought of them being in the same house – and the same bed – all the time. Sometimes when I had been thinking in such a fashion I found myself speaking out against Mr Nicholls as well, but I always wished afterwards that I had not because it was not fair after what he had promised me. Even so, such thoughts kept coming back, and in the end I had the idea that I might be able to stop such a thing coming about if only I could put Madam against Mr Nicholls, and so I used to tell her things about him – some true and some made up.

I started very gently but, as she seemed to believe me and to want to know more, I became bolder and bolder until in the end I was saying some awful things about him. At first, I had not known how she would take such tales, and I thought she might tell me off, but slowly we seemed to be drawn together, and she talked to me more than she had ever done. Still, though, I could not bring myself to like her any better. I had a long memory for the wrongs she had done me in the past, and as well as that I did not know what she might force Mr Nicholls to do in the days to come.

149

Then Spring came, and once again she was off on her travels. When she told me she was going she said she could not tell me for exactly how long, but that it would be for quite a while. She said she would be glad to get away from everything for a while, and I knew by how she said it that she meant every word. In truth, life could not have been easy for her at that time – not that that bothered me – for, all else apart, I knew that Mr Brontë and Mr Nicholls were not speaking and that must have made for some very awkward times between the three of them.

Anyway, off she went and I looked forward to some happy meetings with Mr Nicholls, but they turned out to be few and far between because for most of the time he just was not his old self and, when I think back, they were of my making and not his. His mind seemed always to be somewhere else, but he would not tell me what he was thinking and I just had to put up with it. Once, as a joke, I said that I thought he was pining for Madam, but he snapped at me so badly that I soon learned that there was little laughter in him. Truth to tell though, we did have one or two times together when things were much as they had been, and they made up for everything – so much so that all my old hopes started to come back to me.

Then *she* was back in the Parsonage, and everything went back to as it had been, until all Mr Nicholls seemed to be able to say – and he did not seem to care who heard it – was that he had had enough of it all. Even so, I did not sense how badly he had been feeling until the day he met me in the lane and told me he was leaving!

At first I thought it was just another of his moods, but when I saw that he was in earnest my head went round and I was like to have fainted had he not taken hold of me. There were a few folk about so we could not linger any longer than it took to settle upon a time to meet later in the Church, and it was there that he told me that he had already given his word to take another job miles away. It was an awful shock, and once I had taken his words in I could scarce stop weeping, and clung to him as if to root him to the spot. But it was no good – his mind was made up and all was settled.

All I could think of was what was to become of me, and if we

150

should ever see each other again, but his answers were of no help and it became evident to me that it was likely to become a case of 'out of sight, out of mind'. That hurt me very much, and I all but refused him when he asked for a last meeting, but I did not and two nights later we met on the moor and said our farewells. Of course, I was tearful again, but I had come a little way to accepting what was to happen for I could not believe that this was to be the end of us altogether after all we had meant to each other. That feeling was made even stronger by his seeming so very sad at our parting, and for, I think, the very first time, I knew that he *really* cared for me.

So away he went, leaving a great hole in my life and the Parsonage and our house. I thought of him day and night, and sometimes when I was home I would go into his old room and wonder what he was doing and who he was with. His spirit seemed to linger in there, and sometimes it was almost as if we were together again – but we were not, and my world was empty and had no meaning.

As for how things were in the Parsonage, probably the least said the better. Madam went about as if bewitched, and things were very bad between her and Mr Brontë, especially as he seemed forever to be calling Mr Nicholls to her. There seemed to be no chance of them coming together either as they could be apart in the same house all day if they so wished. They did not even meet at meal times because ever since I had been at the Parsonage I had never known Mr Brontë do other than take his meals alone. His children did not care in the old days, because they could do and say much as they pleased with him out of the way, but now, with her sisters and brother all dead, Madam also ate alone. I never knew how they could do it because, whenever possible, we had always eaten together in our house and they were happy times with everyone talking 13 to the dozen, and Father smiling and keeping an eye on everything.

Then, only a week or two after Mr Nicholls had gone, they were both taken very ill, with Mr Brontë again having some kind of fit, which sent him blind for a while, and her ending up having to be blistered.

It was all very miserable, especially as she kept us running up and down stairs all the time as if we had naught else to do but wait on her hand and foot. As far as I was able, I looked after Mr Brontë myself and left her to the others, but there were things that she would allow only me to do and I came to hate my work. That is not to say, though, that things were much better when I had finished my work and had my supper because I lacked company outside of the family. My one good friend had gone into service with a family in Keighley, and I seemed to have no interest at all in lads after Mr Nicholls. Many was the time that I just wandered about on the moor thinking of past and happier times, or I would sit upstairs in a dream for so long that someone would come to see if I was all right.

Then, of all things, I began to hear talk of Mr Nicholls being seen about in Haworth, and all of a sudden my hopes were raised that he had come back. I even made so bold as to ask Madam about the truth of the gossip, but she said she did not know what I was talking about – though something in her manner made me suspect that she knew more than she was letting on. I started to walk to places where they said he had been seen, but I never set eyes on him.

In August she went off again, that time up to Scotland as I recall, and life became so much easier at the Parsonage with just old Mr Brontë and Miss Aykroyd to look after and I felt happier with her away than I had been in a long while. Only much later did Mr Nicholls let it slip out that he had met her on her way home and that they had had two nights together – in Harrogate, I think he said. Had I known that at the time I do not know what I would have done – especially as I still wandered about at nights hoping to catch sight of him – but I never did.

Then the Summer was gone, and once more my worst time of year was nearly upon us. I became quite down, and had many daydreams of moving away to service elsewhere – perhaps even to where Mr Nicholls was – but I could not face leaving my family, and in any case as far as I knew Mr Nicholls had made no move to see or write to me since he left. I liked to think that there was a good reason for that though, and that is why I did not *really* believe the gossip of him being seen about, for I just

152

knew that he would *never* have come back to Haworth without somehow letting me know.

That is why I was so angry with him when many years later he finally got round to telling me that he had been meeting Madam on and off ever since he left, but they were not able to resolve the differences between him and Mr Brontë. In the end it would seem that though Mr Nicholls had become more and more displeased with the way things stood he was forced to leave it to her to carry on trying to wear down her father's objections to their marriage because by then, he said, he was set upon seeing everything through to a close. Only years after that talk with him did I get to *know* what he meant by that, but I must say now that I had my thoughts at the time but chose to take no notice of them.

[*GG*] Relations between Charlotte and Nicholls were very strained for the three days following her return from her visit to Ellen Nussey. She must have known that she was out of favour with Nicholls, and must have expected to be. However, she could have had no idea of the intensity of the emotions which were churning away within him. Then, when he did finally get to see her alone, I think that she must have been shocked by the vehemence of his verbal attack, and stunned by his charges. Of course, Nicholls had no idea that she did not want to marry Taylor, nor that George Smith felt similarly about her, but Charlotte did and her thoughts must have raced while Nicholls ranted on,

I think it safe to say that she had virtually come to terms with the probability that she was destined to become an old maid, and that the prospect would not have been to her liking. The possibility of marrying Nicholls must therefore have entered her mind more than once and that, I suggest, is why she accepted his proposal, albeit with an initial appearance of reluctance.

However, having accepted, it must have taken only a short time for her to realize that she was faced with two immediate, and major, problems.

153

Firstly, and although she was not certain, she had a very good idea of how her father would react to the news. Hitherto, Mr Brontë had made it abundantly clear that he did not wish her to marry at all. However, there had been an unspoken agreement that if she ever felt so inclined it would be into wealth or rank – preferably both. Neither had ever considered for one moment that marriage to a curate might become a subject for discussion.

Then there was the question of how to put a brave face on the matter when telling her friends and acquaintances because, as we know only too well, she had been at pains over the years to let them know her opinion of such lowly creatures as curates.

In the event, her father did not disappoint. When she told him the news he, quite literally, had a fit! She wrote to Ellen about it: '. . . Papa worked himself into a state not to be trifled with, the veins on his temples started up like whipcord, and his eyes became suddenly bloodshot.' She had to back-pedal hurriedly, otherwise he would probably have dropped dead in front of her. As it was, he used 'such epithets' about Nicholls that her blood 'boiled with a sense of injustice'. In order to calm him, and buy time, she was forced to promise that Mr Nicholls 'should on the morrow have a distinct refusal'.

Charlotte may have placated her father, but then she had to face Nicholls and he, also, was livid. He told her that he would tolerate the situation no longer, not even temporarily as she had begged; he had had enough and was leaving. She and her father could do exactly as they wished. He retired to his lodgings in a fury, and sent a letter of resignation to Mr Brontë who replied with 'a hardness not to be bent, and a contempt not to be propitiated'. The two men did not meet.

It was only when his temper had cooled that Nicholls realized that he had burned his boats rather prematurely. He knew that he could not live for very long on the small amount of money at his disposal, and certainly he could not afford to travel far. It must have been an agonizing decision for him to take, but in the end he was forced to eat humble pie by writing to Mr Brontë asking if he could withdraw his resignation. However, the reply stated that he could do so only 'on condition of giving his written promise never again to broach the obnoxious subject' to him or his daughter. Nicholls' rage flared again at that, but he had no option but to accept the stipulation while he determined his future.

Mr Brontë's reaction had been much as Charlotte had anticipated, but then she was forced to think very hard about how to explain the situation to everybody, because she knew that the facts were bound to come out. Eventually she decided that the only thing to do was to portray the whole matter as such a romantic story that everybody would understand that she really could not have helped being swept off her feet.

Her letter to Ellen, of 15 December 1852, is a gem. It is so patently a work of romantic fiction, that one cannot help but be amused. When considering what she wrote, it should be borne in mind that Nicholls was almost thirty-five years of age at the time. This was no lovesick adolescent, but just listen to Charlotte as she tells the tale to her friend: 'He entered – he stood before me. What his words were you can guess; his manner – you can hardly realise – never can I forget it. Shaking from head to foot, looking deadly pale, speaking low, vehemently yet with difficulty – he made me for the first time feel what it costs a man to declare affection where he doubts response.'

There is more in the same vein. It is a masterpiece. I doubt very much, however, whether Ellen or anyone else was taken in by it for one moment, and one can but wonder how Charlotte could ever have imagined that they would be. Nevertheless she had to start the story somewhere, and that letter was the blueprint for the account which she gave to the world.

Charlotte's story of Nicholls' proposal has been accepted as the truth by every writer about the Brontës whom I have come across. Nobody appears to have doubted it nor, although it could almost be a scene from *Jane Eyre*, to have recognized her literary style. It was the tale to which she adhered for the rest of her life, and I think that in the end she came to believe it herself.

After the Christmas of 1852, Charlotte decided to go ahead with a planned visit to the Smiths and Nicholls was left to face the adverse local reaction that the knowledge of his proposal had engendered.

The people of Haworth had never liked him, and because of

155

the, now open, hostility which he was experiencing from all sides, Nicholls stayed away from both the Parsonage and the church, even to the extent of procuring a locum-tenens for Sundays. John Brown made no bones about his feelings, saying that he 'should like to shoot him'. Martha, also, was said to have been 'very bitter against him' although, as she tells us, her reasons were very different from those of her father.

Some confirmation exists of the tactics which Martha says she used in order to drive a wedge between Charlotte and Nicholls – and it comes from Charlotte's own pen. In her letter to Ellen Nussey of 4 March 1853, she wrote that Martha had told her of certain 'flaysome' looks which Nicholls had given her mistress, and which had 'filled Martha's soul with horror'. Then, on 6 April, Ellen was informed, bluntly: 'Martha hates him.'

Of course, none of that helped Charlotte to resolve her dilemma. She had tried, ceaselessly, to persuade her father to change his mind, but he was adamant and called the whole matter 'degrading'. Then there was the fact that nothing which she said or did could dispel the dark cloud of anger and despair which hung over Nicholls. She felt absolutely torn between father and lover, and so she did what she normally did when she was in any state of emotional turmoil or indecision – she went on her travels.

In April she stayed with Mrs Gaskell, in Manchester, and took the opportunity to propagate the story of Nicholls' 'proposal', just as she had during her visit to the Smiths a couple of months before. From Manchester she went to Ellen.

She returned to the Parsonage somewhat refreshed but, hardly surprisingly, she found that nothing there had improved during her long absence – in fact, if anything, the situation appeared to have worsened. Nicholls seemed now to have no intention of trying to appease her father, and was rude and abrupt with him in public. Charlotte described it as 'a dismal state of things'.

Nicholls now obtained a curacy at Kirk Smeaton, near Pontefract, which, although also in Yorkshire, was some fifty miles from Haworth. He left on 27 May 1853, and Charlotte told Ellen she was desolate: 'he is gone – gone – and there's an end of it.' However, even as she wrote, she knew that she had no intention of allowing his departure to be an end of anything.

Unknown to her father, Charlotte corresponded with Nicholls after he resigned, and also met him on the several secret visits that he made to Haworth during that summer of 1853. He would not take up his new post until the August, and so he had decided to stay with his friend Grant, who was the incumbent of the next parish to Haworth. The rumours which Martha heard of his having been seen about the village were therefore true.

Chapter Thirteen

'My bone cleaveth to my skin, and to my flesh, and I am
escaped with the skin of my teeth.'

Job 19:20

Christmas 1853 came, and it was another miserable one,
especially as Madam did not go away. She just moped
about the Parsonage, and seemed to have no interest in anything
except being as bad-tempered as she was able. To tell the truth, I
came very close to putting in my notice at that time, but I bit my
tongue and went off home for what was left of Christmas
contenting myself with thinking about what a cheerless time
she was having stuck in that big cold old house with naught but 2
old people for company – both ill and crochety – and her father
not speaking to her either. It is a terrible thing to say, but I was so
pleased at the prospect that I almost sang my way down the lane.

As it had turned out, things had been so arranged that I did
not have to go back to work until 2 days after Christmas Day,
and I went in bent upon being full of cheer, and rubbing it in
about what a happy time I had had, to what I thought would be
a sick-at-heart Madam. To my great surprise though, she was
as full of cheer and smiles as I had meant to be, and greeted me
as if I was her best friend. She said she could hardly wait to tell
somebody, and then went on to tell me that her father was no
longer against her seeing Mr Nicholls, and that he was coming
back to Haworth as soon as possible.

Even after such a long time, as I write this the thoughts that I
had then come flooding back as if it was but yesterday. At first I
just could not take it in and thought it was a joke. Then, to my
surprise, I was not angry and miserable that I was to lose Mr
Nicholls, but rather my spirits were raised higher than for a
long time at the thought of having him back, because I

158

remembered his words that though things might be difficult for us for a time I should trust him and that naught would ever come between us.

Within just a week or so I saw him again! He turned up at the Parsonage all smiles and almost as if nothing had happened. She had warned us when he would be coming, and all morning I was aflutter with every sound on the path. When, at long last, he did arrive I had to hold myself back from running out and throwing myself into his arms. I heard them talking in the passage and then, with a big smile all over her ugly face, Madam was leading him down to see her father. I stood by the kitchen door with the others, just looking, but when he saw us he gave us a big wink over Madam's head. Well I say he gave it to *us*, but I knew that it was meant only for me and ,I could have kissed him for it.

He left that same day, but he came back a few times over the next couple of months, although I was never able to say more than a few words to him, and then only when others were about. Then, almost before we knew what was what, he and her were betrothed and Father said that he was coming back to his old job. All in all, I could not have been more happy, but there was a great disappointment in store for me. All along I had thought that he would come back to stay in our house, but now Father said that that was not to be – he was going to live at the Parsonage even before they were wed.

At first I could have wept, because I knew that with him under Madam's eye all the while there would be very few meetings between us. However, I soon overcame my feelings and comforted myself with the thought that I would probably *see* more of him if he was living under the same roof as me.

I knew that he did not love her – very much the other way, in fact – so I was sure that he had his own good reasons for going into it, and I trusted his promise that nothing would ever come between us. In the meanwhile, though, he was back and the wedding was arranged and that, of course, caused a great deal of talk in the village about it all.

Not one person thought of it as a love match, rather that Mr Nicholls was just after her money and his job back. In fact there

159

was so much gossip that it would not have been possible for some of it not to have got back to Mr Nicholls and her, and it was him who first told me that a little of it had come to his ears.

It was taking terrible chances I know, but I had told him that I would like us to keep on meeting for as long as we could, and he had said that that was what he wanted as well. The only trouble was that folk now took far more notice of him, and also the nights were much lighter, so it was not possible to meet out of doors – and that only left the Church and the School, and even then it was not easy.

We managed to meet about once a week, and it was at one of those times that Mr Nicholls told me that he had heard that the villagers were saying that he was only after her money. Oddly enough, that did not seem to bother him at all though. In fact he seemed quite pleased, and said he would rather they thought that than that he was in love with her, because then he would have felt that they reckoned him for an idiot. As it was, he thought that with Haworth folk being what they were they would tend to look up to him for it and be on his side.

Of course, Madam got to know about the talk as well – there never seemed to be *anything* that she did not get wind of – but she *was* put out.

One evening, after I had cleared all up after supper in the Parsonage and was walking down the lane to our house, I came upon her in the Churchyard fussing about with some flowers. It was lovely weather, and I had felt that I just had to get out for a few minutes, but I had nowhere to go really so I was quite content to stop a while when she called over to me.

We sat together on the wall, and she went chattering on about this and that, and asking me questions about my family and some of the villagers. Then she got on about the wedding and to my surprise she said she was unhappy as some of her so-called friends did not seem to wish her well. She said that one in particular had saddened her very much and, although she did not name her, I soon put 2 and 2 together that it was Miss Nussey. Then I could not believe my ears when she went on to ask *me* what I thought about it! Quizzingly, she said that from some of the things I had said to her in the past, and from bits

160

she had heard, she did not think I liked Mr Nicholls very much – and then I had a job not to burst out laughing when she said that if I knew him better I would be bound to like him!

Well, for a moment I was nonplussed – it had all come upon me so quickly that I did not know what to say to her. As it was, I pretended to be thinking on what she had said, and all the while she watched me with her face all bunched up in that way she had.

In the end I said I was sure she was right, and made haste to explain that anything I had said to her in the past about Mr Nicholls had only been the passing on of what had been said to me and what I thought she should know.

She seemed well pleased at that, but once again she asked me what I thought about the wedding. This time, though, I had had time to get my answer ready, and I told her what I thought she wanted to hear. I said that they seemed very suited, and that with Mr Nicholls being a clergyman and all, just like her father, I had no doubt but that they would be very happy. To my surprise, though, that did not seem to please her as much as I had thought it would. Her lips pursed, and I could see that she had her own doubts and had not been duped by Mr Nicholls as much as he thought she had.

I was at our house a few evenings later when Father came in and said there was quite a to-do going on up at the Parsonage, and asked me if I knew aught about it. Well, there were so *many* happenings there at that time that I did not rightly know which one he was talking about, so I said as much and then he went on to tell us. He said that Mr Brontë had told him that he was bent upon safeguarding what he called his 'wilful daughter' from Mr Nicholls, in spite of herself, and as best he could, and so he had listened carefully when some of her friends had spoken to him on the quiet about a way to stop Mr Nicholls from getting his hands on her money. Mr Brontë had then spoken to her about it, but she would have none of it and so he was getting the friends to speak to her themselves.

Well, I had never heard of such a thing. As far as I knew, once you were wed everything of yours passed to your husband, and what did that matter if you loved and trusted him? Mind you, I had never quite thought it fair that it should be the Law, but that was how things were and it had never bothered me overmuch. I must say though that her standing went up in my eyes, and I thought that if she had said that she would have naught to do with it I must have misjudged how she felt about Mr Nicholls. Anyway, I told Father that I would keep my eyes and ears open and the matter passed off.

As it happened, I learned naught more about it, and I did not dare to speak to Mr Nicholls about it for I knew that he would be very vexed if he did not know already, and then it would probably have come out that Father had been speaking out of turn and *he* would be in trouble. So I just let it be.

Whether or not it had anything to do with it I do not know, but Madam went off on her travels again around the end of April. She said she was going to see some of her friends to tell them about the wedding, but I did not see why that could not have been done by letter rather than gadding around the country leaving her father and Mr Nicholls at loggerheads – and I thought she just wanted to get away from all the arguments. Mind you, *I* was pleased to see her go and so, I think, was Mr Nicholls – although he did not say as much.

I must say it was wonderful for me and him to have the Parsonage almost to ourselves at times. Of course, we had to be careful, but the girls were only allowed upstairs when I said so, and Miss Aykroyd did not know half of what was going on around her.

Then, and quite quickly it seemed, she was back again and did not I know it! She was in a bad temper from the minute she walked in the door, and it just seemed to get worse with every day that passed. All her friendliness to me had gone out of the window, and there were times when I could have hit her. Just because Mr Nicholls was now staying at the Parsonage everything had to be done differently and just right so that she could show off to him, and she ran us ragged with her sharp tongue. Well, that is to say that she *tried* it on with me, but I was having none of it. I just listened, bit my tongue, forced a smile – and then did what *I* wanted. My days of being frightened of *her*, or of losing my job, were long gone and I think Madam knew it.

162

I had noticed that she had been a bit snappy with Mr Nicholls as well when she thought that no one was in earshot, but one morning they had a row such as I had never heard. They had gone into the sitting room a few moments before, and I had heard the door shut to behind them.

Well, that got me going straightaway, but I could do naught about it except to wonder what they were up to. Then I heard Mr Nicholls' voice raised so high in anger that I went into the hallway to see what the matter was, and shortly after he flung out of the room shouting something at her over his shoulder.

The next thing I knew he had rushed out of the Parsonage, leaving the door wide open, and was stamping down the path. I asked the girl who was cleaning the passage what had been going on, and she told me that him and her had had a right set-to, but she did not really know what about except that it seemed to be something to do with money. She did say, though, that he had a face like thunder when he passed her.

For a time after that work was a real misery because there was such an awful air about the Parsonage. Nobody seemed to be speaking to anyone else, Mr Nicholls took what little food he had on his own, and even I could not get a pleasant word or a smile out of him whenever we had a few moments together. With him in such a mood, and others about nearly all the time, I was not able to find out what the row had been about. All I had to go on was that it had been something to do with money, and the only thing I could think of was that it was somehow connected with what Father said Mr Brontë had told him.

Mr Nicholls never stepped outside the Parsonage for days. He kept to his room and put it about that he was ill, but I knew for a fact that he was not and I wondered for how long he would be able to bear being cooped up in such lovely weather.

One day, though, a doctor came to see him, and for a moment I thought that he really *had* got something up with him. I could not bear not knowing, so I asked Madam outright. After all, and leaving all else to one side, I thought it only right that we should know if there was a sickness in the house which could be passed on to us, and that was how I put it to her.

I had expected to be snapped at, and I had made up my mind that I would stand up to her, but she did not seem at all put out by my question and said that I could calm my fears. With a little smile – the first I had had from her for ages – she told me that he was not ill at all. It was just that he was thinking too much about matters to do with the wedding, and that he would soon be all right again. Then she went on to say that he was really something of a big baby who just needed to be noticed all the time. Well, that did not sound like Mr Nicholls to *me*, and in any case I did not think it proper that she should be talking to me about him behind his back like that.

Later on, I told Father and Mother of what had passed between us, and Father said that he had been told by one of the ladies who helped at the Church that Madam had said as much to some of them as well.

Anyway, there was some kind of meeting in Mr Brontë's room one day, and after that things were a little better in the Parsonage, and Mr Nicholls seemed to be back almost to his old self. I was able to have only one long time together with him though, and for most of that he just went on and on about *her*. It seemed that he had overheard two ladies gossiping in the Church, and so had learned that Madam had been calling him to folk. He was very bitter about that, but when I saw that our time together was being wasted by so much talk I put an end to it in the only way I knew how.

That was to be our last meeting for a while – and so I was glad that we had made the most of it – because, all of a sudden, all the talk was of the wedding taking place as soon as possible! Then it came out that it was to be at the end of June, and I could not understand what all the rush was about, and nor could the village – because they only got betrothed in the April. I had seldom heard of such a thing, save when the lass had found herself with child, and I could but join in all the wondering.

I do not know whether she thought she had told me – but she had not – but Madam seemed to take it that we all knew when the date of the wedding was fixed. In fact, it was Father who told us that it was set for, of all the days of the week, the last

164

Thursday in June, and it was only from him that I learned that Mr Nicholls and her were going to Ireland afterwards.

That bit of news pained me more than I can say. I had come to accept the wedding, but the thought of him and her going across the sea to places that Mr Nicholls had told me such lovely tales about brought tears to my eyes. How I wished that it was *us* getting wed and going off. It just did not seem fair, and the only way I was able to calm myself was with the thought that once they were back Mr Nicholls would see to it that there were changes – though I could not think what they would be.

I had thought that I would have to put up with Madam being all cock-a-hoop as the wedding day came nearer, but she was very quiet and I soon understood why. Somehow I had had a picture in my mind of a great day of merrymaking, with the Church crammed to the rafters with folk, and all of us given time off to go as well, and bells ringing out and then eating and drinking and music – oh, I do not know *what* I thought, but to be sure I did *not* picture what I found was *really* planned. It seemed that Mr Brontë would not be in charge of the service – as we had all taken for granted – and that but 5 people *in all* were to be allowed into the Church! I could not believe it, nor could anyone else at first. It seemed such a hole-and-corner business, and almost as if it was something to be ashamed of.

Of course, I could see Mr Nicholls' hand in all that, and later on he told me that I was right, and that it was his way of getting his own back for all that her and the old man had put him through. I must say, though, that *I* was not put out because I would not be there. I had pictured myself having to watch him at the altar being married to her, and I do not think I could have borne it.

So, in the end, the only way that I was caught up in it was seeing that all was right for the wedding breakfast and then, after that, when we waved them off to Ireland. I must say about *that* that it quite cheered me up, for never had I seen a bride and groom look so unhappy.

Then they were gone – for 6 weeks Madam had told me – and once again I felt an emptiness in my life for a time, especially as it was so quiet at the Parsonage. The only good things were that

165

there was far less work, and the weather that July was so lovely that my spirits were lifted far higher than I could ever have thought. I had pictured myself moping about day after day, wondering where they were and what they were doing, but to my surprise I hardly gave thought to them, and was out and about quite a lot.

The first 2 weeks passed and little of moment took place, and then Mr Brontë was taken quite poorly. As I had expected, he had been very quiet after they had gone away, and I used to feel so sorry for him sitting there alone for most of the time with only goodness knows what thoughts for company. One morning, though, he could not even get out of bed, and he told me that he felt most unwell. I ran across the lane to Father's barn and he came straightaway as he was, dust and all.

Well, to keep a long tale short, we *did* have a time with him for the next week or so. Father told the Church Council, and they saw to it that a doctor came in, and some of their wives came to see Mr Brontë, but all the real and nasty work was left to us servants, and that was not right, for we were not paid to be nursemaids and some of the work was not fit for young girls. Even so we stuck to it, but the old man *was* in a state, and we were kept busy looking after him, and cleaning up after him, and trying to keep the air in his room sweet for visitors. I spent hours with a feeding-cup with him, coaxing him to drink, and wiping his mouth and nightshirt, and I tried to keep his hands and face clean, but right from the start I made it clear that the men had to see to the rest for it was not fitting work for a woman.

In the end, Father told me that one of the Council men had written off to one of the addresses that Madam had left with Mr Brontë telling them that her father was in such a state that he thought they should come back straightaway. It did not seem that the letter had got to them though, because there was no answer and no sign of them until the day when, of all things, *I* got a letter from Madam!

Such a thing had never happened before in all my time at the Parsonage, and I thought that at last she was owning up to it that I was in charge there. The letter is by my hand as I write this, and I see that it is dated 28 July 1854, and was posted in

Dublin. In it she told me that they would be back in Haworth in 4 days, and I did not know whether to laugh or cry.

I was pleased that I would be seeing Mr Nicholls again, and that *she* would then be there to look after her father, but I felt that she would probably be worse than ever now that they were married, and I did not look forward to being bossed about by her in front of him. On top of that, I still had a strong feeling that there was trouble in store and I wanted no part in it.

[*CC*] In November 1853 Charlotte received a shattering blow to her last hope of a stylish marriage, when George Smith's mother wrote to tell her that her son was engaged to be married. How much Charlotte was hurt can be seen from her extraordinary letter of 'congratulation'. 'My dear Sir, In great happiness, as in great grief – words of sympathy should be few. Accept my meed of congratulation – and believe me Sincerely yours, C. Brontë.'

It was surely this blow that finally prompted Charlotte to take decisive action. Enough was enough; time was not on her side, and her father just had to be made to see her point of view – which was that he would *have* to agree to the marriage *and* to reinstate Nicholls. So she finally nerved herself for the fray and confronted Mr Brontë, but here again, although the outcome is a matter of fact, we can only conjecture about the actual words which were spoken. However, on all the evidence available, it would seem that she told him that she had been seeing and writing to Nicholls, and that she was determined to marry him. The ultimate threat was probably that if her father did not agree to her demands she would marry Nicholls anyway and leave Haworth.

It must have been a difficult encounter for both of them, but whereas Charlotte would have had the consolation of feeling better after having had her say, her father must have been aghast at her manner and what he had heard. Bad enough to learn that his daughter had been defying and deceiving him, but to be threatened by her would have been intolerable, especially as he had neither forgotten nor forgiven the way

167

in which Nicholls had treated him in public. It would appear that he refused, angrily, to change his mind, but this time Charlotte was determined to stand her ground, even at the risk of provoking the old man into another seizure.

Once he saw that her mind was made up, I have little doubt that Mr Brontë was brought up short by the prospect which he faced if he remained obdurate. He had suffered two strokes, his sight was poor, and he was a man very jealous of his home comforts. Therefore the idea of being left alone and totally dependent upon village servants would not have appealed to him at all. So, although he huffed and puffed, there was never any really doubt about the final outcome and he was forced to admit defeat. Grudgingly, he agreed that Charlotte could 'continue the communication', and gave notice to the assistant curate who had replaced Nicholls, with the latter taking up his old post as soon as possible.

Mr Brontë was not alone in his doubts about Nicholls' motives for marrying his daughter. Ellen Nussey had voiced her disapproval openly, and others had also made their reservations known – albeit more circumspectly. At first, Charlotte took their innuendoes very badly, but gradually she came to appreciate that they had only her best interests at heart and listened to them when they came to her with a proposal to safeguard her capital.

Under normal circumstances, the law decreed that upon marriage everything which a woman possessed passed to her husband, and she would own nothing in her own right. Now Charlotte had some £1,700 invested, which would be worth approximately £60,000 in present-day values, and her well-wishers had been anxious that Nicholls should not get his hands on it. They therefore suggested to Charlotte that a marriage settlement be drawn up to protect her assets and discovered, somewhat to their surprise, that they were pushing at an open door.

The idea was that everything should be paid into a trust, and that Joe Taylor, the brother of her old schoolfriend Mary Taylor, would be the sole trustee. All the investments would be transferred into Taylor's name, and he would receive all the proceeds arising therefrom. Those dividends, et cetera, would be paid only to Charlotte, unless she nominated somebody else in writing.

There would be a clause specifically forbidding Nicholls to meddle in those arrangements, and no money was to be made available to his creditors. Should Charlotte predecease him, the capital would remain in trust for any children or grandchildren, unless Charlotte had left written instructions to the contrary. If there were no children or written instructions, all the trust funds were to be paid out as if Charlotte had died intestate and *unmarried* (my italics), and therefore, should he still be alive, her father and not Nicholls would be the beneficiary. Were Charlotte to be left a childless widow all the trust funds would revert to her.

Those proposed conditions made it quite clear that it was not intended that Nicholls should ever get his hands on his wife's money, and are evidence, should it be needed, of how little he was trusted by anyone concerned.

There was one potential drawback to such an unusual settlement, however. It would have been quite possible for Nicholls to have disputed it after the marriage, and there was a fair chance – in the male-dominated society of those days – that he would have won the day. Such a possibility could be avoided only by obtaining his written agreement to the proposed arrangements. One can imagine the trepidation with which Charlotte raised the subject with him and, according to Martha, her fears were well founded because the most frightful row ensued. Nicholls was livid with rage at what he termed the conspiracy against him, and vowed that he would call off the marriage rather than put his name to such an insulting document. He stormed off, leaving Charlotte to wonder what would happen next.

For days he sulked and brooded upon the options open to him, but once his anger had subsided, he saw that it was essential to ensure Charlotte's continuing silence, and that he could do this only by marrying her. In any case, his own financial situation had been improved considerably recently owing to some scheming by Mrs Gaskell. Upon learning that a rich patron of writers, Richard Monkton Milnes, intended to

169

provide Charlotte with an annuity of £100, she somehow persuaded him to pay it to Nicholls instead.

Her motives for such meddling are unclear, but the extra £100 would allow him to retain some dignity as her husband, whilst he bided his time. Nevertheless the humiliation of it all still rankled, and he continued to avoid company until he felt that he could face the world again with some degree of composure.

In order to explain away his prolonged absence from his duties, Nicholls had let it be known that he felt ill, and thought he was going to die. He even went so far as to consult a doctor, and that saved Charlotte a great deal of embarrassment when she was asked where he was. However, she was unable to resist reporting that Dr Teale had informed her betrothed that 'he had no manner of complaint whatever except an over-excited mind – In short I soon discovered that my business was – instead of sympathising – to rate him soundly.'

The marriage settlement was signed and sealed by Charlotte, Nicholls and Joseph Taylor on 24 May 1854, and Charlotte was delighted. She was also cock-a-hoop at her success in, as she saw it, having bent both her father and Nicholls to her will. Now she used every opportunity to belittle Nicholls to her friends, not realizing the light in which she revealed herself by such behaviour. In a letter to her friend Catherine Winkworth, she told her that: 'I cannot conceal from myself that he is *not* intellectual; there are many places into which he could not follow me intellectually.' In writing that, she chose to ignore the facts that Nicholls had received a far better education than she, and that he was a university graduate. In any case, was that a proper way in which to write about the man with whom she was supposed to be in love, and whom she was to marry? Thoughts come unbidden, but to voice them is a conscious act.

In June, she told Miss Wooler that he was: 'A man never indeed to be driven – but who may be led.' However, she was soon to discover just how mistaken she was on the latter count, because he was already, quietly but firmly, setting the pattern for what was to follow.

For one thing, he now saw an excellent opportunity, in the

proposed marriage, to put an end, finally, to Charlotte's friendship with Ellen Nussey. Charlotte tried to put a brave face on it by telling her friend constantly of how highly Nicholls regarded her, but Ellen was not deceived. She knew full well what Nicholls really thought of her, and even Charlotte herself was sometimes hard put to it to explain certain matters.

One example is when, as soon as she had become engaged, she had wished, as was only natural, to see Ellen. She was dying to tell her friend all the news and gossip – but it was not to be. Nicholls would not hear of it, and Charlotte had to try to explain away her disappointment. She wrote to Ellen saying that she had hoped to see her, but that 'Arthur as I now call him' had said that 'it was the only time and place when he could not have wished to see you.'

The implication was that he was so in love that he wanted Charlotte all to himself at that time. The reality, however, was that Ellen was the very last person whom Nicholls wished to have around during such a delicate period, and Ellen knew it. Their dislike was mutual, and she was not to be allowed any opportunity to disrupt events. Nicholls wanted Charlotte sealed safely into wedlock, and was not prepared to take the chance of Ellen putting more doubts into his fiancée's mind at that late stage. Indeed, I would suggest that, had he been allowed his way completely, Charlotte would have been kept in *total* isolation until the day of the wedding, and then the service would have been held in the middle of the night, with nobody else present – and he officiating!

In the event, Charlotte rebelled and, as we have seen, she went to visit Ellen. However, that made Nicholls only more determined to end their friendship as soon as possible.

The wedding finally took place on 29 June 1854, and the arrangements were very much in accordance with Nicholls' requirements. The service was conducted by the Rev. Sutcliffe Sowden – a friend of his – and the only other people present were Ellen Nussey and Margaret Wooler. There was no 'best man' and, in the absence of Mr Brontë, it was Miss Wooler who gave away the bride! I find it all quite weird.

The often inaccurate Mrs Gaskell – who relied heavily upon

what Charlotte told her – has it that, on the evening before the wedding, Mr Brontë made it known that it was his intention to stay at home whilst the others went to the church. Apparently he gave no reason, and therefore the casual observer might very well have wondered why he should have come to such a decision – especially if all was sweetness and light as Charlotte and the 'authorized version' would have us believe. His only surviving child was to be married, and in his own church almost adjoining the Parsonage. One would even have thought that he would have wanted to conduct the service!

Were what Mrs Gaskell related true, that incident alone would have served to illustrate how Mr Brontë *really* felt about Nicholls, but I fear it is not. It is something that Charlotte fed to Mrs Gaskell to make it appear that her father was absent by choice – which would have been bad enough – but, according to Martha *and Charlotte herself*, he was not.

The *truth* of the matter is that it was never intended that he should be there, and Charlotte made that quite plain in her letter to Miss Wooler, dated 16 June. She wrote that: 'Yourself, E. Nussey and Mr Sowden will be the only persons present at the ceremony.'

There was no *physical* reason why Mr Brontë should not have gone. He was quite well at that time, and the church, in which he had preached twice in one day only a short time before, was nearby. No, as I have said, he was not invited.

A fortnight before the wedding she had told Ellen that her father was easily depressed. We can understand why.

Chapter Fourteen

'Her feet go down to death; her steps take hold on hell.'
Proverbs 5:5

It was quite a to-do when they got back, and we all had to help bring in their things, but I saw at once that neither was very happy. Not only that – they both looked tired, with her seeming quite unwell with a pale face and great dark rings under her eyes.

I had expected her to be quite gay and full of talk, but she said hardly a word save that she did not want anything to eat or drink and was going straight upstairs to lie down. From the looks of her, that did not surprise me at all and so off she went. Mr Nicholls said he would have something though, and that gave me the chance to have a few quick words with him.

After his meal, which I served myself, Mr Nicholls said he was going for a walk to stretch his legs after the journey, and I saw him going off towards the moor. It was a lovely day and I longed to be going with him, but there was so much to do that I just had to get on with it.

Later, around supper time, he was still out and so I thought I would show willing and I crept upstairs to see if Madam wanted anything. I tapped gently on the door, not wishing to awaken her, if she was asleep, but straightaway she called out for me to come in.

I was surprised to find that, apart from taking off her bonnet and shoes, she was dressed much the same as she had been downstairs. From the look of the bed and the pillow, I could see that she had been lying down, but I doubt whether she had slept much because she had already undone some of her boxes and started to unpack.

I asked her how she was, and whether she had enjoyed herself and if she wanted me to bring her anything. She did not answer

173

me directly though, but wanted to know where Mr Nicholls was. When I told her he was up on the moor she seemed to give a sigh of relief – although I could not be sure – and said that she would love a cup of tea, but that she would have it downstairs and, if my duties allowed of it, I should bring a cup for myself and join her and she would tell me all about it.

Well, I had thought that she might like some tea, so I already had the kettle stirring on the stove, but as I made to go down, all of a sudden – as if she had just thought of it – she asked me how her father was. That seemed a bit late to me, for it was the first time she had mentioned him since she got back, but I told her he was much better and that I would tell her all about it in a minute.

Whilst I was saying that, though, my eyes strayed to the opened boxes and I thought I would hang up some of her clothes out of the way before I went downstairs. I told her that the kettle was on, and that tea would be ready shortly, and then I said that I would just hang up a few of her things before I went. I began to lift a couple of dresses from the box nearest to me but, quick as a flash of lightning, her temper changed and she snapped at me to leave things be.

It was such a quick change of mood that it shocked me and I just dropped the dresses back, but not before I had seen that under them, opened, was Miss Anne's book that I had found and it looked as if Madam had been reading it.

Well, the way that she had spoken to me made me go so red with temper that she must have noticed it because straightaway she was all smiles and saying that she was sorry that she had snapped at me, but she was tired and the things could be left until she had recovered from the journey. That was all very well and good for her, but for me the harm had been done and any kindly thoughts that I may have had for her went right out of the window. I thought of saying that I would not be able to take tea with her, but I bit my tongue because I wanted so badly to know what had happened in Ireland.

I went downstairs and made up a little tray and took it into the sitting room. Then I was just about to go up and tell her that all was ready when she came down.

By then she had changed her dress, and it seemed to me that she had splashed her face as well because she looked a bit better than she had and seemed more lively.

Anyway, I poured the tea and straightaway she started telling me about how she had been thrown from a horse in Ireland, and she went on and on about it until I had quite had my fill of hearing the same thing over. What *I* wanted to hear and talk about was Mr Nicholls' family and their house, so I only made as if I was interested and waited whilst she finished about the horse and started on other matters.

The trouble was, though, that she kept coming back to the horse, and it was evident that it had given her a great fright and she was not going to talk very much about anything else. That being so, I did not stay as long as I had been going to. Instead I made up a tale that I had to see to the supper and gathered up the things and went to the kitchen.

Later, after supper and when I had washed up and put everything else to rights, I went to the sitting room to say I was popping home for a minute, but nobody was there. At first I thought she must have gone to see her father, but then I heard her coughing in her bedroom and so I went up there as quietly as I could.

The door was ajar, and she was sat upon the bed with something in her hands. At first I could not see what it was, but then, as I tapped at the door, I saw that it was Miss Anne's book that she was so intent upon.

My tap seemed to startle her because she looked up sharply, closed the book quickly and laid it face down, but not so quickly that I did not see that she had come nearly to the end. She made no mention of it, but just said that she supposed I was off home for a while. I said I was, if that was all right, and then asked her how she thought Mr Brontë looked, for I felt sure that she would have been in to see him by then, but to my surprise she said that she had not seen him yet but would do so in a minute.

When I got back downstairs I could hear voices from Mr Brontë's room. I listened at the door and I found that it was Mr Nicholls in there with him. I waited about for quite a while, hoping that he would come out, and all the while being careful in case Madam came down, but he did not. She did not come down either, and I thought how odd it was that Mr Nicholls should have gone to see the old man and not his daughter.

Later, as I lay in bed, I wondered why it was that she seemed to have made straight for Miss Anne's book as soon as she got home – putting all else to one side, even seeing her father. It was evident that she must have read it before in all the long while she had had it, so why go through it again and so soon after her honeymoon?

I thought and I thought, and then I recalled how she had gone on and on about the bother with the horse. The way she told it, Mr Nicholls seemed to have done little to help her, and I thought that perhaps it had come into her mind that he had not wanted to! Had he, I wondered, brought about the trouble in some way in order to try to get rid of her as he had done with Master Branwell and probably Miss Emily as well? And was she having the same thoughts as I was? I tossed and turned until I could hear the cocks crowing, and I knew that I would be fit for nothing at work.

When I had to get up, only a short while later, as I had expected I was tired and out of temper with the world, and if Madam had said just one word out of place to me she would have known all about it, and I would have been out of there for ever. As it was, though, she could not have been nicer and smiled and talked to me whenever our paths crossed. I hardly saw Mr Nicholls though. He was in with Mr Brontë for the longest time, then he was in and out of the Church, and then, shortly after supper, I saw him walking her towards the moor.

They went on those walks, at different times, nearly every day after that and they were gone for ages, which made me wonder why, for she had never been one to do much walking for walking's sake – not like Miss Emily. In point of fact, I had begun to wonder just what they *were* up to up there until, at the end of the week, she said to me – in such an odd manner – that she was weary of so much walking and could not understand why Mr Nicholls seemed so bent upon dragging her along for miles, but that she did not like to displease him. That set my mind at ease in one way, but in another it made me think about him as much as the bother with the horse had – which was something that she had told me about again and, indeed, seemed to tell of to anybody who would listen. If she did not want to go, why was he making her go up on the moors with him, and taking her to places where very few other folk went? I knew what he had done in the past, and I could not help but begin to wonder what he was about now.

It was not until they had been back for over a week that Mr Nicholls and me managed to set a time and place for our first meeting. It was very hard to get a word alone, with her always about, but he was able to whisper out of the side of his mouth and that night we met in the Vestry.

There was so much that I wanted to know that, aside from a kiss when we sat down, we did naught else but talk and from what he said I did not think that the visit to his family's home had gone very well. He told me nearly all they had done, and what they had seen, but, oddly enough, he did not say a word about the bother with the horse until *I* brought it up. Even then, though, he did not answer me. Instead he sat upright and asked me how I knew of it, and his lips came together tightly when I said that she had told me and was telling everybody else. He was not at *all* pleased, and said that she talked too much, and then he went on to something else – so I never did hear his side of the tale.

Things settled back into a rut very quickly, and Madam seemed to take to the duties of the Parish almost as if Mr Nicholls was already in charge as of a right. She was out and about calling on folk in the village all the time which, from what Father said, was not very much to the liking of most of them, and when she was not doing that she was having folk back to the Parsonage, which just meant more work for all of us there. It was as if she could not bear to be alone.

Only on their walks did I see Mr Nicholls and her together for very long. In fact it began to seem to me that she wanted to be with almost anyone but him – and that he felt the same about her – whereas *I* would have given the moon and all of the stars to have been with him for as long as he wanted.

Then she started to go on about having Miss Nussey over to

177

stay, and I wondered what Mr Nicholls would have to say about *that*. At one of our very few meetings, I asked him about it and, as I had expected, he knew nothing about it and was up in arms at the notion. He said he had told her time and time again that he was not having 'that woman' – as he called her – to stay, and that she was like to drive him daft if she did not start listening to what he told her.

Him having said that, and so firmly as well, perhaps you can picture how I felt when one day she told me that Miss Nussey *was* coming and, what was more, there would be a friend of Mr Nicholls stopping at the same time. I could not *wait* to get Mr Nicholls' side of it but, as I have said already, our meetings were so few and far between that I had to bide my time.

When I *did* get the chance, he did not seem at all put out though. All he did was to pat me on the shoulder and tell me that he knew what he was about and that I should trust him. Now that was all very well and good for him, but I thought that I should know what he had in mind, and I told him so. That did not please him at all, and when I saw his face set I wished I had not said anything, and so I told him quickly that I was content to let things be.

So Miss Nussey and Mr Sowden came, and he and her seemed to be together nearly all of the time – so much so that I dared to ask Madam if they were walking out. She thought that *very* funny, and gave quite a laugh, saying that they were not, then her face changed and she said that she wished she could have more of Miss Nussey to herself but that that did not seem to be possible. That made me wonder just what *was* going on, and it became even more of a puzzle when Miss Nussey took me to one side one day.

Now apart from the time when I thought that her and Madam were laughing at me behind my back, I had always liked Miss Nussey and she had often had a word with me. This time, though, it was different for she made it plain that I was to say naught to anyone of our talk, and then she went on to ask me if all was well between Madam and Mr Nicholls!

Well, I did not think that that was a proper thing for her to be talking to me about, and I needed time to think of what to say;

so it was a moment or two before I gave her my answer. However, seeing that I was not of a mind to say aught, she told me that no one would know of anything that I said to her, it was just that she was worried about her friend. That made no difference to me though for, whatever she said, I was not going to take the chance that she might talk out of turn and get me into trouble, so I just answered that they both seemed to live together very well and left it at that. I do not think that she was overpleased with me, but that did not bother me at all.

So they came and went, and Madam seemed very sad at their going, and then, all of a sudden it seemed, Winter was nearly upon us and, as usual, my spirits began to droop. To tell the truth, I was very, very down all round then because I just could not see an end to my way of life, and I made up my mind that I would *have* to speak of my feelings to Mr Nicholls. That was easier said than done though and, as I remember it, it was well into October before we had some proper time on our own and a chance to talk.

For a change, he seemed quite full of cheer, and asked why I had such a long face which, he said, did not become me. Well, for a start, I told him, I had not taken much enjoyment from waiting on him and her, and Miss Nussey and Mr Sowden, without knowing what was going on. He sighed at that, as if I wearied him, and then, as if speaking to a child, he asked me when I would ever learn to trust him, and said that I had his word for it that Miss Nussey would never be over again.

I did not really know how he could be so sure of that, but I did not say so. Instead, I went on to tell him how I felt.

By then they had been married for about 4 months, and whilst *their* lives had changed *I* just went on, bored to death, doing the same old things. In fact my work was even harder now that Mr Nicholls was living in the Parsonage, and Mr Brontë and Miss Aykroyd could do less and less for themselves. My meetings with him were now far fewer than before, and even when we did meet we seemed to be in fear and trembling of being found out. He was not the same then as he had been, with his moods and secrets, and that made me wonder what his feelings for me *really* were.

179

Every day I had to watch as him and her went off for long walks together, and each night I had to go to my lonely, cold bed with the thought that they were sharing the same one whilst all *I* had to look forward to was mooching about, usually on my own, with my only prospect being another day of hard work. I showed him my hands, and asked him how *he* would like such rough work day after day, with naught to look forward to but a few hasty meetings held in secret – but he said naught.

Then I reminded him that he had said that nothing would ever part us, but all I saw was that we seemed to be drifting apart and my life ahead looked bleak indeed.

When I had finished, I was sorry in a way that I had said anything for I did not want him to think me a scold, but it just had to be said and I looked at his face to see how he had taken it, and whether there was any comfort there for me. I hardly expected to find any, but I was very taken by the way he was looking at me. He told me that he could quite understand how I felt, and that *he* was not very pleased with his lot either. His face set as he said that he hated being with her nearly all the time, and the way she was always trying to make plans for them.

In particular, he could not stand her going on and on about having children. It seems that she had a bee in her bonnet about that, and had begun to talk about it from the minute they were married, and just would not stop because she feared that she was becoming too old. For his part, though, he did not want any children, and the whole business was something that they had begun to argue about on their way to Ireland, and the rows still went on. That had started him wondering just what sort of a mess he had got himself into and, more to the point, how he was going to get out of it, and he had not enjoyed himself at all when they had been with his family.

I asked him if he had any plans of his own and whether he had me in them somewhere, and said that he should tell me if he had so that I knew what was in his mind. He said that he could not – it was best that I did not know, especially as he was not sure about them himself. He said that he had thought up a plan when he was in Ireland, but he had had to change his mind and now, though he was sure of the outcome, he did not know how he was going to work it all out. Once again he told me to be patient and that I could trust him, and I said that I would for I knew by the way he looked that he meant what he said and I had faith in him, although I dreaded what might be in his mind.

That night we made love in a way that had not happened for a long time, and I was very happy for I knew that he could not be making up such feelings.

[*GG*] For Charlotte, the honeymoon had clearly been a traumatic experience.

Firstly, she received quite a shock when she arrived in Banagher and discovered how much superior Nicholls' ancestry was to her own. She described the house belonging to his aunt as being 'very large and looks externally like a gentleman's country seat'. Obviously, it was very different from the Parsonage which, according to Lady Kaye-Shuttleworth, and up to 1850 at least, 'never had a touch of paint or an article of new furniture for 30 years'. Charlotte wrote that Nicholls' male relatives were well educated, and the females 'strikingly pretty'. His aunt was 'well-bred', and had been brought up in London.

All in all, Charlotte must have felt very much out of place, but perhaps she understood then why Nicholls had been so unsettled when he had returned to Haworth after his holiday.

Then, after staying for a week at Nicholls' family home, the couple set off for the west coast, with Nicholls alert for any opportunity to put the next step of his plan into action – for, such as it was, he had one.

Many months before he had accepted that marriage to Charlotte was a necessary expedience, but even then, I feel, he also knew that eventually she would have to go the way of her siblings. His problem was finding the best way to rid himself of this thorn in his flesh.

There is reason to believe that at one point he had experimented with small doses of poison, but he had known all along that her death would need to be achieved in such a way as to ensure that no suspicions were aroused. There would certainly have been comment had yet another mysterious death occurred at the Parsonage so soon. That she would have to go was certain, but how?

In the absence of a better idea, he had decided that the honeymoon would be spent in Ireland, and he would see what, if anything, could be accomplished there. Then, when the time actually came, he was even more determined that a way to dispose of her should be found because the honeymoon served only to increase his dislike of her. She was bad enough in small doses, but being with her for twenty-four hours a day was an ordeal which he found intolerable.

However unlikely, it is possible that he might conceivably have endured her inconsequential chatter and her attempts at intellectual condescension when in Haworth. However, seeing her in his old familiar surroundings convinced him beyond all doubt that her days should be numbered. He knew that most people, but his family in particular, were wondering why on earth he had married this weird little woman from England – especially when he got on so well with his 'strikingly pretty' cousins. The suspicion that he was being laughed at behind his back gnawed away at him, and was something which he found hard to bear.

What *really* sealed her fate however, was when she began to go on about their starting a family before it was 'too late'. Being married to her was bad enough but, having witnessed the straits to which Mr Brontë and others had been reduced in similar circumstances, he certainly had no intention of being saddled with a young family. He had made it quite clear to her that he was not interested, and now the subject was a bone of contention.

From Banagher, the couple headed for Killarney. Nicholls had a general idea of the area, but had learned some details from his friend Sutcliffe Sowden, who had been there with his brother. Part of the journey was through a remote region and therefore a guide was hired. Then all three set off, on horseback, for the beautiful, but wild, mountain pass known as the Gap of Duloe, and it was there that a heaven-sent opportunity for Nicholls arose.

We have the story from Charlotte's own pen, in a letter to

Catherine Winkworth dated 27 July 1854. She told of how they had arrived at a part where the track 'was now very broken and dangerous'. The guide had warned Charlotte to dismount but, for reasons about which we can only surmise, she ignored his advice – and Nicholls did not intervene. Now, I do not know what Charlotte was doing on a horse in the first place because, as far as I can discover, she had never ridden in her life. That being so, one would think that any normal and considerate husband would have ensured that his wife heeded the warning of a professional guide – but not Nicholls. If the pun may be forgiven, he was never one to look a gift-horse in the mouth!

Let us take up Charlotte's account of what happened next: 'We passed the dangerous part – the horse trembled in every limb and slipped once but did not fall – soon after she (it was a mare) started and was unruly for a minute – however I kept my seat – my husband went to her head and led her – suddenly without any apparent cause – she seemed to go mad – reared, plunged – I was thrown on the stones right under her – I saw and felt her kick, plunge, trample round me!'

Despite all that, she escaped serious injury – and a good try by Nicholls came to nothing.

We really should try to analyse this incident, in an effort to imagine what really happened.

The guide was in front, with Nicholls at the rear and Charlotte tucked safely between them. They came to the dangerous part and the guide suggested that Charlotte should dismount. Quick as a flash, Nicholls saw a possible chance and grabbed it: 'I shouldn't bother dear, it doesn't look that bad to me.' Silly Charlotte stayed put, and the guide shrugged his shoulders and continued on his way. Then her horse slipped but, to Nicholls' disappointment, did not fall. However, it was enough to frighten Charlotte, who made as if to dismount, but Nicholls had already done so and was at her horse's head: 'Stay where you are my dear, I'll lead her along this stretch.'

We do not know what he then did to the horse, but it seems more likely than not that he did *something*, because it was already past the dangerous part and was being led by the head. Even Charlotte stated that there was no *apparent* cause for the

183

animal's subsequent behaviour, but that it seemed suddenly to go mad.

Picturing the scene as she described it, we then have the mare rearing and plunging while Nicholls, apparently, was trying to control her. Suddenly Charlotte was thrown on the stones directly under the horse. Then the horse was kicking and plunging, and trampling all round Charlotte. If she did not cry out when she was unseated, she would surely have done so when she felt herself under those flailing hooves – yet Nicholls is supposed to have noticed nothing of his wife's predicament. It is beyond belief.

It seems that Nicholls was continuing to torment the mare in some way, in the hope that Charlotte would be killed, or at least badly injured, before the guide returned to see where they were. However, to Nicholls' dismay, he came back too soon.

As was only to be expected, the 'accident' frightened her very much, and that is borne out by the fact that her recounting of the incident takes up more than a third of her letter. Not only that, if one looks at the actual document, the tension which she experienced in reliving the episode is only too apparent in the deterioration of her handwriting. She must have had her suspicions of what Nicholls had been about. Obviously she felt the need to tell somebody of what had happened, but she was unable even to hint at her fears. The implications terrified her, and she saw quite clearly that her days could be numbered.

Enough was enough, and Charlotte decided that she would be safer at home. The letter to Catherine Winkworth was written at Cork on 27 July but, and in spite of anything which Nicholls may have had to say, on the very next day they were some 150 miles away in Dublin. It was from there, as we know from Martha, that Charlotte wrote to her telling her that they were coming home and would be in Haworth in four days.

The excuse given for their early return was that Mr Brontë was not well. However, he had been indisposed for at least a fortnight and that had not bothered Charlotte in the slightest until the incident with the horse – and she admitted as much to Martha. She told her in the letter that even if she *had* been at Haworth when her father was ill 'it would not have done much good – and I was sure that you would do your best for him'.

So home they went, one partner more fearful than she had ever been in her whole life – and the other determined to do better.

It would seem that one of the first things which Charlotte did upon her return from her honeymoon was to encourage as many visitors as possible. That, however, left her little time for writing or reading because, as we have seen, her husband expected her to accompany him on long walks across the moors in addition to everything else.

Charlotte was not at all enthusiastic about those expeditions, and that was, I believe, because she was afraid of being alone with Nicholls in that vast wilderness, or anywhere else for that matter, and it was a source of relief to her that so many people were responding to her invitations to come to the Parsonage. More than anything else, however, she longed for Ellen to come to stay.

Nicholls, of course, would have felt very differently. Obviously it was evident to him by then that Charlotte would have to die at Haworth after all, and he needed time to think and privacy to allow him to pursue his plans. Although he had a very good idea, he had not, at that stage, decided for certain how Charlotte was to meet her fate. All he knew was that, this time, he would need to be very, very careful. That was almost certainly one of the reasons for his institution of the custom of the walks on the moors; it was a desolate area, and accidents could happen there – especially if they were given a helping hand!

He knew that with Ellen on the premises he would be restricted in his actions. Nevertheless, he also realized that it would appear most peculiar should he been seen as the one who was keeping the two friends apart indefinitely. It was an awkward dilemma.

However, from what eventually happened, he seems to have found a partial solution to the problem. When a visit could be postponed no longer, Ellen Nussey would be allowed to come but, at the same time, he would invite someone else to stay who would keep her occupied and away from Charlotte as much as possible. He floated the idea to his friend Sutcliffe Sowden, and the latter agreed to make up a foursome should the need arise.

He told Charlotte of the arrangement and she was not at all pleased. Not only would she have resented not having been

185

consulted, she would have realized that there would be none of the long private conversations with her friend which she had anticipated with such eagerness. She would also have known that Ellen would not like the idea of being palmed off on to one of Nicholls' friends. However, any protests which she may have made were ignored and she was forced to put a brave face on the situation. On 9 August, she wrote to Ellen and told her that Sowden was to stay with them the next time she came to visit. The excuse she made was that Arthur had said, 'he wished us to take sundry long walks – and as he should have his wife to look after – and she was trouble enough – it would be quite necessary to have a guardian for the other lady.' Thus Ellen was put on notice and, as far as Nicholls was concerned, she could like or lump it.

One can well imagine Ellen's feelings upon receiving that letter. She wanted so much to see Charlotte and have a good gossip but that, seemingly, would not now be possible and she would probably have had a good idea why not. Also, she would have resented Nicholls' high-handedness and what, to her, would no doubt have smacked of condescension. Therefore, she decided to make no reply, and not to accept any further invitations to the Parsonage.

Now Charlotte knew Ellen very well, and of how she felt about Nicholls, and she would have anticipated her friend's reactions. However, she had been unable to conjure up a more plausible excuse for why Sowden would have to be present whenever Ellen came. It was no surprise to her, therefore, when her friend did not answer. She wrote again, proposing a particular date, but Ellen replied that it would not be convenient for her.

That, then, was how matters rested for over a month, and the situation seems to have caused Charlotte great concern. She decided to take the initiative.

On 14 September, she wrote once more: 'Mr Nicholls [no longer 'Arthur', you will have noticed] and I have a call or two to make in the neighbourhood of Keighley . . .' She went on to say that they would be doing so on the 21st, and that: '. . . we wish so to arrange as to meet you there and bring you back with

186

us in the cab.' It was suggested that they should pick her up at the railway station.

The extent of Charlotte's longing to see Ellen again is obvious: 'We shall be very, very glad to see you, dear Nell, and I want the day to come.' She really was in an impossible predicament. On the one hand she was trying to placate the old friend whom she yearned to see, while on the other attempting to conform with the terms set by her husband, which she knew were unacceptable to Ellen. All that she could do was to try to present those conditions in the best light possible and trust that her friend would read between the lines.

In the event, that last letter did the trick and Ellen went to Haworth – but she was never to see Charlotte after that.

It would be more than interesting to know what took place during that visit of Ellen Nussey to the Parsonage. We know that relationships were strained, to say the least, and there must have been quite an atmosphere. Nicholls had not wanted Ellen there in the first place, and I doubt whether he would have bothered to disguise his feelings. For her part, we know that Ellen distrusted Nicholls and, were such a thing possible, she probably detested him even more. If some sixth sense warned her of the danger which he posed to Charlotte, her intuition would have been strengthened by the marked difference which she noticed in her friend. However, she was unable to discover what was going on because rarely were they left alone, and when they were Charlotte seemed loath to discuss her problems.

Of course, we can only surmise about Charlotte's thoughts, but I think that she now became convinced that Nicholls was merely biding his time for a suitable opportunity to arise in order to try again. She must also have had her own ideas about her recent 'illnesses', but she did not know what to do to protect herself. After all, she had no real evidence to support her fears, and Nicholls was putting on a good show of affection to the outside world.

She knew that Ellen would have believed her, but she realized that little would be achieved by confiding in her. Her friend would have wanted her to leave Nicholls, but if she did that a reason would have to be given publicly, and that

187

she could not do. Charlotte had declared consistently that she was happy in her marriage, and she and Nicholls presented a public image of wedded bliss. It would have been impossible, therefore, for her to have left him suddenly without causing a great deal of just the sort of gossip and speculation which she had always dreaded. Not only that, she knew her friend very well indeed and was only too aware that Ellen would have had difficulty in keeping any confidences to herself.

One would think, though, that either or both of those consequences would have been a very small price to have paid had it meant saving her life, but things were not as simple as that. Charlotte had always been very jealous of her public image, and she was a proud woman. Then there were the practicalities of life to be considered. Had she left Nicholls she would have been homeless, and any whiff of scandal would have ensured that not many doors remained open to her. Even those who might have been prepared to take her in initially would not have wanted her as a permanent guest. Then there was her father; he would have raised the roof had she left, with unforeseeable consequences.

Had she not been responsible for Anne's death, Charlotte could, of course, have gone straight to the authorities, but she was, and that was the end of the matter. A counter-accusation by Nicholls, who would then have had nothing to lose, would have resulted in the exhumation of Anne's body and the discovery of the poison which, beyond a reasonable doubt, could have been administered only by her sister.

Even had she been completely innocent of any wrongdoing, and with her accusations supported by the evidence of Anne's diary, Charlotte would probably have found it very difficult to interest anyone in what she had to say.

Her thoughts seem to have gone around and around, with her tiredness and depression preventing logical conclusions, until all she felt capable of was to hope against hope that she was mistaken in her suspicions about her husband. From her actions, it is obvious that she wanted to do nothing which might alienate him, and thus provoke the very outcome that she feared.

We, and men in particular, may find it very difficult to understand her confusion and inability to act. However, many women behave similarly in such situations. There are untold numbers of battered wives who stay with their husbands, even when they are in mortal peril. Charlotte was just such a one. She carried on from day to day, fearful but not knowing what to do about it, whilst all the time Nicholls increased his dominance over her.

Chapter Fifteen

'For my soul is full of trouble: and my life draweth nigh
unto the grave.'

Psalms 88:3

From now on, little changes began to take place in the
Parsonage, but the first only came to my notice when, one
day, Madam took me to one side and, almost in a whisper, asked
me to take some letters to the post for her and not to tell *anyone*
that I had done so. Of course, I said that I would, especially as it
got me out of the Parsonage during the day, but I wondered
what was going on because up till then she had always made
such a big thing of marching off with all her letters in her hand
for folk to see.

Then I noticed that Mr Nicholls was always by her as she
opened her letters, and he would put out his hand to read them
himself when she had done so. One day, in my hearing, she said
that there was naught in them to interest him, but he said sternly
that *he* would be the best judge of that and took them off with him.

I wondered what was going on all of a sudden, because up till
then he had been content to let her read just snippets out to
him, and he had even seemed bored by them. Now he not only
read every word of the letters coming in but, whilst I was
cleaning in the passage, I saw him standing over her as she was
writing one of her own and he was telling her, almost word for
word, what she was to put. It was evident that she did not like
that at all, but she seemed to be putting up with it and I was
struck by the change in her. Only then did it come to me,
though, that the letters that she had given me to take on the
quiet must have been some that she did not wish him to see.

That got me thinking hard, for I did not know what to do,
but in the end I made up my mind that I should tell Mr

Nicholls what she was having me do – because all my feelings were for him and I owed *her* naught.

He was *so* pleased when I told him, and said that I had been right to do so as he thought it very underhand of a wife to send secret letters. Then he told me that if it happened again I should give them to him first and *he* would see to it that they went off after he had read them. Of course, I said I would, but I begged him to be careful in the opening and resealing of them for I did not want anyone telling Madam if they found they had been opened, for *I* would get the blame.

So that is what happened from then on, because she began to ask me to take her letters more and more. It seemed to work all right, but only later did I find out that sometimes she gave letters to one of the other servants to take for her; so Mr Nicholls did not see them all.

It was about that time that something else happened that seemed to upset her greatly. When I went down one morning I found Miss Anne's old dog, Flossy, dead in the kitchen. I must say that it quite upset me as well, especially as, by the look of it, it had died in great pain. That did not prepare me for how Madam carried on though. When I told her she burst right out crying in a manner that I had never seen on her before, not even when Master Branwell and Miss Emily died and she was making it up. I just could not understand it, for she had never made much of the dog, but there it was – she had tears streaming down her face and rushed straight back upstairs and did not come down again all that day.

Another change that happened was that they hardly went out together any more, except for the walks up on the moor, and I even heard her making complaint about that, but in such a fearful manner that was so unlike her that I had to look twice to make sure that it was her who was speaking. Mr Nicholls would have none of it though and, in a harsh manner such as I had never seen him use to her before, he made it quite clear that it was his wish that she should go with him, and that he would not take 'No' for an answer.

I could not understand any of that, especially as because when they first came back from Ireland she had been out and

191

about everywhere in the village – in fact folk had got fed up with her calling and playing the Lady with them. Before she was wed, as well, she did not seem to be at home for 5 minutes at a time, and was always gadding off somewhere. Now, though, all that was changed and, as I have said, she left the Parsonage only with Mr Nicholls, and even then only to go up to the moor, and I did not know why. What I *do* know is that being cooped up in the Parsonage did not agree with her because she seemed to be complaining all the time – although not so much with me.

They had some visitors though, because just before Christmas, as I remember it, Madam got very excited for a change and started putting on all her old airs again because Sir James Somebody or Other and his wife were coming for a day. Well, you never saw such a to-do. She had us slaving away from morn till night, and you would have thought that the Queen herself was coming – and for a month at that!

Then, all of a sudden it seemed, yet another Christmas was upon us. I had not looked forward to it all that much but, as is often the way, I enjoyed it perhaps more than most. I was not able to meet Mr Nicholls though, which was a bitter blow to me, but he seemed so busy all the while, and she seemed to watch his comings and goings as never before. In a way, it was perhaps just as well though, because it always seemed that his mind was far away and not on what he was – or should have been – about!

After Christmas it was *awful* – especially as I had had such a good time at home during my time off, with lots of folk coming and going all the while. The Parsonage seemed so dark and cold and quiet, and everything was in such a mess that my heart sank. Nevertheless we got down to it, and soon started to get things to rights and warm ourselves up in the doing.

It took us 3 or 4 days to have the place back to near normal though, and matters were not helped by Madam starting to stand over us again and poking her nose into what we were doing, and telling us how to do it. It got to such a pitch that I nearly told her that if *she* had lifted a finger over Christmas there would not have been so much for us to do and, as she was

192

so good at everything, the place would be as she wanted it – but I kept quiet, smiled at her sweetly, and thought my own thoughts!

Next morning, though, Mr Nicholls told me that she was not well, and would not be getting up. I asked him what was up with her, but he said that he did not know – she just felt out of sorts. He did not seem at all put out, and said that he was not going to send for a doctor.

Later on I went up to see her, and I must say that she did not look all that good. She wanted naught to eat or drink, and did not seem to want to talk to me, so I made up the bed whilst she sat out and then left her to get on with it!

After a day or two she seemed all right again, but even so I was very surprised when she came to me and said that her and Mr Nicholls were going away for a few days, and told me how to look after her father and Miss Aykroyd, as if I did not already know all about that and far more than she did – talk about teaching her grandmother to suck eggs!

She said they were going to stay with the Sir James and his wife who had come to the Parsonage just before Christmas, and I wondered why Mr Nicholls had given his agreement to that, because he would not go anywhere else.

Anyway, off they went, and I must say that I was pleased to see the back of them for a time and to have things a little easier for a change. They were only gone for a little while though, so it seemed that no sooner had they left than they were back again. Madam looked a little better than when she went, but within a day or two she seemed quite poorly. She said she had a cold. Over the next few days she just dragged herself about and was very quiet, and she began to go to bed in the afternoons. Then she started to be sick, and I wondered what was going on – for it seemed that she had something more than a cold.

The first thing that came to my mind, especially after what she had said to Mr Nicholls about having children, was that she was carrying, but when I thought about it I could not really believe that. For a start, she was not that far off 40 and, if I was to believe Mr Nicholls, they had done nothing of that sort for quite a while anyway. Then, of course, the other thought that

193

came yet again – and hot on the heels of the first – was that Mr Nicholls might be up to his old tricks.

I may have been very much in love with Mr Nicholls, but I was not a fool, and all along – whenever he spoke of being patient – I had thought that, somehow, he might be going to do away with her, but I had shut my mind to such a thing because I did not wish to be a part of it even in thought. If that *was* in his mind though, the way that she had kept on and on about the bother with the horse in Ireland made me wonder if the same thought had come to her. Now she was always, it seemed, being ill and I thought it little wonder that she was so quiet.

Of course, it would have been much easier for him to poison her now that he lived in the Parsonage, and I began to think back on how he seemed to have been so mindful of her well-being of late. Since she had become ill he had taken to making her drinks himself and carrying them up to the bedroom, with one for himself, after she had had her afternoon rest. Not only that, I noticed that he always washed the cups himself. I did not like to see a man doing such things – especially him – and so, 2 or 3 times, I had offered to make the drinks and told him to leave the dirty cups, but he had just said that it was all right, and that he did not wish to give me extra work, and carried on.

I do not know what *she* made of it all *really*, but one day when we were alone in the bedroom she said something – I cannot now bring her real words to mind – that made me believe that she thought she was with child. She did not come right out and say so – it was just something that I picked up on – so I did not think it my place to take her up on it, but I thought: 'If that's what you think, Madam, you had best think on.'

Some days later Mr Nicholls and me managed one of our few meetings, and I took the chance to ask *him* about it. It did not come out very easily, after what he had told me, but I had made up my mind to ask him and so I nerved myself and did so. What, I asked him, did he think ailed his wife, and could it be that she was carrying a baby? That did it! He took his arm from me, looked at me as if I was mad, and then asked how the 'D——' could I think such a thing, and went on to say what I thought was a very bad thing for a man of the Church, that

194

if she was it would have been an Immaculate Conception! Well, I said that there was *something* up with her, and I thought it high time that he had a doctor in because folk were starting to talk.

When I think back, I see that he never did answer any of my questions straight out, and I now know why. I did not know for certain at the time, but certainly I had a good idea of what he was about – I just shut my mind to it.

Then, as if there was not enough going on, Miss Aykroyd took very ill. Mind you, she had not been her old self for a very long time – and that was to be expected, because she must have been well over 80, and had not really done anything around the house for years. Even so, she had been very kind to me, especially in my early days at the Parsonage, and I had not minded looking after her as well as Mr Brontë. Now, though, it was not just old age but something far worse, and it made me sad to see her in such a way. She could keep nothing down at all, and sometimes there was blood in what came away from her, but when I told Madam and Mr Nicholls how bad she was neither of them seemed very bothered, and I could do naught but clean her and her bedding and see that she was warm and comfortable.

Perhaps it was to have been expected with all that I had been doing, but then, of all things, *I* was taken ill, and in very much the same way as Miss Aykroyd – although not so bad. Even so it frightened me, for it was rare for me to be so unwell as to have to take to my bed, and I did so only when I felt I could go on no longer.

Before I did, though, I told Mr Nicholls and Madam what I was about, and the next thing I knew Mother and my sister Tabitha – who is about 7 years younger than me – had turned up to look after things. Seemingly, Mr Nicholls had told Mr Brontë about me and he had told him to ask if Father could arrange for some help to come in and look after us all.

Well, it was almost worth being ill to have no work to do and to be fussed over by Mother, but I was glad when I was up and about again for it was no pleasure being in the same room as Miss Aykroyd all the time.

195

I do not know if what I had said to Mr Nicholls had anything to do with it but, some time in the February, he brought in a doctor for Madam – from Bradford of all places. How I wished, though, that somebody would bring in a doctor, *from anywhere*, for poor Miss Aykroyd – even from the village – because she just got worse and worse, and to tell the truth we were all tired of cleaning up after her. I feel very ashamed of that now, but it was not a nice job and I could see no end to it. Came the day, though, when she just passed away in her sleep, which was a shock to me when I found her like that, although I knew that for her it was a blessed release.

I rushed and told Mr Nicholls and Madam, but he was not put out about it one whit, and Madam was so ill herself that she seemed not to take it in properly. The only one who showed anything for her was Mr Brontë, and he was very tearful about her with me, and we both cried when she was laid to rest in the Churchyard, by the garden wall of the Parsonage, on that cold February day. We were the only ones who did though. Mr Nicholls just looked stern, and Madam said she was too ill to come, and I was not at all surprised by that because by then she was in a really bad way.

To tell the truth, she was very much as Miss Aykroyd and me had been, but far worse than me. She was taking hardly anything, and that only from Mr Nicholls, and she just brought it all up again and got weaker and weaker. Mind you, I did have some help with her from Mr Nicholls, who seemed very put out by her state. He helped me change her bedding, and it was him who cleaned and fed her, and that was a good thing because *I* could not have done it. It had been bad enough with poor Miss Aykroyd – but at least I had felt something for *her*.

Having said that, I could not but help feel sorry for Madam. She told me that she was not sleeping at nights, and little wonder at that for I knew that she had read Miss Anne's book again, and by then she must have had her thoughts about what was happening to her.

All in all then, there was a very strange, quiet air about the Parsonage in those days and, as we could not open the windows for long as it was so cold, there was always a terrible smell of sickness, damp, rot and other things about it. I *hated* it all, especially as the smell tended to linger on me, and I had to have a strip wash every night to try to get rid of it.

I had had a feeling of trouble in store when they came back from Ireland, and there had been a little already, but now it was so strong that I just knew that we were all caught up in something awful and felt the doom that hung over us. I did not know it then, but things were moving to a close.

[*GG*] We have seen that Nicholls had been examining Charlotte's mail, both incoming and outgoing, for some time, and we know that sometimes he censored her letters. Nevertheless, Charlotte was managing to smuggle a few out, with Martha as the principal intermediary. It was an arrangement which Nicholls had anticipated long before Martha told him of it, and he had realized that it was unlikely that he would be able to end the practice. He therefore decided to minimize the dangers of those which he feared most, and they were the ones to Ellen Nussey.

Charlotte was told that she should instruct her friend to burn *all* letters which she received from her, and Nicholls stood over her whilst she wrote. Once again she was placed in an impossible situation with Ellen, and this time she was not able even to attempt an excuse.

Her letter is dated 20 October and, obviously referring to a previous communication of which Nicholls *did* have knowledge, she wrote: 'I'm sure I don't think I have said anything rash – however you must *burn* it when read. Arthur says such letters as mine never ought to be kept – they are dangerous as lucifer matches – so be sure to follow a recommendation he has just given – "fire them" or "there will be no more", such is his resolve. I can't help laughing – this seems to me so funny. Arthur, however, says he is quite "serious" and looks it, I assure you – he is bending over the desk with his eyes full of concern. I am now desired "to have done with it . . ." '

One cannot help but feel pity for Charlotte. She did her best to keep it light with her 'I can't help laughing' and 'this seems to me so funny', but she did not succeed. She wrote, also, of

Nicholls having eyes 'full of concern', but although they were probably full of something it certainly was not concern. In any event, she contradicted herself immediately because it just is not possible for a husband who is snapping at his wife to 'have done with it' to have his eyes 'full of concern' at the same time.

That incident alone should serve to convince us that all was not well between Charlotte and Nicholls, and it goes a long way to corroborate what Martha wrote.

Of course, Charlotte's letter served merely to confirm everything that Ellen had ever thought or suspected about Nicholls, and I imagine that her comments about him on receiving it were hardly ladylike.

Predictably, she declined to give the required undertaking, and her refusal brought forth more threats. Charlotte wrote again: 'Dear Ellen, Arthur complains that you do not distinctly promise to burn my letters as you receive them. He says you must give him a plain pledge to that effect – or he will read every line I write and elect himself censor of our correspondence.' She went on to tell her friend that she should: 'Write him out his promise on a separate piece of paper, in a *legible* hand – and send it in your next.'

What is one to make of *that*? *I* find it almost unbelievable.

Ellen's reply was sarcastic, and shows quite clearly that she knew that Nicholls was virtually dictating Charlotte's correspondence. She addressed it: 'To the Revd. The Magister', and it reads: 'My Dear Mr Nicholls, As you seem to hold in great horror the ardentia verba of feminine epistles, I pledge myself to the destruction of Charlotte's epistles, henceforth, if you pledge yourself to *no* censorship in the matter communicated.'

That letter now bears a note stating that: 'Mr N. continued his censorship so the pledge was void.' It also carries another comment which we shall discuss a little later.

There is further confirmation of Martha's allegation that Nicholls told Charlotte to whom she was allowed to write. In January 1855, Mrs Gaskell complained to Catherine Winkworth, who was a mutual friend, that Charlotte – usually so meticulous about her correspondence – had not answered her last letter. Mrs Gaskell had not heard from her since the previous September – and she was never to again! Nicholls had no intention of allowing his wife to communicate with such a notorious gossip.

Early in 1855, Nicholls found himself in something of a predicament. The persistent Sir James Kaye-Shuttleworth had been going on and on about him and Charlotte going to stay with him and his wife but, as we know, Nicholls did not wish to go *anywhere* at that time. In this particular case, however, he realized that constant refusals might jeopardize his plans for his own future.

He knew that he was going to do away with Charlotte, but he could not foresee what would happen after that. He thought that it was more than likely that, with his daughter dead, Mr Brontë would boot him out, and then it would not be at all a bad thing to have a friend in high places – especially one who could offer him a living. In the event, Sir James did indeed offer him the living at Padiham. He declined it, but in the nicest possible way because, even as he spoke, he must have hoped that the offer would remain open for just a little longer!

Martha had her suspicions that Nicholls began to poison Charlotte just after Christmas but, were that so, it is hard to understand why he had delayed for so long. The probability is that he decided to wait until the depths of winter because then the likelihood of her death being attributed to natural causes would be so much greater. However, an alternative explanation may be that he postponed the final reckoning until after he had conducted a few dosage trials with whatever poison he intended to use. It is rather curious to note that Anne's dog, Flossy, died in early December. Now the dog was old, and could have gone at any time but, especially as that was so, it would have made an ideal guinea-pig.

On 19 January 1855, Charlotte managed to get a letter out to Ellen and told her that: 'My health has really been very good ever since my return from Ireland till about ten days ago, when the stomach seemed quite suddenly to lose its tone – indigestion and continual faint sickness have been my portion ever since.' Now such symptoms in a woman, and especially one recently married, would, in those times, have tended to

199

indicate pregnancy. That had obviously occurred to Charlotte who continued: 'Don't conjecture – dear Nell – for it is too soon yet though I certainly never before felt as I have done lately. But keep the matter wholly to yourself – for I can come to no decided opinion at present.' She went on to say that she was 'rather mortified to lose my good looks [sic!] and grown thin as I am doing.' Now I am a mere male, without a comprehensive knowledge of such matters, but I must admit that growing thin is not something which I associate with pregnancy!

Was Charlotte pregnant? Most writers seem to be firmly of the opinion that she was, but I wonder. We have only the word of Mrs Gaskell for what may be merely a *canard*, and we have seen already that she was not the most reliable of biographers. We cannot know whether she was surmising as a result of what Ellen Nussey told her, or simply repeating something put about later by Nicholls.

Whatever her condition, from that moment on Charlotte had no direct contact with Ellen. Nicholls took over the writing of her correspondence completely, and it must have given him great pleasure to tell Ellen, on 23 January, that *he* was answering her letter, 'as Charlotte is not well'. He wrote that his wife had said that 'it will not be possible for her to visit you earlier than the 31st', adding the rider that he did not think that it would be advisable for her to do so even then 'unless she improves very rapidly'.

Six days later he wrote to Ellen again. Charlotte was still unwell, she was bedridden, and he had sent for a doctor from Bradford, 'as I wish to have better advice than Haworth affords'. The physician in question was a Dr MacTurk, who was said to be very competent, but summoning him was simply a part of Nicholls' strategy, and a ruse employed by other poisoners over the years.

The plan, which is put into operation in the early stages of the poisoning, is to consult a respected doctor who does not know the patient, and preferably one who practises outside the area. Then, in a manner similar to that employed by Charlotte with regard to Anne, a false idea of the nature of the illness is

200

planted in his mind by the poisoner, and his agreement obtained that this is probably the cause of the indisposition. Thus a medical history of the supposed ailment is established and may be quoted to a *local* doctor.

Mrs Gaskell's account informs us that, after Charlotte had been ill for some time, Nicholls sent for a doctor who 'assigned a natural cause for her miserable disposition – a little patience and all would go right.' Against that, however, we must set Nicholls' letter to Ellen, of 1 February: 'Dr MacTurk saw Charlotte on Tuesday. His opinion was that her illness would be of some duration, but that there was no immediate danger. I trust therefore that in a few weeks she will be well again.' It was a peculiar letter by any standard. Having implied that the doctor expected Charlotte to be indisposed for a fairly long time, Nicholls thought that she would be recovered in just a few weeks. Admittedly, it could be argued that 'some duration' is a relative term, but medical men of my acquaintance tell me that they would use it only when months rather than weeks were involved.

There is no mention in Nicholls' letter to Ellen of 'a natural cause' – very much the opposite in fact – but that is not to be wondered at, because even if Charlotte *had* been pregnant, and that seems unlikely, Ellen Nussey was the last person whom he would have told.

To realize the importance of that letter in the order of things, one must ask why Nicholls was bothering to write to Ellen at all, because normally he would not have wasted a stamp on her. The answer is that it was just another tactic in his strategy, and one that has been used by murderers through the ages. Relatives, friends or acquaintances who might become concerned at not hearing from the victim have to be appeased before they become inquisitive. Ellen was just such a person, and Nicholls followed the classic pattern.

The friend has to be placed on notice that the victim is ill, but at the same time she must be reassured that it is nothing serious. In that way, there is no rush to the bedside, but on the other hand the friend is not totally unprepared when informed that there were complications and the patient is dead.

201

Here, therefore, we have Nicholls warning Ellen that it might be a long illness, but that there was no *immediate* danger and, despite what the doctor has said, *he* expected her to be up and about in a few weeks.

Had Ellen discovered that Charlotte was seriously ill, or even that she was definitely pregnant, there can be no doubt but that she would have hastened to the Parsonage. So in his next letter to her was Nicholls lying to keep her away or telling the truth? On 14 February he wrote: 'It is difficult to write to friends about my wife's illness, as its cause is not yet certain.' He wrote that although, according to Mrs Gaskell, the doctor had 'assigned a natural cause' over a fortnight before, and despite the fact that, at around the same time, Nicholls had appeared reasonably confident that Charlotte would soon be well!

As with so many of the mysteries surrounding the Brontë family, various people had motives for lying and therefore it is nigh impossible to establish the truth with certainty. What is puzzling, however, is why so many writers airily perpetuate 'facts' which, as only a little research would have shown, are nothing of the sort. It is this casual approach that has allowed the many Brontë *canards* to go unchallenged for so long.

Where the truth of a matter is in doubt, and not able to be established by any other means, we must fall back upon circumstantial evidence.

Charlotte had been quite happy to intimate to Ellen the *possibility* of a pregnancy, so surely she would not have hesitated, nay would she not have been overjoyed, to have told her friend had it been confirmed? However, nothing of the sort ever happened.

When, eventually, she managed to get a faintly pencilled message out to Ellen all that she wrote about herself was: 'I am not going to talk about my sufferings, it would be useless and painful.' That pathetic note does not read as if it is from a woman who is expecting her first child by 'dear, patient, constant Arthur' does it? It is more like a cry for help from a Charlotte who knows her fate and is resigned to it.

202

Chapter Sixteen

'Are not my days few? cease then, and let me alone, that
I may take comfort a little.'

Job 10:20

Thinking back, nothing was ever the same after Miss
Aykroyd passed away, although I did not notice it so
much at the time because I was so out of sorts with myself. The
feeling that trouble was on the way had stayed with me, and
things were not helped by that February being so bleak.

It got so that I *hated* being in the Parsonage more and more,
and it was terrible getting out of bed on those cold mornings,
with frost even up the inside of the windows. I was only really
content at night, when I had had my wash and was snug and
warm in bed with my thoughts.

My parents must have had words about me because once
Mother asked me if I was all right, and if I needed a doctor –
and I knew that she would not have said such a thing unless she
had talked about it with Father first. I told her I was just down,
what with one thing and another in the Parsonage and the
weather and all, and knowing how I always felt about Winter
she let me be after that.

What I could not understand, though, were the changes
that had taken place in Mr Nicholls. All of a sudden he
seemed very happy with life, and though he seemed to have
barely any time for me he spent hours and hours with
Madam, waiting upon her every wish. He did everything
for her, and I used to hear him talking to her for such long
times that I wondered what he could find to go on about all
the while. Sometimes, when I made an excuse to go into their
room, I would hear him comforting her, and saying that she
would soon be better and suchlike, but I could tell that he

had changed from what he had really been saying when he heard my knock.

Whenever we had the Parsonage more or less to ourselves, which was a lot of the time by then, I tried to get him to pay some attention to *me*, but no matter what I said or did he always had some excuse for why we could not meet properly, and he never so much as pecked my cheek. It got to such a state that I began to worry that I had done something wrong in his eyes, but then, around the middle of the month, all became clear to me.

I remember well that it was a Saturday, because I had taken to leaving the Parsonage earlier than usual on Saturdays, and on that particular one I was going out with my sisters. All morning I had worked hard so that I could get away on time, and so I was not at all pleased when, after weeks of paying little heed to me, Mr Nicholls asked me to wait a while as he wanted a word with me. Any other time I would have been filled with joy, but then I was just cross. I thought of all the times when *I* had tried to have a proper meeting with *him* but it had not suited him and he had put me off, but now, when *he* wanted to, he expected me to be at his beck and call.

As it happened, I did not have to wait for very long, but at one point I thought I would be there for ever. I heard him come leaping down the stairs, and he went straight into Mr Brontë's room and shut the door. Whenever that had happened before the big upset between them it had usually meant that they would be in there together for ages, and so my heart sank as I thought of my sisters waiting for me. I need not have worried, though, for he was out of the room almost as soon as he had gone in, and I saw him coming towards me with a great smile on his face and waving a bit of paper in the air.

He pulled me into the sitting room, sat me down at Madam's writing desk, and put a pen in my hand. Then he laid what I found to be more than one bit of paper before me and told me to sign my name where his finger was pointing.

I did not do so though. Father had always dinned it into us all that we should never sign *anything* without reading it inside, outside and upside down first, and understanding what we were putting our names to, and I was not going to change the habit of a lifetime, even for Mr Nicholls.

The pen was still in my hand, but I made no move and that seemed to anger him a little. Once again, but in quite a sharp voice this time, he ordered me to sign where his finger was, but his manner was not to my liking and so I put the pen down with a bang and looked up at him. He had some colour in his cheeks, and his eyes held a look of wildness such as I had never seen in them before, and that made me wonder all the more about what I was expected to put my name to.

I looked more closely and saw that the papers were thick, such as I had seen only in important letters and the Church papers with seals on that Mr Brontë sometimes had on his table; so I knew that what was in front of me was of some moment. It was no good – I could not sign such a paper without knowing what it was all about and so I told Mr Nicholls that I needed to read it first. That, though, was not at all to his liking. He took up the papers quickly and just looked at me hard with his mouth pursed in such a way that I knew he was cross with me. We just looked at each other for what seemed the longest time, but was probably only a minute or two, then, with a grim smile, he said that it was his wife's Will. He went on to say that that was all I needed to know, but he would tell me in secret that it got him out of an agreement that he had been made to sign and she was leaving everything to him.

He put the papers before me again and this time I had a close look at where I was supposed to sign and saw that I would be putting my name as a witness to having seen Madam sign the paper. There was what looked like her signature, and I found that Mr Brontë had already signed as a witness, although I knew that he had not *seen* her sign it. Knowing how Mr Brontë regarded Mr Nicholls, I wondered how he had come to do so, but I thought that if *he* had felt able to sign then there was no good reason why *I* should not – so I did, but not without some worries about whether I was doing the right thing.

As soon as I laid the pen down Mr Nicholls took up the papers again and waved them about to dry the ink. Whilst he was doing so, he told me to say naught to anyone about it and he

205

would see to it that I did not suffer for my pains. He kissed me gently, and I knew then that I would do anything for him as long as I was sure that I meant anything to him – and I was. The way he held me, I dare say that the kiss could have led on to other things there and then, but my sisters were waiting and so, much against my feelings, I drew back from him and said that I had to go.

From that moment on things between Mr Nicholls and Madam changed totally.

As far as Mr Nicholls went, he began to act very oddly, and was out of the house more than he was in. I often wondered where he went and what he was about, for he seemed always to have a queer look on his face and spent far less time with Madam than before. Sometimes he left her almost totally alone for days, except for seeing to some of her meals and washing some of her cups and plates. There were no more long talks between them – in fact I never heard even a kind word come out of him to her – and Madam became more and more down. She seemed to live for his visits, and sometimes when I was in her room and he came with her tray I saw her face light up in such a way that I almost felt sorry for her.

I did not, though, because she was slowly wearing me down even more than she had done when she was up and about. At that time I was having to do nearly everything for her, and the washing and cleaning alone was taking up nearly all of my days. It was work that was in no way to my liking, and I told Mr Nicholls so, but his only answer was that I should put up with it for a little while longer and all would be worthwhile.

That, of course, got me to thinking again of what he might be about, and I am sure now that Madam must have felt the same. I had thought the matter of the horse very odd, and I had sensed that she did too. Now I saw that all the talking that had been going on between them must have been about the Will, and surely that must have made her think all the more, especially as he got ready some of the things that she ate and drank. But even with that, and on top of her knowing what had happened to Master Branwell and probably Miss Emily, the silly woman had somehow allowed herself to be talked into

206

leaving everything she had to him, and so giving him a very good reason to get rid of her.

I made up my mind that I would try to keep an eye on him whenever he was in the kitchen and so I started to do things differently. Up till then I had told him when the food was ready, and had then gone elsewhere whilst he fussed with getting the tray just right before taking it up. Now, though, I took to doing jobs in the kitchen whilst he was there.

It was plain that he did not like that, and he would send me on little errands to get me out of the way for a few minutes. That could not go on though, and I was usually there, but working in such a way that it must have seemed to him that I could not see what he was doing all the while. I managed a sly look his way every now and then though, but it was a little while before I saw anything untoward, and even then I could not swear to what was going on.

He always had his back to me, and all I saw was his arm and elbow go up as if to the pocket of his waistcoat. Then they went down again and I saw the elbow move about a bit – as if something was being shaken or stirred – before the same raising of the arm and elbow as there had been at the outset. Then, out of the corner of my eye, I saw him looking at me over his shoulder before he began busying himself with getting the things on the tray to his liking. I witnessed that several times, and even though, as I have said, I could not swear to it in a Court of Law, I knew in my own mind what he was up to and I wondered if I should do anything about it.

I thought and I thought, but always it came back to me that I should do naught. After all, I was not *sure* of what was going on, and my feelings for him were such that I could never get him into trouble. Even if I had gone to Father and he to the Justices, I doubt whether they would have taken my word against his. In any case, what would there have been in it for me? Mr Nicholls had shown me naught but kindness and affection, whereas Madam had made my life a total misery at times over the years, especially when I was naught but a slip of a girl. I had never liked her, whereas I had been drawn to Mr Nicholls from the

207

moment I first saw him, and I had his promise that I would come out of everything well.

Mind you, I did not know what exactly he meant by that, but I had my dreams and I was not willing to put them to one side, and also open myself up to all kinds of bother by pointing the finger at him. In the end I made up my mind, once and for all, that I would side with him come what may.

At times, though, that was easier said than done, because she really was sinking fast and there were times when it was nigh impossible not to feel sorry for her and for me to harden myself against her. By the end of February she was just skin and bone, and being sick all the while and with her bowels very loose. There was blood mixed in with whatever came away from her and I knew that she could not go on much longer like that. As I have said, sometimes her looks were so piteous that I could have taken her in my arms and comforted her, but I just thought on and let her be.

It was about that time that Mr Nicholls took to sleeping in the little room next door that had been Miss Emily's, and I could not blame him for that because it sometimes made me feel sick just to go into the big bedroom. He explained it away by saying that he was getting no sleep with her tossing and turning and moaning. That meant, though, that there was no one with her all night, and on some mornings I just dreaded what I would find when I went in to her.

Mr Nicholls, for his part, seemed to go near her as little as possible now, and to my mind it was evident that things could not go on like that for much longer. I said as much to him, and told him that I thought that she should have a night nurse, but he would have none of it and turned to go, but I was set on having it out.

What I had said was not out of concern for *her* but for *me*. It did not bother me if she was on her own all night, but what *did* upset me was having to wash her, be at her beck and call for the smallest thing and clean up that awful stinking room in the mornings. He had said that he was not willing to take on a nurse, so I asked him why, then, could he not get me another girl to help me with the bedroom work? I looked at him straight

208

and wondered what he would say, but I did not have to wait more than an instant for his answer. Straightaway he said that he would see to it, and with that he was off.

'The girl that he got was such a little mite though that I could not give her such work to do. Instead I took an older girl from downstairs and started the new one in much the same way as Miss Aykroyd had taught *me*.

Life now became a little more bearable for me but, as the weeks dragged on, Madam just got worse and worse. Mr Nicholls hardly went near her and nor did I. Apart from doing what had to be done first thing in the morning, I kept away as much as possible and took no heed of any shouts or banging down. What was going on was none of my business.

What got me to thinking, though, was why there were no letters or callers for her. I would have thought that, surely, if only for the looks of it – because I do not think that anybody really *liked* her – folk would have been asking how she was, and certainly I had expected Miss Nussey to come over long before this, even though her and Mr Nicholls did not get on. But no one came, not even a doctor by then, and she just lay there day after day, mostly on her own except for when Mr Nicholls took her food and Mr Brontë was able to get up to see her.

I was not at all surprised, then, when early on a Saturday morning – that was the last day in March as I recall – I was shaken by Mr Nicholls who told me that she had died in the night. He looked tired and grim, but not put out, if you know what I mean, and we exchanged no words of sadness at her passing – for the truth of the matter was that we were both glad she was gone. Instead, he put his arm around my shoulders and gave me a little hug, and then went off on some errand. For my part, I was up and into her room as fast as my legs could carry me. I knew that Miss Anne's book must be in that room somewhere, and I had made up my mind to have it.

When I got to the door, though, I must say that I stopped for a moment before going in because I did not really want to see her dead, but then I nerved myself and opened the door. However, the sight that met me was not at all what I was prepared for. There was no body there, the windows were wide open, all the bed-sheets and coverings and the palliasse were tossed in a pile in the corner, and the rest of the room looked as if a gale had swept through it. All her clothes were higgledy-piggledy, her boxes were open with things hanging over the sides, and her writing-desk had been brought up from downstairs and now lay unfolded on the floor with her papers strewn about and a secret drawer open and empty.

It was as plain as the nose on my face that somebody – and it could only have been Mr Nicholls – had been looking for something and I wondered what it was. As far as I knew, he did not know of Miss Anne's book and so it could not have been that, but I wondered if he had found it by chance during his search.

I did not really know where to start looking for it myself, for everything was in such a mess, but before I began I went to the little room where Mr Nicholls had been sleeping and there, on his bed – and as I had expected – was what I took to be her body, covered with a sheet. Then, although it was not something that I *really* wanted to do, I felt that I just had to have a last look at the woman who had given me so many hard times over the years. I drew the sheet down from her face very slowly, and even though I had been afeared at what I would see I was really taken aback at the sight that met my eyes, because there was none of the peace of death that I had heard so much about. Her head was little more than a skull with very little hair on it, her eyes were wide open and staring at me, and her lips were drawn back as if she was ready to leap up and bite me. Never do I wish to see such a sight again, but it still comes back to me from time to time.

Quickly I pulled the sheet back up. I found that I was shaking, and my first thought was to get out of there as soon as I could – but I did not. Instead, I had a good look through Mr Nicholls' things – very carefully, and putting them back as I had found them. Mainly I wanted to see if Miss Anne's book was there, but I was always inquisitive and also going through his things gave me much pleasure. As it happened, I found little of moment although I was very pleased to find the pocket-book that I had given him years before wrapped in a silk kerchief at the bottom of a trunk.

I did not find Miss Anne's book though, and so I left and after having a quick splash and getting dressed I hurried downstairs for a cup of tea to settle my mind after what I had seen. Then I went back upstairs and started to put the big bedroom to rights. First I took all the bedclothes downstairs and emptied the palliasse out the back for the straw to be burned. Then I set about hanging her clothes where they should have been and tidying up generally – but all the while I was keeping an eye out for Miss Anne's book, not knowing whether or not I was on a fool's errand and Mr Nicholls had it already.

It took a long time, but I *did* find it, though it was simply by chance, and when I came across it I knew why Mr Nicholls had not – if, indeed, that was what he had been looking for.

My find came about like this. When I had put everything away, I began to sweep the room – moving things as I went. I must say that I did so quickly and not very gently because I was so vexed at not finding the book, and also I wanted the job over and done with as soon as I could so that I could have a little breakfast before seeing what else was to be done and how Mr Brontë was. So I knocked the broom very hard into corners, without heeding the paintwork as I usually did – not that that mattered very much anyway as it was so bad – but when I came to a corner from where I had pulled the bed out a small part of the board that skirted the room came away – and out fell the book!

That bedroom had been made a little bigger a few years before, and Mr Brontë had gone on about the shoddy workmanship of the men who did it – in fact he had had them back twice at least to put some things right. Because of that, I was not at all surprised to see that this small bit of board seemed not to have as many nails as there were holes for them, so it came away easily. It had covered a lovely little hiding place that Madam must have found at the time, for there was the book. I had a look and a bit of a feel round in the space to see if anything else was hidden there. There was not, so I just picked up the book, hid it under my apron and took it to my room. Later, when I popped home, I went out the back and wrapped it in an old bit of canvas and then hid it in the little shed where the kindling was kept – Madam was not the only one to have her own little hidey-hole!

Having the book made a great deal of difference to how I felt. Even though I thought such a lot of him, I did not *really* know what Mr Nicholls' true feelings for *me* were, nor what he had in mind for me, but now I had the means to bend him to my will if need be.

After her death there was a great deal of talk in the village, and I was really surprised to find how few folk had known how bad she was. It seemed that Mr Nicholls had told no one, and Father in particular was very much up in arms about it for, although *I* had told him, I do not think that it had sunk in as to how poorly she really was.

He said to us, and others, that in his post as Sexton he would have thought that he would have been told by Mr Nicholls or Mr Brontë how bad things were. He also went on and on about there being no postmortem examination by the doctors, and said that too many folk to do with the Parsonage had died in such a short while that he could not, for the life of him, understand why nobody else could see that something was amiss. Mother told him to hush, lest he found himself in trouble, but he did not listen to her and only stopped when someone at the Lodge warned him in like fashion. When Mother told us of that I was pleased, for I did not wish to see Mr Nicholls harmed in any way, and by then it was all water under the bridge anyway and no one could bring them back.

I did not go to the funeral. Even had I been asked I could not have brought myself to have done so, and I must say I wondered how Mr Nicholls, a so-called man of God, could have gone into the Church with so much blood on his hands, so to speak. He did though – well I do not suppose he could have stayed away really – and I was told that he moved many folk to tears by what he said to them – but that did not surprise me at all because he always was such a lovely talker. For my part, I stayed at the Parsonage and saw to it that the food and drink was all in order for the Wake.

It was *so* quiet and peaceful in the house once the funeral was over and done with. Mr Brontë hardly moved out of his room anyway, and with only him and Mr Nicholls to look after my days were much easier and more pleasing than they had ever been – especially with not having *her* sharp tongue going on and on, and her poking and prying with her eyes everywhere. The weather was getting better by the day as well, and so I started the Spring cleaning a bit earlier than usual. I had all the windows opened, except those in Mr Brontë's rooms, and saw to it that the house was cleaned, scrubbed and polished from top to bottom until it smelled sweeter than ever it had.

As for me and Mr Nicholls, I find it very hard to put into words how happy we were with her gone. Now we could make love more or less whenever and wherever we liked, and I found out how much better it was in a bed. We were even able to have some meals together, and I felt quite the lady of the house – it was almost as if we were wed.

All the while, though, I wondered what he had it in mind to do now that he was free of her and had her money. I half-expected that he would up and go back to Ireland and so, after a couple of weeks, I asked him straight out what he was going to do.

He must have been waiting for me to say something, for he did not seem a bit surprised and said that he had been going to tell me anyway. With a smile, he said that the way things were now suited him well, and that he saw no reason to leave unless I wanted him out of the way. That made me burst out laughing, which I suppose was not really right in the light of all that had happened in that house, but I was so happy that I was like to have died with joy.

Of course, I still had my secret dream that some day he and I would wed, but for the time being I was more than content to leave things be and see what would happen next.

[*CC*] As there is no evidence of a pregnancy, and having disposed of that myth, we may now attempt to discover what *really* ailed Charlotte.

According to Martha, the reality was that Nicholls was

proceeding quietly with his deadly plan, and one is able to plot his steady progress from a calendar of letters:

21 January: 'Indigestion – loss of appetite – and such like annoyances' (Charlotte)

23 January: 'Not well' (Nicholls)

29 January: 'Continues unwell' (Nicholls)

1 February: Illness will be of 'some duration' (Nicholls/ MacTurk)

14 February: '. . . completely prostrated with weakness and sickness and frequent fever' (Nicholls)

27 February: 'I am reduced to great weakness – the skeleton emaciation is the same' (Charlotte)
'My sufferings are very great – my nights indescribable – sickness with scarce a reprieve – I strain until what I vomit is mixed with blood' (Charlotte)

30 March: 'My dear Daughter is very ill, and apparently on the verge of the grave' (Mr Brontë)

31 March: Dead.

All that time Nicholls was penning letters supposedly dictated by his wife, and censoring the few of which he was aware that she had written herself. He ensured that there were many favourable references to himself, and that it was made clear that it was by *her* wish that no doctors outside Haworth were now being consulted. Dr MacTurk is heard of no more: he had served his purpose. Charlotte was now under the supervision of the Haworth practitioner Dr Ingham – who had been well primed with the 'opinion' planted on Dr MacTurk.

Dr Ingham appears to have been as well suited to Nicholls' purposes as the credulous Dr Wheelhouse had been. For one thing, he was apparently in the habit of prescribing for patients whom he had not examined. Around 20 January, when Charlotte herself was beginning to feel really unwell, she wrote a short note to the good doctor: 'I regret to have to disturb you at a time when you are suffering from illness, but I merely wish to ask if you can send any medicine for our old servant Tabby.'

214

It is obvious that Charlotte – who quoted none of Tabby's symptoms – took it for granted that he, ill or not, would do as she had requested, so we may presume that it was a common practice of his. As it happened, Tabby was dead within a month – little wonder then that Nicholls stayed with Dr Ingham!

I think that Tabitha's death destroyed whatever little faith Charlotte may have had in Dr Ingham. She wrote to Joe Taylor's wife, Amelia, and told her: 'Medicine I have quite discontinued. If you can send me anything that will do good – do.' In her next letter, she told her friend: 'The medicines produced no perceptible effect on me but I thank you for them all the same. I would not let Arthur write to Dr. Hemingway – I know it would be wholly useless.'

I find all that very contradictory. After telling Amelia that she had 'quite discontinued' taking medicine she went on, in the next breath, to ask her to send some – and took it! Obviously it was only Dr Ingham's medicine, administered by Nicholls, that had been discontinued.

There are other aspects of the letter which I find quite peculiar. It is very odd that she should beg for any sort of medicine from a friend and yet, we are asked to believe, she would not allow her husband to write to a doctor. That contradiction apart, she was in no position to forbid Nicholls to do anything.

Of course, the complete explanation is that few of the letters contained Charlotte's own words, whereas Nicholls' involvement is quite apparent. He was ensuring that no blame for what was to come could be attributed to him, and therefore Amelia and the world were told that it was at his wife's request that Dr MacTurk's services were dispensed with and Dr Hemingway not consulted. She alone is held responsible for discontinuing with the medicine prescribed by Dr Ingham whereas Nicholls, by inference, is shown in a favourable light as encouraging her to seek other remedies. In reality, of course, Nicholls probably did not care from whom she received medicines if he was dosing them all!

The fact of the matter is that, at the end, Charlotte was doomed. With visitors forbidden and her mail censored, she was kept in virtual isolation by a husband who hated her and was plotting her death. There was no one to whom she could have appealed. Tabby was gone and, much as he detested Nicholls, her father would probably have thought her hysterical. She might, of course, have turned to Martha, but I think that she sensed that she could no longer trust even her.

Until Charlotte's 'illness' became much worse, Martha had presented her usual friendly, but somewhat servile, face to her mistress. However, her attitude had changed abruptly once Charlotte became *really* ill, and especially after the Will was signed, and Charlotte could not but have noticed that she was no longer the apparently willing and obliging Martha whom she had always known. We cannot know what construction she placed upon her servant's change of attitude, but I am convinced that it was that change which finally broke Charlotte and left her feeling completely abandoned.

Her mental and physical torment can be only imagined as she lay there for hours, neglected and utterly alone. She *must* have suspected by then what Nicholls was up to, but she seems to have hoped against hope that she was wrong. It would appear that she dreaded the sound of Nicholls' footsteps upon the stairs and yet, at the same time, from what Martha tells us, she lived for his visits.

As the weeks passed, and she sank lower and lower, who knows what apparitions from the past were conjured up in her fevered mind. Whatever her transgressions, she went a long way towards expiating them during those last grim days.

According to Martha, it was during that period, when Charlotte felt so isolated, and was so very, very vulnerable, that Nicholls took advantage of her state of confusion.

I can imagine that, since the time of their honeymoon, he had been on and on at her to rescind the marriage settlement. Always she refused, steadfastly, to do so, and his anger had been evident in the increasingly hostile attitude which he had adopted, and which had frightened her so much. Now, however, all that changed and, with a suddenness that threw her off guard completely, Nicholls began to devote himself entirely to her needs. He showered such affection upon her that she, in her loneliness and despair, began to think that perhaps she had misjudged him which, of course, was just what he had hoped for.

He seems to have lost no time in pressing home his advantage. Martha tells us of the soothing words which he whispered to Charlotte as he spooned more dosed broth down her, and of the pathetic gratitude with which she responded to his ministrations. Soon she appears to have been his to do as he would with, and then he had no trouble whatsoever in persuading her that it was only right and proper that she should make a Will in his favour, thus circumventing all the provisions of the marriage settlement. As we know, the witnesses were Martha and the almost blind Mr Brontë and I have often wondered whether the old man realized what he was signing.

Under the terms of the Will, Nicholls was the sole beneficiary unless his wife left children. Had that been the case, he would have had only the interest on the money invested at his disposal, with the principal passing to any progeny on his death. It was fairly standard wording, and had caused Nicholls no problems. He had known that there would be no offspring, and had agreed that those provisions be included merely to humour Charlotte in her imagined pregnancy. What if, though, despite all the evidence to the contrary, there was the slightest possibility in his mind that Charlotte *might* be pregnant? That would have been a strong additional motive for getting on and killing her as quickly as possible before the child was born.

Making the Will was a fatal mistake on her part because Charlotte Nicholls, née Brontë, died just six weeks later – in the early hours of Saturday, 31 March 1855. The accommodating Dr Ingham certified the cause of death as being 'Phthisis 3 months'.

Not being a medical man, I had to look up the definition of 'Phthisis'. Apparently it means 'wasting', and is a general term applied to the progressive weakening and loss of weight occasioned by all forms of tuberculosis, especially that of the lungs. There is, however, absolutely no evidence that Charlotte was suffering from tuberculosis; not even the possibility is mentioned anywhere. I think, therefore, that we may take it as read that, relying upon the family's medical history, Nicholls planted the idea of tuberculosis in Dr MacTurk's mind, just as Charlotte had done with the doctor called to Anne, and that either MacTurk or Nicholls did the same with Dr Ingham.

It would have suited Nicholls very well to attribute his wife's illness and death to consumption – but only after she had been disposed of safely. He had not wanted well-wishers beating a path to the Parsonage while he was poisoning her, and that may be why he never referred to tuberculosis in any of his correspondence. For just the same reason, the probability is that he persuaded the doctors not to distress his wife by mentioning the then deadly disease, and encouraged her in the idea that she might be pregnant.

Obviously, Dr Ingham was not sure of what had killed Charlotte. He guessed, and he guessed at tuberculosis because he had been pointed in that direction. However – and as in the previous deaths – there was no postmortem examination, nor were any official questions asked. One cannot help but wonder what would have happened had someone in authority acted upon what Martha states her father was saying.

Nicholls must have been elated after his wife's death. Not only had he rid himself of her, but it was only a matter of time before he would have his hands on her money and other possessions. There was also the possibility of more, once he had had the opportunity to go through the papers of her siblings at his ease. However, he had his priorities, and one in particular gave him great pleasure. He could not wait to tell Ellen Nussey of Charlotte's death, and wrote to her only a few hours after it occurred!

I read his letter with a sense of incredulity. No mention was made of tuberculosis, instead he told Ellen that: 'Charlotte died last night of exhaustion. For the last two or three weeks we had become very uneasy about her, but it was not until Sunday evening that it became apparent that her sojourn with us was likely to be short. We intend to bury her on Wednesday morning.'

That letter was written on 31 March. Charlotte's 'illness' had started at the beginning of January, and by mid-February she was 'completely prostrated with weakness and sickness and

218

frequent fever'. A week later she wrote of her 'skeleton emaciation', and of blood being mixed with her vomit. Nevertheless,
according to Nicholls, it was to be at least another two weeks
before 'we' became 'very uneasy'.

It makes me wonder what it would have taken to *worry* him!

It will also be noticed that, although he had had five clear
days in which to do so, Nicholls had not told her closest friend
that his wife was at death's door – that news came to her from
Mr Brontë on the day before Charlotte died.

Ellen arrived at the Parsonage just before lunchtime on the
Sunday, and was asked by Mr Brontë to stay over until the
funeral. That she did, but she left Haworth immediately after
and never saw Mr Brontë or Nicholls again.

From Nicholls' point of view, the situation after Charlotte's
death was very satisfactory and at last he was able to contem-
plate his future with equanimity. In fact, only one thing
prevented him from being a completely happy man. That, of
course, was the fact that, try as he might, he had been unable to
find Anne's book. He had searched for it high and low,
ransacking Charlotte's possessions, the room in which she
had died and, later, the rest of the house, but with no success.
Whilst he was doing so he must have wondered whether the so-
called diary had simply been something that Charlotte had
invented in order to substantiate what Anne had told her, or
whether Martha had come across it after Charlotte's death and
now had it hidden away. She had never mentioned it though,
and he did not like to raise the subject in case, by doing so, he
told her what she might otherwise not have known, so he
decided to let sleeping dogs lie for the moment. *Should* Martha
have it he would be no worse off than he was already, because
he felt sure that she would never act against him unless he
crossed her – and that was something that he did not intend to
do. If, however, the book was still hidden away somewhere in
the house he would have plenty of opportunities to continue to
look for it because, if possible, he intended to be around for
some time to come.

Nicholls had no vocation, and he was not ambitious. All that
he had ever wanted was a quiet, comfortable life, and he had

been considering how that might now be achieved. He had no great love for England or the English, and his first thoughts had been of returning to Ireland. There he would have been amongst his own kind, and away from all the unhappy and unpleasant memories of Haworth, the Parsonage and the Brontës. However, he knew that he would still have to earn his living, and that was easier said than done for a Protestant clergyman in the south of Ireland. It was true that he had Charlotte's money, but that would not keep him for life, and it was not enough to make an adequate investment in a business.

Thinking things over, he obviously realized that he could, however, really scoop the kitty if he stayed at the Parsonage and played his cards right.

There were two main considerations which led him to that conclusion, and the first was old Mr Brontë. He was nearly seventy-nine years of age, and not very robust. Seventy-nine was a good age, even by today's standards, and he could not have been expected to last for much longer. With his own savings and from what the deaths of Emily and Anne had yielded him – for both had died intestate – he had a reasonable amount of capital. There was also the furniture, and other possessions, in the Parsonage, plus some potentially valuable memorabilia which had belonged to his family. Nicholls reasoned that all could be his if only he could also persuade the old man, somehow, to make a Will in his favour.

The other matter which I think gave him food for thought was his, then largely intuitive, feeling that, in some way or other, there was still a lot of money to be made from the works of the Brontë sisters.

He therefore decided that, were he allowed to do so, he would stay.

Chapter Seventeen

'Behold, these are the ungodly, who prosper in the world;
they increase in riches.'

Psalms 73:12

W hat happened next was that, of all things, I began to feel
very tired – almost as if life was draining out of me. It was
hard work to put one leg before the other, and I could hardly keep
my eyes open. Looking back, I see now just how much the things
that had happened had taken out of me. What with looking after
the Parsonage, Mr Brontë, Miss Aykroyd and Madam, and being
ill myself, it had all been too much for me.

Once again, Mother was the first to notice how quiet I was
and said I looked as if I needed a rest. Then she must have had a
word with Father, because the next thing I heard was that he
was going to have a word with Mr Brontë. The upshot of it all
was that it was arranged that I should go to stay at Mrs Dean's
Almshouses in Leeds for a while, and Mother said that she was
going to see to it that everything in the Parsonage was taken care
of whilst I was away.

I must say that it was not a prospect that pleased me greatly,
for I felt too tired to go anywhere and I had looked forward to
some time alone with Mr Nicholls, but even he said that I
should go, and so I did.

When I came back I felt different again, but there was a shock
awaiting me because, of all people, Father had taken to his bed.
I had never known him do that before and so I knew that
something must be badly amiss, but even so, when I saw him I
could not believe how ill he had become in such a short while.
He was as white as his pillow-case, and was having great trouble
in breathing, with the air making terrible sounds as it went in
and out. Not only that, he had a bowl by him and was all the

221

time coughing and spitting into it, so that I felt sick to watch him and to hear it.

Of course, it all meant more work for Mother, but she made no complaint, although it was evident to me that *I* should have to go back to work straightaway as she had enough on her plate. That did not bother me though, because I felt quite my old self again – and I was dying to see Mr Nicholls.

It was lovely when I did, and he hugged me so close that I thought he would never let me go, and one thing led to another so that us meeting again was all that I had looked forward to.

Then it was a case of getting the Parsonage back to rights as I liked it, and for that I needed help. Mother and my sister Eliza had done their best whilst I was away, but a lot of the little jobs had been left to one side, and I knew that it would take it out of me again if I tried to do it all myself,

I spoke to Mr Brontë about it, with Mr Nicholls there, and it was agreed that I could keep the young girl from the village who had been taken on so that I could deal with Madam when she was ill. That is what I had hoped for because she was one of my friend Milly Oldfield's young sisters, and I knew she needed the money. Before I went away there had been talk of getting rid of her after Madam's death, and I had half-expected her to be gone when I got back, but Mr Brontë saw that I needed the help and Mr Nicholls would back me up in anything.

So we kept young Emma on, and me and her worked wonders. She was not very big for her age, but she was strong and willing and was a great help to me. I made sure that she was treated a lot better than *I* had been at her age, and she paid me back by being cheerful and ready for anything. Most of all, although Mr Nicholls and me were always careful, I felt sure that she would keep her mouth shut – even with Milly – if she saw or heard aught that she should not have done as she was so grateful to me for keeping her job.

The weeks went by, and once the Parsonage was as I wanted it life became very pleasing and I was content for the first time in a long while. Only Father gave me anything to worry about for he seemed to be getting worse every time I saw him, and he had shrunk away to only half the man he was, and it seemed such a shame to see him lying there in bed with the weather outside so lovely. The doctor kept coming in, but he did little or no good, and in the end we all knew that Father was not going to get better.

He died on the 10th of August, 1855, when he was but 51 years old. The Doctor said he died of 'dust in his lungs', and that was hardly surprising because of his work. His going hit us all very hard indeed for he was a very gentle and fair man, and always heard us out and, even though Mother gave us hard smacks from time to time, he never laid his hand upon us – not like most of the fathers in Haworth who seemed to be very heavy-handed. But that was only a part of it for he was a man who was very much above the others in the village and looked up to by most. For a start, he had had a very good schooling and had more books than I have ever seen outside of the Parsonage. Even after me and my sisters had left school he took it upon himself to give us lessons, and made sure that we could read better than any of the other children.

I had never really thought of him properly until I saw him lying there in his coffin, and then I was so overcome that I just burst out crying and I sobbed so much that it seemed as if my tears had been bottled up for years.

Oddly enough, Mother showed little of what I knew she must be feeling, and I put that down to how worried she must have been about money, and I am so glad now that I was able to help her with that. Father's younger brother William took over his job as Sexton, and I know that he helped Mother from time to time as best he could, even though he was married and had 2 young lads of his own.

Needless to say, the funeral was a very sad affair, but we were all surprised by the number of folk who turned up, which was far more than for any of the Brontë funerals, due, in part, to the many Freemasons who came, some of them from Lodges quite a way away. Mother was overcome by the number who spoke to her and shook her hand, especially as some of them were far above our station in life.

Once I got over Father's death a bit, I think that the rest of

223

that year of 1855 was the happiest time of my life, especially as everything had been so awful at the start of the year with me so full of troubles of different sorts. Even after Madam was dead I had thought that Mr Nicholls might leave Haworth and, though he told me he would like to stay, I knew that Mr Brontë did not like him and I had wondered if he would be told to go.

Nothing happened, though, and we all settled down to a life that, after a few months, seemed as if it had always been the same. If anything, Mr Nicholls was more loving towards me than he had ever been. He was always putting his arm around me or holding my hand, and our lovemaking just got better and better now that we could be together longer and there was no need to watch out for Madam or anyone else coming. I still felt that it was grand to share a bed with Mr Nicholls for a whole night, instead of just a short time for making love, and at those times I felt that we were *really* together. Sometimes I would awaken very early and just lay there looking at him sleeping, with his hair all anyhow and, the beard apart, looking quite like a young lad. At times like that I often wondered what was in store for us both, and how things would end up – but then I put such thoughts from me and just took enjoyment from life as it was at each moment.

One moment when I was *more* than pleased, though, was when Mr Nicholls came to me one day and gave me 10 gold sovereigns that he had put in a little leather bag with a drawstring. Laughing, he said that Madam's Will had gone through all right, and the money in the bag was my 'witness fee'. It was the most money I had ever had all at one time in the whole of my life, and I laughed as well when I recalled how I had dithered before signing my name. The trouble was, I did not know what to do with it there and then. Mr Nicholls offered to put it in a bank for me, but I was not having that. I did not trust banks, and in any case I would have been afeared to go into one. I did not want my family to know about it either, because although I knew I had done nothing wrong I was sure that they would think I had. It would have been nice to have bought myself some things, but I dared not do that because that would also have brought questions that I was better without. In the end I hid them away safely with Miss Anne's book, and it was a little nest-egg that gave me great comfort to have by me.

Mr Nicholls was also very free in giving me little sums of money whenever I wanted to buy things for the house. Mind you, I think he got it from Mr Brontë in the first place, but whoever it came from I was able to replace many things that had served their time and get others to bring a little brightness to the place.

It was about that time, as I recall, that Mr Nicholls spoke to me about Miss Nussey who, it seemed, had written to him saying that she thought that Mrs Gaskell should write down the story of Madam's life. That was a good one, I thought, seeing as how most folk never knew what she was *really* like – but I let Mr Nicholls go on. Anyway, Mr Nicholls had written back, and told her that him and Mr Brontë did not agree with what she had said.

Afterwards, though, Mr Brontë had managed to read her letter for himself, and he had then told Mr Nicholls that he had changed his mind, and that he would write to Mrs Gaskell. Well, Mr Nicholls had not been very pleased about that, and he had taken the old man to task about it, saying that Madam had been *his* wife, and it was not Mr Brontë's place to agree or disagree.

Seemingly they had had quite a few hard words about it, but in the end Mr Nicholls had realized that he could not stop the old man from writing, and in any case he had come round to his way of thinking. There could be quite a lot of money in such a book – and that would rightfully come to him – and also it might give him the chance to get his hands on the letters that Madam had written to Miss Nussey that he had not seen. He knew that Madam had been able to get some out of the Parsonage when she was ill, and there were also others that he thought might show him up if folk got to see them.

He had already been in a good mood for quite a while by then, but the prospect of getting some money *and* having the letters back put Mr Nicholls in even better spirits, and in fact he was far happier than I had *ever* seen him, and it warmed my heart to have him so and to hear his laughter.

His good spirits also made him far more lively, and he gave much more time to his Church duties and was pleasant to all. To my surprise, he seemed even to have warmed to Mr Brontë, and would spend hours with him reading to him and humouring his every fancy. That was something that I could not understand at all, for each had used such harsh words about the other in the past that I had never thought to see them in company together as they were, let alone seeming to get on so well.

By then, though, I should have known Mr Nicholls well enough to have seen that there was always a good reason for everything he did, and such proved to be the case with Mr Brontë. Within what I recall as being only a short time after Madam had died, Mr Nicholls told me one night, with a great smile on his face, that somehow he had got the old man to make a new Will, and that almost everything would come to him!

I looked at him with an even bigger smile on *my* face, for I was quite sure that he was pulling my leg. Being civil with each other was a marvel in itself, so I just could not believe that Mr Brontë would ever leave all his things to Mr Nicholls. Somehow, though, Mr Nicholls had managed to get him to do so, and he showed me the Will, and then I was even more surprised because I saw that *I* was to get £30 when the time came! Mr Nicholls pointed that out to me, and said that it was him who had told Mr Brontë that I should have something – but I was not sure that that was true, for Mr Nicholls would say anything that suited him, and I knew full well that Mr Brontë had always had a soft spot for me. Even so, I gave every sign of believing him, and in ways that I knew would please him.

Things settled down again after that, and we got into a way of living that was very pleasing to me and, I think, Mr Nicholls, but I do not think that Mr Brontë was very happy. Mr Nicholls kept as many people as possible away from the Parsonage so that Mr Brontë hardly saw anyone else save me. I was as kind to him as I could be, for I had always liked him and, as I have said, I think he always felt something for me as well. Whenever

226

possible, I would sit and talk to him about the old days and that would bring back memories to him and we would enjoy a laugh together. I also saw to it that he had all the little treats that he liked so much, as they seemed to mean so much more to him the older he got. Even so, there were times when he told me that he felt as if he was in gaol, and that he had never thought he would ever come to such a pass. What surprised me, though, was that he would sometimes speak against Mr Nicholls just as he always had, and that made me wonder all the more why he had signed the new Will.

He cheered up a lot, though, when Mrs Gaskell came to see him and Mr Nicholls about writing the book about Madam. To my surprise, Mr Nicholls was very forthcoming to her. I knew that he saw that there was money in the book for him, but even so I was not expecting him to put himself out quite so much. Then she said she wanted to talk to me, and Mr Nicholls told me that I could but that I should watch my words. Well, that was easier said than done, for she kept on about so many different things, but I was careful and more or less told her what she seemed to want to hear.

As for me and Mr Nicholls – well, it was a time of such happiness for me, and we carried on, more or less, as a married couple when no one was about. There was never any mention of us really getting wed though, and although that was a secret dream that I still had I was more than content with the way things were for the time being, even though others seemed very put out.

I had always thought that folk would start talking about us sooner or later, and I would not be at all surprised if there had not been a few nods and winks long before that, but I had not realized just how much gossip was really going on until I was told about it by Mother.

Looking very stern, she took me to one side one evening when I went down and said that she thought that we should have a talk , and that we should walk out so that we could be on our own. That made me wonder even more about what seemed to be bothering her, but we put on our coats and bonnets without another word and walked along the lane towards

Change Gate. After a while she began speaking, very slowly, and then I learned what was worrying her.

I had known that Father had always been against Mr Nicholls and I think that, like some others, he had thought that there was something going on between us long before it really was. Now, though, from what Mother told me, it seemed as if he had really *known* something, and I wondered who had been talking.

Anyway, Mother said that Father had not thought it right that I should be living alone in the Parsonage with Mr Nicholls, and that he had been going to have a word with me but then he was taken so ill. Seemingly, though, it had stayed on his mind and, towards the end, he had made Mother promise that she would speak to me. She had told him that she would, but had put it off and put it off, but now, though, folk were talking all the more and she just thought that I should know of it and, in view of what Father had thought, that I should tell her what I was going to do about it.

Well, she had quite caught me on the hop, and I suppose it was because I felt so guilty that I had been getting more and more angry the longer she went on. I felt sorry for *her*, for she was only doing what she thought was right, but she was the nearest one to hand and so all my anger spilled out on her. I said that for one thing I was *not* alone with Mr Nicholls – Mr Brontë was there – and in any case Haworth folk would make tittle-tattle about aught, as she well knew. For my part, I told her, I could not see what was wrong with living with 2 clergymen, and if folk had anything to say they should say it to them, or the Church Council or to my face, instead of gossiping behind our backs.

Mother seemed a bit put out by the way I had turned on her and she started to get cross with me back. She said that that was all very well and good to say, but I knew they never would, and Father had thought there was something to it all anyway, and he had had the good name of the family to think about, especially with him being Sexton and all, and he had been fed-up with the sly digs. Now that *really* got me going. I said that the good name of the family had never seemed to bother him when he was

228

carousing with his cronies at the Lodge, or in the bars of the public houses, nor at those times when he had had to be brought home because he could not manage on his own. In any case, I was 28 years of age, and I would do as I wished. On top of that, I pointed out that I was taking good money into the house now, and if I left the Parsonage where was I to go to get so much, because I certainly was not going into a mill nor moving away into service with another family.

Mother was very quiet when I finished and when I looked at her I saw she had tears in her eyes and I knew I had gone too far. Then, in her soft voice, she said that I should know that Father and her had only been thinking of me and my good, and she thought I should say 'sorry' for what I had said about him and for how I had spoken to her. That I did, and readily, for I had said it all in temper and had wished the words back as soon as they were out, and I gave her a little hug and a kiss and we made up.

As for the future, Mother told me that she had kept her promise to Father and said her piece, now on my own head be it. However, she went on to tell me what I already knew – that Father had disliked Mr Nicholls, or 'that black-hearted Irish-man' as he had called him, on sight – and she warned me that if I had the notion that he would make an honest woman of me one day then I was a dunderhead. That made me go very red, but I let it pass and no more was said of the matter.

Something of our talk must have rankled with Mother, though – unless she did it just out of concern for me and my health – but the next thing I knew she had been to Mr Brontë behind my back and arranged for my sister Eliza to 'give me a hand' as she put it.

I was not at *all* pleased about *that*. Not that I minded having some more help, especially from Eliza as she was but 4 years younger than me, and we had always been good friends. No, it was because I thought she had been put there just to stop the talk, and probably in the hope that she would keep an eye on me and Mr Nicholls as well. Another thing that did not please me was when I found out, quite by chance, that our Eliza had been taken on at the same pay as me. By then I was getting 3/10d a week, after all the years I had been there and all that I had done for the Brontës. That was bad enough, but to have our Eliza coming in new and getting the same made me very cross – but not with her, because I was glad for her sake. I did speak to Mr Nicholls about it though, but he said to leave things be and that he would make sure that I did not lose out in the end, so I said naught more to anyone.

Of course, I also told him what Mother had had to say, but it did not seem to bother him at all. He said that if the people of Haworth had nothing to gossip about they would make something up, so we might as well be hanged for sheep as lambs and I agreed – although we were always more than careful when Eliza was about for I was not *that* sure of her.

I have said that Mr Nicholls was not bothered about any talk there might be, and that was in keeping with his general manner at that time for naught seemed to put him out, but then, very soon after, I saw him in such a temper as I had never seen even in his worst times with Madam.

As I remember it, I was working in the kitchen when he came storming in with a face so black with anger that I did not know what to say. He said he wanted to talk to me and that I should come to his study straightaway, and with that he stormed off. Eliza was with me at the time and she asked me what was wrong, but I did not know, and had to say so, as I hurried after him wondering if I was at fault somehow.

When I got to his room he snapped at me to shut the door and then, in a low voice but one that was full of rage, he began to pour out such words as a clergyman should not, to my mind, have even *known* of. I sat down in alarm, and just let it all go over me until I could get some sense out of him. Then, when he had calmed down a little, I got the story.

It seemed that he had said something to Mrs Gaskell, like that he would see to it that she would not lose by it out of the book she was writing as long as she let him see it first and changed anything not to his liking. That, he said, had not pleased her, and she had told him that she would not permit anyone to even *see* the book first, let alone change anything in it. As for not losing by it, she said she had it in writing from Mr

Brontë that *all* the money from the book was to be hers anyway! He said he had asked her what on earth she was talking about, but she had just said the same thing over again and had told him to see Mr Brontë if he did not believe her.

At that, and still not thinking that what she had said could possibly be right, he had rushed up to Mr Brontë's room and had asked him for the truth of the matter. Seemingly, Mr Brontë had not at first taken in what Mr Nicholls was talking about, but after a while he recalled that he had indeed told her that she could keep any money from the book, and that had so angered Mr Nicholls that he wondered how he had stopped himself from hitting what he called 'the b—— old fool'. Instead, he had tried to make him understand what could have been done with the money which, as he said, had been handed to Mrs Gaskell on a plate. Even if him and Mr Brontë had not kept it for themselves – which, without doubt, Mr Nicholls would have done – he had pointed out that so many things could have been done with it in the Parsonage and the Church and the Parish that just cried out for work on them.

It had all been of no use, though, and so he had gone back to Mrs Gaskell and told her that it was evident that Mr Brontë was not himself and had not known what he was doing when he said that she could keep all the money, and that she should take no notice of what he had written, and in any case *he* was Madam's next of kin and only he could make any agreements.

Mrs Gaskell, though, would have none of it. She said that she had only taken on the job of the writing because of her understanding with Mr Brontë and she was holding to it. As *she* saw it, Mr Brontë was quite in order to ask for a book to be written about his *daughter*, and to tell her whatever she needed to know to write it, and Mr Nicholls had come forward of his own free will to tell her other things. It was in vain for Mr Nicholls to say that he would not have done so had he known that he would not be having any of the money. That, she said, was something that he should have spoken about a long time before and now it was too late. Mr Nicholls told me that he had said that he would see a lawyer about it, but she just said that he could do what he liked because she knew she had right on her side.

After thinking about it – I do not know if he ever did see a lawyer – he came to see that there was nothing he could do, but he was very bitter about her and Mr Brontë and things were never the same between any of them after that.

It was all so sad, for it soured things in the Parsonage for a while, but after a few weeks things were back as they were.

I do not know where the next few years went to. It seems now that I just settled into a life of contentment and the weeks and months just rushed by. Of course, folk carried on gossiping, and there were still some of the older women who would not come to Church any more, and would shun me in the street and shops, but in the main the villagers came to accept things as they were. I did not care either way, though, for I was happy.

Only one thing bothered me slightly, and that was that, although we were to all intents and purposes a married couple, Mr Nicholls never ever talked about us really getting wed. I brought the matter up a few times because, truth to tell, sometimes the tittle-tattling got me down a bit, and anyway it would have been lovely to have been Mrs Nicholls and everything legal. Every time, though, Mr Nicholls just put me off, saying that we were all right as we were – were we not? – and that we should leave things as they were for a while and see what happened, and I just did not feel able to keep pushing and risk souring things.

Of course, I always wondered if the reason why he did not wish to wed me was because of the difference in our stations in life, and once I said that to him. To give him his due, he seemed really taken aback at the notion and said that such a thing had never been in his mind – but even so I always wondered. I could do naught about it, though, so I just let it be – thinking that he always seemed to know what he was doing and he always seemed to have my good in mind – and all the while things just drifted on.

I always felt sorry for Mr Nicholls, though, for from some of the snippets that got back to me it seemed that folk blamed him for the way things were rather than me, and many were also speaking out against him for keeping Mr Brontë so close. They

232

did not seem to give heed to the truth that he was now keeping to his bed all the time, and was far too weak to do anything or see folk for very long at a time. Looking after him meant a lot more work for me of course, but it was a labour of love for by then he was like a Grandfather to me.

Then, in the Summer of 1861, came the awful night when he was taken very bad. He could hardly breathe, but worse than that he was taken by fits for hours on end, with his whole body twisting and turning and him shouting out about the pains in his belly and his chest. Me and Mr Nicholls tried everything to soothe him, but it was no good and in the end I had to go for Dr Ingham. *He* could do nothing, and I wondered why we had bothered, but it would have looked bad for us had we not because Mr Brontë died that day.

His passing saddened me beyond all measure, and I sobbed my heart out at his funeral. Mr Nicholls did not seem to mind though for, after all, the pair of them had always been at loggerheads. He told me that his mind was more on what would happen next, and I must say that that was something that was very much to the fore of my thinking as well.

[*CC*] After Charlotte's death Mr Brontë was forced to think at length about the situation in which he found himself. Nearly blind, and not in very good health, he had to face the prospect of living with a man whom he detested, but upon whom he was compelled to rely because, for quite some time, Nicholls had carried out most of the parish duties, even though it was the old man who received the minister's stipend.

He could, of course, have rid himself of his assistant by the simple expedient of giving him notice, but then he would have had to go through all the tedious business of finding a replacement and I doubt whether he would have felt up to it. That apart, he had to acknowledge the fact that Nicholls was invaluable to him in his personal life, because it was he who dealt with the practicalities of everyday living at the Parsonage, including the running of the household. It seems that eventually, therefore, he decided that, if Nicholls *wished* to stay, he

233

would retain the Devil he knew – but it still went very much against the grain.

No words on the subject of Nicholls' remaining or going ever passed between the two men. For a few days after the funeral each waited, not a little apprehensively, for an approach from the other. When that did not happen, it was tacitly assumed that things would go on very much as before, but Mr Brontë was pleasantly surprised at the solicitous attention which he began to receive from his son-in-law.

Now, what other means of persuasion Nicholls employed are not known, but the fact remains that his efforts were completely successful insomuch as, within only three months of Charlotte's death, he had managed somehow to coerce the semiconfused old man into making a fresh Will. It was probably a combination of kindness and threats which did the trick because, although Mr Brontë seems to have resigned himself to spending what remained of his life with Nicholls, I doubt very much whether he would have agreed easily to bequeathing most of his worldly goods to him. One suspects that his greatest fear was that Nicholls and Martha would leave if he did not do as he was bid. As before, when Charlotte made such a threat, the possibility of being left alone in that grim house – at the mercy of complete strangers – would have terrified him.

Mr Brontë's Will was dated 20 June 1855. Apart from some minor bequests, including one of £30 to Martha Brown, Nicholls was the main beneficiary. He was also the sole executor. Mr Brontë referred to him as 'my beloved and esteemed son-in-law', a description which I find rather ironic considering their mutual dislike. It suggests that Nicholls had more than a little to do with the drafting.

We know that the mere thought of Nicholls marrying his daughter had almost caused the old man to have a stroke, and nothing had changed, or would change, over the years. In 1860, that is to say five years after Charlotte's death, John Greenwood, the Haworth stationer, remarked: 'Aye, Mester Brontë and Mr Nicholls live together still, ever near but ever separate.'

Ellen Nussey wrote to Nicholls shortly after her friend had died. She suggested that Mrs Gaskell should be asked to

234

undertake a reply to a 'tissue of malignant falsehoods' which had appeared in an article in *Sharpe's London Magazine*. Obviously intent upon letting sleeping dogs lie, Nicholls told her that Mr Brontë and he did not feel inclined to take any notice of the article.

It is also obvious, though, that he had *not* consulted Mr Brontë because when, in the following month, the latter, somehow, found out about Ellen's letter and Nicholls' reply there were heated arguments between the two men, and Mr Brontë wrote to Mrs Gaskell contradicting what his son-in-law had said and asking her if she would, in fact, write Charlotte's biography. He went on to say: 'Mr Nicholls approves of the step I have taken.' However, we have it from Martha that Nicholls neither knew or approved of what came later: 'Whatever profits might arise from the sale would, of course, belong to you.'

It seems that Nicholls was torn between avarice, and wanting the whole world to forget about the personal lives of the Brontës and him – well, for the immediate future anyway. The more publicity there was, the greater the danger that someone would start to wonder about so many deaths in the same household. He did not like anybody to visit Charlotte's grave, nor to pay any kind of tribute to her. Strange behaviour indeed for a husband who, we are asked to believe, was so devoted to his wife.

Another example of Nicholls' peculiar attitude to Charlotte's memory concerns John Greenwood's, the aforementioned stationer's, last child. When Nicholls learned that it was proposed to name it 'Brontë', in memory of Charlotte, he refused to perform the christening. Greenwood therefore went to see Mr Brontë who, as we know, was bedridden by then, when he knew Nicholls to be out, and subsequently the old man performed the ceremony secretly in his bedroom, using his water jug for the purpose. Nicholls discovered what had happened when he went to enter the details of the next christening in the register. According to Greenwood, he was furious and 'stormed and stamped, and went straight home to the Parsonage to Mr Brontë to ask him for his reasons in going directly against his wishes'.

235

The only thing which could tempt Nicholls into showing any interest in the Brontë family, or relaxing his arbitrary rules, was money. That is why I believe completely Martha Brown's assertion that he knew nothing of Mr Brontë's arrangement with Mrs Gaskell until it was far too late to do anything about it. For instance, he jumped at the chance of having Charlotte's oft-rejected *The Professor* published after her death, in spite of a statement by Mrs Gaskell's daughter that he had a 'sullen, obstinate rooted objection to any reverence being paid to Miss B. one might say at any rate to people caring to remember her as an authoress . . .' His avarice invariably overcame his natural caution, and his jealousy that the three Brontë sisters were being acclaimed for works that owed a lot to him.

G. Smith, Elder & Company published *The Professor* in 1857, and Nicholls even wrote a preface. He was well paid for the book and therefore, thinking that he was on to a real money-spinner, he looked forward eagerly to the financial negotiations that he anticipated in connection with Mrs Gaskell's biography of Charlotte.

He was cooperation personified in the writing of it. Mrs Gaskell said that he 'brought me down all the materials he could furnish me with'. He even wrote to Ellen Nussey asking whether she 'would allow us to see as much of her correspondence . . . as you might feel inclined to trust me with.' What effrontery from the man who had demanded an undertaking that she burn all his wife's letters to her!

Mention of these demands reminds me that earlier I referred to a note that was penned on Ellen's reply to the second letter on the subject from Charlotte. At that time I wrote that it bore another comment which I would mention, a little later. The second note reads: 'Mr Nicholls and Mr Brontë were the very first to break his (Mr Nicholls') objections – by requesting the use of CB's letters for Mrs Gaskell.'

How Ellen's letter to Charlotte came back into her possession, thus allowing her to write the notes, is not known; certainly it is highly unlikely that it was returned to her by Nicholls. One strong possibility that comes to mind is that it was purloined by Ellen Nussey when she had ample opportunity to sort through Charlotte's belongings while staying at the Parsonage during the period between her friend's death and her funeral.

Be that as it may, Nicholls discovered that he had underestimated Ellen; she supplied the letters but, wisely, she sent them direct to Mrs Gaskell. She also furnished her with other information, and thus the writing of the biography was able to begin. Only when it was well under way did Nicholls discover that old Mr Brontë had relinquished voluntarily the possibility of either of them receiving any cash from the proceeds, and then he was fit to be tied. The remembrance that he had so lowered himself as to write a begging letter to Ellen Nussey was bad enough, but the discovery that he was to gain no advantage from having done so was infuriating.

The Life of Charlotte Brontë was published in March 1857, and was the subject of much criticism. Mr Brontë said it was not true that he was eccentric and had a temper, and Nicholls thought that he had been portrayed as being unsympathetic to Charlotte.

However, the strongest attack came from Mrs Robinson's solicitors, who objected to what they considered to be the libellous story of the supposed affaire between her and Branwell. Mrs Gaskell was forced to remove it from subsequent editions, and was also compelled to issue a public retraction and an apology in *The Times*.

There were other protests, and complaints about inaccuracies, because Mrs Gaskell was very gullible, and far from objective in certain areas. It is clear that she was essentially a romantic novelist, and any statement made by her should be taken with a large amount of salt.

Although he may have been angry at what Mrs Gaskell wrote, and disappointed – to say the least – at having gained nothing for himself out of the book, Nicholls did not pursue the aspects of it which concerned him, but continued with his policy of drawing as little attention to himself as possible. Beholden to nobody, he led a quietly pleasant life, and bided his time until the happy day when his father-in-law would die.

As the months went by, a peculiar relationship developed between the ill-assorted trio in the Parsonage.

In 1856 Mr Brontë was an ailing and reclusive seventy-nine-year-old. Nicholls was a handsome man of thirty-eight and Martha was some nine years younger. The only description of her which I have been able to discover was written four years later by Mrs Gaskell's daughter, Meta, who stated that she was 'a blooming, bright, clean young woman'.

She and Nicholls were to be together in that house, virtually alone, for some six years. He had probably had affaires before going to Haworth, had been married until only recently and, as we shall see, years later he married again. A virile man, he had a healthy sexual appetite as, indeed, had Martha, It was a very cosy arrangement, but one which attracted attention and gossip in the village and did nothing to reduce Nicholls' unpopularity. John Brown, in particular, was not pleased.

As for Mr Brontë, he existed in a world almost entirely of his own making, hardly knowing which day was which or what was going on around him. There is no reason to doubt Martha's assertions that she was kind to him and saw to his needs, for which he was almost pathetically grateful, but there is reason to suspect that her motives were not entirely altruistic.

We have seen that Mr Brontë had bequeathed £30 to her, but I came upon something which made me wonder whether she was wheedling money out of the old man while he was still alive. What I found was a curious little letter which he wrote to her in July 1856. Now, they lived in the same house, and saw each other on a daily basis; so one would think that there was no necessity for letters to pass between them – but this one was different.

If there was ever an envelope it was probably addressed 'To Whom It May Concern', but what we know for certain is that the note reads: 'The Money contained in this little Box, consists of sums, given by me, to Martha Brown, at different times, for her faithful services to me and my children. And this money I wish her to keep ready for a time of need.'

Now what is to be made of that? At the time the note was written, Martha had worked at the Parsonage for some sixteen years, so why should it suddenly have been deemed necessary to have a letter confirming that the money in a box was hers – if, in fact, it was? Why should anyone have thought otherwise? Indeed, who was even to know of the very existence of the box if she chose to say nothing of it? It is all very peculiar.

One wonders whether there is any significance in the fact that Mr Brontë apparently wished her to keep the money 'ready for a time of need'. We know that he hated Nicholls, but he seems to have been genuinely fond of Martha. Did he, perhaps, envisage a time when his son-in-law would dismiss her, leaving her with no immediate means of support – or that, if she *had* received the money legitimately, Nicholls would demand to know from whence it had come and try to claim it for himself?

The only alternative explanation, and the one which I consider the most likely, is that it was Martha herself who felt the need for such a letter, which was written at a time when the old man was confused and so completely vulnerable that he would have put his name to anything. Whether she had been obtaining the cash by fair means or foul, but especially the latter, she had no idea what the future held for her, and she must have realized that when the old man died it might become very necessary for her to be able to prove that the money was hers.

It is not surprising that she never mentions this extra nest-egg in her deposition. We shall never know half of the chicanery that went on under that roof.

Nicholls apparently kept Mr Brontë a virtual prisoner, censoring his mail as far as was possible and fulfilling those of his social engagements which took his fancy.

One example of the state of affairs is displayed in a letter written by the old man to a Haworth couple who had invited him to dinner. He thanked them for their invitation, but then added, 'I never go out at night, nor indeed by day, to any parties. Mr Nicholls will, however, do himself the pleasure of visiting you at the time specified.' That was a little unfortunate for the hapless couple who, had they wanted Nicholls there, would presumably have invited him in the first instance. As it was, they were saddled with him willy-nilly because he was so pleased to get out of the Parsonage occasionally.

239

His continuing unpopularity in the village ensured that he received very few, if any, invitations in his own right, and even those people in what would normally be regarded as his social circle were never on intimate terms with him. For instance, Dr Ingham gave Nicholls' Christian name as 'Abraham' when he recorded Charlotte's death, and did not know what the 'B' represented. Nicholls soon protested about *that*, and a correction was inserted upon the death certificate.

By 1860 Mr Brontë was completely bedridden. Mrs Gaskell and her daughter visited Haworth and found him unshaven, but with 'such a gentle, quiet, sweet, half pitiful expression on his mouth'. They had a conversation, but then the old man asked them to leave 'in five minutes or so'. From what he went on to say, Mrs Gaskell became acutely aware that, 'he feared Mr Nicholls return from the school – and we were to be safely out of the house before that'. She also told Mr Williams about the visit, commenting that: 'Mr Nicholls seems to keep him rather *in terrorem*. He is more unpopular in the village than ever.' Nothing, therefore, had changed.

The Revd Patrick Brontë died on 7 June 1861, aged eighty-four years. His death certificate states that he died of 'Chronic Bronchitis, Dyspepsia, Convulsions 9 hours.' It is signed by the good Dr Ingham, and so we cannot be at all sure of the *true* cause of death. It was *probably* from natural causes, but who knows? Perhaps Nicholls finally became impatient and helped him on his way; it would have been in character.

Chapter Eighteen

'My beloved spake, and said unto me, Rise up, my love,
my fair one, and come away.'

Song of Solomon 2:10

Of course a meeting of the Church Trustees was called after
Mr Brontë died to see who was to take his place, and that
was what Mr Nicholls seemed to be thinking about all the time.
He told me that he felt sure that he would get the job, and I
dared not tell him what my Uncle was saying for, if you listened
to him, Mr Nicholls would be the last one to be chosen. Uncle
said that from what he could gather the Trustees were against
him, which was all that really mattered, but in any case so were
most of the villagers. Looking at me straight, he said that *I* had
not helped Mr Nicholls' chances either by staying on at the
Parsonage after his wife died – but he would say no more about
that for I was old enough to know what I was about, and it was
not really his business anyway.

Well, nothing happened for a while, and because of that Mr
Nicholls became even more sure that he would soon be in charge,
and he was always going on about the changes he would make
both in the Church and the Parsonage – and I could not help but
keep hoping that a change in my standing would be one of them.

Came the day, though, when the Trustees had him up before
them and told him that they had chosen somebody else – and
when he came back he was in a temper such as I had seen on
him only once or twice before. He almost spat out the words as
he told me what they had said. Seemingly, they had told him
that he could stay on in his present job if he wanted to, but he
would have to leave the Parsonage when the new man came. If
he did not wish to stay in his present job under somebody else,
they would be obliged if he would at least stay on and run

241

things until the new man had arrived. Mr Nicholls gave a bitter laugh when he told me that. He said that he would see them all in Hell first – and would leave when *he* wanted to, and that would be just as soon as he could get away from what he called 'this miserable place', and everyone in it. With that he slammed off up to the moor, and I had no chance to ask him where *I* stood in all that.

No real chance arose in the days straight after that either, for Mr Nicholls started going through the Parsonage like a man with the Devil prodding him. He began upstairs and went through everything as if he was Mother with a fine-tooth comb looking for nits. First of all he emptied the room where Madam had died, and then he began to put things in there that he said he would be taking with him. When he was done, though, there were still a lot of things left over and so I thought that I would have *my* share and I asked Mr Nicholls if I could take a few things. He said I could, except for some he had put to one side, and so I did – and more than a few! After all, I thought I had earned some more pickings in view of all I had done for the family over the years, and all for only a few pence a week at that.

I had the things taken to Sexton Cottage, where Mother put some of them into use. Most of them, though, especially all the books, letters, drawings and papers, were sealed up tight in some boxes and put in one of the back sheds.

As for the things that he had put to one side, after Mr Nicholls had looked at them all more than carefully, they were taken away by the carter – either to people who he had had in and had bought them or to the Auction Rooms at Keighley. Tom Oliver, the carter's son, tried to talk to me, but I would have none of it. I wondered then what I had seen in him at the time, and felt sorry for his wife who I had heard was carrying again, poor soul.

Soon the Parsonage began to look really bare, and there was little for me to do for it was a waste of time cleaning too much with folk in and out all the while, and not caring what they knocked against with the things they were carrying either. With time on my hands, I had more chance of watching what Mr

242

Nicholls was about, and at first I could make neither head nor tail of what he was up to as he acted very oddly indeed.

As I have said, he had been through everything very carefully, but even after a room was quite bare he did not seem content. I heard him tapping on walls and floorboards, and saw him peering into cupboards and every nook and cranny. Why, once, I even caught him looking up a chimney with a lamp, but when I asked him what he was after he just grunted and said that it did not matter.

I must indeed be a simpleton because it was only when I saw the piece of board in front of where I had found Miss Anne's book lying away from the wall that it came to me that it *was* her book he was looking for and, though I felt a bit guilty at seeing him waste so much time, I could not help but smile as I watched him carry on in the same way all over the house.

Only one good thing stands out in my mind about those few black weeks, and that was when Mr Nicholls came to me with the 30 gold sovereigns that Mr Brontë had left to me in his Will. They were in a bag such as the one that held the 10 sovereigns that I had had after Madam's Will only bigger, and I lost no time in hiding them away with the others and Miss Anne's book, for I thought that from what I could see I should soon have need of them.

Then came the evening when Mother asked me what it was in my mind to do when Mr Nicholls was gone. Would I stay on with the new man if he wanted me, or was I going to start looking about for a new place? Well, I did not know what to say to her, for the truth of the matter was that I just did not know. Mr Nicholls had been so distant of late that I had not felt able to ask him what was in *his* mind for me, if anything, and so I just said that there seemed to be plenty of time and I was just thinking on and waiting to see what happened – which was true.

That did not seem to please Mother or my Uncle, and I could not blame them for being out of patience with me for it was evident that there was *not* plenty of time, as anyone could see by the rate that the Parsonage was emptying. There was nothing for it, come what may, I would have to have it out with Mr

243

Nicholls, though that was not something I looked forward to with the mood he was in.

On the very next morning I went in search of him and found him upstairs going through the things that it seemed he was going to keep. I got very little welcome from him and that made me cross, but it also gave me cause to wonder if I was doing the right thing in bothering him at a time when he was so much out of sorts. For two pins I would have turned on my heel and left, but I overcame my fears and managed to get it out that I needed to talk to him at length. With that I sat on one of the boxes that he had got tied up and just waited, but not without a little fluttering inside.

He looked up at me from what he was doing with some papers and I saw that he was unsmiling – as indeed he had been for the past weeks. I had not been able to get above a word or two out of him at a time, and certainly there had been no lovemaking, or anything near it, to set my mind at rest that all was well betwixt us, but I had tried to make allowance for him as I knew that he had been hurt at not getting Mr Brontë's job, and had been so busy as well. Now, though, I felt that things had gone on long enough, and I had made up my mind that I was going to have it out with him.

Anyway, he just asked me, in a nice enough voice though, if it could not wait as he had a lot on his mind, but I said it had waited long enough and he knew by the sharp way that I spoke that I meant it. So he stopped what he was doing and sat on another box across from me.

It had been in my mind to lead up to things gently, but when it came to it I could not wait and just came out with it and asked where he was going when he left the Parsonage, and if he had given any thought to me.

At that he looked at me straight, drew a long deep breath, and said that he was going back home to Ireland, and that he was so sorry that he had not thought until then of how I must be feeling. He said that he had kept meaning to talk to me but, what with one thing and the other, the days had just slipped past. I waited for him to go on, but he stopped and just looked down and fiddled with a loose thread at his cuff, and so I thought it up to me to say something and I came out with all that I had bottled up inside me.

I told him that I did not want to be parted from him, and of how I had felt about him from the first time I clapped eyes on him – as if he did not know that already. I reminded him of all that we had gone through together and then – I just could not help myself, though it had not been my intent – I told him that it was only out of my love for him that I had kept silent about what I knew of his part in the death of Master Branwell and perhaps Miss Emily's, and what I suspected about the others, and because I trusted him when he said that one day it would all be worthwhile, and that had made me hope that the time would come when we would be wed – or at least living together openly somewhere far from Haworth.

He looked up sharply when I spoke of his part in the deaths and made as if to speak, but I just put two fingers on his lips, gave him a loving look, and asked him to hear me out. Then, at the end, I told him that I had seen Miss Anne's book years before and that I now had it hidden away safely.

I stopped. I had said all that I wanted to say, and now I waited all a-quiver to hear from him.

It was a long time coming, and I began to think that I had gone too far, but then he came over and sat beside me. He put a hand to each side of my face and gave me such a long, loving kiss that I felt myself shaking. Then, in a soft voice, he said that he was so sorry that he had not made time to speak to me before. He asked me to forgive him, and told me that he should have known how worried I would be not knowing what was in his mind. With his arm around my shoulders, and looking straight into my eyes, he then went on to say that he had never thought other than that we should leave together, and he just wished that he had made that quite clear to me sooner – although he had thought that I would take it for granted. As for our being wed, that had *always* been in his mind, but he had thought it best to leave it to one side for a time to see how I got on in Ireland, for he did not intend ever to leave there again and that would cause trouble between us if I wanted to and he did not.

245

I could not help it – I just burst out sobbing and clung to him tightly with tears streaming down my cheeks. For quite a while I was not able to say a word, for he had been so loving and had done away with all my worries.

When I began to calm down he gave me one of his lovely Irish kerchiefs to dry my eyes and face with, and then I just sat there snuffling and taking great gulps of air whilst trying to smile at him until I could speak. Then I told him how pleased I was that he had taken away all my fears – not only that he did not want me and would leave without me, but of all the gossip, and probably worse, that I would have had to face alone when he was gone. I told him again how much I loved him, and said that, come what may, he could trust me always.

From that moment on I really *was* happy. There had been times before when I had felt that my life could never be better, but now I knew such *deep* contentment that I felt I could bear anything that might lie ahead. Only one thing bothered me, and now I shall never know the truth of it. To this day, I often wonder how he would have answered me had I not told him first that I had Miss Anne's book. How I wish that I had kept my mouth shut about it and let him speak first – I could always have brought up what I knew later. But it is no use crying over spilled milk, then or now, and I just got on with things.

It was just as well, though, that I felt able to deal with other matters after our talk, and that I had nerved myself for one of them, for I had a terrible time with Mother and my Uncle when I told them what was to happen. To write of all that was said would take an age, so I shall just content myself with saying that it all went much as I had feared. Uncle was thunderstruck and Mother burst into tears. Uncle then started to rant on alarmingly, and was so beside himself with anger that at one stage he said I was little more than a common whore and that he had always thought as much. Then Mother said how sad I had made her, and agreed with a lot of what Uncle had said, saying that Father would have said the same. What seemed to bother them most, though, was not my happiness but that there would be a lot of talk in the village.

Well, Mother may have been sad, but that was as naught to

how sad *they* made *me* – yes, and angry too at some of the things that Uncle had said against me. Yet it was no more than I had expected, so I was steadfast and just told them that I was sorry for all the trouble that I was bringing to them and asked that we might part without more hard words when the time came.

The thought of telling them had been a great burden on my mind, and so once it was over and done with my spirits rose again and I was able to enjoy getting ready to leave in full. I must say, though, that things between us were never to be the same again.

When it got nearer the time for us to go, Mr Nicholls made sure that there was nothing left in the Parsonage that he wanted to keep or sell, and he let me have my pick of the rest which I gave to my family on the understanding that some of the things were still mine should I ever want them back. After that I wanted to clean the Parsonage from top to bottom for the new people before we left. It would not have been such a big job, for now most of the rooms were quite bare, but Mr Nicholls would not hear of it. Apart from bearing a grudge against the Trustees and the new man, whoever he might be, he said that the world should see what a pigsty the Brontës had lived in, despite the airs and graces that Madam and her father had put on.

As it turned out, though, we were busy enough before leaving without taking on extra work anyway, what with seeing to the plans for moving ourselves and the things to Ireland and all, but I could not help but notice that the talk in Haworth had started already. In fact, several folk had the gall to ask me if it was true that I was going with Mr Nicholls, and then sniffed as if at a bad smell – and there were many such in the village – and walked away with their noses in the air without another word. I did not really mind, though, for it was no more than I had expected from that narrow-minded lot, nor was the silence that I had to bear whenever I popped home. As for Mr Nicholls, he got much pleasure from shocking everybody, saying that it was but a small return for the misery that he had suffered at their hands over the years.

At long last the day of our leaving came, and it was one of mixed feelings for me. I was sad to leave my family, especially as Mother and Uncle were so nice to me after all the hard words, although they said nothing at all to Mr Nicholls and acted as if he was not there. On the other hand, I cannot tell you how happy I was to be off at last, and how much I was looking forward to seeing Ireland and making a new life with Mr Nicholls. The only so-called friend who bothered to see me off though was Milly Oldfield, and I promised her that I would pay for her to come and see me in Ireland when we were settled in, which made me feel very grand. On top of everything else, and for the very first time, I was able to wear the Forget-Me-Nots brooch that Mr Nicholls had given me all those years before. He noticed it straightaway, and gave me a little peck on the cheek saying that those days seemed such a long time ago now.

[*GG*] From what Martha tells us, it would appear that Nicholls was greatly surprised when the Church Trustees did not offer him the living of Haworth following Mr Brontë's death, and this surprise is shared by most of the Brontë biographers. He had been running the parish, virtually single-handedly, for years, and there had never been any question of his ability to do so.

However, and despite the 'testimonial of respect' that Charlotte said the people of Haworth had presented him with in 1853, the Trustees had their very own good reasons for not preferring him. Not only did they know of his general unpopularity, but they were not at all pleased about his relationship with Martha. It may well have been that one or two of them were also perceptive enough to have their suspicions about the Brontë deaths.

We do not know whether the Trustees gave him any reasons for not wanting him as their Minister but, all in all, Nicholls decided that the sooner he was out of Haworth the better for all concerned. He rampaged through the Parsonage, and then sold most of the furniture and other possessions. Within four months he was back in Ireland.

Ellen Nussey wrote to George Smith: 'It was a shock to me discovering that he had been ransacking his wife's things, so speedily after losing her – unfavourable impressions deepened still more, afterwards, by what seemed a most selfish appropriation of everything to himself, and when there were near relations living both of Mr and Mrs Brontë's side.' One suspects, however, that Ellen's sentiments were not entirely altruistic. Doubtless she, too, would have welcomed a few mementoes!

In her deposition, Martha makes it quite clear that she hoped that Nicholls would marry her once Charlotte was out of the way, and certainly she was not prepared to allow him to disappear from her life just like that. She wanted some form of confirmation that he was actually going to where he had *said* he was going, because she had no intention of losing the goose and the golden eggs. It seems, also, that she had an additional incentive for wanting to leave Haworth. In such a small community it was inevitable that there should have been rumours about what was going on between her and Nicholls, and the villagers had not approved. There was not much that they could have done about it before, but now circumstances had changed. They had seen to it that Nicholls was not offered the living, and now that he was about to depart Martha was not prepared to be left behind to face the music alone. Had she allowed him to go without her she would have been jobless and with no guarantees for the future. As she tells us, even her own mother and uncle would not have been very sympathetic.

As for Nicholls, he must have wondered whether there would ever come a time when he would be free from ties with Haworth and the Brontës. Whatever his feelings about his lover – and she had been a good companion and a faithful ally – I do not think that he ever had any intention of marrying her. However, he did not want to tell her that just then because he realized just how dangerous it might be to have an embittered Martha at large. Reluctantly, therefore, but putting a brave face on it, he decided to take her to Banagher with him.

249

Chapter Nineteen

'My days are past, my purposes are broken off, even the
thoughts of my heart.'

Job 17:11

Just as Madam had done, I found the journey to Ireland
both exciting and tiring. Never in my life had I been so far
from Haworth, or been on a boat, or seen so many new things. I
could not help but remember how I had wished it was me when
Mr Nicholls took Madam on the same journey, and now I could
not believe that it was really happening to me. Indeed it *all*
passed like a dream – and seems so even now – from which I did
not awake until we came at last to the home of Mr Nicholls'
family at Banagher.

This was something I had been dreading. As it happened,
though, everybody was very nice to me – much nicer, Mr
Nicholls told me, than they had been to Madam. On the way
over, I had asked him what he had told them about me and how
he was going to pass me off, but he told me not to worry. They
already knew of me from his mention of me over the years, and
now he had told them that I was a good friend who was coming
with him to help him set up his new home. They had asked no
questions, and he had said no more.

It was a grand house where the family lived, and I was given a
bedroom the like of which I had never seen before – or, indeed,
since. I was so glad that I had talked Mr Nicholls into taking me
over to Keighley before we left, where I had spent some of my
sovereigns on buying new clothes and other bits and pieces that
he helped me to choose, for I did not feel at all out of place.
Indeed, Mr Nicholls told me that I settled in with his family,
and they with me, far easier than Madam had done. Seemingly
she had also bought new clothes, but she had not asked for any

250

help from him and so she had looked very much out of place there and all the time seemed bent upon making folk believe that she was far grander than she was.

We stayed at the house for just over 2 months, and during that time Mr Nicholls showed me lots of places and we had many long talks. First of all, we spoke about what he was going to do for a living, and he told me that he had already made up his mind that he *was* going to leave the Church, which he had never really liked. He said that he had talked it over with his family and friends, and they had all said he could do worse than become, of all things, a farmer!

That was something that I had *not* expected, for I had not thought that he would wish to work hard and dirty his hands, but after he told me the ins and outs of it I saw that it did not have to be like that for him; so I said that if that was what he wanted I would be happy to be a farmer's wife – for I had never known a poor one in spite of all of them always carrying on as if they did not have a penny to bless themselves with.

Then, little by little over the weeks he told me what he said was the whole story of the deaths in the Brontë family – although I suspect that still I do not know everything – and of the feelings of everyone at the time and the parts they played. Of course, I already knew some of it, and suspected some more, but even so I was taken aback by some of the secrets he seemed to feel free to tell me then – and others that he has dropped since – and to this day I do not really know how I think of him all in all. He has told me, he says, of everything that led up to the deaths, and the way he puts it I feel when he is speaking to me that there was little other that he could have done. Later, though, when we are apart, doubts come to me and sometimes I see him as the 'black-hearted Irishman' that Father called him. So I had my doubts about him then, and still do, but I can speak only as I find and he has always been good to *me*, and I know that he loved me once even if he perhaps does not do so now.

Anyway, during the time with his family he was out and about, sometimes for whole days, looking at farms, and there seemed to be so many for sale that I wondered why and whether

251

he was doing the right thing. I put that to him, gently, but he told me not to fret – it all depended upon how much money you had behind you to run things and how you went about doing them, and he knew full well what he was about. So he carried on looking, and then the day arrived when he came in, all happy and excited, saying that at last he had found what he wanted, and he was sure I would like it as well. He wasted no time, but the very next morning he took me off to see it and I loved it – Hill House – just as much as he did, and so he shook hands with the farmer and the deal was done.

As soon as all the paperwork was settled, Mr Nicholls took on 4 men to help him with the farm, and 2 girls to give me a hand with getting the house to rights after the workmen had finished making it sound and painting it as we wished. When I say that he took on the girls, by that I mean he brought some to see me and took them on after I had chosen the ones I liked – which made me feel very grand and much happier than I would have been if he had just taken them on without asking me – and I thought him very caring for doing so.

Well, Mistress or not, for such was how they addressed me, I was not going to be another Madam. I worked alongside them and as hard as they did, and we cleaned that house from attics to cellars until you could have eaten off the floor. Then Mr Nicholls sent to England for the things that he had kept from the Parsonage to be sent over, and in the meantime we went out buying other things – which was a great joy for me. I must own up to it, I have always liked shopping and spending money – but then I felt even more happy for, to my mind, I was setting up my very first home of my own and I wanted everything to be right.

In the end everything was finished just as we wanted, and the place looked lovely – as I had always thought that the Parsonage could have looked had enough money been spent on it, instead of in dribs and drabs – *and* there were curtains to the windows. My girls had worked very hard and so I gave them some extra money without telling Mr Nicholls. I had been very surprised when he told me how little they and the men would work for. My wages at the Parsonage had never been very good, but theirs were so miserable that I felt quite shamed each week when I paid them and I wanted them to know that I was pleased with them. What Mr Nicholls did with the men was up to him.

At first it did not seem possible that all the work at Hill House was finished, and that we were in our own home at last. Mr Nicholls and me had separate bedrooms, which had been his suggestion, and I must say that I did not take to the notion at first. Then, though, he told me that that was how all the best folk went on, and I could have mine painted and made as I wished, and could use it as my own little sitting room as well, and so I agreed for, after I had thought about it, I liked the thought of having somewhere of my very own.

For those first months we lived as happily together as two people ever could, and Mr Nicholls started saying that if we were to be wed we should start about setting a date. Something now held *me* back, though, for, little by little, I had begun to have doubts about the whole business.

At first, it had all been new and exciting, and there had been so much to do that I hardly had a moment to think. Then, once we moved in, I enjoyed being Mistress in my own house – especially when Mr Nicholls was away on business – and learning things about the farm, and keeping chickens and all manner of things. Slowly, though, as happens in most lives, we settled into a way of life – but it seemed to have more bad about it than good for me.

We always got up very early, and I did not mind that one whit for I had done so all my life, but then Mr Nicholls was out for most of the day and I found myself doing very much the same as I had done at the Parsonage – but amongst strangers. In the main, the only folk I saw during the day were the girls, and sometimes one of the men, and what with me being from England and their Mistress as well they did not seem able to let themselves go with me. I tried to talk to them, and to learn as much as possible about their lives and the places thereabouts, and to be as friendly as I could, but it was no good – I did not understand half that they said, nor them me, and there was always a bar between us.

I found myself becoming more and more lonely and

253

homesick. I missed my family and Milly Oldfield more than I had ever thought possible, and even started thinking more fondly of Haworth and the folk there. The weather did not help either, but then I never was happy in the Winter. In truth it was far warmer than Haworth at that time of year, but it seemed to do nothing but rain, so that the yard was like to a quagmire. I could not go out, and there was mud everywhere so that I started to see the newness going from our lovely house far sooner than I had thought.

Sometimes we went into town in the little horse and trap that Mr Nicholls had bought, but whilst he knew everyone and enjoyed himself nobody spoke to me unless they had to and I stopped going. As for Mr Nicholls' family, they were always very nice to me and I got on well with his cousins, but they were far above me in station and I never really felt fully at ease when we went there, especially with us not being wed and all – not that I could see things changing much when we were. Some of his cousins had told me of how they had felt about him marrying Madam, and I may have been wrong but I had little doubt that they would not feel much different about me.

It was going on for Christmas 1862 when I knew for sure that I could stay in Ireland no longer. By then I was homesick beyond recall, and nothing that Mr Nicholls or his family tried to do to cheer me up could make me feel any better.

Looking back, I think that, in a way, it was probably Mr Nicholls himself who had started me thinking in earnest of going home. In the August he had gone to England on business and had then stayed with his friend Mr Grant at Oxenhope, near Haworth. They had gone into Haworth several times and when he came back he told me that he had seen my Mother, and made me laugh with some of the things that were going on in the village and what folk that I knew were getting up to. That started me thinking of home again, though, and as thoughts began turning towards Christmas I missed being there with my family, and remembered only too well all the good times that I had had shopping and getting presents ready and going to parties and dances and suchlike with my friends. I do not think that I have ever been so miserable and, all in all, I was sorry that

I had come, but I did not know how to get out of it, and in the end I had to have a proper talk with Mr Nicholls to see how he would feel if I went back.

It was not something that I looked forward to, for I must say that he was very loving to me all the while, even when I was out of sorts and not good company, and I could not have wished to have been treated more kindly – although, being the worrier that I am, I often wondered how much of that was real and how much because of what I knew and because I had Miss Anne's book. Then there was the feeling that he and his family might think secretly that he was marrying beneath him, and I did not want to hurt him in that way. No, I loved him far too much to force him into a marriage that he did not want, and certainly I did not wish him to come to think of me as he had of Madam – and end up as she had done.

Anyway, one night I told him most of how I felt, and then sat back and waited to see what he would say.

I suppose that, in my secret thoughts, I had really expected that he would be pleased at the idea of getting shut of me, and so I looked at him closely for any signs of pleasure, however much he might try to hide them, but I saw none – in fact very much the contrary. Either he was a better actor than I knew he could be or he showed real feeling, but to this day it pleases me to think that the second was the truth for he seemed really put out and looked at me for a long while with what I felt to be real sadness all over his face.

In the end he said that he truly did not want me to go, and would be most unhappy if I did. He spoke of how well we got on together, and asked if there was anything – anything at all – that he could do to make my life happier. For example, would I like to go back to Haworth for visits from time to time, or have my sisters or Milly Oldfield over to stay when the weather was better? Little did he know that I had already thought of those things, and some others, but I had come to see that whilst they would help they would not answer my needs in full. I told him that, and we talked on for quite a while, and in the end he came to see that I was in earnest and said that if going back was what I really wanted he felt too much for me to stand in my way – even if he could. He wished, though, that I would think on for a while longer to see if I changed my mind, especially with the coming of the better weather. If I did not, we would have to come to some agreement for the future. I did not know what he meant by that at the time, but I let it pass for there had been enough deep talking for one night.

Well, I let a month or so go by, and in that time Mr Nicholls did everything he could to make me happier, and I felt so sorry for him when I just had to tell him that I was sure that I wanted to go home. Again he seemed very sad, and I thought that I saw a tear in his eye, but he told me that he would stick to his promise not to try to hold me against my will, and would do all that he could to help me. He said that we should talk about what I was going to do and where I was going to live when I got back, for he thought that things might be hard for me in Haworth on my own, and he did not wish to see me in want, so he would see to it that I was never in need of money. There was a great deal more in that vein, but it is enough to say here that what we settled on pleased us both.

Mr Nicholls came all the way to the boat with me, and we stayed overnight at an inn. That night we made love for what we both believed, in our deepest thoughts, would be the last time and it was something that I shall never forget. There was such gentleness and passion mixed that next morning I felt drained. When it came time for us to part I hung on to him crying so much that I was like to change my mind, but I knew that things had gone too far for that.

Almost the next thing I knew I was back in Haworth for Christmas, but it was not the joy that I had expected. Everything was as if I had never left, with all the stares and the nudging, and the gossip and jeering that I knew was going on.

The last straw came when, after only a few weeks, Mother asked me what I had in mind to do with myself, for she did not know that I had some money of my own and also that Mr Nicholls had seen me right when I left. She kept on and on about me getting a job as soon as possible and trying to live down my past, as she put it, until I felt I would scream every time she opened her mouth. My Uncle was not much better either. He said that there was no chance of me getting my old job back at the Parsonage as the new man, a Mr Wade, had brought his own servants with him – as if *that* bothered me, for I could never have faced going into that house again.

Anyway, that was that. Already I was missing Mr Nicholls and, oddly enough, Ireland, and what with that and everything I had come back to I made up my mind to leave Haworth. I wrote to my sister Ann, by then Ann Binns, who was living with her husband Ben in Saltaire, and asked if she could put me up for a while until I had sorted things out. We had always got on well together, so I felt sure they would have me – and they did.

Well, I was there for quite a time, and Ann and Ben were very good to me, but all along I kept thinking about what I was going to do with myself next because I did not want to outstay my welcome.

I thought about going into service somewhere away from Haworth and all the tittle-tattle, but somehow I did not fancy being amongst folk I did not know. The whole thing went round and round in my mind, and I began to feel quite bothered about it all, but then it was all settled by a letter from Milly Oldfield.

She told me that old Dr Ingham's housekeeper had died and that he was badly in need of somebody to take her place, and said that she had thought of me right away.

Now I knew the Doctor, and he knew me well enough, and I was sure that he would take me on. Not only that, I knew that his house – which was the old Manor House by Cook Gate – would be much easier to take care of than the Parsonage, but I could not make up my mind whether I wanted to go back to Haworth again. All of my being yearned to be back where I belonged, but I wondered if I could stand all the talk.

For two whole days I thought on it all the time, and could not sleep for it, but in the end it was Ann who decided me. After I had told her what was bothering me she said I should go back and give it a try. If I did not like the work or anything else I could always leave and I would be no worse off than I was then. On the other hand, if all went well it would be the answer to all my worries.

That did it. I wrote to Dr Ingham at once and it was but 2 days before I had his answer. He told me that he was still in need of a housekeeper, and asked me to be good enough to go and see him as soon as I could. Well, not to make a long story of it, that is what I did and we got on very well together. I had never thought much of him as a doctor, but he was always quite a nice man and I was sure that he would be a good employer.

Within a week I was living there and everything went very smoothly. I wrote and told Mr Nicholls what had happened and he seemed very pleased for me. Not only that, he asked me to go over to see him in the Summer and that made everything perfect.

The year 1863 was quite a good one for me. All went very well at the Manor House and, better still, Mr Nicholls sent me the money to go to Ireland. He met the boat in, and I must say that my heart seemed to give a turn when I saw him there waiting for me, and looking quite as handsome as ever. We hugged and kissed each other without a thought for what the other folk might think, and tears of joy rolled down my cheeks. I would swear that his eyes were not quite dry either.

It was a time that I shall never forget. Hill House had quite settled down after all the work we had done on it, and all the folk there seemed really pleased to see me again.

My old room looked just as I had left it, and Mr Nicholls had seen to it that there were flowers everywhere, but, truth to tell, I did not spend much time in it. During the day we were out and about, and at nights we cuddled up together in Mr Nicholls' big bed just as we had done before.

At the start I was quite shy with him, for it had been a long time since we were last together in that way. Soon, though, we were every bit the same as we had been before I left and we made love as if we had never parted.

It was all too good to last and it seemed that no sooner had I got there than I was packing again to go back to Haworth. I had dreaded leaving, but I knew I could not stay. Mr Nicholls saw me to the boat as before, and I clung to him so tightly when it was time to part as I had a feeling that I would never see him again. We kissed for the last time and I turned to go aboard the boat, but then I burst into a flood of tears and hurried up the gangway without looking back.

By the time we were leaving I had calmed myself and I was able to stand by the rail on deck and wave him goodbye. He waved back, very slowly and, I thought, sadly, and then I watched until we were out of the harbour and I could see him no longer.

Life went on quietly back at the Manor House for the rest of the year and soon it was Christmas and the New Year and my spirits began to lift a little with the thought that Spring would not be *that* long a-coming.

I kept writing to Mr Nicholls, and he to me, but as usual his letters told nothing of his feelings for me and sometimes I wondered whether he was afeared of putting them into words. That did not bother me though for I *knew* how he felt and I looked forward so much to seeing him again in the Summer.

So all was going quite well until one of the worst days I've ever had when I had a letter from him which changed my whole life.

He told me that he would always love me and look after me, but went on to say that, as I knew only too well, it was not in his nature to be without the company of a woman and, as I had made it quite clear that I was not coming back, he was going to wed his cousin Mary Bell – who I had met and got on well with. He hoped I would understand and that I would feel able to go to the wedding – for which he would send me some extra money.

Well *of course* I understood how he felt – I felt the same, for it is not in the nature of a person not to have some loving – but all the same it was a black day for me. I cried on and off for most of it, and at one point I made up my mind to go back to him if he would have me – but then I knew it could not be. One thing I was sure of though, and that was that I would not go to the wedding – for that I could *not* have borne – and in any case it would not have been fair to Mary. In the end I wrote to him saying that I *did* understand how he was placed, and giving him and his wife-to-be my best wishes. Then I said that I hoped that *he* would understand why I did not feel able to go to the wedding and I asked him to make up some excuse for me.

On the day he was to be married I went to Haworth Church and thought about what was happening at that time in Ireland, and what Madam, whose body lay not far from where I sat, was thinking about it all. I went over all that had taken place since I had first known him, and I think it was then that the notion first came to me to write it all down – though I have not done so until now.

After that time nothing was ever the same for me, and I think that it had a lot to do with the illness that befell me at the end of 1864.

To this day I do not know what was up with me, but I was very poorly indeed and not able to do any work at all. Dr Ingham was not much help. He was very kind, and kept dosing me with this and that, but I could see that he did not know what ailed me and I was getting no better. That bothered me greatly because, the illness to one side, I was doing no work – just lying in my bed and being looked after.

In the end I told him that I thought it would be better if I went home to my Mother and my Uncle, so as not to be a burden to him and the other servants, and that perhaps the change might help.

I must say that that seemed to take a load off his mind and certainly he agreed right away. He saw to it that Mother was told and that I was taken to Sexton House in a carriage – wrapped up so warmly that I could barely breathe.

Of course, I was bothered about losing my job were I to be away for too long, but he put my mind at ease by saying that he would get by until I was better.

He kept coming to see me, but I took none of the medicines that he left. Instead I had Mother's broths and cooking, and with her nursing I slowly began to feel better and was able to go back to the Manor House in the February.

I had kept writing to Mr Nicholls all that time – much to Mother's annoyance as, in her mind, he had led me astray and then rid himself of me – and so he knew all that was going on and was very pleased that I had been able to go back to work.

Later in the year, though, Mother became ill and no matter what Dr Ingham or anybody else did for her she seemed to get no better. I was very worried about her, because there was not really anybody in the house who could nurse her all the time, and in the end I just had to ask the Doctor if he would let me go home and look after her.

Once again he was very good. He said that he too was very worried about her, and that he thought she should have someone by her.

Well, sad to tell, nothing that I or anyone else could do was enough to save her and she died in 1866. Of course, her death upset me greatly, especially as I kept thinking that perhaps she had caught what ailed her from me, but I must say that Mr Nicholls was very kind. He sent me the money to go over to Banagher and I stayed with him and his wife in Hill House.

I had thought that it would be a very uneasy stay – with what had passed between Mr Nicholls and me, and with Mary no doubt having her own thoughts about it – but we all got on very comfortably together and it was to be the first of many such visits.

I kept on at the Manor House, but all the while I was plagued by illness – which Mr Nicholls put down to Haworth being so cold and damp. Although I was barely 40 I felt worn out at times and nowhere near my usual self, and in the end I just had to give up working.

As always, Mr Nicholls was kindness itself at that time. He made sure that I had enough money, and had me over to Ireland whenever I felt like going. Once he even wrote asking me to go to live at Hill House, not as a servant but as my home, but I did not feel that I could do that. Instead I stayed in turn with members of my family – mostly my sisters.

The time came, though, when I felt that I could not carry on putting on others and that I really needed somewhere to live of my own. I said as much to Mr Nicholls and he was quick to agree. He said that I should find a place to rent that I liked and he would see to everything else.

Well, I looked and looked around Haworth and in the end I set my heart on this little cottage in Stubbing Lane and I moved in here in 1877. I do not think that Mr Nicholls thought much of my choice, nor was he very happy about me living alone, but

261

it suited *me* and I have been very happy here. One thing I know made him laugh – on a whimsy I named it 'Bell Cottage' and the name makes me smile many a time. Many of the villagers cannot fathom the name. I am often asked about it, but I just smile. For those who *have* worked it out it just adds to their notion that I am no better than I should be anyway, and they know what *they* can do and all!

There is little left to tell. Mr Nicholls still writes to me, and I to him, and he makes sure that I have enough money to live comfortably, with no need to work. Not only that, every year he invites me over to Ireland and sends me the money when I decide to go. I enjoy my visits, although I do not go every year. Mary and me get on very well, and now me and her are like sisters. I still love Mr Nicholls in my own quiet way, but we are both content with the way things have turned out, and it pleases me to see how he has got on. He has bought another farm since I left and seems to be on the way to becoming rich, not only from them but from what he tells me has come his way from the writings of the Brontës and other bits and pieces. I do not begrudge him that for one moment for, as I have said, he looks after me well enough.

For my part, I quite enjoy my little life, and I even have a gentleman friend in Keighley who I see from time to time, though I shall never feel for him as I do for Mr Nicholls. Sometimes he talks about us getting wed, but I have made it plain that I shall never do so. Mr Nicholls has spoiled me for other men, and in any case I am too set in my ways now to live with somebody else.

Still, enough of all that, which has naught to do with what I set out upon. I have told the *real* story of how the Brontës lived and died, and in doing so I have eased the burden which has lain upon my mind these many years – although I shall never be proud of the part that I played, and I often pray for forgiveness.

As I have said to Mr Coutts, I do not want to harm Mr Nicholls in any way, shape or form, and so I do not want what I have set down to be made known until we are both dead and have gone to make our peace with God, if such be possible.

Then Mr Coutts can make such use of it as pleases him or those who come after him.

[Signed]   Martha Brown

I swear on my Oath that what I have set down here is the whole truth, and I give full Authority to Mr James Coutts, of Messrs Coutts and Heppelthwaite, Solicitors, of Palmer's Buildings, Conduit Street, Keighley, in the West Riding of Yorkshire, and his Heirs, being members of the said Firm, to use both what I have written and that said to have been written by Miss Anne Brontë in any way that he or they may see fit, but only after my Death and that of Mr Arthur Bell Nicholls, of Hill House, Banagher, King's County, Ireland.

Signed this Eighth day of January in the year of our Lord One Thousand Eight Hundred and Seventy-eight.

Martha Brown

Signed by Martha Brown, in our presence who in her presence, and we in the presence of each other (all being present at the same time) have hereto subscribed our names as Witnesses.

James Coutts   Solicitor,
                                      Mere House,
                                      Midhope Street,
                                      Keighley,
                                      West Yorkshire

Edmund Beasley   Solicitor's Clerk,
                                      21, Cottage Lane,
                                      Keighley,
                                      West Yorkshire

[*CC*] Nicholls' arrival with yet another English woman must have caused quite a stir in Ireland, and though Nicholls was nothing if not plausible, and had a good tale ready, there would have been many who wondered why he had brought a 'housekeeper' all the way from England. One thing that pleased him greatly, however, was that, at long last, he had been able to give up the cloth, which was something he had wanted to do for years. Now that he had enough money to go into business that is exactly what he did. As Martha has told us, he bought a farm and moved into Hill House with her. There, once the dust had settled, he was able to give his full attention to the problem which he thought she might pose.

I suppose that, initially, he must have given thought to murdering her also, but if he did he would soon have realized that it just would not have been a feasible plan. Killing off a healthy servant girl was an entirely different kettle of fish from disposing of sickly Brontës, and anyway he still felt a strong affection for her. Little by little, therefore, he was forced to the conclusion that whatever happened would need to be by mutual consent. A happy Martha would be a safe Martha – but he could not decide what, precisely, should be done.

In the event he found that no problem existed. Martha had faced the reality that Nicholls would not marry her voluntarily – despite anything which he may have said – and she had no wish to force him and thus risk the fate which had befallen Charlotte. In any case she was desperately unhappy and homesick in what was to her a totally alien environment, and longed to be back with her own kind. As she says, within a relatively short time, she and Nicholls came to an amicable agreement about money and she summoned up the courage to return to Haworth and her family.

For Nicholls it was the ideal solution. He was delighted, and once she was safely out of the way he wasted no time at all in fulfilling another of his long-held ambitions. He courted and married Mary Bell, one of those 'strikingly pretty' cousins of his upon whom Charlotte had remarked during their honeymoon.

For the rest of his life Nicholls lived in quiet obscurity, and continued to have a horror of publicity. The only times he broke his silence was to write a few letters to England about his first wife.

264

However, readers will not be surprised to have learned from Martha that he *did* keep up a correspondence with her. Nor will they have been totally unprepared for the news that she visited Nicholls and his wife regularly, and for quite long periods, although we are not told how Mary felt about that!

I am surprised that nobody else appears to have commented upon this incongruity. Nicholls did not write regularly to anyone else, why then to a former servant? He did not receive regular visits from anyone else, why then from Martha – and who financed her trips? They, of course, knew the answers to those questions and now, thanks to Martha, so do we.

As one would expect, Ellen Nussey was one with whom he *did* sever all ties, but that did not bother her, especially as she also now had money on her mind. In the years after Charlotte's death, she ran hither and thither trying to capitalize upon her friendship with her erstwhile friend, and upon the letters which she had received from her.

She asked George Smith if he would publish Charlotte's letters but was told: 'The right to print those letters (otherwise the copyright in those letters) belongs to Mr Nicholls, not to you. The letters themselves are your property and Mr Nicholls cannot claim them from you, but you cannot print them without his permission.' He went on to say that he did not think that such permission would be easy to obtain!

A month later Ellen wrote again: 'I have some letters which most people in his (Mr Nicholls') place, would give almost a fortune to possess.' She continued: 'If you think it right you can give him a hint that he has not all the power on his side . . .' However, George Smith was not in the blackmailing business and he would have none of it. In any case, he had done enough running around after Charlotte, and he was not going to make the same mistake with her friend. That apart, he had no wish to antagonize Nicholls as the latter possessed most of the Brontë papers, including manuscripts and letters, and if there was money to be made from them George Smith wanted to be the one making it.

At what, though, was Ellen hinting? Just what did 'some letters' contain which was, apparently, so dangerous that it made her think that Nicholls would be prepared to pay 'almost a fortune' to suppress them? It would have been most interesting to see how Nicholls would have reacted had Ellen's remarks been put to him, but Smith *would* not write and Ellen *did* not. Referring to Nicholls, she told Smith: 'His notes to me became less and less civil in time till the time of Mr B's death when I ceased to write at all.'

Nicholls, of course, was blissfully unaware of all of this and carried on with his life as a farmer and country gentleman. Meanwhile, the manuscripts, books, letters and other documents which he had taken with him from the Parsonage lay undisturbed in cupboards in Hill House for over thirty years.

Upon the walls of the house were drawings by the three sisters, and the idealized portrait of Charlotte by George Richmond. However, what Nicholls treasured most was the famous profile portrait of Emily, which Branwell had painted when she was seventeen. Originally it had been part of a group painting of the three sisters, but Nicholls had mutilated the canvas, cutting out Charlotte and Anne. That action alone, I feel, speaks volumes for where his true feelings had lain.

Martha Brown died at Haworth on 19 January 1880. She was fifty-two, and was buried in Haworth churchyard, near Tabitha Aykroyd.

What may be considered surprising to some, who do not know her story and regard her simply as a former servant, is that she left a Will. It is dated 13 April 1875, and was written on one of her visits to Nicholls' home at Hill House, and witnessed by him and his wife. In it she left the sum of £20 to her niece Ellen Binns, of Saltaire, Yorkshire, and bequeathed the residue of her estate to be divided equally between her five sisters – Ann, Eliza, Tabitha, Mary and Hannah – or their progeny. Her executors were her brothers-in-law Benjamin Binns, of Saltaire, and Robert Ratcliffe, of Haworth. Probate was granted, in London, on 5 February 1880, only seventeen days after she died.

In the period following her return from Ireland, Martha sold a few of the hundreds of articles which she had acquired, one way and another, from the Parsonage over the years. However, the bulk of the inscribed copies of Brontë novels, paintings, drawings, letters and clothes went to her sisters, who often sold items to collectors.

With Martha's death Nicholls' last link with the Parsonage was severed, and after he received news of the death of his former lover he no doubt sat on many a night reliving the events since 1845. I can picture him smiling as he remembered all that had happened. He had experienced some tight scrapes, and there had been worrying times, but he had enjoyed himself along the way. All in all, he had had a good life.

Arthur Bell Nicholls lived until he was nearly eighty-eight years of age, and died peacefully on 3 December 1906.

The Brontë saga had ended.

267

Epilogue

'And it was in my mouth sweet as honey: and as soon
as I had eaten it, my belly was bitter.'

Revelation 10:10

While considering, and writing, this book, I often wondered what poison – or poisons – Nicholls used.

In Branwell's case, the assumption that it was laudanum
came easily to mind, but what of the others?

Time and time again, I was struck by the similarities between
the Brontë deaths and those in the 'George Chapman' case. For
those unfamiliar with the case, let me state the bare facts.

Severin Klosowski, alias George Chapman – still regarded by
many as having been 'Jack the Ripper' – was a London publican
who, between 1897 and 1902, murdered three women by
poisoning them.

The first was a Mrs Mary Isabella Spink. She was separated
from her husband, and she and Chapman, as I shall call him
from now on, lived together as man and wife. If one excepts the
after-effects of her frequent drinking bouts, Mrs Spink had
enjoyed good health all her life until Chapman obtained the
lease of the Prince of Wales Tavern, in Bartholomew Square,
off London's City Road. After only a few months there her
health broke down completely, and she began to suffer from
abdominal pains and severe vomiting. A Dr Rogers was called
in, but she became weaker and died on Christmas Day, 1897.

Dr Rogers certified the cause of death as 'Phthisis' – shades
of Charlotte!

He was to say later that he was influenced by Mrs Spink's
emaciated state, but he had made no attempt to ascertain what
had *caused* the wasting.

The second victim was Elizabeth Taylor, who also purported

268

to be Chapman's wife. An enthusiastic cyclist, she was in good health but, after a time, she too became thinner and began to waste away. Although she was attended by several doctors, none could understand her symptoms. In the main she was under the care of a Dr Stoker, who was so pleased when his patient became a little better that he discharged the nurse. Only two days later he was surprised to find that Elizabeth was dying.

She expired on 13 February 1901, aged thirty-six. Dr Stoker stated that her death had resulted from 'exhaustion from vomiting and diarrhoea', but he did not know what had *caused* the symptoms. As with Mrs Spink, no postmortem examination was made.

This case, also, has similarities with Charlotte's. Nicholls told Ellen Nussey that 'Charlotte died last night from exhaustion', and it will be remembered that she strained 'until what I vomit is mixed with blood'.

Chapman's third victim was Maud Marsh. By then he was the lessee of the Monument Tavern, Union Street, Borough, and Maud answered his advertisement for a barmaid. Soon they too were living as man and wife.

It was not long after that she began to suffer excessively from sickness, vomiting, diarrhoea, abdominal pains and general distress. She became so ill that she was admitted to the nearby Guy's Hospital, where she was seen by several doctors. However, all were puzzled by her illness, and all diagnosed differently. Incipient cancer, internal rheumatism, and acute dyspepsia (the last reminiscent of Mr Brontë) were all thought to be possible causes. Nevertheless, whatever treatment she received appeared to have been efficacious, and she was sent home. Only later was it realized that the improvement was due solely to her having been out of Chapman's clutches.

The symptoms recurred shortly after her return to the Monument Tavern, but Chapman did not want her to go back to Guy's and so our old friend Dr Stoker was called in. He seems to have shown no surprise that Chapman had acquired another 'wife' so soon, nor that she was displaying the same symptoms as the one who had died the year before.

269

Chapman then left the Monument and took the lease of the Crown, also in Union Street. Dr Stoker continued to visit, but his treatment was ineffective and the patient failed rapidly until she was able to swallow only liquids.

On one occasion Chapman prepared a brandy and soda for Maud, but she was very weak and left most of it. Both her mother and the nurse drank a little, and soon they too were stricken with vomiting and diarrhoea – but still nobody, not even the doctor, suspected foul play.

Only later did the victim's parents become suspicious, and they consulted their own general practitioner, a Dr Grapel. At first he thought that Maud was suffering from ptomaine poisoning. However, on his way home, he decided that arsenic was involved, but only *after* he had learned of the patient's death did he telegraph Dr Stoker and urge him to look for that poison. What had happened was that Chapman had taken fright after the visit of Dr Grapel, who seemed to be on the right lines about the mysterious illness. He had therefore administered a much stronger dose, which caused Maud's sudden demise on 22 October 1902.

Had it not been for Dr Grapel's telegram, I am sure that the good Dr Stoker would have certified 'Phthisis', or 'Marasmus', or 'Exhaustion' – or perhaps even 'Spots before the Eyes' – as the cause of death. As it was, even he was placed on enquiry. He refused to sign a death certificate, and held an unofficial postmortem examination. Initially nothing was revealed to account for the unexplained death, but analysis of some of the internal organs disclosed the presence of arsenic.

Then an official postmortem was carried out. Once again some organs were analysed, but this time large quantities of antimony were found. Arsenic *was* present, but only as an impurity in the antimony.

As a result, the bodies of Spink and Taylor were exhumed. Spink's body – coincidentally considering the other suspicions about Chapman – was exhumed from a grave in the Roman Catholic cemetery at Leytonstone where, under the name 'Mary Chapman', she had been buried near the remains of one of 'Jack the Ripper's' victims, Mary Kelly.

270

Large quantities of antimony were discovered in the corpses of both of Chapman's 'wives', but what surprised everybody was the remarkable state of preservation of the bodies which the poison had induced.

Had it not been for Maud Marsh's parents, Chapman would have escaped detection just as Nicholls did. Certainly none of the many doctors who attended Chapman's three victims was of any help to them. What chance, therefore, did the Brontës have?

Chapman was executed on 7 April 1903. Nicholls did not die until more than three years later, and I like to think that he read the reports of Chapman's trial. If he did, he no doubt felt a great deal of sympathy for him: 'There, but for the Grace of God . . .'!

Antimony was a poison employed by many other murderers, including William Palmer, the infamous Rugeley poisoner who was hanged in 1856. That was only a year after Charlotte died, and no doubt gave Nicholls a few nervous twitches!

It was also much favoured by homicidal doctors. In 1865, and only four years after Mr Brontë had gone to meet his Maker, Dr Edward William Pritchard was hanged for the murder of his wife, his mother-in-law, and possibly a maid-servant, with the use of antimony. His victims displayed the same symptoms as had Chapman's, and the Brontë children had some symptoms in common with all of them.

I was particularly interested to read that Maud Marsh had complained that her mouth and throat 'burned'. The nurse said that the doctor examined Maud's throat 'and said it was raw'. That put me in mind of the time, in 1852, when Charlotte had complained about *her* mouth and tongue, and when Dr Ruddock said, of the pills which he had prescribed, that 'he never in his whole practice knew the same effect produced by the same dose on man – woman – or child'. *He* never bothered to ascertain the reason either.

Another physician, Dr Targett, who had Maud Marsh under observation at Guy's Hospital for over a fortnight, had various ideas about what ailed her. In the reports on his evidence, he is quoted as saying that he 'thought she was suffering from

271

peritonitis. Before she left the hospital he thought she might be suffering from *tuberculosis*. (My italics.) The possibility of any irritant poison never presented itself to his mind.' In fact, he had no idea what the trouble was, nor did any of the doctors involved in all the Brontë deaths.

Antimony was a very popular poison in Victorian times, for a variety of reasons. It is colourless, odourless, practically tasteless and easily soluble in water. Also it was cheap, costing only twopence an ounce in the late nineteenth century [about 33p in today's values], and it should be borne in mind that a mere two grains might be a fatal dose. Even Nicholls could afford it! The main symptoms of antimonic poisoning are also those of gastroenteritis, and it was frequently diagnosed as such in those days.

One of the symptoms is that the victim has a great thirst, and I am reminded that that was something of which Emily often complained. Antimony is an irritant, and a depressant. The irritant nature is such that if a little is applied to the skin a pustular rash will appear, just as was visible in Charlotte's mouth and, almost certainly, in Maud Marsh's throat. Certainly antimony is known to *irritate* the throat, resulting in the same persistent coughing which affected Branwell and Emily.

All in all, therefore, it would seem that antimony was the principal poison which Nicholls used. It is possible, though, that on occasion, and especially in Branwell's case, he employed a cocktail of poisons which included antimony – as did Palmer.

Almost certainly, we shall never know the precise causes of the Brontë deaths. All that I can hope is that Martha Brown and I have established sufficient reason to doubt those given on the death certificates. Only exhumation of the bodies, and analysis of the internal organs, offer any possibility of accurate diagnoses. I am not, of course, suggesting that anybody should rush out and dig up the Brontës! However, churches and cemeteries are often disturbed for building, road-widening and other reasons. Should anything of the sort occur at Haworth or Scarborough, I would hope that the opportunity would be seized to try to establish, once and for all, how the Brontës *really* died.

Such a disturbance would not be without good precedent. So

many changes have taken place at the Parsonage, the church and Haworth village since the time of the Brontës.

Mr Brontë's successor, the Rev. John Wade, did not have a very high opinion of the Brontës and deplored the literary pilgrims who kept appearing at the Parsonage. He had the house cleaned up, decorated and enlarged, after stating flatly that he refused to live in 'a pigsty'. Later additions were the lawn and trees, in place of the sparse clumps of grass and the few blackcurrant and lilac bushes which the Brontë children knew. The gate through which the family coffins passed is no longer in use, and the Parsonage itself is now a museum, run by the Brontë Society.

Mr Wade also had the church, or more properly the chapel, demolished, with the exception of the tower – to which a storey was added to accommodate a clock. The new chapel was built in 1879 and, at Mr Wade's behest, trees were planted in the churchyard.

The Black Bull has been altered somewhat, but Branwell would still recognize it. He might, however, have a little more difficulty with the village. Generally speaking, the centre of Haworth retains its original outline, but it has become a literary shrine to the memories of the Brontës, with the usual souvenir shops and the like.

So there have been many changes, but they are not so apparent at night. Only then is it that one feels fully the atmosphere of the place. Branwell complained to Francis Grundy about 'having nothing to listen to except the wind moaning among the old chimneys and older ash trees . . .', and Mrs Gaskell observed: 'The wind goes piping and wailing and sobbing round the square unsheltered house in a very strange unearthly way.'

Go to Haworth in the winter, on one of those dark nights when the black clouds seem to touch the hills, and the wind comes screeching off the moors. Stand in the graveyard, amongst those close-packed headstones, and watch the trees being bent and twisted in all directions. Then look at the darkened Parsonage, and imagine what could be happening there.

Do the spirits of the Brontës still linger in their old home, I wonder? Do those of Anne and Nicholls return from their distant graves? Does Branwell still tap, vainly, at the windows to be allowed in? Are all those long-gone characters now reconciled in death, or do the recriminations which were hurled back and forth well over a century ago still continue? Perhaps the publication of the secret truths revealed in this book will allow them all, and especially Martha Brown, to rest in peace.

Appendix A

To those already familiar with the story of the early life of the Brontë family this appendix will add little to their sum knowledge – although I shall make some comments which are pertinent to Martha's story.

For readers who come fresh to the tale it will prove sufficient for the purposes of this book. If they then wish to explore the subject in greater detail there are innumerable sources to which they can refer, the most important of which are listed in Appendix B.

The father of the family, Patrick, was born on 17 March 1777, at Emdale, in the parish of Drumbally Roney, County Down, Northern Ireland. His parents, Hugh and Eleanor, were poor peasant farmers whose surname was Brunty, Prunty or Bruntee.

Patrick was apprenticed first to a blacksmith, then to a weaver. However, he must have acquired some education along the way because he was teaching in a local school by the time he was sixteen. Later he became the tutor of the children of the Reverend Thomas Tighe, who was the vicar of a nearby village.

Mr Tighe encouraged young Patrick to go to university in England, and it is possible that the vicar, or one of his friends, lent him enough money to do so or provided an annuity.

In 1802, at the age of twenty-five, Patrick became an undergraduate at St John's College, Cambridge, where he was enrolled as Patrick Branty. He received financial help from his college, and from some wealthy fellow students, but he also earned a little by coaching others.

It was at that time that he affected the name of Bronte, or Bronté, and it is perhaps worth noting that Lord Nelson had been created Duke of Brontë only a few years earlier. However, it was not until much later in life that Patrick went a step further and adopted the diaeresis which was to make the name Brontë.

He graduated in 1806, and was ordained as a minister of the Church of England. After holding several curacies, in Essex, Shropshire and Yorkshire, he became the minister at Harts-head-cum-Clifton, near Bradford, Yorkshire, and it was while he was there that, in 1812, he met Maria Branwell. She was from Penzance in Cornwall, but was staying locally with her uncle and cousins. On 29 December 1812, they were married in Guiseley Church, Maria being twenty-nine years of age and Patrick thirty-five.

Their two eldest children, Maria and Elizabeth, were born at Hartshead, but then Patrick was appointed perpetual curate at Thornton, in the West Riding of Yorkshire, and it was there that the now famous children appeared on the scene. ('Perpetual curates' enjoyed much the same status as vicars.)

Charlotte arrived on 21 April 1816; Patrick Branwell – known always as 'Branwell' – on 26 June 1817; Emily Jane on 30 July 1818, and Anne on 17 January 1820.

Within only a few weeks of Anne's birth, Mr Brontë was appointed to the perpetual curacy of Haworth, roughly fifteen miles away, and the family moved into the Parsonage there.

Mrs Brontë died on 15 September 1821, of an internal cancer. During her illness she had been nursed by her sister, Miss Elizabeth Branwell, who also cared for the children to whom she was known as 'Aunt Branwell'.

With six young children on his hands, Mr Brontë made strenuous efforts to remarry, but with no success. Therefore, in 1823, Aunt Branwell returned from Penzance to manage the house.

Maria, Elizabeth, Charlotte and Emily were later sent away to the Clergy Daughters' School at Cowan Bridge, some twenty miles from Haworth. By all accounts, it was a very austere place, with few comforts.

In February 1825, Maria was sent home because she was ill. She died on 6 May from what was diagnosed as tuberculosis. Elizabeth died on 15 June, supposedly from the same disease.

Not surprisingly, Mr Brontë removed the other two girls,

Charlotte and Emily, from the school and brought them back to the Parsonage.

A middle-aged widow from the village, Tabitha Aykroyd, was engaged as cook and general servant, and was to stay with the family for thirty years. She was also something of a nurse to the children, who called her 'Tabby', and it has been whispered that, in addition, she enjoyed a more than friendly relationship with their hot-blooded father!

For the next six years they all lived at Haworth Parsonage. Mr Brontë gave Branwell some tuition, and Aunt Branwell taught the girls. They also received drawing and music lessons from outside tutors.

It was during that period that the children invented dream worlds about which they wrote miniature books. Branwell and Charlotte created the imaginary kingdom of 'Angria', while Emily and Anne conceived 'Gondal'.

In 1831, Mr Brontë decided that the girls needed more advanced tuition and Charlotte, who was then nearly fifteen, was despatched to a school which had recently been started by a Miss Wooler. It was in a large house named 'Roe Head', at Mirfield, about fifteen miles from Haworth, and it was there that Charlotte made her two lifelong friends, Ellen Nussey and Mary Taylor. Much of what we know about Charlotte comes from the letters which she wrote to Ellen, who kept them all.

Charlotte left 'Roe Head' after eighteen months, and for the next three years the children were all at home together again, with Charlotte giving her sisters lessons.

In 1835, Charlotte became a teacher at 'Roe Head', and took Emily with her as a free pupil. Within three months Emily was back at the Parsonage. She had lost both weight and colour, and was said to be homesick. Anne took Emily's place at the school.

Until that time, Branwell had been receiving painting lessons from William Robinson of Leeds, but early in 1836 he set off for London and the Royal Academy School. However, he was back in Haworth in only a couple of weeks. The story was put about that he had been robbed on his journey, but the truth was that he had indulged in riotous living at an inn in Holborn – for he was already drinking and gambling. In that particular instance, though, there is reason to believe that the explanation for his conduct was that he became unsure of himself and his talent after seeing the famous paintings in the London galleries.

Upon his return to Haworth, Branwell was persuaded to become a Freemason, and was initiated into the Lodge of the Three Graces in Haworth. The Worshipful Master of the Lodge was Branwell's friend John Brown. Brown, a stone mason, was also Mr Brontë's sexton, and the father of Martha Brown. Branwell was secretary of the Lodge for a year, and it is amusing to note that he was also the secretary of the local temperance society.

In 1837 Miss Wooler moved her school from 'Roe Head' to Dentsbury Moor. Anne left in December of that year, and Charlotte twelve months later.

As for Emily, in September 1838, she took a teaching job at a girls' boarding school, Miss Patchett's, at Law Hill, near Halifax. She stayed for only six months.

Meanwhile, Branwell, financed by Aunt Branwell, had, in June 1838, rented a studio at 3, Fountain Street, Bradford, and had set up as a portrait painter. The venture was not a success, and Mr Brontë called him home in May 1839 – probably because he had heard of his son's excesses. Certainly Branwell was heavily in debt.

In April 1839, Anne was engaged as a governess by a Mrs Ingham, of Blake Hall, Mirfield – a position she was to hold until December of the same year. Charlotte secured a similar situation a month after her sister – with a Mrs Sidgwick of Stonegappe, Lothersdale, about eight miles from Haworth – but she was back home within two months.

Just for a short time, therefore, they were all at the Parsonage together again. Then, in January 1840, Branwell was employed as a tutor by a Mr Postlethwaite, of Broughton-in-Furness, but he lasted for only six months.

May 1840 saw Anne installed as governess to a family named Robinson, of Thorp Green Hall, Little Ouseburn, near York. Indirectly, that appointment was to have far-reaching and damaging consequences for the Brontës.

After kicking his heels at home for a couple of months,

Branwell managed to be taken on as a clerk by the new Leeds–Manchester Railway in September 1840. Initially he was based at Sowerby Bridge, Halifax, but in the following April he was promoted and sent to Luddenden Foot, also near Halifax, as clerk-in-charge.

During March 1841, Charlotte took another position as a governess. This time it was with a Mrs White, of Upperwood House, Rawdon – about fifteen miles from Haworth – and on this occasion she held the post for nine months.

In 1841, therefore, Charlotte, Anne and Branwell were all away from home, leaving only Emily at the Parsonage with her father, but that situation was soon to change.

In the autumn of 1841, Charlotte persuaded Aunt Branwell to finance some tuition abroad for her and Emily, in order that they might become reasonably fluent in some foreign language. The intention was that they would then return to England and open their own school.

Thus it was that, in February 1842, the two sisters became boarders at Le Pensionnat Héger, in Brussels. Charlotte was twenty-five and Emily twenty-three.

The future looked quite promising for them, but not so for Branwell. In April 1842, he was dismissed by the railway company because of his frequent absences, and some question over his keeping of the accounts.

That, however, did not bother his sisters overmuch – especially Charlotte and Emily, who were making good progress. Originally they had intended to stay at Le Pensionnat Héger for about six months only but, in September, the Hégers suggested that they stay on for a similar period as teachers. Charlotte would give instruction in English and Emily in music and, although they would receive no pay, their board and lodging would be free and there would be no charge for any tuition which they received.

Charlotte was delighted with the idea, but then Fate took a hand because Aunt Branwell died on 29 October 1842.

The sisters returned to Haworth in November, and there was a family conference. Eventually it was decided that Charlotte would return to Brussels alone. Anne would go back to Thorp

279

Green Hall, and would be accompanied by Branwell, who had been engaged as tutor to the Robinsons' young son. As for Emily, she was more than content to remain at home to run the Parsonage and look after her father.

So, in January 1843, Charlotte went back to the Hégers, but she resigned at the end of the year and returned to Haworth. Homesickness was given as the reason for her resignation, but the truth of the matter was that she had fallen head over heels in love with Monsieur Héger, and his wife had realized the situation.

Over the next two years Charlotte was to write passionate, and sometimes pathetic, letters to her 'only joy on earth', but never did M. Héger respond as she would have wished.

Once she was back from Belgium, Charlotte persuaded Emily that they should continue with the original plan and, in 1844, they opened their school – but at the Parsonage. That does not appear to have been the intention when the idea was conceived, but circumstances had changed. No longer was there any possibility of financial support from Aunt Branwell – although they had inherited shares from her, they did not wish to sell them – and there was growing concern about Mr Brontë. His eyesight was failing and, rumour had it, he was drinking far more than was good for him.

It was felt that using the Parsonage would solve both problems. Although not ideal for such a project, the accommodation was free and the sisters would be able to keep an eye on their father.

Unfortunately, and despite their enthusiasm and the distribution of many circulars, everything came to naught. There were no applications for places and the venture was abandoned.

Then, in late May 1845, the Reverend Arthur Bell Nicholls arrived on the scene.

He was the new curate, twenty-seven years old, handsome, but impecunious. A black-bearded Ulsterman, he had been born in Crumlin, County Antrim, of Scottish parents, on 6 January 1818. Orphaned at the age of seven, he was brought up by an uncle, Dr Alan Bell, who was the headmaster of the Royal High School in Banagher, King's County. He graduated from

Trinity College, Dublin, in 1844 and was ordained the following year.

It will be seen from this brief history of the earlier years of the Brontë sisters that little of note had occurred until 1845, the year at which Martha's account begins. Until then their lives had followed patterns which, if continued, would have destined them for obscurity. Had they known what the next few years were to bring they might very well have settled for what they had.

Appendix B – Bibliography

ADAM, H.L. – *Trial of George Chapman* (William Hodge & Co. Ltd, 1930)

BARKER, J.R.V. – 'Subdued Expectations: Charlotte Brontë's Marriage Settlement' (*Brontë Society Transactions* 19.1 & 2.33, 1986)
The Brontës (Weidenfeld & Nicholson, 1994)

BENTLEY, P. – *The Brontës and Their World* (Thames & Hudson Ltd, 1971)

EDGERLEY, C.M. – 'Causes of Death of the Brontës' (*British Medical Journal* 2 April 1932)

FRASER, R. – *Charlotte Brontë* (Methuen, 1988)

GERIN, W. – *Emily Brontë* (Oxford University Press, 1971)

GRUNDY, F. – *Pictures of the Past* (Griffith & Farrar, 1879)

HANSON, L. and E.M. – *The Four Brontës* (Oxford University Press, 1949)

LEYLAND, F. – *The Brontë Family* (E.J. Morten, 1973)

PARRISH, J.M. and CROSSLAND, J.R. – *The Fifty Most Amazing Crimes of the Last 100 Years* (Odhams Press Ltd, 1936)

PETERS, M. – *An Enigma of Brontës* (Robert Hale & Co., 1974)

WILSON, R.L. – *The Brontës* (Ward Lock Educational)

WISE, T.J. and SYMINGTON, J.A. – *The Brontës: Their Lives, Friendships and Correspondence* (Basil Blackwell Ltd, 1932)

Acknowledgments

The research for this book was carried out over many years and I consulted numerous people along the way. Unfortunately, as a result of other books intervening, and several moves, some of my records have gone astray. I must apologize, therefore, to those whom I have omitted from mention, but if they will contact me I shall ensure that their assistance is acknowledged in due course.

My deepest debts of gratitude, however, are to:

John Morrison – a staunch friend. Although he has long held his own suspicions about how the Brontës really died, he has, over the years and with uncomplaining patience, allowed me to sound out my ideas to him. Generous to a fault, he has provided me with much material.

The Brontë Parsonage Museum – with special thanks to Dr Juliet Barker, Ann Dinsdale, Jane Sellars and Kathryn White who were more than helpful and replied to my many enquiries with unfailing courtesy.

The late Dr F. D. M. Hocking – a noted pathologist and the most entertaining of friends. Ever down-to-earth, and with an impish sense of humour, his help with the medical aspects of the Brontë deaths was invaluable. He is sorely missed.

Angela Skinner – of Truro Public Library – who was always supportive, and constantly suggested and sought out books and information that she thought would aid me in my research.

My thanks are also due, in alphabetical order, to:

James Ansbro – of County Mayo, Republic of Ireland – who was most helpful with my enquiries concerning Charlotte Brontë's honeymoon route.

Alison Carpenter and *David Webb* – both of the Bishopsgate Institute Reference Library – who were, as always, friendly and efficient in answering my questions.

Finally, it would be very remiss of me were I not to pay tribute to:

David Blomfield – my editor. Knowledgeable, friendly, patient and humorous, his logical mind and many suggestions saw us through several difficult patches. It was a great pleasure to work with him again.

Nick Robinson – my publisher – and his excellent team for their enthusiasm, guidance and hard work. Their forbearance with the many idiosyncrasies of an aged author is much appreciated.

Lightning Source UK Ltd.
Milton Keynes UK
UKOW031157160912

199090UK00001B/4/A